VILLA NORMANDIE

VILLA NORMANDIE

KEVIN DOHERTY

TCMG Books

First published in 2015 by Endeavour Press
as a Kindle ebook
This edition published in 2015 by TCMG*

Pre-press production
www.ebookversions.com

Front cover design Endeavour Press

ISBN 978-1512112900

A CIP catalogue record for this book is available from the British Library.

*The Corporate Marketing Group Limited Registered No. 2652455 England
Registered office: Knoll House, Knoll Road, Camberley GU15 3SY

For Roz, ma belle femme, with love and thanks

Hervé

I stepped into the shade of the café awning and placed my hand enquiringly on the back of the empty chair.

'Is it free, Monsieur? May I sit here?'

I sat down before he could answer either question. I can do that kind of thing at my age and get away with it. A little trick I learnt from you, my friend. In any case, what was he going to do – tell a bare-faced lie and say the chair was taken? I knew better; he was always alone.

He smiled in that tight way the English have and returned his attention to the folder of handwritten notes he was forever poring over. I'd never seen him without that folder all week.

Claude brought my usual coffee and shook my hand. We exchanged a few words while the Englishman continued burrowing through his notes, then Claude departed to serve a family of tourists. It's high season; he has to keep on his toes.

I cleared my throat.

'Are you in Caillons on holiday, Monsieur?'

But what holidaymaker sits in a churchyard staring at graves and tombs?

I addressed him in French. I knew his French was perfect; I'd heard him use it many times.

'I'm not on holiday,' he said. 'As I suspect you know.'

Now he set the notes down and looked properly at me. It was quite unsettling, that direct gaze. I'd never realised how blue his eyes were. For all my watching, I'd never come

1

face to face with him.

'How would I know that?' I protested.

'Because you've been following me almost since I arrived. Wherever I go, I look around and there you are. Like my shadow.'

'I live here, Monsieur, that's all. You'll always see me hereabouts. Everybody knows old Hervé Meslin.'

'You're Hervé Meslin?' he said. 'Hmm.'

He leafed through the folder until he found the page he was looking for, then he read through it and several others without so much as a word to me. He hunted some more and found another page. He took out that single sheet. He was determined not to let me see anything else, not so much as a stray sentence. Not at that stage of our acquaintance, anyway; I sensed there were certain tests I would have to pass for that to happen.

He gave me the sheet. The paper was very old and turning brown at the edges.

'It's a map of Caillons,' he said. 'But Caillons as it was. Old Caillons.'

I could see that. A map that had been drawn by hand in pencil. Drawn by a very careful and precise hand. My heart turned over as I saw those old street names again. I traced each of them with a fingertip.

'They're all there,' he said, as if to reassure me, as if I might be checking for omissions. 'All the old names – rue du Verger, rue des Châtaigniers, rue du Centre, route du Littoral, rue de l'Épinette.'

I was captivated. 'Even rue du Maréchal Pétain.'

'Even that. And look,' he said, stretching across to place his finger on the map. 'Here's place Dupré where you and I are right now, sipping our coffee on this heavenly morning. Things weren't so heavenly back then, though. Not with Jürgen Graf stamping about.'

My head shot up so fast I heard the bones in my neck crack. Where had he got that name from? When was the last time I'd heard it spoken except by you or me? And God knows, we hesitated to utter it. Here I am a whole lifetime later but the smell of my own urine still brings back the terror I felt that day in the old schoolhouse. As clearly as if it was yesterday. Graf, a devil incarnate. Nothing heavenly about that black soul.

I remember opening my mouth. I remember no words came out.

'Of course,' he continued placidly, 'it wasn't called place Dupré in those days. It was place de l'Église.' He glanced over towards the church, the source of the old name. 'Exactly as the map has it.'

I finished my coffee and wiped my lips before lighting a cigarette; at least we can still smoke à l'extérieur in this land of liberté.

The cigarette helped. I found my voice.

'I'll tell you the trouble with France,' I said. 'We forget our own history. "We've honoured our dead," we say. "Renamed a few streets and that's that. What more can the dead want from us? Let the past be past." So a street name is all there is for someone who gave everything.'

He seemed to understand. He made a sympathetic face. Then he let us sit in silence for a while before dropping another of his little bombshells.

'The truth is, Jeanne Dupré was a cold-blooded killer, as ruthless and vicious as any Marseille gangster. As ruthless as Jürgen Graf.'

I sat up very straight. Maybe he meant it, maybe not; maybe it was one of his tests. Whichever, I couldn't let it pass.

'She did what was required, Monsieur. Nothing more. Is England occupied by an invader that slaughters and destroys, enslaves you and takes every bite from your mouth? Don't judge Jeanne Dupré quickly or harshly. What would you have done in her place? Ask yourself that.'

'Hmm.'

In the days and evenings that followed we fitted fragments of the story together like stones in a wall. I drew on my own memories and the memories of a whole village and on a childhood in which tales of that dark time floated around me like pollen. But him – where did his information come from? Well, from those closely written pages, certainly. But where had *they* come from?

We dined in many places as we talked, but never in the restaurant of the Villa Normandie. We never entered the villa's panelled hallways or felt its rich carpets cushion our steps or gazed across its chandeliered expanses at the guests who come to stay from all corners of the globe. What would Jeanne Dupré have made of those people today, shiny with wealth, to whom the Villa Normandie is just another hotel? Fancier than most, more luxurious, a unique jewel in their itinerary, but still only somewhere to pass through for a few nights, where room service and courtesy come by credit card. A far cry from the living home it once was.

We've seen other changes too in Caillons. Time passes, the world moves on.

'Rue du Phare is apartment blocks now,' he said on that first day.

'People need homes. Caillons has expanded.'

'Le Manoir is a shopping complex.'

'People need shops.'

'The Atlantic Wall – just mouldering bunkers covered in graffiti.'

'I told you, Monsieur – ancient history, long forgotten.'

Then he threw me off balance again.

4

'I don't suppose you know where the icehouse is.'

'The what, Monsieur?'

All I got was that English smile.

'And then there's this,' he said, turning towards the plaque at the corner of the square behind us.

I had no need to look; I know well enough what it says.

Place Dupré
Hélène, Isabelle et leur mere, Jeanne,
massacrées par les nazis

I showed off my little bit of English: 'Hélène, Isabelle and their mother, Jeanne, slaughtered by the Nazis.'

'But was that really what happened, Hervé? Is that the truth? I wonder. You see, there's a thing about truth. Sometimes we can't get down to the bare wood. Sometimes there are things only God knows. Well, only God and the dead – and the dead aren't giving much away.'

'I'm not sure I follow you, Monsieur.'

'Just my mind wandering. Pay no heed.'

Wandering? Had that mind ever in its life had a single aimless, wandering thought?

'You haven't told me your name, Monsieur.'

'Oh, haven't I? It's Stephen Benedict. And to answer your original question, let's just say I'm here on family business.'

Benedict. The name meant nothing to me. Not then.

'Family business, Monsieur? What kind of family business?'

Once again, no reply. He slipped the map back into the folder.

'I don't know if we'll get to the bare wood,' he said, 'but I think we'll do a fair job. I think we'll get along very well together, Hervé Meslin.'

I supposed he meant I had passed his tests.

1

Jeanne Dupré rose at six, her usual hour. But this was six o'clock German time. Now it was the time in France too. Even from the first moment of waking, her country bent the knee to the German occupier.

Hélène and Isabelle were still asleep. Jeanne paused for a moment in their side of the windowless loft that was the cottage's upper room, divided only by a curtain fixed to a roof beam. The sleepy aroma of her daughters summoned up a time now lost forever. She listened to the girls as she had done for all their lives, knowing the individual sound of each. Isabelle was murmuring in her sleep, dreaming of whatever a child in occupied France could find to dream about. Beside her in their shared bed, Hélène, just fifteen and the elder by two years, breathed evenly and gently, a troubled soul but for once untroubled in her dreams. Perhaps her dreams were ones in which she wore no steel leg brace, she walked always upright, her left leg did not drag. Perhaps she ran. Danced en pointe like her adored Chauviré on the stage of the Paris Opéra.

Jeanne padded softly downstairs, bare feet on the bare boards of the open stairs, their treads worn concave and smooth by the many generations of her family, the Rochards, through whose ownership this small cottage, La Croisette, had passed. Now it was all she had.

She crossed the downstairs room and bent down to poke at the embers of the fire. When she had coaxed enough life into it she set water to boil for coffee. Or what had to pass for coffee – a concoction of chicory and ground acorns and who knew what else. It tasted like burnt rope.

She left the downstairs window and shutters closed. She stepped out of the nightshirt – Michel's nightshirt – stood naked by the deep sink and began washing her body, top to toe. The water from the sink's only tap was earth-cold. Winter was worse, of course; winter mornings were purgatory compared to this fine May morning with the promise of warmth to come.

The soap slipped from her hand and skittered across the floor.

This fine May morning.

How could she have thought that?

She pressed a knuckle against her eyes to clear her vision and retrieved the soap. The throb behind her forehead spiralled higher. The soap had left a pale green slick on the boards. She scraped it up carefully, worked it to a weak lather, thinking only of that task and nothing else in the whole world, head down, no tears.

Soap was not to be wasted. This small portion, now placed safely to one side where the water would not devour it, was the household's only slice and it was growing thinner by the day. A fresh one would cost her dear. If that crook Gaspard Baignères could be persuaded to barter, he would demand four eggs. He would settle for two, but two eggs were an entire meal in this house.

This fine May morning.

Nothing fine about what this morning would bring.

She dried herself briskly with the nightshirt. Where was Michel this morning? Were the skies blue over Germany or wherever they had sent him?

There was a small square of mirror. She avoided it. She knew how she looked. Skin and bone, barely a woman's shape at all. She rarely menstruated any more. It was not a question of age; she was still young enough. It was a question of food, the absence of food.

Besides, in the mirror she would see only shame.

Still damp, she dressed quickly in the clothes she had laid ready last night: her best knickers and vest, a decent underskirt, her Sunday blouse and skirt, her only jacket – deepest burgundy, the same one she had worn for Isabelle's baptism and Hélène's confirmation and then Isabelle's too – the black headscarf her mother Colette Rochard had worn as a widow, made of finest Alençon lace. No stockings, but there was no help for that. And finally her good shoes, her only pair of good ones, which she would not put on until immediately before leaving, saving their leather. Who could afford to repair leather shoes these days?

The coffee pot spluttered, water hissed into the fire. Life had set its heart on carrying on. Jeanne opened the window wide and folded back the shutters. The gulls were sweeping up from the bay, scraps of white against the blue sky. Such a fine May morning.

In place de l'Église, in the gravelled front courtyard of the mairie beneath its huge red banners with their black swastikas, Oberleutnant Jürgen Graf was inspecting the three stakes of freshly stripped pine that had been driven into the ground on his orders the previous day. They stood a metre and a half apart in a line parallel to the building's frontage. Each was as thick as a man's thigh; each stood a good head taller than a man. Half their length again was rooted deep in the sandy earth, each one packed tight with rubble and a cubic metre of concrete. They shone clean and white in the deep shade of the mairie.

'Solid as the Reich Chancellery,' said Graf to the man who waited behind him, a small anxious person, bespectacled and colourless.

This was Leutnant Ernst Neiss, secretary to Major Klaus Ebermann, and he really did not want to be here. It was all very distasteful. He was too hot, he was always too hot in this country, he was clammy with sweat even at this early hour, and he was miserable. He nodded his agreement to Graf's words. He would have nodded agreement to anything in order to get away from those three pale stakes and what they portended.

'Now you see why I wanted good German concrete,' said Graf. 'Not the useless shit the French use. Now you see.'

'Yes, Herr Oberleutnant.'

Neiss did not see. Neiss did not care. Neiss thought it made no difference what the damned stuff was. All he wanted was a signature for those three cubic metres that Graf had made him requisition. Since this new oberleutnant had arrived in Caillons last month it had been one new idea or fancy notion after another.

Graf braced himself and kicked the flat of his boot hard against each stake. The three heavy blows echoed around the square. Each stake stood firm. He nodded with satisfaction. A whiff of his cologne rolled through the air. Neiss moved back a pace.

Graf scraped his steel-shod heel across one of the concrete beds.

'It'll last forever. Like our thousand-year Reich.'

'Yes, Herr Oberleutnant.'

Graf planted his fists on his hips and flexed his back. 'Things are changing here, Neiss. These French savages and their so-called Resistance, they've got away with too much, too many German lives taken. That's over. I'll show them the iron grip of Reich authority.'

'Yes, Herr Oberleutnant.'

At last Graf scribbled his signature on the top chit of the block of forms that Neiss held out to him. The leutnant scuttled away.

Graf turned his attention to his nine riflemen. They stood at ease in the square, grouped in their three-man details, smoking and talking quietly. He called them to attention. No parade-ground histrionics; one quiet command was all it took. He felt a surge of pride to see their perfectly drilled response. What a superb machine his Wehrmacht was. What a privilege for Jürgen Graf to be part of this great *thing*, not simply a body of fighting men but a whole ideology – and to be a leader as well. His own father, the clockmaker, could not have measured a fraction of a second's difference between the men as they snapped to attention, heads up, shoulders squared, backs straight as flagpoles.

He went from man to man, took each weapon and inspected it, drawing back the bolt of each Karabiner, checking each action and breech. If there was a speck of grit, a smear of surplus oil, they knew he would see it. But all was gratifyingly clean.

As he checked each rifle he looked the owner in the eye, man to man.

'Remember your fallen comrades today,' he urged. 'Do your duty in their honour.' He slapped the weapon back into its owner's hands. Then, heels snapping together, he thrust his right hand forward in the salute that he knew gladdened his men's hearts. 'Heil Hitler!'

'For my fallen comrades!' came each reply. 'Heil Hitler!'

One final command to all when the inspection was complete and the men relaxed again.

Around the perimeter of the square he had become aware of movement, a slow, reluctant stirring, like wildlife in undergrowth. The vermin that infested this place were emerging from their dens, assembling for the show. Slackers and wasters, every one of them, always hanging about the lanes or the port; they were the ones not called up for Service du Travail Obligatoire, STO, the programme of compulsory work for the Reich in Germany or its foreign provinces, its conquered territories. Always they were there in the background, like the bad breath they exhaled. They slouched on street corners or parked their bony arses on café stools, watching, taking everything in, whispering together, their eyes following every move but their gaze sliding away as soon as anyone looked directly at them. Piles of rags and berets and greasy caps who never did a stroke of work from one day to the next.

But this morning they would see how German fighting men went about things. And what French treachery brought about.

He checked the clock on the mairie. The timepiece, an elegant Henry-Lepaute, was the only good thing he had come upon in Caillons. He wondered what condition the mechanism was in, if indeed the original mechanism was still intact. But it kept good time, he had noted that over the past month, and at present it told him there was time for a smoke.

He sauntered to the edge of the square – big, loose, confident strides as if he owned the whole of Caillons and who would dare argue? – tapping an Eckstein on its packet to tamp the tobacco into place, a habit of his, and lit up, gazing across the bay as the smoke curled above him in the still air.

The sea sparkled as if laid with jewels, so bright it made him blink. He set his shoulders and drew deeply on the cigarette. No cloud broke the perfect arc of the sky from horizon to horizon. Summer was arriving early; it would be a glorious day. He could feel the heat rising from the cobbles already.

Hitler weather, they called a day like this in Germany.

11

He turned to survey the square. The red banners on the mairie shone vivid and beautiful in the sunshine. Well, this foreign land was Reich land now, as much as Germany was. And half of Europe. All of it Lebensraum. So Hitler weather he would call it here too.

Ideal for the task ahead.

There was a sound from behind Jeanne, from the stairs. An uneven sequence repeated – shuffle, step, shuffle: Hélène, descending. Michel had fixed a board along the edge of the steep stairs so that she could steady herself. Jeanne heard the swish of her hand as it moved down the board.

'Maman, I'll go with you.'

Mother and daughter kissed.

'No,' Jeanne said, still holding her. 'It's no place for a child.'

'I'm not a child.'

'Pierre won't want you there.'

'He's my uncle. Your brother. We're his family. We should all be there. Even Isabelle.'

'No.'

'Papa would go with you if he was here.'

'But he's not. And he wouldn't want you to go either.'

She wiped sleep from Hélène's eyes. They were as dark as her own, the irises almost black. She stepped back and held the girl at arm's length. Her beautiful Hélène, on the verge of womanhood. She inclined her head so that their foreheads were touching. They were almost the same height now, mother and daughter. Michel should be here to see her grow up.

'I need you here with Isabelle,' Jeanne told her. 'When it's over, the two of you will go to school as on any other day. You'll walk through the same streets you always walk through – no hiding in back lanes. Go right through place

12

de l'Église with your heads high.'

'You forbid me to go but you expect me to hold my head high afterwards.'

'They'll be watching you.'

Hélène gave her a sideways look. 'Who, Maman?'

'The ones who creep beneath the Nazis' jackboots. They pretend to honour France but they betray her. You and Isabelle will show them what it is to be a proud daughter of France.'

'France, always France.'

'Yes, of course.'

'And you, Maman?'

'Me?'

Hélène drew back. 'Are you a proud daughter of France when you clean and polish in the Villa Normandie for your Wehrmacht major? Our own home that they took from us? You wash floors for the ones who stole our land and our home and made my father into a slave. You clean the shit those Nazi boots drag in. For what – a slice of meat, a crumb of cheese?'

'Meat and cheese that help keep us alive. Hélène –'

'You want me to shut up? Why? In case I tell you what Caillons says about you and your Nazi major? About the other things you do for him?'

She might as well have slapped her mother in the face. And she knew it. But knew it too late, of course. A child's prerogative, to regret too late. As soon as the words were uttered Jeanne saw the agony in her daughter's eyes. But the words could not be taken back and there was nothing Jeanne could say to them. No answer that was worth the breath, no denial, no protest, no anger. There it was, the damage was done and no help for it any more than for the lack of a fine pair of silk stockings.

So she drew Hélène to her again and pressed her cheek

into her daughter's sleep-tangled hair, as much to hide her own sorrow as to comfort the child. For a moment the scent of warmth and sleep filled her nostrils again. Then Hélène slipped from her arms. Jeanne heard the rusted latch of the door scrape open and the bucket rattle as her daughter shuffled outside to feed the poultry.

From above there came the sounds of Isabelle stirring – bedsprings creaking, light footsteps crossing the upper floor. So different from Hélène's laborious shuffle.

'Maman,' said Isabelle as she came downstairs, 'Hélène didn't mean any of that. She just says these things.'

'I know.'

'Hatred becomes a habit. We begin by hating the enemy. When that gets us nowhere we start to hate ourselves.'

'Hélène hates herself?'

'She's looking for reasons. Her leg is one reason. This morning you're another – and of course she's upset about Pierre. I'll make sure she doesn't go to place de l'Église until it's all over.'

Jeanne raised her daughter's hand and kissed its open palm. Isabelle followed her sister outside. The whisper of the sea, soft and peaceful today, briefly entered the house, then ceased as the door closed.

To Jürgen Graf they were vermin, slackers and wasters, mere piles of dirty rags. To Jeanne some of them were hypocrites who had abandoned France. To themselves they were the ordinary people of Caillons, each trying to get by in their own way.

Hodin knew he was the best baker in Normandy. Or used to be. Nowadays he and his wife spent half their night sweeping the floor for every precious speck of spilt flour that could go back into the morning dough. Dust went in there too, of course.

14

'No harm, no harm,' he told his wife. 'Dust is what we are, why not eat it?'

Every now and then he trudged up into the bois de Caillons when Mercier the carpenter was at work in his sawmill. There he filled hessian bags with sawdust. A few fistfuls of that went into every batch as well. The people of Caillons saw him with his hessian bags. They knew what was in them. They knew what was in his bread. It was never the same bread as he baked for the Germans. But the people of Caillons had to eat.

Old Voinet the charcutier skinned, boned and dressed any carcass that came his way these days, big or small. Some he presented as themselves, some became fine pâté and saucisson. Mule, dog, cat, squirrel, field mice, wild birds of every variety. He cheated no one, he owned up to what he was offering. As for the hungry Caillonais, they were grateful he was offering anything at all.

Pauthier the greengrocer was a man in despair. He bought from anyone who had a few square metres of land to grow anything on, in principle allowed for their own needs and no more – but principle and practice rarely walked hand in hand these days – and he marked up the produce and sold it on. But the people of Caillons knew this. So why bear Pauthier's mark-up, modest as it was? Why not go straight to the grower or grow a few things of their own? Many did; more each month, in fact.

That was the first cause of Pauthier's despair. The second was his wife Mathilde, a seamstress whose tongue was as sharp as her shears. Beneath her lively fingers, odds and ends of curtains and worn-out clothing miraculously reappeared as new garments, but beneath the onslaught of her tongue Pauthier was clipped and snipped into a figure of misery and defeat.

All of them gathered in place de l'Église that bright sunny

morning with the shadow of the church spire and the mairie falling across the square – Voinet and Hodin and the Pauthiers, bald Coeffeteau the stonemason, whose cranium was as polished and hairless as any block of finely dressed granite, Mercier and the men from his sawmill, Sulac the thatcher, Fromentin the painter and glazier, Descamps the blacksmith, and the rest of the village tradespeople and workers. There would be no trade today, even for those few customers with money or coupons to buy with.

The fishermen and their boat hands and their wives climbed the long hill up from the port and joined them, leaving their nets and lobster pots and the mussel bouchots until another day; no great loss, since most of the seafood only went into German bellies anyway. Sulot from Café du Marché was there, with his five unmarried sisters and their string of snot-nosed children. Old Musset the postman stood leaning on his pushbike, scratching his beard and lost in thought. Mirabaud the halfwit leered and pestered the women until they or their menfolk batted him away. Farm labourers, even the ones employed on the collaborationist farms and thus themselves also regarded by some as collabos, soot-stained railway workers, the village schoolteachers and the postmistress, even Delalande the one-armed tinker who wandered from village to village sharpening knives and mending pots and who had arranged his peregrinations to bring him to Caillons that morning – they all came.

Some exchanged little nods of recognition and a handshake or a kiss on the cheek. Some kept their own counsel, some spoke quietly together. Many of the women held rosaries, slipping the beads slowly through their fingers to mark each Pater Noster and Ave. The women wore headscarves or had covered their heads with traditional shawls that they wore crossed and pinned on

16

their chests. Men removed their caps or berets and squinted into the sunshine, assessing those tall pine stakes so shockingly white.

All told, the people numbered over two hundred. At first they held to the pavements but as their numbers swelled and the time approached they moved into the square itself until they occupied its lower half, directly across from the mairie. Perhaps some communal instinct emboldened them, an unspoken determination that the morning belonged to them, however hideous the banners and flags that defaced their beloved squares and municipal buildings, however raucous the occupier's marching songs.

Among the last to arrive was Gaspard Baignères. His pushbike had no brakes, so he skidded to a halt in a cloud of dust and leapt off in one practised move. He took off his oilcloth cap and stuck it in a pocket. Indifferent to the resentful glances that followed him, he pushed to the front and took up position squarely opposite the three pine stakes. He produced a whole pack of Gitanes and lit one. A couple of boys sidled closer, ready to pounce on the butt when it fell. He paid no heed, his nose buried in his little notebook that everyone knew so well. He stroked his thick grey moustaches as he read. There was hardly a man or woman who did not have a debt listed in that book, a weekly payment, a promise of a task owed or a valued possession on pawn: the ring they had sworn never to part with, the silverware, the bolt of cloth hoarded from better days.

But even Gaspard looked up when a small frisson went through the crowd, like a ripple passing across the bay of Caillons. Along ruelle de la Baie, which met the downhill path from La Croisette, came Jeanne Dupré. Her step was firm, her gaze level and unwavering as she passed the Villa Normandie, never giving it so much as a glance, and entered the square. She looked as collected as if she was doing nothing more than coming to Sunday mass in l'Église de Notre Dame de la Mer. She was even attired accordingly, in neat burgundy jacket, black skirt and plain white blouse, her auburn hair hidden beneath a black headscarf. The way the headscarf shimmered as the sunlight caught it told Gaspard it was very fine lace, best quality and not cheap. Where had she been hiding that?

As she drew closer, he saw that she was carrying not a prayer book or a missal as he had thought but a small bouquet of flowers. They were violets, Napoleon's own flower. An offering of flowers for the flower of France.

Proud, that was how Jeanne Dupré looked to him this morning. From her earliest years there had been a haughty side to the young Jeanne Rochard. The mature woman had mustered all her dignity for this day. Her heels clicked on the cobbles as she passed. He inclined his head in salutation but she seemed not to notice; or more likely chose not to. She stationed herself almost directly in front of him, so close he could see her shoulders tremble. A thin vein beat rapidly on the side of her throat.

The square was silent now. Even Mirabaud the idiot was still, his gaze fixed on the ground. The only sounds were the cries of gulls over the bay, a dog barking somewhere and the distant braying of a mule.

Then came one further sound, magnified between the walls of the mairie, the church and the Villa Normandie, a sound to which few if any of the Caillonais had ever paid much heed before, even though it was always there, sixty times in every hour, through every day and night of their lives.

It was the crisp metallic clunk as the minute hand of the Henry-Lepaute, its original mechanism still very much intact, nudged forward.

The time was five minutes to seven.

Now it all began.

First, a commotion at the mairie, at the rear of the building where the holding cells were located. The first prisoner to be brought out was young Louis Fougeret, a boat hand. He was followed by Guillaume Raynal, a labourer who had worked the land of Jeanne and Michel Dupré and Pierre Rochard before the Germans came. Last to appear was Pierre Rochard himself.

Graf prowled back and forth as each man was half dragged, half marched by two Wehrmacht troopers to the stakes and tethered there. They had to be dragged because they seemed close to death already, their legs crumpling, their faces bloody and beaten, as purple and raw as anything on Voinet's marble butchery counter, the gunshot wounds sustained on the night of their capture bound in dirty rags.

Gaspard put his notebook away and lit another Gitane; the boys who had moved in on him earlier once again materialised.

The Wehrmacht men were efficient, he gave them that. A matter of seconds and the prisoners were bound securely in place, notches in the wood guiding the ropes so that each man remained upright.

Père François Lachanau had followed them from the cells, reading aloud from his breviary. Now the priest stepped closer as the guards withdrew. Gaspard knew the form. So did every other old soldier like him who was there that morning, all Catholics to a man. There would be only prayers here in public. Since the prisoners were not facing death through illness, they would not be anointed; and though the priest still wore his purple stole over his black soutane, he would already have heard their last confessions and administered the Eucharist in the cells, in whatever moments he had snatched out of Graf's gaze. It was a wonder the oberleutnant tolerated his presence now.

As Lachanau raised his right hand and began to make the sign of the cross above each man, a piercing cry rose from somewhere in the depths of the hushed crowd. Gaspard turned to see a very old man, thin and as twisted as an apple tree, being held tightly in the arms of his tiny wife. The cry and the choking sobs were his. The pair were the Fougerets, mother and father of Louis, their only child, born late in their lives and now to be taken from them.

Recognising his father's scream, Louis lifted his head and howled like an infant.

On Graf's command the nine riflemen advanced in single file into the forward half of the square. There they formed their three details of three shooters, two men standing, the third between them with one knee to the ground, each trio facing a stake and its prisoner. Another word from Graf and the troopers shouldered their weapons. The noise that filled the square now was the rattle of nine rounds being chambered.

The minute hand slipped forward again. Seven o'clock began to toll.

Graf called out for Lachanau to withdraw. But the tall figure of the priest did not budge, broad back turned on the oberleutnant. Lachanau had managed to calm young Fougeret and seemed in no hurry to abandon him.

Graf called again.

Lachanau took a step sideways. But it was only in order to pray over Pierre Rochard, tethered to the central stake. The priest's back remained resolutely turned on Graf. Gaspard smiled behind his moustaches. It was eloquent, his old friend's silent back.

The seventh strike rang out. The oberleutnant called a

third time. He drew his pistol, a Luger. There was again the sound of a firearm being primed, this time Graf's. Père Lachanau reached the end of the prayer and made the sign of the cross over Rochard a final time. Only then did he bother to turn unhurriedly and face the German. He closed his breviary and walked directly to him, stopping only when the Luger was pressing against his ribs. He looked down at Graf and then up at the clock.

'Running late, Oberleutnant,' he growled. 'Sloppy.'

Everyone in the square heard and understood, for he spoke in French. He pushed against the Luger.

'Go on, shoot. You came from hell to be here and you'll be back there soon enough. So you've nothing to lose. Heil Hitler and fuck you.'

Graf simply laughed. 'I won't shoot you today, Priester. I'm not hunting old black crows today.'

He holstered his weapon and ordered the guards to get the priest out of the way. Lachanau warned them off with a glare and strode to the side of the gravelled courtyard under his own steam.

Graf turned to his riflemen and issued another order. They laid their cheeks against their weapons and peered along the sights, settling themselves into their aim.

'*Allons enfants de la Patrie ...*'

The melody was thin and uncertain, the voice that carried it was weak, but the words and tune of the Marseillaise were unmistakable. And these days, illegal. Gaspard peered to see more clearly. Yes, it was Pierre Rochard. From the corner of his eye he saw Jeanne Dupré's shoulders sag for an instant, then she drew them squarely back. Her face was hidden from him by the headscarf but it was clear that her gaze was locked on her brother, and his on her.

That one line of the song was all Pierre Rochard managed. Gaspard did not hear Graf's next order. None of those watching in the square did. The roar of nine rifles drowned it. The bodies of the three men jumped like puppets as three bullets hammered into each. Graf called further orders and the process was repeated twice more in rapid succession. Nine bullets in each man, each body now slumped on its stake. Movement passed through the crowd as hands made the sign of the cross and rosaries were pressed to lips.

Graf produced his pistol again, strode into the courtyard and administered the coup de grâce to Pierre Rochard. He acted so swiftly, the cloud of gunsmoke was so dense, that no one saw whether it was needed or not.

Gaspard dropped the Gitane butt on the cobbles. One of the boys grabbed it and disappeared into the crowd.

Then came a new voice.

'*Le jour de gloire est arrivé ...*'

Gaspard's ears were still ringing from the gunfire so that he was unsure at first whether this fresh singing was only in his imagination. But no, it was real. It came from somewhere behind him and to his right, a solitary male voice deep within the crowd. He glanced around at the densely packed throng. Nothing, no clues. Every face was impassive.

'Enough!' roared Graf. 'This is forbidden by Reich law!'

He marched to the corner of the crowd behind Gaspard. But the singing rose again. Two voices this time, in quick succession, one from the far edge of the crowd, the second answering from its centre.

'*Contre nous de la tyrannie, l'étendard sanglant est levé ...*'

'*L'étendard sanglant est levé!*'

Graf changed direction, brandishing the Luger as if he might shoot into the throng. The inscrutable wall of faces confronted him wherever he turned, each face wearing the

22

same bovine expression that the Caillonais specialised in for the Germans.

Then Jeanne Dupré stepped calmly forward, walked past Graf and on to the line of riflemen, through the now thinning mist of gunsmoke, and into the courtyard. Not so white and clean now, those three stakes.

Graf made no move to stop her. The singing faded to nothing. Jeanne nodded her thanks to Lachanau, who now stood beside the dead men. She laid the bouquet of violets at her brother's feet, returned to the square and ascended the steps to the church. As the door closed behind her, the minute hand of the Henry-Lepaute nudged forward with a loud clunk.

Gaspard looked up. Eight minutes past seven.

As he mounted his pushbike, he turned his gaze to the Villa Normandie. On the balustraded gallery stood the motionless figure of Major Klaus Ebermann in his crisp summer uniform of white tunic and gold epaulettes, watching everything.

Jeanne stayed in the church for mass. It could not be a mass for the dead, which Graf forbade for résistants, but the small church was as full as it would have been for that. She did not take communion, for God knew and saw all: 'Domine, non sum dignus.' Lord, I am not worthy. And it was true; she was not worthy. There were enough sins on her soul without adding sacrilege.

She departed straight after the service. Her duties in the Villa Normandie awaited and she had to change into her work clothes; the day was no different from any other in that regard. As she came down the steps she could not help but glance across to the mairie. A horse-drawn wagon waited while Graf supervised the removal of the bodies. There would be no Catholic burial for them: another of his

23

edicts; instead they would be consigned to a communal pit.

She looked away as Graf turned, for she knew his eyes would be on her. She heard his guttural bark of laughter. Still she did not look up, not even when Mirabaud the halfwit came skipping to meet her.

'Poor Jeanne,' he wheezed. 'Poor Pierre. Poor Mirabaud.'

Her action in the square had been foolish. She saw that now. It had drawn Graf's attention. She should have let the crowd disperse before paying her respects to Pierre. His death was public but her mourning was a thing better done in private. Instead she had made it a spectacle, and at the moment of Graf's humiliation. He would not forgive her that.

As she climbed the path from ruelle de la Baie, she saw that La Croisette was quiet and unoccupied, the shutters and door closed. She wondered if Isabelle and Hélène had done as she said. Perhaps that too had been a dangerous idea.

She lingered for a moment by the little kitchen garden she had made, seeking solace among the herbs and seedlings, the healing comfort of new life. Wood pigeons called nearby, the same creamy notes over and over. Despite their raids she had lettuce, cabbage, carrots coming up, dandelion, wild roquette and rosettes of cornfield mâche for her salad bowl, even tomatoes on the vine by the south wall. Later there would be potatoes that she could store in the coolness of the larder to see her family through the winter. It was rabbits and snails she had to worry about now. But they too might find their way into her cooking pot. She knew where plump white mushrooms, the ones her mother called champignons de couche, grew in the third field, the field that was always damp and shaded by the marching line of tall pines. One day soon she would make pigeon pie with onions, carrots and mushrooms.

She reached the cottage doorway. A small glint of dully

24

reflected sunlight on the windowsill to her right caught her attention. It could have been any innocent thing, a chip of pebble, a protruding nail; the sill caught the sun's rays at this hour. But whatever it was, it was not flat but was resting on edge, propped against the shutter. Her stomach tightened. Someone had placed the thing carefully in that position.

She slipped out of her shoes to save them from the dew-damp grass and stepped barefoot to the windowsill. Now there was no longer any question what had been left for her to find. It was not a shard of glass or any other accidental thing.

'My God,' she whispered. 'Do I have the strength for this?'

She was trembling. Her gaze searched the landscape beyond the cottage, past the plane trees and the ancient elm, and finally to where the land plunged abruptly to the shore a full hundred metres beneath. Beyond the cliff the sea met the sky in a razor's edge of silver. No human being moved anywhere, none was to be seen behind her towards the village or beyond the cottage towards the headland. But someone had been here at her home, someone had chosen their moment.

She reached out to the windowsill and picked the thing up.

She felt the sun on her, warmer now as it climbed higher. Such a fine May morning. Alas, a morning with Pierre dead and Michel lost to her.

But a morning with her duty crystal clear.

2

François Lachanau, for all his seventy-odd years, still cut a formidable figure. Built like an ox and the best part of two metres tall, he looked like the former boxer he was, with his deformed and mismatched ears, his bent and flattened nose and his fists like a pair of coal shovels.

It was over forty years since love of his saviour had supplanted his love of the ring. The heavyweight champion of Normandy hung up his gloves and exchanged his gold championship belt for a holy stole, his embroidered silk robe for a plain black soutane, and became Père François Lachanau, and in time the curé of the parish of Caillons.

He knew every man, woman and child in the village and the port and in the scattered cottages and smallholdings of the surrounding hinterland. Through four papacies he had baptised these folk, confirmed them, married and buried them. He confronted their sins and foibles with infinite patience and compassion, heard their confessions and absolved them, for he recognised himself and his own failings in these ordinary people. Occasionally he saw Jesus in them too.

In short, he was a people's priest. Far more than he would ever be Rome's.

This morning he burst into the upstairs drawing room of the Villa Normandie like the prizefighter of old storming into the ring. With three members of his flock just despatched to their maker, he was in no mood to dance attendance on Major Klaus Ebermann.

'You asked to see me, Major. It better be important. On this of all days –'

He broke off. He removed his biretta, raised his head and sniffed the air noisily.

'Hot wireless valves.'

He crossed the room in a couple of strides and pressed a hand to the top of Ebermann's wireless set. He bent down and sniffed loudly again. It was a theatrical performance.

'Hot valves, hot dust. Catching up with the news, Major? Whose version? You're a man who wants the truth, not the twaddle your ridiculous Herr Goebbels peddles. So I'd guess you were listening to the BBC, to Radio Londres. Like I do myself. Lawbreakers, both of us.'

Ebermann shut the door that Lachanau had left open. Old Madame Guinard was rattling crockery in the dining room. Lachanau smiled to himself. The old woman worked for him as well as for Ebermann. He knew she liked nothing better than a sly eavesdrop; obviously the major too was wise to her little ways.

He closed in on Ebermann again, towering over him.

'Germany's losing this war, Major. North Africa is gone. You were routed in Russia – Kursk, Stalingrad, all that slaughter for nothing. Now Italy's slipping from your grasp. Perhaps Herr Goebbels doesn't listen to the BBC. How long can you hang on? A year? Less? You and your comrades may be as fat and comfortable as geese here in France, but the world will tear your livers out – that's what happens to fat geese. Your so-called Atlantic Wall won't protect you then. The whole world's out to get you. Britain and America and their allies will drive you back into Germany, then Germany itself will fall – implode, like a rotting cowshed in a storm. Boum! And just as full of shit. You're finished, Major. The Third Reich's finished. Your Führer is finished.'

'Thank you for your analysis, Monsieur le Curé, but it's not why I wanted to see you.'

Ebermann spoke calmly enough. If Lachanau's words had stung, the major was not prepared to be riled or to rise to them. But a redness rimmed his eyes that Lachanau had not seen before.

'I wish to raise a private matter, Monsieur. Something personal, not Reich business. I look to you as a priest to respect its confidentiality.'

He led the way to the balustraded open gallery that overlooked the villa's grounds. Birds fussed in the groves of laurel, sparrows rushed in nervous gangs from tree to tree. Sunshine slanted through the poplars, their morning shadows stretching across the lawns.

François Lachanau had known the Villa Normandie throughout the decades he had spent in Caillons, had always loved it. He knew the precise path the sun would take above the old house and towards the sea. He knew how the shadows of those poplars would slip over the lawns through the afternoon and evening. He thought of the Rochards, whose home it was when he first came to Caillons, and then the Dupré family – Jeanne Rochard as she had been, elder child of Jacques and Colette, and Jeanne's husband Michel and their daughters, who had inherited the house on Colette's death. Then came the day the Germans marched into Caillons and seized the grand house as their Kommandantur, leaving Jeanne and Michel with only a fraction of their land and the labourer's cottage where the Rochards had started more years ago than anyone could remember. He thanked God that Jacques and Colette had not lived to see that day.

His fingers caressed the wooden crucifix that hung over his chest. Nothing lasted, nothing but God's love. Empires crumbled, owners of great houses were usurped, the usurpers were themselves washed away like driftwood, humble village priests left nothing behind – unless they had sown the love of Christ in men's and women's hearts.

'Well, Major? I haven't got all day. What's on your mind? Spit it out.'

Ebermann avoided his gaze. 'As you know, the garrison has no Catholic chaplain, no confessor.'

'Of course not. You're all too busy being Nazis.'

'I want you to hear my confession.'

'Ah.'

Lachanau raised the crucifix and kissed it. So the Catholic in Ebermann had not yet been goose-stepped to extinction.

But a weight settled in his heart, not the jubilation that the request should have brought. He knew the answer he had to give. The only one he could give.

'Major, I've prayed for you to ask this of me. I'll take your confession any time you like. But it must be a full confession. Otherwise contrition isn't complete. Here's how things stand with you. Your country is prosecuting an unjust war, a sinful war. Remember your Augustine and Aquinas. You're party to that sin. I can't absolve you unless you renounce that as well as your own sins. Do you understand? A full confession means renouncing this war. Continuing to take part in it is simply returning to your sins, like a dog to its sick. Proverbs 26:11.'

'You're telling me to betray my country.'

'I'm saying you've stolen mine. You turn our men into slaves –'

'Your own government sends them to us.'

'A puppet government elected by no one but your masters. It offers our sons as sacrifice – but unlike Abraham's God, your Reich takes them, and greedily. You work them to death in your factories making armaments, on your farms to feed your people while mine starve, on your railways, in your coalmines. Forced labour, only worth keeping alive while they can work, and when they die you take more from my country. These sins are yours as much as your Reich's.'

'Those decisions aren't mine.'

'So? Every life squandered, whether German or French, ally or foe, is on your soul as much as on your Führer's. Every Jew you send to the gas chambers –'

Ebermann looked up sharply. 'I've sent no Jews anywhere, Monsieur. I'm a German, not a Nazi. The two aren't the same.'

'Does the difference matter?'

'To me it does, Monsieur. Of course it does. And it should matter to you as well. I know about the Jewish children that are sent to Caillons, the ones you and certain other Caillonais give shelter to and protect. Have I tried to take them? No, I have not. I'm no Nazi, Monsieur, no Jew-killer. Be thankful for that.'

'You want me to be thankful that you spare the lives of those who've never done anything to deserve death? To be thankful that you spare the innocent? A strange kind of mercy. And you want a pat on the back for it?' Lachanau fixed the German with a bleak stare. 'You serve the killers, Major, so their crime is yours too. The exceptions you make are neither here nor there. Your wife back home in Germany has a murderer for a husband, your innocent children have Cain for their father. Such beautiful children – as beautiful as the children in the death camps.'

'All my country wants –'

'Never mind your country. Get out of mine. Is that so much to ask? You can't serve two masters, your Führer and your saviour. Your Führer will take you to hell with him, you and that creature Graf. I implore you, I *beg* you, to serve your saviour. Renounce this war and I'll take your

30

confession. It'll be my joy to absolve you then.'

But Ebermann only shook his head. He stood for a moment longer, as if hoping that the priest might relent, then returned inside.

Lachanau raised the wooden crucifix and kissed it again. To turn a man away from his saviour's grace, that was no easy thing. The enemy was not Ebermann. It was not even the Reich. The enemy was Satan. And he had been in training for a very long time.

'I'll pray for you,' Lachanau told the major as he returned to the drawing room. 'Just like I'll pray for the three young men who died today at the hands of your Reich.' He paused at the door, biretta in hand. 'Of course, those deaths too count among your sins.'

The Wehrmacht barracks were located in an old château a few kilometres inland from Caillons. The place was still known by locals as Le Manoir. It sat in the middle of a wide expanse of flat meadows and farmland, the plain of Le Manoir. Like Jeanne and Michel Dupré, the château's owners had been dispossessed by the Germans but had chosen to flee abroad. The Germans had gutted the place, installed bunks and latrines, and billeted themselves in rooms that had once known grand balls and elegant soirées dansantes.

A water tower stood in the farmland of the château outside the barbed wire and watchtowers, and near it a barn, an ancient structure far older than the water tower, built in the Norman style with great beams, open sides and eaves so low a man had to duck to enter beneath them. In the cool of this shady barn waited Gaspard Baignères.

Executions by firing squad followed a reliable pattern. The human body, tethered upright, upon receiving the force of a volley of bullets and as life departed, collapsed in one of three ways: both legs might buckle symmetrically; or flop to the right; or to the left. Three possibilities per condemned man, therefore, each with odds of two to one against.

Three condemned men, so the same speculation three separate times. If an enterprising individual had his wits about him and possessed sufficient mathematical skill, he could open a book and make good money. Particularly if he allowed only accumulator bets with potential returns that were temptingly large to his punters but from his own point of view reassuringly elusive.

Gaspard lit a Gitane. He was that enterprising individual.

The young German gefreiter for whom he was waiting entered the barn. These Boche boys all looked the same to him, these pale hatchlings. Same mother's milk complexion, same nervous eyes trying to look brave. Mighty conquerors who turned out to be lonely boys far from home. Except their bullets killed every bit as effectively as anyone else's, their pale mouths gobbled up as much French food. And of course their Reichsmarks were as good as anyone's.

Wiedemuth, this gangling young trooper was called. A name that, like the dozens of unspellable and unpronounceable Boche names Gaspard had entered in his notebook over the last week, sounded like a dog throwing up. Prausmüller. Hauptmeier. Nettlestroth. Not one without a crossing-out or a correction as he had taken their bets.

Wiedemuth clattered to a halt before him. He held out the betting slip, a half page from Gaspard's notebook, and smiled uneasily.

'Good lad,' said Gaspard, and winked at him. 'Well done.'

Wiedemuth, who spoke no French, nodded. Gaspard nodded back. Wiedemuth smiled again. The boy even

32

looked like the specimen of Hitlerjugend on the Reichsmark notes that Gaspard began counting into his soft hand. It was not a hardened soldier's hand, he noticed; these boys the Boche were sending were barely trained.

One minute and the transaction was done. Gaspard sighed. It hurt to part with good solid Reichsmarks but perhaps it was no bad thing to have at least one winner when all your punters were armed.

'Off you go, then. Back to the rest of your litter. Chop-chop.'

Wiedemuth clomped off in his heavy boots, tucking his winnings away. Gaspard watched him go. Good money in stout hobnails like those if he could get his hands on a few pairs.

He jammed his oilcloth cap on his head and cycled off to his next appointment.

Madame Guinard begrudged every meal she prepared for Major Klaus Ebermann. So it was with reluctance, some months back, that she had allowed Jeanne Dupré to show her how to make the German dish called gebrannte Mandeln. Jeanne had been insistent; the sickly sweet concoction of baked almonds, melted sugar, vanilla and cinnamon was the major's favourite dessert, she had assured the old woman.

'It fills the whole house with its stink,' an exasperated Marie Guinard complained to her friend Mathilde Pauthier, the sharp-tongued seamstress. 'But if she says he likes it, who am I to argue?'

'Who indeed?' frowned Mathilde, her thick black eyebrows drawing together. 'She should know what he likes, that one. There's a lot she must know about him.'

'No end, Mathilde.'

'There's talk, Marie. About him and her.'

'Not from me, Mathilde.'

'Nor me, Marie.'

Marie Guinard had her hands full on the morning of the execution. From the Villa Normandie she hurried to Père Lachanau's house in time to prepare his breakfast after morning mass and his visit to Ebermann, then back again to the Villa Normandie to set lunch for the major. She had scarcely removed her shawl when Jeanne appeared, already at work, her hair tied back, her feet bare.

'My condolences, Jeanne. I'll remember Pierre in my prayers.'

'Thank you, Madame. The major has a request for dinner tonight. He asked me to let you know.'

Madame Guinard rolled her eyes. 'Too important to ask me himself? So what does he want?'

'Blanquette de veau followed by gebrannte Mandeln.'

'Imagine,' Madame Guinard told Mathilde later. 'Her own brother's not even cold in the ground and she's giving me Ebermann's dinner order.'

'Imagine indeed,' said Mathilde. She licked her lips. 'Where did you get the veal?'

Only the collaborationist farms, whose job was to feed the occupier, were allocated fuel for agricultural machinery. Other farmers had to fall back on the methods of earlier centuries: horses and oxen. But draught animals needed food. Of which there was not enough. It was a circle of doom: feed the animals to work the land, and the people went hungry; feed the people instead and there was nothing for the animals.

So the Caillonais who owned draught animals had been forced to slaughter them, which was more humane than letting them starve; and then butcher them, with or without old Voinet's help; then salt and store what they could; and eat, sell or barter the rest. It was a once-only harvest. The farms shrank and thereafter produced only what could be persuaded out of the soil by human labour. Subsistence farming had returned to Caillons.

Jules Descamps the blacksmith could name every horse he had shod since the fall of France. This was because the list was short. The last French horse was three years ago; even the last German horse was over a year ago, a hunter owned by Major Ebermann's predecessor. So nowadays Jules repaired hand ploughs and other small farm equipment and tools, he mended gates, buckets and tubs, mangles and pushbikes, he made kitchen utensils and nails and hammers, and he fashioned the occasional item for Père François Lachanau's church. It was enough to get him by. Just.

'You'll do them today?' said Gaspard. 'It must be today.'

'They'll be ready within the hour. But why are you bothering?'

'You don't want the work?'

'Of course I do.'

Gaspard handed over the cash. French francs. These days worth twenty times less than they used to be, thanks to the thumbscrews the Germans had applied to the exchange rate.

'What about some Reichsmarks?' suggested Jules.

'How would I get my hands on those?'

Gaspard swung his leg over the pushbike and headed back down the shady lane. 'Make sure you get the names right,' he called over his shoulder. 'I've had enough trouble with names this week.'

Jules cut three lengths of iron chain to size, each long enough to encircle a man's upper arm. He stoked up his forge and heated the saddle nameplates. Each was about the length and width of two fingers. Each would form a bracelet when linked to its length of chain. He opened the

35

box of steel letter punches. On one nameplate he punched the name of Louis Fougeret, letter by letter, on another that of Guillaume Raynal, and on the third that of Pierre Rochard. All of them spelt exactly right. Exactly as Gaspard had written them.

3

Hélène and Isabelle did not encounter Oberleutnant Graf that morning, but later they did see the wagon that carried the bodies to the pit behind Jacques Colinet's barn. The wagon and the bony horse that drew it were also Colinet's.

'There he was, that horrible man Colinet, with that old nag of his,' Isabelle told Jeanne that night, 'plodding along rue des Châtaigniers at morning break. The whole school saw, all the pupils as well as Maître Péringuey and Maîtresse Lavisse. How could we not? There he was, the collabo, taking Pierre and Guillaume and Louis to be dumped like diseased swine. He'll pay one day. One day all the collabos will pay.'

'A day of reckoning, you mean?' said Jeanne. 'What day will that be? Tell me. And who'll decide who pays? Jacques Colinet has two daughters, growing girls like you, and there's his wife Delphine, she's sick. Then there's his old mother. So many mouths and he has them all to feed. What would you have him do? Besides, better that Jacques Colinet takes Pierre on his final journey than the Germans. So let me know when this reckoning of yours will be. And who'll weigh right and wrong.'

'See, Isabelle?' said Hélène. 'Maman has all the answers. She always does. Our maman is so wise. We're to be proud daughters of France while she skivvies for the Boche and old Colinet shovels quicklime on our own flesh and blood.'

She shuffled off to bed. Shortly afterwards Isabelle followed.

Midnight came. Jeanne sat alone in the downstairs room, in darkness, her shutters and curtains open despite the curfew, watching the path of the moon across its backdrop of stars. She had allowed herself to doze through the evening, making up for the sleep she would miss tonight, trusting her body to wake her in time. She was now wearing a rag-tag assortment of Michel's old clothes: battered leather blouson, black trousers, black woollen cap, work boots he wore in the fields, several pairs of his thickest socks to make the boots fit. The trousers were baggy and too long; she had tucked their cuffs inside the outer layer of socks. The jacket was too wide in the shoulders and reached to her hips.

She was glad of the heavy clothes, for it was cold in La Croisette now, the fire having enough life to last the night but no longer throwing out any warmth. Isabelle and Hélène would sleep through until morning, exhausted by the day's emotional toll. Even so, Jeanne waited another hour before zipping the jacket up to her throat and stepping outside, drawing the door softly behind her, careful that the rusty latch did not scrape.

It was warmer out of doors than in. She stood listening in the doorway and watching the darkness, her eyes already adjusted to the night. The land was never silent or still. It bore too much life. She heard the whir of crickets, the muttering of her chickens in their sleep, small scufflings in the hedges. Tiny scraps of inky black flashed past overhead – La Croisette's bats, whose tenure of the cottage and its outbuildings went as far back as that of the Rochards. She stood motionless in the midst of all this struggle for life, her senses at high pitch, until she was sure no human movement or sound intruded.

The chickens flapped in alarm when she invaded the henhouse, squawking and filling the air with a flurry of loose feathers that assailed her face and lips. She cupped a hand over her nose and mouth against the hot stench that rose from the bucket of decomposing straw and chicken droppings destined for the kitchen garden's compost midden. When the birds accepted she was not a fox and settled back in their roosts, she crouched to the far end of the low shed, pushed some birds aside, lifted a plank and withdrew the bundle of oily cloth. It was as long as her arm. She laid it across her knees and unwrapped the submachine gun, a German MP40. She slipped two filled magazines into her pockets, one on each side to prevent them clanking together, replaced the cloth and the plank and returned outside. She gulped lungfuls of clean air and scrutinised the countryside and outbuildings again as she passed the leather strap over her shoulder and hefted the weapon along the inside of her arm. There was a time when the weight had almost been too much for her, but now she hardly noticed it. She had carried her children and grown accustomed to their weight. A submachine gun was no different.

As she negotiated the fields, she kept close to the stone walls and high earth-banked hedges, crossing open ground only when she had no choice. Doing so left a trail through the long grass but it would be gone by daylight. Only the damp third field, the one that never dried out, would hold the pattern of her passing for a few hours longer; and before then the roe deer would obscure it as they returned to the bois de Caillons.

She paused beneath the plane trees and again by the old elm, remaining motionless for several minutes and scanning all around, not letting her gaze focus on any detail but alert for any shift in the blackness. All she saw was the glow of fireflies and the silent glide of an owl, a shadow sweeping across the stars. All she heard was the sound of the night and the wash of the waves as she drew near to the headland.

To those who knew no better, there seemed to be many tracks leading down the steep cliff face to the shore, interlaced and cutting through the mass of gorse and shrub. But in fact most of them were false, doubling back to the top or petering out in tangled undergrowth. Some descended a tantalisingly long way before marooning the explorer among dense thickets of buckthorn and fierce juniper. All were narrow and uneven, their surface broken by roots and branches to trip the unwary. In daylight, descent was difficult and frustrating; at night it could kill.

But she had known these tracks since childhood. After making a final check that she was not being followed or observed, she jumped down to a path that looked no different from any other. At once she was lost from view from above. She followed the trail unhesitatingly.

She had no idea when the icehouse had been made. Nature had begun the job but some unknown generation of the Rochards had finished it. A split in the limestone face, obscured by undergrowth, led to a narrow tunnel that ran back at a shallow angle, then turned sharply to burrow deeper into the cliff, finally ending in a room-sized chamber. Only when a person reached the chamber could they stand upright. Meat and game had hung here once, in a time when there was enough of either to store, packed about by blocks of ice lowered from the headland on ropes. The depth of the tunnel and its sharp bend provided natural insulation, enhanced by a heavy elmwood door at the entrance to the chamber itself.

When she arrived, the first men she saw were Jacques Colinet, the man who had taken Pierre's body, and Marcel Voinet, son of old Voinet the charcutier. Beside them sat Charles Meslin and Luc Clavier, formerly a boat hand and a railwayman respectively but now true maquisards. Like Michel, they had received their STO call-up papers; unlike him, they had preferred to take their chances in the hills, hiding in the woods and the thick scrub, the maquis, living off the land and anything Jeanne and the others could spare from their own meagre rations.

These four were seated on low stools and wooden boxes around the upturned crate that served as a table and on which burned a hurricane lamp. A person could scream themselves out of voice in this chamber and never be heard outside; all the lanterns in Caillons could burn here and their light not be detected. But the wick of the lamp was turned low and tonight's business would be conducted in quiet voices – no one who came here took foolish chances; and those who took foolish chances would never be brought here.

Behind Colinet and the others stood Gérard and Paul Leroux, both fishermen, like their father and every Leroux before him. The younger brother, Paul, was a new face here; he had never been invited to join them before. He had proven himself as a messenger and watcher, and now he had been judged ready for duty in the field. Tonight's action would be his first.

She kissed cheeks with each of the six. Though Charles Meslin greeted her readily enough, she knew he would be her problem tonight. She passed him the packet of rabbit meat she had brought. She saw other small packages on the shelf of rock behind him and Clavier.

'Forgive me for today, Jeanne,' said Colinet as they kissed. 'I had no choice.'

'Regarding Pierre? Nothing to forgive.'

'Your daughters saw me. I was made to take that route, right past the school. Graf's orders.'

'Not your fault, Jacques.'

Colinet nodded unhappily.

'How's Delphine?' she asked.

'Weaker every day. God doesn't make it easy for her.'

Jeanne set the MP40 against the wall where the others had already propped their weapons – German guns like hers, stolen or seized in previous actions, and British Sten submachine guns that came in by parachute from England. She pushed an empty cider barrel into place and sat down next to Meslin.

'I thank all of you for being in place de l'Église this morning,' she said. 'Particularly Charles and Luc.' She nodded at Meslin and Clavier, the two maquisards. 'We know the risk they took in being there. But there are things to say tonight. Hard things.'

'Like what?'

'Pierre, Louis and Guillaume are dead because we were betrayed.'

She let the statement sink in.

'You have proof of this?' said Charles Meslin.

'It's my strong opinion.'

Meslin raised an eyebrow.

'I'm not saying the traitor is one of us,' she continued. 'I'm simply reminding us to be on our guard. When we attacked the rail convoy that night, the Germans were waiting. How come? How did they know? They turned the tables on us. We achieved nothing except the loss of three of our best résistants.'

'And you lost a brother.'

She might have lost a husband by this time too. Six months had passed since she had seen Michel off at Gare du Havre. Six weeks now since his last letter, scrutinised by the German censors to make sure it contained no clue to whatever work he was doing or where he was. Perhaps he too should have fled to the maquis.

And it seemed she might be losing her daughters as well, in spirit if not in body, the way Hélène was talking these days; Isabelle, for all her robust common sense, might not be far behind.

She set the bitter thoughts aside; her mind had to be clear tonight.

'We were sent into a trap,' she said.

'What are you suggesting we do?'

'We leave it to Danton. I'm confident he shares my suspicions.'

'Has he told you that?' Charles Meslin asked sharply.

'No.'

'So it's another of your opinions.'

'If I can see the danger, Danton can see it even more clearly. Hear me out, Charles. We don't know where or at what level the traitor is operating. Only Danton can see the full picture. He knows more than any of us. We carry on with our work – and that includes tonight. Above all, tonight.'

'What if we're betrayed again?' It was Paul Leroux, the new member, anxious that his first action might turn out to be his last.

'That's a chance we have to take. Tonight is our response to what happened today. Our comrades withstood whatever beatings and torture the Nazis employed to make them give us up. We have that debt to repay. We won't be found wanting. Tonight we'll show the Germans that. We'll show them we're not finished, that we're as strong as ever.'

Meslin had been watching her closely.

'You're speaking as if you're our leader, Jeanne, rather than on equal terms as one of us.'

'Do you disagree with anything I've said?'

He turned away.

Paul Leroux looked from face to face.

'Who's this Danton?' he asked.

His brother Gérard threw him a warning glance. 'Quiet,

Paul.'

'Let him ask,' said Marcel Voinet. The others shrugged assent.

'Why not?' said Jeanne. Time was marching on but talk of Danton would suit her purpose.

'We don't know who Danton is,' Jacques Colinet explained. 'None of us knows. That's the point.'

'What do you mean?'

'Danton isn't his real name, which means we can't betray him to the Germans.' Colinet scratched his unshaven chin. 'Look, every cell needs its leader, someone in charge on the ground. But it also needs its Danton – someone above, who sees things from a higher level, as a man does from a hilltop. In a valley you can't see what's in the next valley. We're in our valley. Danton is our eyes.'

Leroux still looked puzzled.

Jeanne took up the explanation. 'There are many Resistance cells across France. Each operates independently and its members know the identities of only their comrades in that cell. If the Germans eliminate one cell, others continue unaffected, undamaged. Or if the Germans capture members of a cell alive and succeed in making them disclose the identities of other members, the worst they can do is round them up and terminate the cell. Again, other cells continue intact. But it's also important to have a network that links cells together.'

'Why?'

'Take what we were trying to do the night Pierre and the others were captured. For years the Germans have been building and extending what they call the Atlantic Wall, their defences along our coast because they fear invasion from the west, a seaborne invasion from Britain or the Atlantic. It's why they shut down the lighthouse, so that it can't guide an invading force. And it's why Caillons and other coastal areas are off limits to outsiders. The Germans constantly move supplies to the coast as the work proceeds – construction material and machinery for bunkers and fortifications but also heavy armaments, anti-tank obstacles, mines. We'll never stop them, but what we can do is deplete their resources and destroy the morale of the Wehrmacht troops that provide safe passage. It wears them down. They'd rather be home with their sweethearts or mothers than risking their lives for cement mixers.'

'The cell attacked this kind of convoy?'

'One of several we've sabotaged. But only when Danton says so. That's why the network is important. Otherwise cells could attack each other by mistake.'

'How could that happen?'

'Each cell has its own territory but there are no maps, no borders, so there's always a danger of overlaps. We could mistake another cell for German reinforcements. Or plan an action only to find that our target convoy has already been attacked further up the line. We'd be endangering ourselves for nothing and laying scarce explosive that has to be retrieved at great risk.'

'Did Danton authorise the action on the night we were betrayed?'

She nodded. 'He did. Also, he's our ears as well as our eyes. We need radio contact with England. Danton sees to that. Radio operators are always at risk of being tracked down and captured, tortured for information. Danton provides a cut-out between us and them.' She gave Leroux a thin smile. 'And he ensures there are replacements if all of us are wiped out. So he'll have someone in mind to replace you, Paul, if you're killed tonight. And me. All of us.'

Leroux was nodding his understanding. 'So this is everything Danton does?'

'Almost.'

'What else?'

'He tells us who takes over if the cell leader is captured or killed.'

'How can he do that if no one knows who he is?'

'He does it like this.'

She placed the coin on the crate. It was what had been waiting for her on the windowsill of La Croisette. None of the men touched it but they all leant forward to see it more clearly, including Paul Leroux. Someone brightened the hurricane lamp.

The coin seemed to be an ordinary one-franc piece, struck in a grey metal, perhaps zinc or aluminium. Leroux saw that its year was 1943. But he also saw that the same side of the coin carried the legend 'Liberté, Égalité, Fraternité'.

'Impossible,' he said.

'Exactly,' someone replied quietly. 'But all the same there it is.'

'If it was issued last year, it should say "Travail, Famille, Patrie".'

Work, Family, Fatherland: the despised Nazi-like slogan of what Père François Lachanau called the puppet government of Marshal Pétain. Coins minted by it bore that slogan, not the old still-potent battle cry of the Revolution.

'Turn it over,' said Leroux.

Jeanne did so.

'Again, impossible.'

On the other side was the profile of a severe-looking Marianne, warrior soul of France and defender of liberty, complete with traditional cap and wheatsheaf. But the words that enclosed her image were 'République Française', not Pétain's 'État Français'. Republic, not state.

Leroux looked at all the men in turn, seeking an explanation, but their attention was fixed on the coin – all

46

except Charles Meslin, who was staring again at Jeanne. In the end it was Jeanne herself who spoke.

'We don't know where these coins originate. For good reasons, we're not told. Perhaps here in France, but I think not – too dangerous. More likely an overseas territory. They're the first coins minted by the Free French, by us in effect, and by personal order of General de Gaulle, our leader in exile. Perhaps they come from England, where he is.'

'They signify that France lives,' said Paul Leroux.

'And that we live too,' added his brother. 'Free French. These coins are here in France, right under the noses of the Boche, exactly as we are.'

Meslin could take no more.

'The coin isn't yours,' he told Jeanne. 'It's your brother's.'

'I can assure you it is not,' said Colinet before Jeanne could say anything. 'I have Pierre's coin. As his second-in-command I regarded it as my duty to take it from his home before the Germans got there. I have it in a safe place. This coin is Jeanne's.'

'We're to be led by a Nazi major's whore?' Meslin thrust his face into Jeanne's. 'If we're looking for traitors –'

Jeanne's knife slammed into the crate, between his legs. No warning; no one had even seen the blade find its way into her hand. Another centimetre and the blade would have nailed Meslin to the wood. He yelped in alarm.

'Danton has made his decision,' she said calmly. There was no anger or strain in her voice; it was as if the knife had been conjured up and planted by someone else. 'We don't pick and choose which decisions we like. The matter of our leadership is closed. I'm no one's whore and I'm no traitor.'

She wrenched the knife free and returned it to its sheath

47

inside the leather blouson. The only sounds in the chamber were Meslin's rapid breathing and the soft splutter of the hurricane lamp. She surveyed the grim faces around her.

'I appoint Jacques Colinet as my second-in-command if he'll accept that responsibility,' she said. 'Jacques?'

'I accept,' said Colinet.

She put the coin away. 'And now we have a rendezvous to keep.'

Le Manoir was a long dark silhouette in the distance far beyond the trees, the blackest thing against the horizon in this landscape where blackout regulations held sway. Jeanne panned her field glasses across the plain and the dark hulk of the château. All was still.

As well as fortifying the château's ancient perimeter walls with barbed-wire fences and watchtowers, the Germans had ploughed a wide killing strip all the way around the outside so that no grass or undergrowth could provide cover for an intruder or attacker. As always, local men had done the work at gunpoint. Heavy machine guns were installed in the watchtowers, which were manned day and night. Powerful floodlights were available to the guards if any suspicious movement was detected. Sirens would blare, rousing a contingent of armed guards from standby duty in the guardroom, to be followed within two minutes by the entire manpower of the garrison. Regular drills ensured that everything functioned without a hitch, as every villager knew, for the Germans made no secret of it. That was their way – nothing left to chance, everything operating like a well maintained machine.

The place was impregnable: that was the message the Germans wanted to send. What were not impregnable, however, were the lanes that led to and from Le Manoir, including the final stretch that ran through the dense woodland of the bois de Caillons and across the expanse of open plain to the château's main and secondary entrance gates. It would have been impossible to make these routes secure, short of posting armed guards along every metre. Aware of this vulnerability, particularly the woodland track, the Germans were careful to avoid any pattern in regard to when their vehicles entered and exited Le Manoir.

But the rail convoys were beyond their control. They came and went according to orders issued by military command headquarters in Paris – and when a convoy was despatched, then Wehrmacht units along its route had to provide protection on the ground, supplementing the guards who rode the convoys. It was this combination of firepower into which Pierre Rochard had led the cell on the night of his capture.

Tonight, however, it was not the rail convoy that the cell was targeting. It was the Wehrmacht unit itself that would venture out to shepherd it.

'There'll be ten or a dozen men at most,' Jeanne whispered to Paul Leroux. 'There are seven of us. These are odds we can handle. Our sympathisers risk their lives to get information to us about convoy movements. We owe it to them to put what they tell us to good use. Tonight we'll do that.'

The night-time dew in the woodland was heavy. Jeanne could feel it seeping through Michel's heavy trousers as she lay flat out on the elevated bank some six metres above the woodland track, among the sweet chestnut trees and oaks. The danger was that the damp would stiffen her joints. In an action like tonight's, slow or delayed movement could be fatal. So she tensed and released her muscles, repeating the process several times. It was something Pierre had taught her.

To her and Paul's right lay Gérard Leroux and, beyond

him, Luc Clavier and Marcel Voinet. Jacques Colinet had taken Charles Meslin with him to the opposite bank on the other side of the track. Jeanne knew he did not trust Meslin and wanted to keep him close.

Around them the sounds of the night continued. A single soft click took her attention. It came from where Colinet lay. All sounds travelled at this hour but particularly human ones. Colinet had clicked his tongue, just once. Jeanne raised the field glasses again. The high doors of the château's main gate had swung open. A pair of blacked-out headlamps, each beam reduced to a narrow strip, appeared, then the doors closed behind the vehicle as it began to accelerate along the lane and towards the woods. She listened carefully to the engine note as it approached. As expected, a light truck. Which meant up to twelve men.

Her plan was simple. All along this stretch through the woods the track was badly rutted, flooding when rainwater gathered in the dip and turned the surface to muddy clay that dried as hard as stone. Tonight she had instructed Colinet and the others to dig logs and rocks into it before laying the explosive, making it far worse than usual. The deep ridges would toss the truck wildly from side to side as soon as it hit that stretch. The driver would have to fight to hang on to the steering wheel and with any luck the men in the rear, ignorant of his struggle, would be cursing his ineptitude. Levels of stress and anger would be high, with awareness of danger and readiness for response correspondingly reduced.

She waited until the truck was in the dip directly beneath where they lay. Sure enough, it bucked and yawed like a boat in heavy seas, crunching up and down on its suspension springs, the tarpaulin roof rippling with each impact. Angry voices carried up through the night.

It was the moment. She raised the upper half of her body

and rammed the plunger down.

The world exploded into flame and heat. She flung herself prone again, hands clamped over her ears and her body pressed flat behind the broad base of her oak tree but she felt the heat and the wind rush over her like a burning ocean. She sensed that objects were flying overhead, crashing through the trees and to earth – chunks of metal or pieces of bodies, impossible to tell which. The truck had become a ball of fire. When she took her hands from her ears she found her hearing impaired but, as if through layers of blankets, she was aware of muffled screams and shouting; the roar of flames reached her as a low crackle. There was movement within the fireball. Shapes detached themselves from the core and collapsed to the woodland floor, still burning.

She looked around for Paul Leroux. In the orange glow she saw him. He had half risen from his cover and was now crouching transfixed, staring at the inferno. She knew the signs. He had to be brought back from the edge, otherwise he would be useless to them, endangering them by his passivity or even turning his weapon on them in his confusion.

She braced herself on an elbow and slapped him as hard as she could. He gasped, looked at her with incomprehension.

'Get down, Paul!'

Her words seemed to reach him from a great distance. He nodded uncertainly. She hauled at his jacket until he slid down. She put her mouth to his ear, not sure if he could hear any better than she could.

'Hold your fire unless it's needed. Don't waste ammunition. Don't show your location.'

But the rattle of a submachine gun, it too muffled by her deafness, drew her attention. She could see no muzzle

51

flashes, so the shooter was not Jacques Colinet or Charles Meslin on the elevated ground opposite. The shooting had to be down by the burning truck, on its far side. No member of the cell had disclosed their position, which meant that the shooter was firing at random into the night and the trees – a combination of panic and playing for time.

Now a second gun opened fire. This time she saw the flashes, on her side of the blazing remains of the truck. As if encouraged, the first gun began again. So a minimum of two men still had to be dealt with. Her choices were straightforward. Reinforcements would be setting out from the château at any second; she could call an end right now and get the cell safely away, or they could finish the job and seize whatever weapons and munitions had survived the blast; after all, at least two submachine guns were still operational.

The first option, withdrawal, was the one that made sense.

She turned to Paul Leroux and found that he was watching her. That was good. He was in control of himself again. She saw the question that had formed in his eyes.

Leroux's weapon was a German rifle, a bolt-action Karabiner 98k. The MP40s and Stens were not accurate as single-shot weapons. To stand any chance of an effective shot, and one that also minimised the risk of revealing their location in the way that submachine-gun fire would, a rifle was the only option. She looked from Paul to his brother Gérard. She sensed he was making the same calculation. Safety or munitions. The others would be doing likewise.

She answered Paul's unspoken question with a single nod. She would not call an end. They would not withdraw. They would finish the job.

Paul Leroux did not rush things. He eased himself into position and lined the shot up from memory, reckoning there was a good chance his target was too frightened or too injured to have moved. He waited for another burst of fire to confirm his hypothesis. When it came, he gauged distance back from the unshrouded muzzle flashes and calmly took the shot. In the dip below them the submachine gun jerked upwards, loosing off a series of rounds that flew high and zipped harmlessly through the canopy of the trees. Then it fell silent.

But as it did so, another burst of fire sounded: the first gunman. This time, however, his fire was returned immediately. Jeanne looked over to the other side of the track in surprise. Even with her impaired hearing she recognised the sound – not Jacques Colinet's MP40 but the unmistakable high whine of Charles Meslin's Sten. One short burst, well placed and enough to do the job, no wastage. There was no reply.

Through the field glasses she saw that both gates of the château were opening, though as yet no headlights had appeared. Soon there would be a stream of vehicles and they would tear along the lane far faster than the truck had done. Some would make for the site of the blast, the rest would fan out across the lanes and fields in an attempt to cut off escape routes.

She guessed that the cell had a maximum of two minutes to complete its work. There might still be survivors, so there was still danger. She was leader, she would take the bullets if any were to come. She made her way down the bank, signalling the others to remain in place and cover her. The heat from the truck was still fierce. No shots rang out but there remained the risk of ammunition exploding. She made a swift assessment of the scene. She saw the bodies of the men that Leroux and Meslin had shot. She saw other corpses, some complete, some not, all of them carbonised, the black flesh already contracted to the skeletons. She saw weapons scattered around. Some might be almost red hot but they would still be functional. She saw steel ammunition lockers – intact, which was good, but potentially lethal if the contents had been heated to the point of instability. Their removal would be a gamble.

She signalled the others to join her and shouted a rapid list of instructions – the weapons she had spotted, handguns still worn by the dead and that should be taken, the ammunition lockers, the cases of stick grenades and egg-shaped grenades, these requiring the most cautious handling of all.

She discovered that her hearing was recovering. She could hear the crackle of the flames, she could hear Colinet directing the others, she could hear their replies.

She heard the groan.

It came from the direction of the bank she had descended, but somewhere to the right, near the truck. She cocked the MP40 and edged cautiously towards the sound.

He was hidden among tree roots, a metre or two above the track, and partly covered by earth and torn-out vegetation, debris flung by the explosion. He lay on his back, arms by his sides. Her gaze went at once to his hands but she could see by the light of the flames that they were safely empty, merely filthy with dirt. An MP40 like hers lay nearby but beyond his reach. She pushed it further away with her foot.

She could not be certain, given the flickering flames and the shadows here in the undergrowth and the dirt smeared over his face, but he seemed to be young, perhaps about twenty. Blonde haired and no doubt blue eyed, a perfect Aryan, one of the boys she had spoken of who should be home with their sweethearts, not sucking the life from France.

Her finger stayed on the trigger of her weapon as she bent down to unfasten the holster on his belt and remove his pistol.

The smell hit her, a rank odour of intestines, blood and faeces. There was a sudden flare-up of flames and she saw that his midriff had been torn open. Not a wound but a gaping hole the width of his torso. She saw now that the dark matter partly covering him included his own innards. The filth on his hands was not dirt but blood. One hand rose weakly from the ground and twitched in what seemed a senseless movement; she thought it a reflex of some kind until she realised he was trying to put his insides back in place.

'Mutti,' he moaned. 'Mutti.' Maman. Mother.

His eyes flickered open. They were indeed blue.

Jacques Colinet arrived beside her. He unfastened the German's tunic pocket and found the boy's Kennkarte, his Wehrmacht identity pass. He squinted at the difficult Teutonic script, twisting the pass to catch the light from the flames. The boy watched him.

'Wiedemuth,' read Colinet. 'Wilfried Hermann Wiedemuth, born March 1925.'

Not even twenty.

Colinet folded the document shut and fingered its thick, cloth-like card, then slipped it into his pocket. He bent down again and took Wiedemuth's pistol, a Luger, from its holster, the task that Jeanne had not managed. The boy's eyes followed him. Colinet undid the German's boots and with an effort pulled them off. The boy groaned.

'Better we leave now, Jeanne. We've collected as much as we can.'

The noise of the flames had lessened. She heard engines racing, still in the distance but drawing closer by the second. Now the German boy was watching her. There was something vulnerable about the stockinged feet in their home-knitted socks.

'Then go,' she told Colinet.

'Jeanne –'

'It's an order. Go. Give me the pistol.'

Colinet passed her the weapon, picked up the German's MP40, then made off. She removed her woollen cap and used it to wipe dirt and sweat from the boy's forehead. He groaned again. She held his gaze.

'Shh,' she whispered. 'Shh, Wilfried.'

The sound of his name seemed to comfort him. She whispered it again. His eyes closed. She spread the woollen cap over his head.

'Mutti,' he moaned.

She released the Luger's safety catch, tugged back the angled leg of the breech mechanism and discharged a single round through the woollen cap.

The racing vehicles were so close now that she could hear the shouts of their occupants. She scrambled up the bank and disappeared into the darkness.

Half an hour later the MP40 and the Luger were safely stowed away and the chickens were grudgingly settling themselves down again.

As she fastened the henhouse door the nausea suddenly swept over her. She doubled over and retched violently. All that came out was a stream of thick spittle. She retched again. The taste in her mouth was sour. She tried to spit the taste out but that only provoked more retching. She wiped her mouth and waited for her breathing to return to normal. Her eyes watered, so that everything around her was blurred.

But the carbonised bodies among the flames were clear enough in her mind's eye, along with her hands driving the magneto plunger home. So was the infinitely sad gaze of Wilfried Hermann Wiedemuth. So was her finger as it closed on the trigger of his pistol.

Lord, I am not worthy.

Gradually the retching subsided. The faintness passed. She straightened up and turned towards the cottage.

Unseen by her mother, Isabelle closed the cottage door, gently so that the rusty latch did not scrape, and crept soundlessly upstairs.

4

In a draughty room at the top of a small castle on Scotland's Isle of Lewis, an Englishman called Daniel Benedict picked up his pen and began to write.

The day outside was bright and dry but a harsh north wind with the bite of Siberia in it whistled around the castle's towers and parapets. The wind rippled the waters of the cold North Sea where they flowed into the harbour at the edge of the castle's grounds, it rocked the big clumsy seaplanes with their boat-like fuselages and strange backward-facing propellers, it rattled the poorly fitting windows of the room, and it caught the cigarette smoke drifting above the man who sat waiting at the other end of the table with a neat stack of large photographic prints by his elbow.

Six weeks, Benedict was thinking as his pen moved across the page; six weeks he had been here. Training, preparing, planning. Making sure there were no omissions or oversights.

In the mornings there was the physical stuff. Shaking off the cobwebs. Running, marching, cycling every rock-strewn road and mossy track of the island from end to soggy end. Then work on the maps, on the intelligence briefings and his own story, his cover – the truthful histories of those who would be his contacts and the fiction of the character he would inhabit for the duration. In the afternoons there was weapons work, mostly handguns, particularly the Browning 9mm but others as well, just in case. The firing range: in daylight, at dusk and at night, both bright moonlit nights, for moonlight shadows were more deceptive than sunlight ones, and dark miserable nights – dreich, the locals up here called them – when the cloud cover was as thick as London fog. And every evening spent with the French Catholic priest flown up from London for the purpose.

Then the identifications. Architectural layouts, photographs – never of good quality – and sketches produced by field agents in what he hazarded were trying circumstances. It was similar to the training given in identifying enemy aircraft, except these structures would never leave the ground.

'What's this one?' the trainer would ask.

'H679.'

'And this?'

'H669.'

But his notes were the thing. They were what it was all about. His notes and his memory. Each week he was taken by boat or sent on foot to stare at sections of the cliffs and rocky outcrops of the island. Never more than a minute in any one location. Nine, ten, a dozen sections at a time. Sprinkled about on the cliffs or beneath them, wherever the engineers could manage, were placed oddments of hardware cadged from the island's naval air squadron: trucks, any vehicles that could handle the terrain, bits of equipment scattered at random over a beach or a clifftop landscape: an old shed, a motorcycle, a defunct postbox, lamp posts. All to ensure variety. Tarpaulins were suspended over cliff faces with outsize letters and numerals painted on them, large enough for him to read from wherever he had been positioned: H622, H134, H636, twenty or thirty such combinations, matching the letters and numbers on the blurred photographs and architectural layouts he had studied.

Two weeks after each viewing session, he did his notes. The same procedure was repeated for four of the six weeks, with the locations, the artefacts and the letter–number combinations always changed. Bringing him to now, here, in this chilly room, with this final set of notes. Whose accuracy was second nature to him but a mystery to everyone else.

He finished work and passed what he had written to the man at the other end of the room. He had no need of the assessment the man would issue after comparing Benedict's notes with the photographic prints. He knew what the assessment would say. The same thing it always said: no errors.

He was ready. Though he had not known it back then, he had been ready ever since the ghost of an ancient ship had begun to emerge from the sandy earth of Suffolk.

'Miserable bloody weather,' grumbled the colonel.

Beneath his window, London's Baker Street was a sea of black umbrellas and soaked raincoats. Curtains of rain pulsed along the pavements and road. People ducked in and out of doorways, squeezing between the stacked sandbags.

'Miserable bloody war,' said the thin man seated at the table behind him.

The colonel sucked on his pipe, which by his calculation had gone out an hour ago. That meant another half hour before he could refill and light it. When he turned from the window he did so stiffly, swinging the right side of his body around. The right leg was a prosthesis. His right hand was also false, made of wood; hence the black glove it always wore. The real leg and hand had disappeared somewhere in the wild countryside of Ireland's County Kildare twenty-odd years previously, vaporised by an IRA bomb. The nasty little Irish war had left him with a healthy respect for the guerrilla tactics of the Irish irregulars – tactics that his own organisation, the Special Operations Executive, had taken to its heart, made its own and developed further in this present war.

He manoeuvred himself into a chair opposite his companion.

'In one hour from now, I'm scheduled to brief the director. One hour after that, he'll brief the PM. This will be the largest invasion force the world has ever seen, three to four million Allied troops drawn from a dozen nations by the time it's at full flow.' There was a file on the table. He eyed it as he spoke, as if his words were addressed to it; which, in a sense, they were. 'In support of that, this operation of ours cannot fail and it must not fail. Not my words. Nor the director's. Churchill's words.'

'They do have a certain ring to them.'

'So your agent is ready?'

The thin man had come prepared with a file of his own. Now he passed it across the table. The colonel opened it and glanced briefly at the photograph.

'Daniel Benedict,' said the thin man. 'Father English and self-made, mother French and a cut above. Our man Daniel was born in London and is a British subject, but Benedict senior's business interests were mostly in France, so that's where the boy was raised and educated. Consequently Daniel Benedict is perfectly bilingual. He also has good German, which is handy.'

'An archaeologist by trade.'

'One of the best. He worked on the excavation of Sutton Hoo in Suffolk –'

'The excavation of what?'

'An Anglo-Saxon ship burial. The finest yet found, apparently. The grave of a royal chieftain or feudal baron.

When the war came, the project was mothballed and he signed up for military service. Someone pointed him in our direction because of his language skills and knowledge of France. To date he's had seven field missions in France, all with Resistance cells, all successful. For the last six weeks he's been on Lewis, preparing for this next excursion. Usual stuff plus a few tailored extras. And cycling.'

'Cycling?'

'Lots of cycling.'

The thin man seemed disinclined to elaborate. The colonel resumed leafing through the file.

'Archaeologist. Well, it takes all sorts. Seven missions, you say?' The colonel chewed on the stem of the dry pipe. He could count on the fingers of his remaining hand the number of agents with that survival rate.

'There's one other thing,' the thin man continued. 'It's not in the file. I've kept it separate. He may have what some psychologists call an eidetic memory.'

'Photographic?' The colonel sniffed. 'No such thing. Myth.'

'Opinion is divided. What's certain is that Benedict can look at a location and commit its every detail to memory – topographical features, both natural and man-made, distances, you name it.'

'You believe this?'

'We've tested him. It's all in the file. He comes through with flying colours. Over and over.'

'Which is why you've chosen him for this operation.'

'We need comprehensive detail, complete accuracy. But we can't send a reconnaissance aircraft, even if it could get back safely. Too much for it to cover. And it would have to do the job in daylight. We can't send an agent with camera equipment. If he's captured, so is the equipment. Same thing if a recce aircraft is brought down. The Germans would know there can be only one reason for our recceing that particular part of the French coast. So Benedict's our camera.'

'Fine unless he's interrogated under torture.'

'Then the usual recourse applies.'

Which meant a cyanide pill. The colonel set his pipe down and cleared his throat. 'He has a code name for this job?'

'Avignon.'

The colonel raised an amused eyebrow. 'As in spurious popes. Very droll. Where is he now? Still up among the heather?'

'In London on a few days' leave.'

'Transport arranged?'

'He'll fly out from Tempsford when the weather lifts.'

The colonel cast a dubious look at the window, still lashed by rain.

'If it doesn't take too long, the moon will still be with us,' the thin man reassured him. 'The forecasters are optimistic.'

'Whose territory will he arrive on?'

'The local agent is Danton.'

'And Danton's sufficiently briefed?'

'Sufficiently and no more. The purpose of the operation but not the reason.'

'I should bloody well think not. I hope the same applies to Benedict.'

The thin man shifted in his chair. He nodded. But in the colonel's experience there were nods and then again there were nods.

'He knows, doesn't he?' he said. 'Benedict knows.'

'I have no reason to believe that.'

'And no reason to doubt it, by the look of you. No one with that information is supposed to be allowed in harm's way. Risk of capture, interrogation.'

'We don't *know* that he knows. Besides, who do we have that compares?'

The colonel mulled it over. He leafed through the file again. Seven missions. Last man standing, seven times out of seven.

Done. Devil take the hindmost.

'Reception committee to meet him?' he said.

'It'll be set up. He'll also have a number of staging posts along his way, contacts who'll give essential assistance.'

The colonel closed the file and gave it a little push across the table with his gloved hand.

'So I can tell the director everything's hunky-dory, and the director can tell the PM.'

The thin man picked up the file and rose to leave. 'Hunky-dory apart from what we can't ever button down.'

'Collaborators, traitors, informers.' It was a familiar refrain. 'And more varieties of communists than you can shake a stick at.'

'Some of the communists are our friends. For the present.'

The colonel harrumphed to himself as the thin man departed. He flipped open the tobacco pouch and at last began the luxurious task of packing the bowl of the pipe.

His gaze fell on the one file still on the table, the file that had lain there throughout the conversation and that he would take with him to his meeting with the director. The file that was the reason for the operation on which Daniel Benedict would shortly embark and about which he was meant to know nothing but probably knew too damned much. But what kind of agent would he be without the knack of finding out what he was never meant to find out?

The cover of the file bore the usual nonsense of 'Top Secret' and its quaint terminological predecessor 'Most

Confidential' – as if such warnings would discourage rather than further incentivise the unauthorised reader. Within these optimistic stamps was the name of the file: Overlord. Almost nine hundred years had passed since England had been invaded by a foreign power. That invasion had come from Normandy. This time, God willing, the tide would flow the other way. There was a satisfying symmetry to that.

And here was another one. The colonel picked up the file. A wry smile crossed his face as he lit the pipe. Overlord. Perhaps a man who dug up the occasional feudal baron was indeed just the ticket.

To the thin man and the colonel he was Benedict or Avignon. But to the drinkers in Le Singe Rouge he was Georges, a regular, in so far as anyone there could be considered a regular. At Le Singe Rouge, regulars came and regulars went.

The club was in a sleazy little back alley off a sleazy little Soho backstreet ten minutes' walk from Carlton Gardens, where the Free French had their official headquarters. Le Singe Rouge served as a sort of unofficial HQ. It had the advantage over Carlton Gardens in that the haughty de Gaulle never set foot there. The Connaught, where le grand Charles lunched every day, was more the general's style. That his people should be free was one thing; that he should actually rub shoulders with them, quite another.

Tonight, as ever, the air in Le Singe Rouge was blue with cigarette smoke and heavy with the fumes of alcohol, not all of it licit and some of it brought in by the drinkers themselves rather than purchased at the bar. No one minded. It meant more at the bar for everyone else in these difficult times. A four-piece band was busy on the corner stage, grinding out a repertoire of jazz and traditional numbers, the latter guaranteed to bring tears to exiled French eyes. Couples shuffled across the cramped dance floor, their preoccupation body contact rather than choreography. The music competed with a hubbub of voices that would grow louder as the night wore on.

Benedict inched towards the bar. There was a pattern to his evenings here. He would settle at a table with a few familiar faces. He would scan the most recent issues of *France* that were lying around and vaguely discuss an article with someone while nine-tenths of his attention was on the ebb and flow around him. No one would ask what he had been up to since he last dropped in, or where he lived, or how he earned his living, or where he had been lately, or even what part of France he hailed from. Nor would he make such direct enquiries of anyone else. A person might be what they seemed or they might not; as might he. So he said little, enough to pass himself, and asked less, but kept his eyes and ears open, scooping up gossip, innuendo, speculation, opinions.

Then he would move on to another table, another group of drinkers, another perspective on the hurly-burly, another conversation.

After a while, names might crop up, always the names of absentees: 'Where's Jean-Marie?' 'I haven't seen Armand for a while.' A head would shake, shoulders would shrug, someone would frown and pour another glass. Someone always knew, but no one would ever say. But it was clear that Jean-Marie would not be coming back to Le Singe Rouge. Perhaps he was an airman who had thrown his lot in with the RAF, perhaps he was lost now, downed in flames. Perhaps Armand was a fellow agent, as unknown to Benedict as Benedict was to him; perhaps Armand had run his final mission. Perhaps one evening someone would remark, 'What's become of that Georges fellow? I don't see him around these days.' The heads would shake. At Le Singe Rouge, regulars came and regulars went.

Sometimes, however, the course an evening took was a little different. Benedict would return from a mission with a further mission, one that was off the record and in its own way every bit as discreet as the official one, every bit as essential. No need to bother Baker Street with it. Those were the nights when he would seek out a face that until then had been only another drinker.

Tonight was such a night.

Pascal was at his usual corner table, reading, or seeming to read, a copy of *La Lettre*. As usual, he sat alone. As usual, he stroked his small beard as he read: a very neat little beard, for Pascal was a very neat little man. As usual, he had before him a single glass of red wine that would see him through the evening.

Benedict took his own drink to the table and sat down. Pascal did not look up from the leaflet.

'Good evening, Georges.' His voice was only just audible over the blare of the band. 'Why don't you join me? Oh, it appears you have.'

'Good evening, Pascal. Thierry sends his best wishes.'

The pamphlet continued to hold Pascal's attention. 'I don't think I know anyone called Thierry.'

'He asked me to buy you a drink.'

'Very kind of him, whoever he is, but I already have one.'

'Then this will cover your next one.'

Benedict set the coin on the table. Pascal's gaze took it in. It was a one-franc piece. Benedict had placed it year side up. The lighting was poor but the engraving was clear enough: 1943; Liberté, Égalité, Fraternité.

Pascal continued stroking his beard. He looked bored. But he did reach out and lazily turned the coin over: République Française.

'Fascinating,' he said. He did not look fascinated. 'But we're all Free French here. Everyone has these little baubles.'

Benedict stood up. 'Very well.' He picked up his drink. 'I apologise for disturbing you.'

'Sit down, Georges. I can't see the band. Madeleine's on soon and you're blocking my view.'

Benedict sat down again. He and Pascal studied one another in silence. He was aware of two figures separating themselves from the smoky crowd at the bar and moving closer. They edged into the shadows behind him.

Eventually Pascal broke the silence.

'Thierry's dead.'

'I'm sorry to hear that. He was a good man.'

'Where did you meet him?'

'In Toulouse.'

'When might that be?'

'I was with him and certain of his companions during a period of a month or so, ending six weeks ago. A friendly visit to give them assistance.'

He could see that Pascal was calculating. He himself had no idea when Thierry had died. Or how.

'Tell me a little more about this visit of yours,' said Pascal.

Benedict provided an account of the actions during the month in Toulouse; he included details that no outsider, no infiltrator or enemy, would know.

'On the final night there was an engagement outside the préfecture and the cathedral, near the fountain. It was hard fought but the outcome was positive. A minimum of eight enemy dead, with no losses on our side. One of the enemy fatalities was particularly important to Thierry, for personal reasons – the man who had tortured and hanged his son.'

Pascal pursed his lips. He said nothing.

68

'Afterwards we regrouped in a basement in the nearby suburb of Colomiers, in a house called Les Aiguades. That was when Thierry asked me to come to you. I had to leave immediately afterwards. I haven't been able to get to London until now, which I regret – all the more because of what you've just told me.'

Pascal seemed to make a decision. 'I was informed that someone had gone across from here. I didn't know who.'

'Naturally.'

'As for the question of timing, Thierry was killed the day after you left. You couldn't have saved him, my friend, if that's what you're thinking. I fear we may have a cuckoo in our nest.' He ran his fingernail over the embossed characters on the coin. 'But to our present matter – why did Thierry send you to me?'

'The two may be one, your cuckoo and the answer to that question. I'm to give you a name.'

The fingertip tapped the coin once and became still. 'Then please do that.'

'Séverin.'

Pascal's face showed no reaction. 'Séverin. You're sure?'

'Perfectly sure. Anatole Séverin. Thierry was emphatic.'

Pascal clucked his tongue, then fell silent again. His head dipped over *La Lettre*, though it was clear he was not seeing words on a page. Benedict knew what was happening. He recognised when one man was trying another, a judge and jury of one, in a court of the mind and the memory. Here is what happened, here is where such-and-such a person was at such-and-such a time; here is what he knew, here is what others knew, here is an unaccounted-for absence, a wrong glance, a hesitation that went unremarked at the time but is laden with implications now.

Such a court, such a judge and jury of one, with no appeal

possible, had no place in a civilised world. But how long since this world had been civilised?

As Pascal had promised, the band had been joined by Madeleine. The strains of 'J'attendrai' drifted over the babble of voices and laughter. 'Day and night I'll wait for you.' The babble carried on, desperate and urgent. Tomorrow we die. If not us, then someone surely will.

Benedict waited too. The court might have further questions for him. He turned in his chair to watch Madeleine. The two burly men behind him seemed to have no interest in music. They watched him.

At last Pascal raised his head.

'I've often wondered about you, Georges, when I see you here or at the rallies. But then, one wonders about everyone, one way or another.' A bone-weary smile. There would be no further questions. The evidence had been weighed, the verdict was in, sentence had been passed. 'Thank you for carrying out Thierry's commission. We needn't mention this again, I think.'

'Indeed not.'

Benedict was about to rise from the table, but Pascal had not finished.

'I dined with le général yesterday.'

'Yes?'

'He says England and the English are no use to us.'

'Does he?'

'That seems to me a bizarre view. England gives us shelter. It gives him shelter. But le général says that the English don't understand us. The English mind, a cold and wintry affair, he says, will never understand the passionate French soul. He says the only reason England helps us is from self-interest – better to contain and try to exterminate the Boche in France than to let the disease spread.'

'Why wouldn't England simply amputate the diseased

part?'

'Le général has a view on that too. Le général has a view on everything. He says that one day, if England thought it necessary, she would do precisely that. He says Churchill can't be trusted. Even worse, the Americans. England is nothing more than a little America.'

'What do you think, Pascal?'

Pascal's gaze surveyed the crowd. 'I don't agree. England is honourable. I can't say about Churchill, but he's only one man. I think England will stand by us because the English believe in doing the right thing. I don't like it when le général says these things. One day this war will end. Hitler and the Boche will be gone and France will be free. There'll be a new republic. Who'll lead it? Le général? Will France and England be friends then? I hope so. I hope France remembers who helped her, I hope the French remember.'

'I'm sure we will.'

'I mention this to you purely as a matter of theoretical interest, Georges, nothing more. As one Frenchman to another. Yes?'

'Of course.'

Benedict nudged the one-franc piece towards Pascal and left to resume his rounds of the tables.

He had fulfilled his private mission. The rest was up to Pascal. And Pascal had reciprocated. His warning, unattributed, would be in the report that Benedict would pass to the thin man in due course.

Half an hour later he glanced across the smoky room in time to see the two men who had stood behind him now moving casually through the crowd, drawing no attention to themselves but making steady progress, like an icebreaker through pack ice. A third man was securely pinned between them, steered by their comradely arms across his shoulders.

71

They were making for the exit. At Le Singe Rouge, regulars came and regulars went.

Benedict looked towards Pascal's table but now there were only the glass of red wine, still full, and the copy of *La Lettre* standing neatly on end like a menu card. No sign of the one-franc piece. No sign of Pascal either. Court had been adjourned.

5

'Herr Oberleutnant,' said Neiss, 'I don't understand.'

'Of course you don't,' agreed Graf. 'That's why you're not an oberleutnant and I am.'

It was the fortnightly screening of the latest films from the Reich's Ministry for Public Enlightenment and Propaganda. The event was Graf's innovation. The salle de réunion in the fishermen's hall down by the harbour was packed, the entire population of Caillons being present, both village and port. Graf had made attendance compulsory. Ration cards and food coupons were stamped upon entry, and absence of the red stamp would mean the loss of next week's bread, meat and cooking oil, the quantities of which were already calibrated at technical starvation levels – quite properly in his view, for these wretches would trade their grandmothers for a way around whatever allowance was set.

He and Neiss stood halfway down the room, where they could see not only the screen but also the Caillonais themselves. It was partly a matter of common sense – who in his right mind would feel safe in a dark place with these animals? – and partly a matter of making sure everyone paid respectful attention during these valuable educational opportunities.

Normally the Ministry's films were a joyous experience for him. Some were in colour, a visual miracle that took his breath away and a testament to the Reich's scientific superiority; but most, like tonight's, were in black and white. Even so, his heart always beat a little faster at the sight of those ranks of marching men in faultless formation, the sound of their stirring songs, the billowing swastika banners, the eagle insignias borne aloft, the vast choreographed gymnastic displays by bare-chested men and athletic women, all so fit and clean of limb. Oh, how wonderful were those sturdy Aryan maidens in their provocative black briefs. And how his spirit would soar as his Führer's rhetoric transported it to heaven as if on the wings of those mighty Reich eagles.

But tonight all was sullied. Tonight these Gallic brutes had destroyed every shred of pleasure – exactly as they had slaughtered his fine young troopers, Wiedemuth and Schmidt and Prausmüller and the others. For that a price would be paid. They would soon see that for themselves.

'The execution posts,' persisted Neiss. 'If you do what you plan, Herr Oberleutnant, what becomes of them? Installed at the mairie on your orders. Most precisely and exclusively on your orders.' His pallid face glistened in the flickering light from the screen. His spectacles slid down his nose. 'It was only with great difficulty that I was able to requisition the construction materials. The Atlantic Wall has priority over all other building works. The special requisition is on file in Paris and Berlin. Now you do this. Questions will be asked. How am I to answer them?'

'You don't. I'll deal with anything from Paris or Berlin. Think of those German mothers, Neiss.'

'Herr Oberleutnant?'

'The mothers of your murdered comrades. They're the ones to keep in mind – good mothers, wholesome and true guardians of hearth and home, the very foundation of our Reich and the new Germany, the comforters of their brave fighting men and the bearers of our future.'

'Yes, Herr Oberleutnant, but –'

'They deserve reverence and honour, Neiss, not the crushing letters I had to dictate to you for Ebermann's signature. As if he cares about my men. They're only names to him.'

Neiss coloured. 'Herr Oberleutnant, you shouldn't speak of Major Ebermann in that way.'

'Those letters will break the hearts of ten good German households. Does he know that? Do *you* know that?'

'Of course I do, Herr Oberleutnant. As does the major.'

Graf grunted, unconvinced. His gaze swept the audience, the faces frozen and stony as the images passed across the screen. His gaze came to rest on Jeanne Dupré.

'Look at her, Neiss. German hearts are breaking while she perches there like a queen between her princesses. I'm not stupid – I know about her and Ebermann. Can you imagine a greater contrast with German motherhood than that woman?'

If Neiss replied, Graf did not hear. His talk of motherhood had brought his thoughts to the woman who had been his own excuse for a mother. An equally poor excuse for a wife to his father.

Murderess.

The film rattled on as his thoughts circled, uneasy, unable to settle. But wherever his gaze went, however bitter the taste of those memories of failed motherhood in the Graf household, he kept returning to Jeanne Dupré and her daughters. A man could loathe a woman. His eyes could search her body and see nothing of any appeal, nothing to stir him. Or so it could seem. He could look at the daughter with her weak twisted leg and be repelled. Or so again it could seem.

But a man could wonder, he could give free rein to his thoughts if only for a secret moment. The mother's filthy little French body. The daughter with her budding breasts.

Weakness that a man could take in hand. A man's mind could probe the thought as a tongue probed a sensitive tooth, recoiling, always withdrawing from the throbbing sore but always seeking it again, wondering and wanting to test the reality against the imagining.

The film was drawing to a close. He told Neiss to fetch the troopers who were waiting outside and walked with measured pace to the front of the room, past the Dupré females, past the old priest Lachanau, whose whereabouts he had noted with special care, and stationed himself by the screen. When the final frames ran through and the screen flickered white and the empty reel clattered, he nodded to the projectionist and stepped in front of the screen. The lights came up, the spinning reels slowed to a stop. The villagers waited, knowing something was coming, anxious as to what it might be. He spun the moment out; well might they fret.

He took the sheet of paper from his tunic pocket and unfolded it.

'The following persons will go to the rear of the hall, where they will be escorted outside for special duties,' he announced.

He watched the effect as the command sank in. Now they knew. The priest knew too. The old black crow began to rise from his chair, his face like thunder. But Graf had anticipated him, had walked towards him and was already within reach, pistol drawn. One swingeing blow and the flat of the weapon smashed into the side of Lachanau's head. He dropped like a felled beast, without a whimper.

Graf felt the shock wave that swept the room. A gratifying result. The woman Dupré cried out and rushed to the priest's aid. Graf ignored her. He read out the list of ten names, pausing after each one. One worthless Caillonais for every fine young Wehrmacht trooper who had been slaughtered. If he had his way, it would be two, even three. But Ebermann had overruled him. Another example of the major's weakness.

Around the room ten men of various ages rose apprehensively to their feet. Oh, they hoped, they prayed that it might not be so, what they feared was to happen, but in their hearts they knew better. And once again he was ready for what would come now, the hands clutching fearfully at the ones who had been selected, the tears, the pleas. He strode towards the two men nearest him, levelled his pistol at them, tore them from the hands that tried to cling to them, and nodded at the contingent of his troopers who were now entering the hall. They marched up the central aisle, rifles and submachine guns at the ready, and seized all ten men, herding them at gunpoint out into the dusk.

As the doors slammed after them, he surveyed the gathering.

'The rest of you will remain here. You will be silent.'

Three minutes passed, during which he and four armed troopers patrolled between the rows of chairs, stopping at intervals to stare at someone or demand identity papers – none of it necessary but it was proper to affirm who the masters were. A child began crying, soon followed by others. These people had so little control over their offspring. One young female unbuttoned her dress and pressed a grubby baby to her breast. He shuddered. They were little better than the beasts in their fields.

Then came the volley of submachine-gun fire in the distance. It lasted a long time, perhaps fifteen seconds. Sobs and half-stifled wails arose here and there in the hall.

'Silence!'

He pictured the scene: the ten men lined up at the very edge of the breakwater as he had instructed, the bodies tumbling into the surf, driven by the force of the submachine-gun rounds, the spreading pool of blood on the water, the tide on the turn, carrying the corpses out to sea. It might be weeks before any returned to shore; if they ever did.

'The curfew will be reinstated in ten minutes,' he announced as the echo of the gunfire faded. 'That allows adequate time to return directly to your homes. Thereafter you will observe the curfew in the normal way – no lights visible, shutters and windows closed. I remind you that it is forbidden to go out without an Ausweiss, a Laissez-passer, which must be accompanied by appropriate identity papers. Following the recent cowardly murder of Wehrmacht personnel, security will be stepped up. Additional armed patrols will be on duty throughout the night. They have authority to open fire without warning on anyone transgressing curfew regulations or suspected of being a threat to civic security. The breakwater is off limits since it is not on the route to any domicile. Consequently, if you hold a night fishing Ausweiss, it is suspended for tonight. That is all. You will leave now.'

Neiss crept nervously into view. Tailed by the leutnant, Graf stalked the hall as it emptied, watching as little huddles supported one another and ragged lines shuffled along with heads bowed, some people weeping, no one speaking.

He turned away from the odours of stale clothing and unwashed bodies. The old priest had recovered consciousness and was being helped by the woman Dupré and someone else, another female, elderly and plump. As this one turned towards him, Graf saw that she was the priest's housekeeper, the Guinard woman who also cooked for Ebermann.

'The major lets these people get too close to him, Neiss.

As if the woman Dupré in his bed isn't bad enough, he has the priest's witch keeping house for him. No fool like a commissioned fool.'

He looked up and down the line of people straggling past. The crippled daughter and her little sister were nowhere to be seen. They had made themselves scarce, no hanging about to help their mother and the priest. Minds of their own, then. How interesting.

'Psychology, Neiss.' He put an arm about the leutnant's shoulders and walked him to the side of the hall.

'Psychology, Herr Oberleutnant?'

'The new science. Of course, the Jews are already trying to take it over. Freud and the rest.'

Neiss pushed his spectacles back in place. 'Herr Oberleutnant?'

'But we can use it too. It can serve the Reich. How? Simple – deny these people the heroics they crave. They're an emotional race, they indulge themselves. Can't help it, it's their degeneracy. They elevate the lowest common murderer to the status of demigod. Religion and singing, mindless prayers, priests and their superstitious rigmarole – all this is pure hysteria, it excites them, emboldens them. So we must sweep it away. No homage to so-called heroes. Let there be no glorious death, only extinction, as unacknowledged as a sackful of drowned kittens. Forget about finding and executing the actual perpetrators of crimes against us – when we succeed, that's the most dangerous moment, because that's what allows these people to turn them into martyrs. So the answer? Couldn't be easier – execute others instead.'

'What others? Who?'

'Anyone. It doesn't matter. Can't you see? That's the point. Choose at random. Like tonight. No glory in that, only humiliation. It tells them they're all equally insignificant. Psychology, Neiss.'

The leutnant frowned. 'And the execution posts?'

'We'll still use them, of course we will, particularly when the numbers are less pressing than this evening. The harbour is convenient on this occasion since we're down here anyway. And it gets rid of the bodies. Besides, we should be creative in our techniques. As with the ovens for the Jews.'

Neiss turned even paler. 'The ovens?'

'I admit we had to work to get them right. Prototype after prototype. Sometimes new ideas take time to refine. But the Reich's scientists are ingenious, they triumphed.' Graf chuckled; he was feeling better now. 'Let's have a walk. Clear the stink of this rabble from our nostrils. Night's the best time for a walk here, once the curfew empties the streets. We'll stroll down to the breakwater. You look like you need a breath of fresh air. Come along.'

'Leave me, Jeanne,' said Lachanau. The strong voice was reduced to a hoarse whisper. 'You must go home. The curfew.'

'Too late,' she said. 'No matter, I was planning to stay with you anyway.'

She had managed to get him to his home and upstairs, where she bathed and bandaged the wound. He had drifted in and out of consciousness as she traipsed up and down with basins of water. She had manoeuvred him onto the narrow bed and tugged off his tattered shoes and pulled the thin blankets around him. The wound was deep, a gash the length of the gun barrel that had made it, but she did not think there was any fracture or break in the skull. He was made of iron.

He touched his bandaged head tentatively. 'I've taken far worse punishment than this in my time.'

'You probably deserved it.'

'It's embarrassing.'

'My being here?'

'No. What I let Graf do to me.'

'So even a priest has his vanity.'

'My guard was down. I'm getting old.'

'You? Never, mon curé.'

It was little wonder that Graf had him in his sights – he had a score to settle after the way the priest had faced him down at Pierre's execution. Just as she too had put herself in the oberleutnant's sights.

There was another worry. Graf's action this evening was not only a new level of evil. It was also clever. It could turn people against the cell and its activities. Such reprisals played right into the collabos' hands. That could prove very dangerous.

Lachanau sighed. 'Who else is here? Madame Guinard?'

'No, I sent her off.'

'Your daughters?'

'They went straight home.'

'So you're proposing to be alone with the priest in his house all night. And here you are in his bedroom. Oh dear. What will Caillons say about you, Jeanne?'

'No worse than it says already.'

'Ah. Now that's something I wanted to speak to you about.'

'What Caillons says?'

'More important, what your saviour is saying. You never come to confession nowadays. You no longer take communion. Precious holy sacraments, vital to your soul. Why are you avoiding them?'

'Perhaps my confession would be too much of a burden.'

'For me?'

'For God.'

'Nothing's too much for him. What would he do for all eternity if he didn't have us to forgive?'

'Say your prayers and go to sleep, mon curé. I'll be downstairs. Call if you need anything.'

Downstairs she found the priest's black winter greatcoat, threadbare but voluminous, and cocooned herself within it in the one armchair. She looked around the room and saw his breviary on the table, a bible and various devotional pamphlets, a simple wooden crucifix on the wall, a small porcelain font of holy water by the door, like the one in his bedroom, a hand-tinted photograph of Pius XII on the wall and opposite it a Sacred Heart. There was little else in the simple room. So this was Père François Lachanau's world.

Her thoughts turned to Michel – still no letter – and her daughters. She prayed for them and asked Christ's mercy on the souls of her fellow countrymen who had died tonight.

She wondered about praying for Wilfried Hermann Wiedemuth, born March 1925, died May 1944, and the other Germans who had died with him.

Then there was the matter of praying for herself. She wondered how far forgiveness could be stretched. But exhaustion overtook her and she was asleep before she could decide on any of these things.

Isabelle was fast asleep, Hélène was sure of it, had been for ages now. She whispered her sister's name one more time, then made herself count silently to one hundred before whispering again. Isabelle's breathing continued undisturbed.

Hélène slipped from the bed and sat down on the floor to strap the steel brace in place. She stayed there to dress, then made her way as quietly as possible down the stairs, concentrating hard on trying to place her feet where she knew the creaks were fewest. Her left leg was the one that needed particular concentration. Sometimes it seemed to have a mind of its own. She could tell it to do this, go there, but it would either decide without warning to drag like a puppy that was tired of walking or suddenly fold in entirely the wrong direction.

The latch of the door scraped as she raised it, so she froze in place, holding the door still closed, to hear if Isabelle stirred. She heard nothing. She stepped outside as quickly as her leg would allow and closed the door immediately so that the sound of the ocean, always so much louder at night, would not fill the cottage. She stood there for a few moments, listening to the night and the sea, then she turned towards the old coastal path, the one that nobody bothered with these days now that the land was no longer worked. In one direction it would take her to the headland and the cliff. In the other it would take her to the harbour and the breakwater.

She set off down the slope. It was the harbour route she had in mind.

Behind her Isabelle stealthily opened the window of La Croisette and unhooked a shutter, pushing it aside in time to catch a glimpse of her elder sister before the shuffling figure melted into the shadows.

When she was sure that Hélène was not about to turn back, she hurried out to the henhouse. Her stomach heaved at the stench as she crept inside. Darkness and heat enveloped her.

The tap-tap on the door was very soft, only just audible over the bubbling of the cooking pot. It might only have been a pine cone tumbling from the tall cypresses that towered over the little cottage.

Gaspard Baignères propped his ladle against the side of the pot and reached up to one of the low roof beams, hooked his hand into the deep hollow carved in it and lifted out the Star semi-automatic pistol. It had been a good friend to him back in his army days in the forests of the high Ardennes and in the horror of the trenches; and many a time since.

He drew the pistol's slide back as quietly as possible, then eased it forward.

The tap-tap came again. Then a third time. It was no pine cone. He switched off the single light bulb and unbolted the door.

The young man who came puffing in was short and slight, smaller than many women. He was half wheeling, half dragging a pushbike even older than Gaspard's. It looked too large for him. A beret was squashed down tightly on his head. Sweat trickled through his hair. He blinked at Gaspard through large tortoiseshell spectacles.

'The Boche are everywhere tonight,' he said. 'It was touch and go. Roadblocks, patrols. You'd think there was a war on.'

Gaspard bolted the door and switched the light on.

'Welcome, Professor. Another stolen vélo?'

The visitor shrugged. 'Property is theft. Anyhow, I'll return it before morning.' He leant the pushbike in the corner, alongside Gaspard's machine.

The spectacles magnified his eyes. When he looked at Gaspard, one eye stared slightly into the distance. It was a disconcerting effect but Gaspard had grown used to it. Now that the visitor had caught his breath the eyes seemed to be focusing on the cooking pot. Gaspard returned the pistol to its hiding place and resumed stirring the stew.

'How's Paris?' he asked over his shoulder.

'Hungry. Starving. Corpses in the streets. People may

84

turn to cannibalism. Rumours are it's already happening. If you've got money and the right connections, preferably German, you swig champagne on the Champs-Élysées and dance all night. Otherwise –' He made a slashing gesture across his throat. 'Only the profiteers and the capitalists are happy, as sleek and fat as mink. And as sharp of tooth. You'd be in your element.'

'I'll stick to the countryside. You're writing?'

'Small things for the magazines that still survive. Essays. Some pieces for the theatre, when I can find somewhere to stage them.'

'Your name in lights.' Gaspard's free hand sketched in the air.

His visitor snorted dismissively. Then the wayward eyes fell on Gaspard's notebook, closed but still on the table where he had left it.

'Ah,' he said. 'A fellow thinker and writer?'

His hand moved towards the notebook but Gaspard retrieved it in time and slipped it safely away in his pocket.

'Scribbles, nothing of importance,' he said. 'We had a little excitement this evening. It's why you had a hard time getting here.'

A little excitement. Ten names, all carefully noted.

He glanced down at his visitor. The wandering eyes were now aimed in the general direction of the cooking pot.

'That smells good.'

'I thought you philosophers didn't need food.'

'You're thinking of ascetics.'

'That's not you?'

Another snort.

'So what are you, then – apart from a Marxist?'

'I resent that simplification. Perhaps an existential nihilist.'

'Aha. Nothing matters.'

'That soup does. Is it rabbit?'

'It's not soup – it's ragoût. Beef ragoût.'

'Beef ragoût made with rabbit?'

'Beef ragoût made with beef.'

Now the visitor removed his beret and sat down at the table. His tongue made a rapid circuit of his lips. He seemed slightly overcome, but that might have been the cycle ride. Gaspard knew he had difficulty with his balance and in judging distances and direction.

'You'll join me?' he asked.

The little professor nodded. Gaspard ladled the stew into two tin bowls and set bread on the table – real bread, the heavy black bread that Hodin had learned to make for the Germans, not the make-believe variety with sawdust. He fetched a bottle of red wine and filled two tin mugs. His guest watched everything closely.

'I don't suppose you have butter?' he asked. 'Existential nihilism can only take a man so far.'

Gaspard set a platter of Normandy butter between them. It was a deep, warm yellow. The little man sighed with contentment and raised his mug of wine in a toast.

'I bring news,' he said.

'We eat first, Professor,' said Gaspard. 'When there's news, always eat first.'

What a disgrace Neiss was. Graf had packed him off to barracks when it was clear that the man was an insult to his uniform and the Reich. Throwing up at the sight of a few bodies floating on the waves – what kind of fighting man was that?

So Graf returned to the harbour by himself. There they were, the bodies, only four or five of them left now, out beyond the lines of wooden bouchots, bobbing gently along, the rest having already been drawn out on the retreating tide; or perhaps some had sunk beneath the surface until they would fill with gas and be impelled upwards again to give some fisherman a lively surprise.

He stepped down from the breakwater to the beach. The moonlight played tricks with colour. It was hard to know whether the surf was still stained red or whether the blood had all washed out to sea. He stood there for a while anyway, enjoying the cool night air. He would check the patrols and the roadblocks shortly but first he was entitled to a few quiet minutes. He had done good work this evening. That smack he had dealt the priest, what a pleasure that was.

He tapped an Eckstein on its packet and dug out his lighter. A light breeze was coming in from the bay, rattling the halyards against the masts of the small boats at anchor in the harbour. He cupped his hands and turned his back to the breeze, sheltering the lighter before flicking the spark wheel.

When he turned, she was there on the breakwater. The lighter remained unlit. He clicked it shut. Beside him was a hut where fishermen stored their tackle and nets. If he had been standing half a metre forward he would have been visible to her. His first reaction was fury. How had she managed to get here despite the curfew? Where were his men? How had she got past them? Someone would take a bullet for this.

Then again, maybe not. Not if there was a good enough reason to keep her transgression under wraps.

He stepped forward so that she could see him. She almost stumbled over the edge of the breakwater in alarm. She turned in her clumsy way, ready to flee, but then she saw the pistol that had replaced the lighter in his hand.

'Come here,' he said.

She did not move. He loaded a round. She jumped at the

sound, knowing its meaning. Still she did not move. He realised she was paralysed with fear, which was pleasing. He lowered the pistol and repeated the command.

She hobbled awkwardly down the steps from the breakwater, following the route he had taken. It took her a long time. When she reached the sand she stopped. Now he could see the wet tracks on her cheeks.

'You've been crying?'

No response.

'Come here. All the way here.'

She picked her way across the beach. For her the soft sand was treacherous. She missed her footing several times, almost falling over. Eventually she arrived. She stared at the ground. He wanted her to raise her dark eyes, he wanted her to look at him.

'Why were you crying? You have a boyfriend? He died tonight?'

She shook her head. 'I wanted to say adieu. I've done nothing wrong.'

'You knew some of these men?'

'I knew all of them. Naturally I did. Caillons is a small place, everyone knows everyone else. That's why I came. And I was thinking about my uncle. That's not against the law.'

'Ah yes. Your uncle was Pierre Rochard.'

She nodded.

'A murderer. A résistant. Executed under the law.'

'Your law.'

'Yours too, now. You're trembling. Are you afraid?'

'No.'

'Are you sure? Aren't you afraid of me?'

'No.'

'You should be.' He held the pistol on her while he produced the lighter again and lit the cigarette. 'You say

88

you did nothing wrong. Not true. You transgressed the curfew. Creeping about like a little alley cat. A lame alley cat. You know the punishment for breaking curfew?'

No response. He held the pistol to her head and made the sound of a shot being fired. Once again she jumped. He chuckled. His cigarette smoke drifted across her face. She clenched her eyes shut. He scanned the harbour from side to side. No sign of life. Nothing on the road above, nothing on the steep path up to the village. His gaze returned to the harbour and the cottages that encircled it. There might be watchers behind every closed shutter. That was how this place was, that was how these people were.

So what? Caillons was his. All of France was his. He rocked on his heels. He pointed with the pistol at the door of the hut.

'Open it,' he told her.

Understanding dawned. 'No.'

He brought the pistol back to her head.

'I see you have a mind of your own. I like that in a young woman. But you know I kill people.'

'Everybody knows that. It's all you're good for, you Boche.'

'Ah, but you won't be the only one I'll kill.'

At last the dark eyes looked directly at him. Her little chest quivered with her sharp intake of breath. He bent down to her.

'First your mother. Then your little sister. I enjoy dealing with females. I have a special talent.' He straightened up. 'Now open the door, alley cat, and let's get inside.'

He took a final drag of the cigarette and followed her into the hut.

Tap-tap.

Gaspard and his visitor froze. The little professor's eyes

89

swivelled in the general direction of the door. Gaspard put a finger to his lips.

It came again: tap-tap.

A busy night. Gaspard shooed his visitor silently behind the stove, where he crouched down in time to grab his pushbike as it followed him.

Gaspard retrieved the Star from its home in the roof beam, switched off the light and cracked the door open.

Jacques Colinet was standing there. Gaspard opened the door a little wider but made no move to admit him. The Star remained behind his back.

'Good evening, Jacques. You're out and about late. Don't let our friendly oberleutnant catch you. You heard what he said – bullets first, questions afterwards.'

'Can I come in?'

'I'd like you to, but …' Gaspard ran a hand over his moustaches. 'Well, you know.'

'Company?'

Gaspard grinned.

Colinet thrust something towards him. Gaspard looked down and discerned the outline of a pair of stout battledress boots. German hobnails.

'Handsome,' he said.

'How much?' said Colinet.

'Owner quite finished with them?'

Colinet nodded. 'Oh yes.'

Gaspard stuck the pistol down the back of his trousers. He switched on the bulb and opened the door enough to let the light fall on the boots.

'Hardly worn,' said Colinet. 'Good as new.'

Gaspard pursed his lips as he examined the merchandise. He nodded thoughtfully and produced a pack of Gitanes. He offered one to Colinet.

'I think we can work something out, Jacques. But you

still can't come in.'

Oblivious to the curfew, Adalard Fougeret, father of young Louis who had been executed with Pierre Rochard and Guillaume Raynal, stood weeping quietly before the three pine stakes in place de l'Église. His feet were aching, his ankles swollen and throbbing because he had walked so much since his son's death, through all the lanes and alleyways of Caillons, remembering his fine boy at every turn – here the little school, there Mathilde Pauthier's garment room where he had bought Louis his confirmation suit, over there the old lighthouse that fascinated the child.

But however deep his grief, he had not taken complete leave of his senses, so when he heard the low growl of an armoured car approaching he pulled himself together and stole away. Not a moment too soon, for as he reached rue du Port he glanced back in time to see the ugly snout of the vehicle rounding the corner from rue du Centre. He headed downhill, planning to cut towards rue du Phare and the lanes that led off from it; he certainly wanted to be nowhere near the breakwater and its horrors.

He had gone only a few paces when he saw the girl. She was right at the bottom of the hill, making her way slowly across the sand, but he knew immediately who she was. Anybody in Caillons would recognise that lopsided hobble.

Then a flicker of light flashed in the darkness near her. Someone was lighting a cigarette. He caught a brief glimpse of a face, though it was impossible at this distance to determine its features. But what he did see was the silhouette of a peaked uniform cap. Hatred rose like vomit in his throat. It was Graf.

Adalard pressed his skinny frame behind an advertising pillar plastered with German notices. If only he had his old shotgun with him he would run down that hill and …

But he did not have the gun. And the thought came to him that he should not even be out at this hour, any more than should young Hélène Dupré. Graf would arrest both of them, the girl first, for he was right beside her, then if he came up the hill he would find Adalard. What would poor Adeline do then, with her husband in the hands of the Boche? Or if Graf shot him on the spot? That was what the German had warned, after all – open fire without warning. Poor Adie. First her Louis, then her Adalard.

He drew his head in sharply and waited. By the grace of God the patrol vehicle sounded further away now. But when he ventured another peep around the pillar, there was no sign of either Graf or the girl.

He was safe. But strangely, so presumably was Hélène Dupré.

He frowned at the empty street. What an inexplicable turn of events. Wait till Adie heard about this. It might even make her forget to chastise him for his folly.

Time to go home and find out.

6

They came for Jeanne at two that morning, arriving in a roar of smoky exhaust fumes and a crash of heavy boots as they vaulted down from their truck and crunched over the cobblestones of the square. They hammered on the door of Père Lachanau's house with the butts of their submachine guns and called out incomprehensibly in their unmelodious language. There were ten or twelve of them, four who came to the house while the rest ringed place de l'Église, their weapons at the ready.

No sooner had Jeanne unbolted the door than it was kicked open, skimming past her and banging against the wall.

'What do you think you're doing?' thundered a voice behind her. The troopers froze, two of them having already pushed their way into the tiny room. Lachanau stood blocking their advance, a huge black-clad figure with his head enveloped in a crown of white bandage.

'Get out of this house,' he roared. 'This is church property. You have no right to enter without permission. Do you know how many laws you've broken – ecclesiastical as well as civil? I'll see to it that Major Ebermann deals personally with each and every one of you.'

Whether they understood every word or not, the troopers got the point; they looked uncertain. Jeanne studied their faces in the half light. More children, not much older than her own Hélène. A squad of Wilfried Hermann Wiedemuths, every one of them blonde haired and blue eyed, as if a factory was punching them out from a template. Why did war hunger so for children?

Lachanau stood his ground but the trooper who seemed to be in charge was determined. He addressed Lachanau but his gaze was on Jeanne.

'We have information that Madame Jeanne Dupré is here. We have orders to find her.'

She laid her hand on Lachanau's arm before he could respond. 'You've found her. What's your business with me?'

'You are to come with us.'

'Are you arresting me?'

'You must come with us.'

She nodded slowly, her hand still restraining Lachanau. *You must come with us.* It was the form of words favoured by this occupying force torn between arrogance and its meticulousness for proper procedure when it had no specific cause for apprehending someone or could not be bothered to articulate one. Or when it wanted to see what a fearful victim might disclose under pressure or interrogation.

'Very well.' She pressed Lachanau's arm as she felt him bridle. She drew his greatcoat closer about her shoulders. 'Back to bed, mon curé. These young men intend me no harm.'

Now that she was in their custody, the troopers were calm and respectful. There was no violence or bullying. They addressed her as Madame. They helped her to board the truck, dropping its tailgate and handing her up with strong arms. They did not close in on her as she sat on the bench between them. If she was suspected of the attack in the bois de Caillons or any other Resistance involvement, they kept the thought to themselves. They did not stare belligerently at her but gazed watchfully out into the night as the truck bumped out of the village and towards Le Manoir, along the lane through the bois de Caillons where the earth and trees were still burnt and blackened. They trained their weapons not on her but on the dark woods and hedgerows.

Soon the truck passed over Le Manoir's killing strip and through the main entrance gate. As the troopers helped her down she glanced up and saw silhouetted against the night sky the watchtowers with their machine-gun emplacements. She was escorted across the compound and down to a cobwebbed basement area with racks where wine had once been stored, and after many turnings and corridors to a cell deep below ground that could well have been occupied by Pierre or his comrades before their transfer to the mairie on their last night alive. There were bloodstains on the walls and floors.

Left alone, she examined her surroundings. It did not take long. There was no furniture. No bed, no chair, no table. No window. There was the door through which she had been delivered, with no handle on its inside, there was one unshaded light bulb overhead, there was a bucket in the corner to relieve herself, God forbid. There was a slot in the door that snapped open when someone chose to peer in. No eyes were ever visible to her. Nothing was said to her. No footsteps approached before the slot opened, none departed after it closed, so her watcher was posted there all the time.

She found it hard to estimate the passage of time. The light went on and off at random intervals. With no reference points, she knew that whatever guess she made would be wrong. Instead she focused on shutting her mind down, as if she was a hibernating animal. The room was freezing cold; she was thankful for Père Lachanau's old greatcoat.

After a period when the cell had been in darkness, the light came on and she heard footsteps approach. The bolts on the door were drawn back. Another of the production line of youths in Wehrmacht fatigues entered. To her shock, she realised she was glad to see him – because she was glad to set eyes on a fellow human being. It was another part of the process. So she rejected the feeling, only to suspect at once that too was prescribed, to confuse her emotions.

Blinking in the light, she watched the young gefreiter. He had brought two upright chairs. There was a pistol at his belt. Unseen hands slammed and bolted the door behind him. He separated the chairs and placed them opposite one another, a metre or so apart, and indicated that she should sit on one. She did, expecting him to take the other. Instead, he knocked on the door, the bolts were slid back, and he departed. His footsteps faded to silence.

She sat there waiting. Nothing happened. No one came to sit in the vacant chair. Time passed. The slot in the door opened and shut. The light went out; after a while it came on again. She watched a woodlouse enter beneath the door, wander across a dark bloodstain and leave again. She stood up and walked about, if three paces in any direction could be termed walking, then returned to the chair. Same chair. So she stood up again and switched to the other one.

Footsteps approached. The bolts slammed back, more urgently this time, the door swung open.

At first Isabelle thought it was a roll of thunder out at sea, where the storms always began.

She had returned to bed but not to sleep. How could she sleep after what she had found in the henhouse? She drifted like a swimmer giving herself to the currents. There were no answers, only endless questions. On and on. All concerning her mother. So many, in fact, that they left no room in her thoughts to wonder what her sister was up to.

The thunder grew louder, drew nearer, but more quickly than any thunder should. She jerked upright in the bed. This was no thunder; what thunder ever sounded like that? Thunder did not march in unison. Thunder did not halt outside La Croisette with a well-drilled final stamp of boots. Thunder did not batter on the door and shout commands.

Thunder did not bring her sister, silent and pale, her gaze vacant and dead, and fling her at Isabelle's feet, and then ransack their home, searching for what Isabelle knew was there to be found.

Oberleutnant Jürgen Graf entered the cell. Jeanne felt no sense of surprise: Graf, master of these little ceremonies, exactly as she had anticipated. He was dressed in formal uniform and peaked cap. In the harsh overhead light his jackboots, leather belt and holster gleamed like mirrors. When he removed his cap, she saw that his hair was pomaded, as though he had recently bathed. His chin and cheeks looked freshly shaved, the skin soft and silky. She caught a sickly whiff of cologne.

He settled himself in the chair opposite her and crossed his legs comfortably, like a man looking forward to a friendly chat. He had brought a pad of paper. He placed it on his lap and folded his hands over it. His fingernails were clean and neatly trimmed.

He gazed at her in silence for a time. She returned his gaze and his silence. There was nothing in his gaze. It was like being regarded by a statue.

'Good morning, Madame,' he said at last. 'I apologise for the basic character of your accommodation. What is your name, please?'

'You know perfectly well what it is. Your men do, and I assume it was you who sent them to fetch me.'

'There are formalities. Please answer the question.'

'Does Major Ebermann know I'm here?'

'That's of no significance. Please cooperate.'

'And if I don't?'

'It's better to cooperate.'

'Better for you?'

'Please don't be tiresome. Your name, please.'

'Am I under arrest? I was told I am not.'

'We simply want to clarify a few things.'

'If I'm not under arrest, I'll leave now, thank you.'

'You can leave soon. Your name is Jeanne Dupré. Correct?'

'There. I said you knew.'

'Dupré, formerly Rochard. Sister of Pierre Rochard.'

'I have no brother. Not any longer. I'm no one's sister.'

'Pierre Rochard, with others under his leadership, was convicted of attacking and killing personnel of the deutsche Militärverwaltung in Frankreich, the German forces in France, and of the destruction of Reich property.'

'He wasn't convicted of anything. He was never tried.'

'He was tried by military court.'

'In secret. That's not a trial under French law.'

'French law does not prevail, Madame. Reich law takes precedence.'

'I'd like to leave now, Oberleutnant.'

'I have only one or two simple questions. The sooner you answer them, the sooner you can leave.' He smiled. 'Free as a bird.' The smile was switched off. 'Did you arrange for the unlawful singing at your brother's execution?'

'Is singing against the law now?'

'That song is.'

'My brother sang, not me.'

'Did you incite others to sing?'

'I heard seagulls that morning. Perhaps you think I conducted their chorus too.'

He sighed. 'Did you know of your brother's activities as

an enemy of the Third Reich?'

'How can a person know something whose existence remains hypothetical unless it has been proven in a legitimate court of law?'

'Did you assist Pierre Rochard in any way?'

'How can a person assist in a hypothesis?'

'The most recent attack on our troops, that too was hypothetical?'

'How would I know? But the innocent Caillonais who were executed on your orders last night, they were real enough. I knew them.'

'And I knew the loyal Wehrmacht troopers who were murdered. So you deny involvement in that attack or knowledge of it?'

'Just as I deny that there is any way in which I can help you.'

Another sigh. 'Thank you, Madame Dupré. That's all for the moment.'

'I'll leave now.'

'Soon, Madame.'

He stood up, replaced his cap, took his pad of paper, which he had never opened or glanced at, knocked for the door to be opened, and left. Once again she listened as footsteps faded into the distance.

Throughout the rest of her detention he returned every hour or so, as far as she could reckon. He always looked as fresh as if he had come directly from the battalion barber. Sometimes he smoked, sometimes not, depending on the length of his stay.

There were always more questions. They were always equally pointless, because he knew he would never get any answers. Which was why he never wrote a single word on his pad of paper. He never even produced a pen.

When at last she was escorted from the cell and back up

to the compound, bustling now with grey-clad troopers and vehicles, the sun was already above the watchtowers. Half the morning was gone. Hélène and Isabelle would be at their wits' end if they heard she had been taken into custody during the night. Even if Ebermann had noted her failure to arrive for work at the Villa Normandie and had uncovered what Graf had been up to, the oberleutnant had been clever – there was no official arrest, she had not been mistreated, merely intimidated, and in the scale of things that counted for nothing.

But what was the purpose of her detention? Someone like Graf did nothing without good reason. The troopers' courteous handling of her, the lack of any serious attempt at interrogation, no violence against her despite the evidence in those bloodstains of its ready availability – none of it made sense.

She stepped through the door a guard opened in the château gate, crossed the killing strip and began the long trek over the plain and back to the village. The question turned over and over in her mind as she tramped along the lanes, the greatcoat now boiling hot and as heavy as lead in her arms, its coarse fabric scratching her skin, while the sun scorched the fields and a stream of Wehrmacht trucks and personnel carriers bounced past her in clouds of dust.

But she found no answers.

François Lachanau would never have wished Jeanne's night of detention on her, nor indeed on any of his beloved flock, but her absence suited him, for he had plans for that night, urgent plans that could not wait, but he had feared that he himself had driven them onto the rocks. As soon as he saw Graf's arm swing towards him in the fishermen's hall he realised his mistake. Even as the blow landed, even as he blacked out, he was cursing his foolishness. It was like a stumble in the ring: too late, no going back.

In the arrival of the troopers, whose racket would have woken Lazarus, he was not sure if he saw his saviour's hand or Satan's. That would depend on what was in store for Jeanne. Graf would be behind it; if it were to rain locusts in Caillons, Graf would be behind it.

But in the meantime Lachanau had his mission to carry out, and that at least he had no doubt was God's will. So when the Wehrmacht truck had gone and its engine note had fallen away, he shed his long soutane and pulled on an old black sweater and a dark beret to conceal the white bandage. He kissed the wooden crucifix and tucked it away beneath the sweater. He went to the larder, opened the weighty sack of fresh mussels and unwound the damp rags in which they were wrapped. They were in fine condition, all of them firmly closed and alive, their salty Atlantic tang healthy and fresh. He rewound the rags, closed the sack, hefted it out to the yard where his old pushbike waited, lashed it securely to the crossbar and pushed off into the night, his long legs folding and unfolding like a giant grasshopper's.

It was a long ride to the home of the brother priest for whom the mussels were destined – an unsteady one too in his condition – so the old man on whom he was calling, even older than young François Lachanau as he called him and long retired from a priest's regular duties, had been in bed many hours by the time he arrived. But after some initial sleepy surprise the old man's eyes widened in delight at sight and smell of the mussels, a bottle was produced to mark the occasion, the exchange of goods for which Lachanau had come was effected, and he was back in Caillons in time for morning mass.

At breakfast Madame Guinard fussed over him, muttering about his injury. He shooed her away, but when she came

101

back to pour his coffee she turned to the news of the seizing of Jeanne Dupré that was the talk of the village and the port.

'What a shock it must have been for you, Monsieur le Curé. They beat the door down, I heard.'

'Not quite, Mother Guinard. It's still on its hinges. See for yourself.'

'Some say she's a Resistance fighter, that Jeanne Dupré, like her brother was.'

'Do they?'

'Others say she's a Nazi-lover, a collabo. There's talk about her and the major.' She shook her head. 'That poor husband of hers.'

'So people talk because she works for the major? But you work for him too, Mother Guinard. And you work for me. Maybe there's talk about you and the major – or you and me. Or you and the major *and* me.'

She retreated to the other side of the room and huffed over a pot of something mysterious that would be his lunch.

Lachanau set his bitter coffee aside and extracted from his teeth a few bits of some substance that had never seen a coffee bean. He would go to the school and speak with the daughters, though in truth he was at a loss for what to say or how to comfort them or put their minds at rest. The Holy Ghost had better be in good form.

By the time Jeanne arrived at the schoolhouse in rue des Châtaigniers, Père François Lachanau had already been and gone.

'Your daughters haven't come to classes today,' said schoolmaster Péringuey, a long-faced fellow who should have been an undertaker. 'Monsieur le Curé was looking for them too. What kind of mother doesn't know where her own daughters are, so that other people have to go looking

102

for them?'

He hastened away as if she might be infectious.

'Maître Péringuey, could I have a drink of water?'

The door banged shut.

She sought the shade of the chestnut trees and rested for a few minutes. It was noon by now. She had walked half the route from Le Manoir barefoot after one of her wooden sabots had broken. She would have to make another. Her feet were filthy, the soles shredded and bloodied. Her body was covered with a film of sweat. It streamed down from her hairline and stung her eyes with salt, it made her dress cling to her back and legs, it cut streaks through the dust that encrusted her bare arms and legs.

She was stared at as she walked through the village. In rue du Maréchal Pétain they watched her pass but no one greeted her. Café du Marché fell silent. One of Sulot's sisters looked up from the table she was wiping, then heaved her bulk indoors. Musset the postman, seated outside, scratched his beard and found something in his satchel that demanded his attention. A knot of women stood gossiping at the top of rue du Port, brawny arms crossed over spreading bosoms; conversations stopped as she approached. In rue du Verger the silence trailed after her, as thick as setting curd.

She understood every stony glare, every dropped gaze, every hush as she passed, and the reasons for them, as various as their sources. To some who watched her she was nothing but a troublemaker like her brother. She might consider herself a patriot, they would say, a résistante, but why resist, where was the point, why oppose the inevitable? The victors were the victors, the old France was dead, Marianne was dead, time to bury the old lady and accept the new reality. Get along with the Germans, make the best of things. But fools like Jeanne Dupré made the Germans despise the French even more.

Then there was the other school of thought. She was no résistante, her little act at her brother's execution was only that, an act. She was a collabo, Ebermann's stuck-up little tramp. One day France would rise again and she would pay for her Nazi nuptials. The people of Caillons would shave her head and drag her through the streets. She wanted to stick her nose in the air? What better way than at the end of a rope from a lamp post?

Ah no, came yet other voices, wearier but equally full of loathing, she was a résistante for sure but never mind whether France lived or died; what mattered was the husband who had died because of her, or the father, the brother, the son gunned down on the breakwater.

In allée de l'Église there was no answer to her knock on Père Lachanau's door. She returned to the square, watching the windows and the balustraded gallery of the Villa Normandie as she entered the church. There was no sign of the priest in the nave, the side chapels or the sacristy. She genuflected, crossed herself with holy water and left, touching a damp finger to her lips for its moisture.

'Poor Jeanne,' crooned Mirabaud the halfwit as their paths crossed in ruelle de la Baie. He too was barefoot today, as he often was, but in his case it was through choice; he claimed bare feet were better in the Somme mud. He had never really left the Somme, the place that had turned his mind; he still danced and sang his way through its trenches and blood.

He bent over to peer at her bloodied feet. 'Poor Jeanne. March on, Jeanne, march on. Poor Mirabaud, poor Jeanne.'

As she ascended the path to La Croisette, she found that her approach had been observed. The door of La Croisette opened. Père François Lachanau, head still bandaged, ducked low beneath the lintel and stepped from the cool shade of the cottage to meet her.

The mysterious creation prepared by Madame Guinard was a broth of some kind. Certainly an animal had been involved, for here were the bones, pathetic little things but bones nonetheless, mired in a swamp of pearl barley, leeks and other green vegetables. Lachanau fetched it, pot and all, and thanked old Mother Guinard as he left the house with it, waving her questions away. He called on Hodin the baker and stood very close over him, whispering about eternal damnation and recounting the baker's lapses from the marital bed with the young wife of old Voinet the charcutier on those forays in the bois de Caillons when Madame Hodin thought he was fetching sawdust. Hodin retreated to the rear of the shop and returned with a generously proportioned pain de campagne.

'No sweepings?' said the priest.

'No sweepings,' sighed the baker. 'No sawdust. Good wholewheat flour and a little rye.'

With these provisions Lachanau returned to La Croisette. He set the fire, warmed the broth and took it and the bread upstairs to where Jeanne lay with Hélène and Isabelle in her arms. He said grace and, bent like a willow beneath the beams of the low roof, refused to go away until he had seen them eat.

It was late afternoon when Jeanne came downstairs.

'Hélène's sleeping,' she said. She set about redoing Lachanau's bandage. 'Now listen to me, mon curé, you'll say nothing to Ebermann about what happened.'

'Jeanne, that's an intolerable suggestion.' He twisted around in his chair to face her, the bandage immediately unravelling. He swept it out of the way. 'A serious crime has been committed, a heinous and unforgivable offence, even under Reich law. Ebermann must be told. Your own daughter, Jeanne.'

She pushed him back down on the chair. 'Exactly as you say, mon curé – *my* daughter, so it's up to me what happens. This is not for Ebermann. And it's not for you, either. Stay out of this.'

There was a glint in her eyes that warned him there was no room for argument. He sighed. He had never tackled Jeanne on the matter of her relationship with the major. He knew no more than he heard from Mother Guinard and the other gossips. Her avoidance of confession did not help. So here he had the one yearning to confess and the other refusing to do so.

He handed the bandage to her. 'Very well. I'll keep my mouth shut. The effort may choke me.'

'You'll also say nothing to Graf. Say and do nothing. Stay away from him.'

He raised his hands in despair. 'Now you really are asking too much.'

'You mean well, mon curé, I appreciate that. But nothing can change what's happened. If you become involved, it will only endanger you further with Graf – you're already a marked man. It will also endanger my daughters. Perhaps even Michel. We don't know how long the oberleutnant's reach might be. So you see, interference from you can only make matters worse. As for Graf's crime, what court would you bring him before?'

'So he'll get away with it.'

'I didn't say that.'

'I don't like the sound of this. Let's have nothing foolish, Jeanne.'

'Graf's time will come.'

'Vengeance is the Lord's, Jeanne. Nothing foolish, I said. Above all, nothing to jeopardise your soul.'

'No more discussion. This is my family's business.

You'll do as I ask?'

He remembered little Jeanne Rochard who never ran to the teachers with her woes, who would have faced down the pope himself if she had felt the need. It was the same Jeanne who confronted him now. He reluctantly nodded his agreement.

Isabelle came downstairs. Jeanne took her hand and sat opposite her at the table.

'Tell me what happened when the Germans brought Hélène home. Tell me exactly.'

'It was as I told you, Maman.'

'There was so much for me to take in. Tell me again. Did they behave correctly towards you?'

'They were loud and fierce but it was all only noise, like they do.' The girl blushed and glanced at the priest. 'I know what you're asking, Maman, but they never laid a finger on me. They said Hélène had broken curfew and she was lucky they hadn't shot her on sight. They said they found her down by the port, in the harbour square. But I think Graf sent them to find her. He arranged everything.'

Jeanne frowned. 'Why do you think that?'

'She says they didn't even ask her name, they didn't ask for her papers, they didn't ask if she had an Ausweiss. Have you ever heard of a patrol that doesn't bother about those things? It was as if they were looking for her. They even knew where she lived and brought her straight here. They had to be acting on Graf's orders.'

Lachanau was nodding. 'You have a very astute daughter, Jeanne. If the patrol had questioned Hélène the whole thing would have come to light. Exactly what the oberleutnant wanted to avoid. Hélène wouldn't have been brought home unless he'd ordered it. She'd be under arrest.'

Jeanne leant across the table towards her daughter to emphasise her next question. 'Did the Germans ask about

107

me? Did they demand to see me?'

'No. They went straight into searching La Croisette. Then the outbuildings. They searched everywhere.' Isabelle paused. 'Almost.'

'Almost?'

'They didn't search the henhouse.'

Jeanne was silent for a long moment. Lachanau waited.

'Why not?' asked Jeanne at last.

'Because I tipped over the bucket of chicken shit before anyone got there. The soldier who went to search the henhouse changed his mind as soon as he opened the door and the stink hit him. He didn't see me watching. The only person who searched the henhouse was me. Long before the patrol got here.'

Jeanne nodded slowly. 'Monsieur le Curé is right. You're a clever one. And now you'll continue to be a wise child and say nothing more.'

The priest took the hint. He collected his empty broth pot. Jeanne walked with him to the bottom of the path.

'There are certain things you didn't hear, mon curé.'

'My ears took a lot of damage in my boxing years.'

'But you did hear what I said about Ebermann and Graf. Stay out of this matter.'

'Under protest I'll honour my promise.'

'It was on Graf's orders that I was taken last night.'

'I assumed as much.'

'He interrogated me several times. But a strange interrogation. His questions went nowhere, as if he was only going through the motions. All night I kept asking myself how to explain this.'

'Now you know. He was warning you off.'

'He was preparing the ground for when I found out about Hélène. Giving me a taste of what he can do if I cause him any trouble. Isabelle's right, he arranged everything. The

108

patrol knew I wasn't here at La Croisette even though it was the middle of the night. That's why they didn't demand to see me. It might even have been the same patrol that came for me at your house.'

'And they knew you were there because Graf saw you helping me home.'

'He's been meticulous, mon curé.'

The priest plunged his hand into a deep pocket of the soutane and withdrew a small circular glass jar.

'What's this?' she asked.

'I almost forgot. It was on your windowsill. It's coffee. Proper coffee. American, I think. Look.' He rotated the jar to show the company name and the drawing of an exotically robed Arab raising a cup to sip from.

She took the jar. 'I've never seen this before.'

He chuckled. 'Perhaps you have a secret admirer.'

He tucked the empty broth pot under his arm and strode off down the slope towards ruelle de la Baie.

Jeanne retraced her steps to La Croisette but lingered outside to consider the unexpected gift. She unscrewed the lid and put the jar to her nose. The aroma brought a moment of giddiness. Then she noticed the flash of something white and withdrew the little folded slip of paper that was buried inside.

The crunch of a footstep on gravel made her look up. She dropped the paper back into the jar, replaced the lid and slid the jar into a pocket of her dress. Leutnant Ernst Neiss stood at the foot of her path, blinking in the sunshine. He took a few tentative steps up the path towards her.

'Major Ebermann wishes to speak with you, Madame. But in the Villa Normandie, not in his office at the mairie.'

'Very well. I'll be with him in an hour.'

'I think he meant now, Madame Dupré.'

'I'll be there in an hour.'

The leutnant blinked a few more times, his face shiny with perspiration. This was a cold-climate German, she reminded herself. Cold climate and indoors, those were his natural habitat. He was melting in this weather. She remembered how she had felt at the school this morning.

'Would you like a drink of water?'

'Thank you Madame. That would be kind.'

She fetched the water and waited while he drank.

'An hour,' she repeated. 'Tell the major I'll see him then.'

Isabelle was waiting for her indoors.

'Why didn't you tell us, Maman? We never guessed. When I think of the things we've said to you, Hélène especially ...' She shook her head unhappily.

Jeanne took her in her arms. 'You were too young. You *are* too young. I'm sorry you even know now.'

'You don't trust us?'

'You say "us" – you've told Hélène?'

'Certainly.'

'Was she in any condition to understand?'

'Not last night, but today.'

'Does she also understand to say nothing to anyone – anyone at all?'

'Of course she does. Maman, don't you think you can trust us?'

Jeanne held her close, this strange and wise little soul that God had sent her; along with Hélène, dearer than her own life.

'Perhaps I know better now,' she conceded.

7

'Line the boys up,' commanded Graf.

The school day was over but on his orders the younger children had been kept behind. Somewhere among these ugly little creatures were the ones he sought.

Now Péringuey the schoolmaster was staring at him in disbelief, his long sorrowful face purple with emotion.

'This is an outrage,' he spluttered. 'I'll do no such thing.'

Graf sighed. He had explained everything so clearly. But these people never knew when to button their lips and do what they were told. They never got any smarter.

He gave one of his troopers the nod. The butt of a machine pistol smashed into the schoolmaster's shoulder blade. He shrieked and crumpled to the floor. The children who were gathered in the classroom, crowded together in terrified silence until now, erupted in screams. The noise cut through Graf like a chainsaw. He swung around to face them.

'Be quiet!'

The fuss subsided. A trooper dragged Péringuey into a corner, where he lay moaning. Graf turned to the other teacher, a weedy woman called Lavisse.

'Line them up,' he told her.

She nodded weakly and spoke to the children. Her eyes were liquid with tears. Her words were delivered too softly and rapidly for him to follow but the twenty or so boys shuffled forward and arranged themselves nervously along the front of the room. They were aged between five and

111

eight, as disreputable a clutch of beggar urchins as he had ever laid eyes on.

Out of curiosity, he strolled the length of the line, studying them to see if he could second-guess the outcome. There were no clues. All were dark haired, dark eyed, he could single none out on that basis. Nor were there any obvious physiognomical indicators – no protruding ears or squat heads. Perhaps the creatures he was looking for were too young for these peculiarities to manifest. He had read that this could take until adolescence.

'This is an instructive lesson,' he told his troopers. 'It's not always as easy to identify the ones we're looking for as the manuals suggest. They're clearly not Aryan, not Nordic, but that goes for all of them – you're not in Germany now. When none of them makes eye contact, how do you spot the shifty-eyed ones?' He picked up a ruler and used it to tilt a chin or two. In each case the eyes were unable to meet his gaze.

'So can we rely on walk as a distinguishing characteristic? They all lumber along like dwarves, they've got their share of bent legs and backs. What you see here demonstrates that the Lebensunwertes Leben, the living ones unworthy of life, can disappear into the crowd like a hidden disease, particularly in a backward country. Do you see how careful we have to be, how thorough?'

The troopers were nodding thoughtfully. Good men all, his Nordic warriors, a credit to the Fatherland.

He turned to the woman.

'Now the sisters,' he told her.

Maîtresse Lavisse clenched her hands together. She moved among the girls and brought seven to the front. They stood by their brothers. Each one instinctively reached for her brother's hand.

'Very touching,' said Graf. He smiled at the woman.

'Now the boys' trousers.'

Maîtresse Lavisse burst into tears. A trooper stepped closer to her. She shook her head vigorously, raised a hand to fend him off, then wiped her eyes, steeled herself and spoke to the line of trembling boys. Her words were greeted by gasps and small cries of protest.

Graf gave the nod again to the troopers. Machine pistols and submachine guns were raised. In ones and twos as they watched each other to see who would go first, the boys, some weeping openly, undid their trousers. Some lowered them reluctantly, some gave up and let them fall to the floor. Some were wearing underpants, disgusting rags grey with age. Encouraging prods with the gun barrels brought the underpants sliding down as well.

Once again he walked the length of the line, slowly inspecting the puny anatomies – twenty-odd pairs of trembling legs and knocking knees, twenty-odd pairs of eyes fastened on the floor, twenty-odd small figures steeped in humiliation.

Twenty-odd tiny penises, shrunk tinier still by fear. And there among them were the two unquestionably circumcised specimens that he sought.

Except there was also a third one. He frowned and checked again, lifting each small appendage with the ruler for a closer look. There was no mistake. Three, not two, shy little foreskinless Zuckerstangen, meaning one Jew more than he had been told. Well, where they were going, three little Jew boys were better than two.

But only the one Jewess, which did accord with his information.

All very satisfactory. He had his Jews. He dropped the ruler back on the table.

'Tell them to dress,' he told Lavisse. 'Tell these three and the female specimen to stay where they are. The others can go back to their places.'

While she relayed the instruction he took a small, cloth-bound prayer book from his pocket and opened it to a page marked by a thin green ribbon. He stood over one of the Jew boys, a quaking thing about seven years old who was still fastening his trousers.

'Recite the Hail Mary,' he ordered.

The boy failed to understand. He wiped a sleeve across his streaming nose. His eyes pleaded for guidance from Maîtresse Lavisse. Now she was letting the tears flow freely.

'He can't,' she sobbed. 'He hasn't learnt it properly yet. He's too young.'

'Too young?'

Graf chose a boy at random from those who had rejoined the other children. He was about the same age as the Jew.

'Recite the prayer,' he told the boy.

This boy also looked to the woman for guidance. But seeing where things were going, she was now beyond guiding anyone.

Graf poked the boy in the ribs. 'Say the prayer.' For emphasis he undid his holster and rested his hand on the pistol.

The effect was instant.

'Hail Mary, full of grace …'

The boy raced through the prayer, eyes closed. It was a gabble but it matched the prayer book.

Graf returned to the Jew.

'Now you.'

The boy understood this time.

'Hail … Mary …'

'Hurry up.'

But nothing more came except random words, some possibly from the prayer, most of them certainly not.

114

Graf shook his head mournfully.

'So here we have two tests,' he explained to the troopers. 'Namely, physical evidence and cultural – in this case using the very same religion they're trying to hide behind and turning it back on them. This one failed both tests. So with a little creative thought we've found a way to overcome our initial difficulties of identification. We now have conclusive proof, scientifically verified by two independent techniques: this little shit's a Jew.' He turned to Lavisse. 'No more lies from you, Maîtresse. Any more asinine excuses and you'll go where this little Untermensch is going.'

The next Jew also failed the test, as did his sister. They too were consigned to the corner, where they huddled against Péringuey.

The third Jew was the most abysmal failure of all.

'H ... H ...'

Graf tapped his fingers on the prayer book, waiting. The boy was white with fear.

Maîtresse Lavisse made a gargantuan effort. 'He has a stammer,' she croaked.

'You were warned, Maîtresse.'

'It's the truth. Hervé Meslin knows the prayer. Don't you, Hervé? He knows all his catechism, every question and answer. Better than anyone else in the school, even the older ones. But he's terrified. Hervé isn't Jewish.'

'Then at least you admit the others are. We're making progress.'

She closed her eyes in dismay. Graf cast an I-told-you-so look at the troopers.

A faint voice called from the corner. It was Péringuey.

'What Maîtresse Lavisse says is true.'

Graf glared at the schoolmaster. No, they never got any smarter. He yanked down the Jew's trousers, almost

115

bringing the boy, who looked near to fainting, to the floor.

'So he was sharpening a pencil and his hand slipped?'

'He had a medical operation. He was having certain problems.'

'What problems?'

'Urinary. He had to be circumcised.'

'Since when do country peasants have the money for doctors and hospitals?'

'The church paid. Père Lachanau arranged it. Hervé is from a good Catholic family. Ask Monsieur le Curé. He'll confirm everything.'

'Why would I trust that old crow?'

'Then get Hervé to say something else, it doesn't matter what, he'll still stammer. It's worse when he's nervous or anxious.'

'And of course he wouldn't fake it, would he? You're very keen to speak up for this one. Are some Jews better than others? Or if you really think this particular one isn't a Jew, then you seem to agree that real Jews should be got rid of. That would be enlightened thinking for someone like you – so enlightened that I can't believe it possible. So it's obvious that this one's a Jew. He happens to be a Jew that you like. I've seen this before. They can be adept at ingratiating themselves with weak and susceptible people. Like you.' He called to a waiting trooper. 'Take the Jew boy. Take all the Jews away now.'

But a sudden cry escaped the boy's lips. A spout of urine, as elegant as ever issued from any peeing cherub, shot forth and puddled on his fallen trousers and the floor.

Graf's eyes popped. Jew piss.

'Scheisse!'

He stepped smartly back. A trooper came forward, grabbed the weeping boy and dragged him over to Péringuey's corner, the trousers trailing about his ankles and leaving a wet shiny track across the floor. The schoolmaster helped the boy pull the trousers up, then took him in his good arm and held him close. He seemed not to care about the urine-soaked clothing. Graf turned away.

'Get these animals out of my sight.'

When the children had been securely deposited in the truck and their wailing was out of earshot, he sat at the table and went methodically through the school records. Péringuey and Lavisse looked on in silence.

The address given for the first Jew showed that he was living with the family Rousselot. According to the register, that was also his name – which was clearly a lie. Since he could hardly have registered in a false name here at the school all by himself, it was obvious that the family – husband André, wife Estelle and André's brother Jean-Marie – were complicit in the crime.

Graf noted the three names.

The Jew brother and sister were being sheltered by the family Lanery. Fernand Lanery was on STO, current whereabouts therefore embargoed – and immaterial in any case, for Agathe Lanery was head of the household in his absence.

Graf noted the name of Agathe Lanery.

So far not a peep from Péringuey or Lavisse.

But when Graf came to the Jew boy with the fake stammer, it was a different matter. The two started up again, like a worn-out mechanism. The boy was a Catholic, not a Jew. His family had lived in Caillons since time out of mind. The child had been born here. Père Lachanau could show the oberleutnant his birth and baptismal records. This excuse, that excuse, yap-yap.

Graf paid no heed. He was too busy striking gold. The stammerer was registered as living in the house of a family called Meslin. Head of household was a certain Charles

Meslin, boat hand by trade. And Charles Meslin, Graf knew, was missing and wanted for evading STO. He was also a suspected maquisard. His spouse Hortense Meslin was the only remaining adult member of the household.

Graf noted the name of Hortense Meslin. Then he copied all five names and their addresses into the arrest warrants that Leutnant Neiss had provided.

He sat back and capped his pen. Péringuey and Lavisse were still whining. He shook his head sadly.

'So you think I was cruel to strip the little Jews?'

A quarter of an hour later the Wehrmacht truck rumbled over the cobblestones of place de l'Église. Deep inside, behind a wall of hefty troopers, cowered little Hervé Meslin and his three Jewish classmates.

Watched by all in the square and those who stepped out from the shops in rue du Centre and Café du Marché, the truck lurched to a halt. The tailgate crashed open. Propelled from behind and helped along by submachine guns in their backs, out stumbled Maître Péringuey and Maîtresse Lavisse, the one still in pain from his injured shoulder blade, the other weeping copiously. Both were as naked as the day they were born.

As Mirabaud pirouetted around them in delight, whooping and clapping, the truck skidded off to make the five arrests.

The one-time pads were kept in the icehouse. Going there in broad daylight was high risk but Jeanne decided on that as the only option, on the basis that she regarded all communications from Danton as urgent.

Even before she had finished decoding the strings of numbers on the small slip of paper from the jar of coffee, she knew her decision not to wait for nightfall had been correct. She put a match to the paper, the code page and her transcription, and crushed the ashes to fine dust.

Jacques Colinet was feeding root grass to one of his two pigs, a heavily pregnant young gilt that went by the name of Pompadour, when Jeanne arrived. He listened to what she had to say.

'Diversions?' he echoed. 'Why draw so much attention?'

'It's not just a drop. Someone's coming in, the aircraft will land. The Germans will have more time to identify the location. Your meadow's the only suitable place but they can get there too quickly. We have to confuse them, throw them off the scent.'

He shrugged a shoulder. It was agreement of a kind but she could see that something was troubling him.

'What is it, Jacques?'

Pompadour grunted impatiently. Colinet tossed her the last of the grass and wiped his hands.

'Well it's Meslin, obviously,' he said. 'This needs all of us and I'm not sure we can count on him. I don't just mean for tonight – maybe we can't count on him at all.'

'You're still questioning his loyalty?'

'Not that.' He looked sharply at her. 'You haven't heard?'

'Heard what?'

He recounted the events at the school and afterwards – the arrests, the schoolchildren running wild through the streets of the village and the port, hysterical with fear, the humiliation of Maître Péringuey and Maîtresse Lavisse – everything that had taken place while Jeanne was at the icehouse.

'All the detainees, adults and children, will be held at Le Manoir tonight. Graf will want his turn with them first, then they'll be sent to the Gestapo unit at Le Havre, probably tomorrow. When the Gestapo finish with them, it's the death camps. Who knows what Meslin might be crazy enough to try – but tonight is when he'd do it, while they're still at the château.'

She too could see the insane logic.

'Then tell him this, Jacques. There's nothing he can do – not even the whole cell could do anything, never mind him alone. It would take a battalion to attack the château. And when his family and the others are being transferred to Le Havre, they'll be within an armoured convoy, heavily protected. Madness to try anything. We need Charles Meslin tonight. If he truly wants to do something, his best way is by being with us. Not by behaving like a fool. Tell him that.'

'Tell a man to abandon his family? How do I do that?'

A shadow moved in the shady kitchen of the farmhouse. Old Mother Colinet had seen Jeanne arrive and had stayed there watching, as an old cat too stiff and slow to hunt would watch a mouse, unable to pounce but unable to tear its gaze away. Jeanne knew the old woman's views concerning the Duprés, first Pierre and now herself, and their malign influence on her son Jacques.

Her gaze went from the kitchen to the shuttered upstairs window behind which Colinet's wife Delphine lay ill, probably dying. Their two daughters would be out in the fields as they were in every spare minute, working like men. These were not easy days for anyone.

The sun was dropping towards the trees in the bois de Caillons. A few straggling gulls were gliding over the bay and the ocean, leaving the land to the rooks gathering in the highest treetops, their hoarse calls echoing against the barn wall. In the pit beyond the barn lay the bodies of Pierre, young Louis Fougeret and Guillaume Raynal.

All of them dead for France. So many dead for France.

She turned back to Colinet. 'I don't know how you'll do that, Jacques. Nor do I care. But there are things a person has to accept. This is one of them. You tell Charles Meslin that, whether he likes it or not.'

The noise of the commotion in place de l'Église had travelled all the way to La Croisette, drawing Isabelle to the village to investigate. Before she got to the end of ruelle de la Baie she already had part of the story from classmates. By the time she reached the square, the schoolteachers had been rushed into Pauthier's greengrocery, where they were cringing among the cauliflowers and potatoes until someone could fetch their clothing. In the meantime coats had been lent. Sympathetic Caillonais, and some with motives less noble, surrounded the pair, providing further shielding – or hoping for a glimpse of something – while Pauthier, who had never seen so many people in his store for years, rushed back and forth in case someone should actually want to make a purchase. The fearsome Mathilde had adjourned her sewing and hastened downstairs: to help Pauthier, she claimed, black eyebrows all innocence, but no one fell for that; she was there to make sure Pauthier's attention stayed on the shop's wares and away from those of Maîtresse Lavisse.

There were children still milling around outside, too excited to go home. These were Isabelle's sources as she gathered all the facts and all the names, the tale of the poor Jewish children and little Hervé Meslin, sifting out the contradictions and filling in the gaps in her forensic way.

She returned home and told Hélène all. The elder sister listened in silence. She had her own miseries but this was worse, even more foul.

'Someone has to do something,' was her verdict.

Jeanne was shown up to the drawing room by Leutnant Neiss, who closed the door behind her and crept off downstairs. She knew this room well, had known it for all her days, the swirling patterns of the hand-knotted Savonnerie-style carpets commissioned from England by her mother, the heavy furniture and panelled walls, the ancient timbers.

Ebermann was standing by the glazed door that opened to the outside gallery. He turned to face her. In his hand was a single sheet of paper. It was folded on itself but she could see the outline of the Reich eagle and swastika showing through. The arrangement of the crest and the lines of text beneath suggested that the document was a letter.

'Please sit, Madame.'

His formality chilled her: the 'vous', that distant 'Madame'. Was this the moment she had always expected? Armed troopers would arrive and she would be returned to Le Manoir; this time she would not walk free.

But that letter; Wehrmacht arrest orders did not come by letter.

'I'll stand, thank you.'

He nodded slowly as if her reply was a complex statement to be weighed with care. He crossed his hands over the folded letter. She knew those hands. They knew her.

He seemed unable to meet her gaze. She realised he was trying to work out how to proceed. Her heart thudded. This was not an arrest. This was something worse.

Michel.

She found she was praying.

'Enemy bombing activity in France has increased,' Ebermann began. 'It has reached an unprecedented level of ferocity, of aggression.'

'Not aggression against French citizens. Aggression against the German occupation. Aggression against you. How often have I told you this?'

'You're wrong. It makes no difference who the target is – bombs don't discriminate. Swathes of French cities have been razed to the ground by British and American bombs. Thousands of French men and women, and children, have been killed. In the last six weeks Lille, Rouen, Orléans, Lyon, Marseille, Saint-Étienne – the list goes on – have all come under heavy bombardment.'

'Why am I here?'

'Even parts of Paris – Sartrouville, Noisy-le-Sec, La Chapelle. Such loss of life, such destruction.'

'Do your propagandists still say you're winning?'

'These bombardments by so-called allies of France are killing more people than German raids ever killed in Britain. Is this how allies behave – by wiping out their friends?'

'Why did you send for me?'

'One of the raids on Paris, the one on Noisy-le-Sec –' His hand lifted from the folded letter, then closed on it again. 'Your husband was assigned to Noisy-le-Sec.'

The room seemed to spin around her. Michel was in France? *France*? All these months? Mere hours from those who loved him, not in Germany or Romania or some other distant German possession.

And Ebermann was talking about bombing raids.

'Madame Dupré? Jeanne?'

He had moved closer. She lifted her head, glanced at him, then quickly looked away, towards the windows and the gallery, where she saw that the sky was still a perfect blue.

'What's happened?' she asked.

'There are rail yards. Noisy-le-Sec is an important transit centre for convoys between France and Germany. Michel was working as a railwayman.' Ebermann looked down at the letter, still folded. 'I'm sorry.'

Her body was stiff, every muscle straining to hold her steady and upright. She kept her gaze doggedly on that heavenly blue sky. How could it still be so blue?

'He died instantly. He wouldn't have suffered.'

She had more sense than to believe that.

'When did it happen?'

'Last month. Five weeks ago.'

'Five weeks? Five *weeks*?'

'It takes time for these things to be communicated. The authorities must collate and verify information and approve its release. Also, many of the bombs missed the rail yards. Many innocent civilians died. That slowed matters down.'

'Innocent civilians? Like Michel, you mean. He was an innocent civilian.'

Ebermann set the letter down on a side table. From a colour photograph on the same table a blonde woman with a kind face smiled out at Jeanne and the world. Her eyes were pale grey, almost translucent. She wore minimal make-up because her flawless pale skin needed nothing to enhance it. Her name was Sophia but Jeanne knew she signed her letters Sofie, and Sofie was what Klaus Ebermann called her. In the other photographs a boy and a girl smiled with their mother's smile.

There was something else on the table. A large cream-coloured envelope. It bore the same crest as the letter. Ebermann picked it up and held it towards Jeanne.

'Michel's death certificate.'

She stared at it. A man's life consigned to a single sheet of paper. Husband, father, friend, reduced to lines of print beneath that hideous crest. As insignificant as the ash she had ground beneath her foot today.

'Where is his … where is he? When will he be returned to me?'

'Regrettably that's not possible. He was buried with the other casualties. There was no choice. Facilities for storage –'

'A mass grave?'

'I'm assured there was a proper Christian committal service.'

He took another step closer. Now he was managing to look directly at her. She saw that there were little knots of red in the corners of his eyes. He still held the cream envelope in one hand. His other hand lifted tentatively towards her.

'Don't touch me,' she hissed. 'You'll never touch me again. Don't blame this on anyone but yourself and those who sent you here. You make the innocent pay for your war.'

Sofie's gentle eyes were watching her. Jeanne snatched the envelope from Ebermann's hand and wrenched the door open. The tears pressed to be released as she stumbled down the long staircase. Her staircase, once. Her home, once.

But the Villa Normandie was lost. Her beautiful Hélène's innocence was lost, in the vilest way imaginable. Pierre was lost. Now Michel.

It was exactly as she had told Jacques Colinet: there were things a person had to accept.

But that France was lost? No, she would never allow that to be one of those things.

François Lachanau was opening the double-leafed front door of the villa when Jeanne rushed past him. He called after her but she raced on.

He found Ebermann seated in old Jacques Rochard's armchair with what seemed like a letter in his hand. The major looked up, startled, as the door flew open. He folded the letter and slipped it into his pocket.

'Graf!' Lachanau bellowed. 'That bastard!'

'Monsieur le Curé, I can see you're upset.'

'Where would you like me to start? With this?' Lachanau

pointed at the bandage on his head. 'This is Graf's work all right – but insignificant alongside his butchery of ten totally innocent men.'

Ebermann stood up. 'We can't allow attacks on Reich personnel to go unpunished. As for your injury, I understand Oberleutnant Graf intervened to stop you inciting opposition to his legitimate response to that attack.'

'Legitimate my backside. Look to your soul, Major. But I'm here on another matter. A matter concerning the living.' A large, blunt finger stabbed Ebermann's chest. 'You made a promise and you've broken it – or Graf broke it for you.'

'What promise?'

'As good as a promise. The Jewish children, of course. So much for your fine words. So much for German promises. Not a Nazi, eh? Not a Jew-killer?'

'The children? What are you talking about?'

'You don't know what your oberleutnant's been up to this time?'

Ebermann seemed genuinely at a loss.

'I wonder about you, Major. Were you really made for war?'

'I hope none of us was. Tell me what's happened, Monsieur.'

In one of the basement cells of Le Manoir, Graf was interviewing Agathe Lanery, who turned out to be a handsome woman. Or had been before the interview. Two troopers held her upright on a chair so that the oberleutnant's blows did not topple her to the concrete floor. At this stage she was down to her vest, her other garments having been torn away as the session progressed. It excited Graf to see each limb and portion of flesh revealed. Slim legs, firm breasts, their areolae large and dark against the pale skin.

She had remained conscious throughout, though now she was showing a tendency to black out, which was a nuisance and would make things take longer. The medic's job was to advise how much more her body could take. Her jaw was probably broken, one eye was swollen closed, a few teeth had been loosened but none had come out. The vest was soaked in blood. All in all, nothing too dramatic, for Graf was holding himself in check. The Gestapo would not be gracious if he delivered them a corpse.

Someone knocked on the door. The radio operator stepped into the room and snapped a salute.

'Heil Hitler! Herr Major Ebermann wishes to speak with you, Herr Oberleutnant.'

Graf mopped his brow. He needed a breather anyway. Before the Lanery woman he had dealt with Estelle Rousselot. It was good and important work, gratifying too, but it took its toll on a man.

He followed the radio operator through the corridors and stairwells to the communications room.

'Heil Hitler!' he barked into the mouthpiece of the RT.

'Release the Meslin woman and child, Graf.'

'But Herr Major –'

'The boy isn't Jewish. Release them.'

'Herr Major, the woman's husband is wanted for evading STO. He may be a maquisard. He may have been involved in the recent assassination of Wehrmacht personnel. His wife may have information on his whereabouts. In addition, we may be able to use her and the child as bait to lure Meslin.'

There was a pause.

'You can hold them for twenty-four hours. Then release them.'

The connection was broken. A burst of static assaulted Graf's ear.

* * *

'That's all I can do,' Ebermann told Lachanau. He returned the radio telephone to Neiss, from whose office in the villa he had made the call.

The priest nodded reluctantly. He had fought his corner as hard as he could. But the match was fixed from the off. He had known that as soon as he heard about the taking of the Jewish children. They were beyond hope. Leutnant Neiss had confirmed that Graf had already informed the Gestapo in Le Havre of their detention; there could be no going back. Beyond hope too were Agathe Lanery and the family Rousselot.

'You have informers among the people of Caillons,' said Ebermann when he and Lachanau were alone. 'Someone told Graf about the children.'

'There'd be no informers if there was no one to inform. You've turned us into a nation of informers, Major.'

They arrived back at the main entrance hall. Lachanau followed Ebermann up the stairs. In the drawing room he took care to close the door.

'Jeanne Dupré,' he said.

A shadow passed across the German's face. 'What about her?'

'Why was she in such a state when I saw her earlier?'

'I told you, none of us is made for war. Husbands and wives least of all. Better to be alone, as you are.'

'I'm not alone. I have my flock and my saviour.' Lachanau kissed the wooden crucifix. 'He'll comfort you too, Major, if you'll allow him.' He shoved his hands into the pockets of his soutane and wandered across to the window.

'Is it Michel Dupré?' he asked.

'Yes. The worst news. He's dead.'

'How?'

128

'A bombing raid – and here in France, I might add. So much for your allies that you hold in such high regard.'

Lachanau returned his gaze to the window. A beautiful evening was arranging its finery over the bay and the warm stone of the village streets. He could see more colours than he could ever hope to name, delicate shades of pink and blue, tones that slipped from gold to pale ochre and back again even as he watched, a dozen varieties of silver. Beauty that only God could create. Beauty beyond man's comprehension.

'I baptised and confirmed them both, you know, Jeanne and Michel. I made them man and wife. I baptised their daughters and confirmed them. So now I must bury Michel.'

'No. It's been done.'

Lachanau became very still.

'Jeanne knows this?'

'Of course.'

The priest tore himself from the beauty beyond the window. He made for the door.

'So even the dignity of burying our own dead is denied us. And still you would blame others for their death. I won't allow you that, Major. What terrors you've brought us. What degradation, what heartache. Are you satisfied? Are you proud of your Führer and your Reich?'

The door slammed shut behind him. Ebermann heard him thumping down the stairs, then quietness descended again on the villa, like dust settling.

With an effort he lowered himself into the armchair. He withdrew the letter from his pocket. It was not Jeanne Dupré's letter but there was the same mighty iron eagle, its claws clutching the wreath of oak leaves and the swastika within it.

He stared intently at the device as if seeing it for the first time. It was the throat of the German people, the volk, that those claws were crushing in their lethal grip.

From the side table Sofie and the children watched as he read the letter again, then let it fall to the floor and buried his face in his hands.

Why did the innocent have to pay?

Hélène forced herself out of bed. She strapped on the steel leg brace and made her way downstairs. She was alone in La Croisette. Isabelle was with the classmates she had met earlier. They would go over and over the day's horrors until curfew, exorcising them with talk and tears. Maman was … well, who ever knew where Maman was? Perhaps better not to know, nor to know what she was doing.

Hélène washed her face to bring some life back to it, scrubbing it with the rough washcloth. She raked the family's comb through her hair until all the tangles were gone. She went out to the far corner of the kitchen garden, to where the wild lavender grew, early this year because of the weather. She picked several sprigs, returned to the cottage and stripped off the flowers, rubbing them into a mash that she squeezed along her arms and throat and between her breasts.

She encountered no one in ruelle de la Baie. In place de l'Église there were a few people, classmates among them, though no Isabelle, a few more people in rue du Centre, including some shopkeepers standing in their doorways, there were the usual time wasters cackling with the Sulot sisters outside Café du Marché and there were others inside with Sulot, and there was a fractious game of pétanque on the dusty pitch at the top of allée d'Acadie where it looked towards the bay.

Some of those who saw her nodded or exchanged greetings civilly enough. Many others looked away. After all, she was Jeanne Dupré's daughter, the troublemaker's daughter.

Unless, of course, Graf had been boasting and his boasts had reached their ears. In which case they were looking away because she was a Nazi bedbug like her mother.

And if Graf had boasted, then her plan was worthless.

She came upon the first patrol in rue de l'Épinette. They slouched against their armoured car, their guns cradled casually in the crook of their arms, and watched with no more than mild interest as she limped past. Someone muttered something and laughed. Someone wolf-whistled. It was no more or less than she had always received. So if Graf had shot his mouth off, they knew nothing of it yet.

She trailed through all the streets of the village and forced herself to go down to the harbour as well. She met two more patrols, with similar results. She felt encouraged by that at least, but as she trudged up the steep hill from the harbour she knew that soon her leg would give up. She would have to stop and rest. Or go home. But she did not dare do that. This evening might be her only chance.

She came to rue du Phare on the very outskirts of Caillons, a forlorn patch of waste ground where the circus used to pitch in the days when the circus still existed. In the distance stood the old lighthouse that gave the road its name, the windows blind and dark, its red cap like flame in the low sun.

There was nothing here. Nothing and no one. Her plan, her stupid plan, was coming to nothing. Tears pricked at her eyes.

A long black Citroën saloon car rounded the corner up ahead. She raised a hand to shield her eyes from the sun's glare. Her heart missed a beat. Graf was in the back seat, wearing dark glasses, the type with little leather flaps on the side. She lowered her hand but opened the palm towards him, a small gesture but he saw it. He leant forward and said something to the driver. The car drew to a halt a few metres past her. She turned and limped back towards it. He climbed out and met her. He seemed to glow with health and cleanliness, a shining ideal of Teutonic manhood. How pathetic she was, in contrast, with her sprigs of lavender.

'Well, little cripple. Back for more?'

She stared into the dark glasses and made her offer: the only thing she had, her body. She set out the terms of the bargain.

He was laughing even before she had finished speaking. His uniform was crisp and fresh, its gold lapel tabs gleaming.

'Why should I do this?' he asked. 'I can have you any time I like.'

'It protects you. I'll never say you raped me. I'll deny it if anyone accuses you.'

'Who's going to accuse me? And who'd give a shit anyway?'

'Major Ebermann. His superiors when he tells them. They'd care that you raped a child. A crippled child.'

He had stopped laughing. The grin was still there, though fading. He tilted his head.

'What makes you think Ebermann would be interested?'

'You do. You've told no one what you did. You didn't tell the patrol that took me home and you haven't told anyone else. If you had, then all the Germans I met this evening would know. But they don't. They might be speculating about it, they might be guessing, but they don't *know*. You arrested my mother to frighten her into not reporting what you did. All this is because you're afraid of the major and what he can do to you if he chooses.'

'Ebermann's a weakling.'

'He can still have you court-martialled.'

'He has to find out first.'

'Oh, he'll find out. Even if I'm dead.'

Graf's eyes were still invisible behind the smoke-coloured lenses. 'Who have you told?'

'With my idea, you don't have to worry. You're safe. You get your little cripple any time you want. Any way you want. You'll like that. You punish inadequacy because you're strong. You enjoy weakness. You despise it in Major Ebermann but mine excites you because you like weakness in women. I don't know why but it doesn't matter. All that matters is for you to be the master. Look how weak I am now, coming back for more, exactly as you say. Begging. Think what you can do with someone as weak as me.'

He was rocking on his heels, as he had done at the harbour. His breathing was audible.

'There may be something in what you say. But you can't have everything. I can't release them all but I might be able to release one – maybe the little Jew boy that they kept saying wasn't a Jew.'

'Hervé Meslin. Very well. What about his mother, Hortense? Her too.'

'Maybe those two. But no more.'

'Tonight?'

'Tomorrow, if you meet your part of the bargain tonight. Payment in full. Do your part tonight and I'll do mine tomorrow.'

His fingers were toying with her breast, encircling it and seeking her nipple. He was standing between her and the car so that his driver could not see. There was no one in rue du Phare to see either.

'That's the only deal you get from me. Take it or leave it. And if you really have taken insurance against your own death – which I'm not sure I believe, but if you have, I understand it, I might even be impressed with such

133

foresight – remember what I told you last time: it won't be only your brains I'll blow out, it'll be your mother's and sister's too. So – you've set your terms and now you've heard mine. Do we have a deal?'

She shuffled closer as her hand reached for him.

The churchyard was deserted except for Jeanne and the dead.

The Rochard tombs were simple rectangular containers set along the churchyard wall and fronted by stone panels. No statues of trumpeting angels, no elaborate bronze muses, only names and dates cut into the stone, the sharpness of the letters blurred in varying degrees by age and weather. Around the fringes of the stones spilled determined clumps of dandelions and purple foxgloves, brilliant in the evening sunshine.

There was a stone bench nearby on which Jeanne sat. She watched the evening shadows as the sun moved across the graves. In one of the elm trees a thrush called for company. Her gaze followed the paths of the bees and butterflies that wandered back and forth through the honeysuckle clinging to the old wall. She felt drenched in its warm scent. When her eyes grew tired, she let them stay closed and allowed her senses to bathe in the fragrance and the soft sounds around her.

She saw a rail yard and lines of weak, exhausted men, worn to shadows. She heard the pounding of ten-kilogram sledgehammers on steel rails, the rasp of shovels in clinker, the thud of pickaxes. She heard the shriek of bombs and saw the blue sky turn black. She saw stone and steel, brick and timber rain down on Michel until all that was left of him was this cream-coloured envelope with its hideous crest.

And love. Love was left.

Sitting there with not a living human soul to hear or see her, she wept herself dry.

Leutnant Ernst Neiss was waiting for her at the foot of the path to La Croisette. He had found a patch of shade beside a hawthorn bush. She wondered how long he had been waiting. What was so important from Ebermann this time? Surely he had no more knives to twist.

'Madame Dupré,' the leutnant said. Then he dried up, though his mouth remained open as if there was the possibility of more words, the hope of inspiration from somewhere. She imagined a German mother telling her little boy not to stand there catching flies. She wondered if he could still hear that mother. She wondered if, like Wilfried Hermann Wiedemuth, he wore home-knitted socks.

Neiss gave up the search for more words. His mouth closed. He blinked slowly at her and pushed his spectacles back in place.

'Good evening, Leutnant. Are you waiting to see me?'

'Yes, Madame.'

'You look thirsty again. Haven't my daughters offered you a drink?'

'There's no one at home, Madame.'

'I see. Then can I offer you something?'

'No, thank you. I must go back.'

'But you haven't told me why you're here, Leutnant. Do you have a message from the major?'

'No, Madame. He doesn't know I'm here. That's why I must go.'

He hesitated, blinked again, then seemed to resolve something in his mind. The missing words finally came tumbling out in an unbroken flow, evidently rehearsed and recited until he had them by heart – probably as he waited

135

beneath the hawthorn.

'My condolences on the death of your husband. I offer you my sympathy. Be assured, what we have in our hearts is not lost in death.'

She stared at him, in her turn lost for words. Somewhere in his recitation she recognised Goethe. The leutnant had applied himself. That German mother had done her job well.

'Thank you, Leutnant.'

But he still stood there, his eyes studying the gravel on the path.

'Major Ebermann received the letter about your husband in today's communications pouch from Berlin.'

'Yes?'

'There was a second letter, Madame.'

Her heart missed a beat. Was there a mistake of some kind?

'About my husband?'

'No, Madame. A letter about the major's family.'

'I don't understand.'

Neiss cleared his throat and looked briefly at her, then his gaze hurried back to the safety of the gravel.

'They're dead, Madame, the major's wife and children. They were on a flight for families of service personnel. There was a failure in communications. The flight was mistaken for an enemy aircraft as it passed over München. München has suffered many times from enemy bombing, you understand, it's a nervous city. The flight was brought down by anti-aircraft fire. There were no survivors. Mistakes happen in war. Perhaps because war is a mistake.'

She stared at him. Then she bowed her head.

'I thought you would wish to know this, Madame, and the major might not have told you himself.'

'He hadn't. Thank you –'

But when she looked up she found that she was speaking to his back, for the leutnant was already hastening in his short little paces along ruelle de la Baie.

8

Jeanne looked up at the cloudless sky. It was a perfect night, the kind of night Michel had loved. They would walk for hours on such a night. The stars were out and the moon was arcing high, colouring the field and the pines that fringed it in shades of blue. There was no wind. The soughing of the ocean rose and fell, a backdrop that was always there in her life, always had been and always would be, Germans or no Germans. A nightingale trilled somewhere in the woods but no other sound disturbed the night. Wherever Graf's patrols were, they were nowhere near.

Jacques Colinet's field was a salt meadow, cropped short by the seven or eight black-faced sheep he still kept to graze on it and on the seaweed they found on the shore. Once there had been a flock of over a hundred; the salt-meadow lambs they produced had been a renowned local delicacy but nowadays, with the flock so reduced, the lambs were never numerous enough to reach any table but Jacques Colinet's own.

But the sheep kept the grass short. Tonight that was the important thing.

She smelt the salt tang of the sea and the sweetness of the pines as she crossed to the east side of the meadow. She could make out the pale forms of the sheep in the inland corner by the pine trees, safely penned by Colinet to keep them out of harm's way. Their black faces, strange voids above their pale bodies in the darkness, seemed to be turned

138

in her direction, watching mutely. She put the first hurricane lamp, as yet unlit, in position. She counted forty steps and positioned the second. Then the third and the fourth. She was glad to be rid of them; carrying them had required her to sling her submachine gun across her back, putting it out of easy reach and leaving her vulnerable. That was why Marcel Voinet was keeping watch in the shallow ditch on the south side of the meadow.

She looked back along the field. All four lamps now formed a line running inland from the coastal end of the meadow.

On the west side, Colinet had also finished setting out his four lamps. They followed a parallel course to hers. He and Jeanne went back and forth along their respective lines, adjusting the locations of the lamps until they matched, and ensuring that the two lines remained true.

Finally, at the southern edge of the meadow, its inland end, in the space between the two lines, they set out the two last lamps, also leaving these unlit for the present.

Everything was ready. They rejoined Voinet and slid silently down beside him in the ditch. If things ran to schedule, they had plenty of time in hand. All they had to do now was watch the night. And listen.

She put Michel from her mind. In the woods, as though aware of her vigil, the nightingale fell silent.

There was a sick, knotted sensation in the pit of Charles Meslin's stomach, and it was nothing to do with the fact that he and young Paul Leroux had spent the last hour flat on their bellies, digging a trench beside the lane that led to the gates of Le Manoir. To dig in that way, with pickaxe and short spade and without the leverage of standing upright, was excruciating. It required the muscles and close-quarter skills of a coal miner, not those of a boat hand

and a fisherman accustomed to the space and open movement that the ocean afforded. Meslin's muscles protested at each lunge of the spade and truncated swing of the pickaxe. Even Leroux, younger by twenty years, was struggling. But they had no choice, because less than half a kilometre across the plain of Le Manoir loomed the German watchtowers with their MG08 machine guns and the unwavering gaze of the guards. In this moonlight there was no need for powerful floodlights to pick out the slightest suspicious movement.

But neither was it the fear of being shredded by machine guns that had produced the sickness in Meslin. The sickness was because of the images in his mind: of Hortense and Hervé, lost somewhere deep in the barracks of Le Manoir, so near yet so far, and at the mercy, if it could be called that, of Jürgen Graf and soon the Gestapo. All evening the images had emerged, crawling through his mind like maggots until finally he thrust his head into the undergrowth and threw up.

'I'm all right,' he insisted to Leroux. 'Ate some bad meat, that's all.'

He trembled as he packed the fat sausages of Nobel 808 into the trench. Explosives were Jacques Colinet's territory but it was all hands to the pump tonight. It angered him that Colinet had forced this job on him. All because Colinet, as second-in-command, wanted to be at the main show.

'We're no more than a sideshow.'

'What?' said Leroux.

'Nothing.'

Sweat dripped from Meslin's forehead and face onto the waxy paper wrapping, the sausage skin as he called it, making it slick and slippery. He shifted position slightly, so that the moonlight fell on his work. He shook his head angrily to get rid of more sweat gathering in his eyebrows and about to spill into his eyes. Leroux saw the movement and heard his grunt. He studied Meslin anxiously. He knew about the arrest of Hortense and Hervé.

'Charles? You're sure you're all right?'

'It's nothing. I'm fine.'

'This explosive – is it stable?'

'Don't you mean am I stable? Pass me the detonators.'

Meslin wiped his hands dry in order to grip the small copper tubes and their cables firmly enough to press them home. Then he rested as Leroux shovelled as much of the sandy soil back in place as he could, flattened it with the spade and scattered the rest so that no telltale humps remained. They slid the spade and pickaxe back in the direction they had come, keeping them close to the ground, then slithered towards them, pushing with their legs and toes and pulling with their elbows. When they reached the tools, they repeated the process. Meslin paid out the reel of cable as he went. Leroux followed, patting it flat and covering it with soil to hold it down and conceal it. All this had to be done with the added awkwardness of submachine guns and bandoliers of ammunition strapped across their chests and backs. Unlike Jeanne's team, they had no one keeping watch for them – something else for Meslin to resent.

By the time they reached the cover of the woodland where they had hidden their pushbikes and the magneto box, Meslin was exhausted and his face and hands were caked in a crust of sandy earth and sweat. He could feel morsels of the explosive trapped beneath his fingernails. He rubbed off as much of the sand as he could, then he hooked the cable up to the magneto terminals and screwed them down tight.

Leroux watched everything closely.

'Where's the plunger?' he asked.

141

'There isn't one. This box is German, it has a crank handle instead. Here on the side, see?'

'Turn the handle and then what?'

'Bang.'

'Yes, but how does it work?'

'It just does. Ask Colinet if you're that interested.'

'What do we do now?'

'Wait for Luc Clavier's explosion. That's the signal to detonate ours. Watch the sky – you'll see the blast before you hear it.'

They both knew that when the moment came, it would be immaterial whether or not there were Germans within range of their blast. If there were, it would be a bonus, but the despatch of a few Germans was not the objective tonight.

Which was why Meslin felt no particular interest or excitement when the main gate of the château swung open, shunting against its stops, the sound echoing across the plain. A moment later a vehicle emerged. He raised his field glasses and brought it into focus. It was one of the staff cars, a long black Citroën with its distinctive inverted chevrons across the radiator grill, headlights blacked out except for a horizontal strip on each. Out of curiosity he kept the glasses on it as it drew nearer.

The sick knot in his stomach drew even tighter. Clearly visible in the moonlight, alone in the car with no trooper in sight to protect him, was the man who had swamped his thoughts, who had taken his Hortense and Hervé from him. Not a man but a monster: Jürgen Graf.

Two kilometres away, Luc Clavier and Gérard Leroux were also finishing their preparations. They too had dug a trench, in their case beneath the sleepers of the railway line where it had to swing briefly inland from the coast to skirt the mighty outcrop of rock known as La Vierge. No convoy was due tonight, not as far as the cell knew. True, their efforts would knock the line out for a few days, but, as with the fate of a few Germans on the plain of Le Manoir, that was only incidental.

Clavier packed the Nobel 808 in place, inserted the detonators and reeled out the cable as he and Leroux retreated a safe distance up the low hill opposite La Vierge.

'You saw how I did it?' said Clavier.

Gérard Leroux nodded.

'Your turn next time, then.'

Their vantage point gave them an uninterrupted view of the sweep of the ocean from west to east – so wide a vista, in fact, that the gentle curve of the horizon was visible. It was this view that had decided Clavier on their location. In his time as a railwayman he had worked this line for sixteen years. He knew every stretch of track and every view that opened to the eye along the way. This was the vista that tonight called for; no other was as good.

Higher up the hill their pushbikes were concealed beside the path that led in one direction to the safety of the bois de Caillons and the unsearchable maquis and scrublands beyond. That was where Clavier would return after the cell met up in the icehouse to review tonight's operation. In the other direction lay the village and the port, Leroux's destination if he could bypass whatever chaos would be reigning by then. In the meantime, like their comrades in Jacques Colinet's meadow and on the plain of Le Manoir, all they had to do was wait. Watch the sky and the stars and the huge bold moon and be patient.

The urge to kill Graf was overwhelming. There were two ways to do it: trigger the explosive or gun him down.

But some surviving shred of sanity told Meslin it could not be done. Either action would draw the entire garrison out from Le Manoir too early; tonight's plan would be wrecked.

Besides, killing the beast would not help free Hortense or Hervé. Meslin could think of only one way to achieve that. The maggots were devouring his brain and it was the only thing he could do before they emptied his skull completely.

He rose to a crouch and pushed the magneto box across to young Paul Leroux.

'You release this catch and turn the handle as fast as you can.'

Leroux looked up at him in alarm. 'What? Charles, wait.'

'You just crank the handle.'

'Charles, what are you doing?'

Too late. Meslin had unearthed the pushbike and was already spinning off into the distance.

The tubby little Westland Lysander, like the bumblebee, seemed not designed for flight. The flattened snub nose looked sheared off and a propeller stuck on as an afterthought, the top-mounted wings actually seemed to rake forward, and the cowled wheels, permanently extended, gave the impression of big clumsy paws pushing through the air.

But like the bumblebee, the Lysander was a deceptive creature. Its stalling speed was absurdly low, its Bristol engine produced little more than a whisper, and it could take off and land on a sixpence, or to be more precise, any small field. In a nutshell, there was no better aircraft for clandestine night flights to the fields of occupied France.

By midnight in England the rain had finally blown itself out and a brisk wind had cleared the cloud. An almost-full moon, only just on the wane, guided the matt-black Lysander carrying Daniel Benedict from its base at RAF Tempsford to its refuelling stop at Tangmere near the south coast.

For Benedict it was a flight over Anglo-Saxon England – from where Eadweard, son of Alfred the Great and king of the Anglo-Saxons, had defeated the Danes in their fortress stronghold a thousand years ago, to where Wilfrid, even earlier, had converted the Saxons to Christianity. All the land beneath him was as dark tonight as it would have been then, not a single light showing, not even when the aircraft passed over London and Le Singe Rouge.

From Tangmere the aircraft headed south-south-east. The gasometer at Bognor slipped past, followed soon after by the pier, a slim moonlit finger pointing the way and confirming they were entering the English Channel.

The pilot was a laconic Mancunian by the name of Tillman. His gunner was a Scot called Smith, as tight-lipped as himself. Lysanders making this kind of run were not usually armed but Tillman had a clear philosophy: no gun, no run. Tonight would be the fourth time the pair had ferried Benedict across. He never asked how many other trips they had notched up; pilots had their superstitions.

The moon made good its promise and stayed with them all the way into the Channel and beyond English waters, showering threads of pale gold on the black waves only feet beneath the Lysander's wheels. The sky became clearer and crisper, the stars multiplied. It was the stars that made the excitement rise within Benedict; they never failed. Perhaps on one thing de Gaulle had a point: perhaps there was such a thing as the French soul; and perhaps Daniel Benedict had a French soul in his Anglo-Saxon body. Perhaps that was why he peered through the darkness in such keen anticipation of the patchwork fields of Normandy.

Meslin cycled like a maniac to Caillons, following tracks and shortcuts that no motor vehicle could take, knowing there was no guarantee that the village was Graf's destination but aware also that there was no way, even with shortcuts, that he could get ahead of the German and ambush him on an open road. He had to hope that by the time he reached Caillons, Graf would still be there. Assuming he had gone there in the first place.

But Graf was there. The Citroën was parked on the overgrown wasteland of rue du Phare.

Meslin hunkered down behind a burnt-out car that was the only cover in sight. He was lucky in his timing. He heard one of the Citroën's doors open. A bark of laughter that could only be Graf's echoed across the empty area, followed by some guttural words of German. Meslin peered out and watched as a slight figure climbed awkwardly out of the car to stand on the dusty roadside. There was a dull gleam of something metallic.

His breath caught in his throat, his eyes widened.

Hélène Dupré.

He pulled back out of sight, stunned. Mother and daughter both Nazi whores. And the daughter not long out of her confirmation veil.

Graf spoke again and Hélène leant back into the car. She whispered something that Meslin could not catch. Graf came into view as he slid across the seat towards her. A tinny ringing sound interrupted them. Graf stretched forward over the front seats. Meslin heard a stream of German and the crackle of RT static.

The girl waited. The call ended. Graf said something to her, a few sentences, but she cut across him, her tone rising and shrill. The German spoke again, more emphatically, and laughed loudly in her face. She wailed as if he had pierced her with a blade. He laughed all the harder, then slammed the car door shut. She limped away, weeping. But there was no mistaking the word she kept repeating through her sobs.

'Papa … Papa …'

Meslin curled his lip. As if anyone cared about her damned papa.

The rear door of the Citroën swung open again.

Graf had taken only one drag of his cigarette when he felt a gun barrel press against the back of his head. A rough hand clamped over his mouth. His silence secured by the gun, the hand travelled down and removed his Luger.

He raised the cigarette slowly to his lips but the hand plucked it from his fingers. His captor, plainly not one to fuss about where his smokes came from, drew on the cigarette and exhaled. A cloud of smoke drifted past Graf's eyes.

'You arrested my wife and son,' the voice said.

Graf digested this information. Only one person fitted it. The bait had been taken. And just in time, in light of his arrangement with the little Dupré cripple. Not to mention Ebermann's interfering orders. Was there anyone in all of France who did not want these people released?

How he would savour informing the major of his success, all the sweeter for Ebermann's timidity. To snare a maquisard and a probable active résistant! Not even the gun at his head was enough to prevent the smile that he allowed himself.

'Monsieur Charles Meslin,' he said amiably. 'How pleasing to make your acquaintance.'

'You're going to release them.'

'Am I? But why should I do that, Monsieur Meslin?'

'I'll kill you if you don't.'

'You'll kill me either way.'

'Call the barracks, have them sent here. No escort, no troopers.'

147

'And then?'

He sensed that Meslin was puzzled by the question, as if he had been asked why the moon rose.

'They'll come away with me. They'll be safe.'

'I see. All of you on the run. That makes sense. And then you'll let me go?'

'Yes.'

'Nobody seems to care about the other Jews. Nobody tries to free them.'

'What?'

'Thinking aloud.'

'Do what I said.'

Graf deliberated his best way forward. He had no doubt how matters would end; but still, care was required. Clearly Meslin was insane, which was helpful. He ran over the man's file in his mind. Minimal education, no trade, worked on boats when the work was there, general dogsbody. Hardly a technocrat.

'I have to start the car engine to use the RT.'

'You didn't earlier. I heard you.'

'That was an incoming call. Outgoing needs more power.'

Meslin went quiet as he thought this over. Graf could feel his breath on his neck. Another cloud of cigarette smoke drifted past.

'I need to be behind the wheel,' Graf added.

'Don't try anything,' the Frenchman warned.

He stepped back to let Graf open the driver's door. It gave the oberleutnant the opportunity to see and take the measure of his enemy. As he thought, a rustic nobody. There would be few reserves of strength in that scrawny frame.

Graf slipped behind the wheel.

'Leave the door,' ordered Meslin. 'Keep your feet away from the pedals.'

Graf noted that the gun was a Sten. Stupid British. They

should be the Reich's friend, not its enemy. Two proud nations together against the degenerates of Europe.

The Citroën's door was hinged at the rear. Meslin was standing against it. The gearstick was mounted on the dash, to the right of the steering column and at the edge of Meslin's line of sight.

'Check my feet,' said Graf. 'Both on the floor, you see?'

It was simple misdirection. Meslin glanced obediently down at the footwell. Graf slipped the gearstick into first, released the handbrake and turned the ignition key. With the clutch disengaged the vehicle suddenly pitched forward, throwing Meslin off balance. Graf's left arm knocked the Sten aside. The gun discharged in a deafening whine. Graf flung himself out of the car and hard against Meslin. They hit the ground. Meslin was on his back: he lacked leverage, just as on the plain of Le Manoir. And his muscles were strained and still exhausted. As the Frenchman stretched for the Sten, Graf put all his power and weight behind a fierce forearm swipe. The blow connected with Meslin's jaw. His head snapped back. Graf knew he had won.

Then everything changed.

The Citroën's engine was dead from the failed start but the slight slope of rue du Phare was enough to nudge the transmission back into neutral. The car was on the move, no handbrake restraining it. Graf saw the inevitable coming. He made a desperate attempt to pull Meslin clear. Too late. The Frenchman's head hit the ground in time for a tonne and a quarter of automobile to roll onto it. The vehicle came to a halt.

'Scheisse!'

Graf kicked the dead man and swore. He would be snaring no wanted man tonight. He would be making no boasts to Ebermann.

He tried to brush himself down but it was a waste of time.

149

A perfectly good uniform was ruined. And where were his patrols? Were they deaf? Or was gunfire simply something they ignored these days?

He heard the deep note of a powerful engine and looked up to see an armoured car rumbling into view.

The burst of gunfire resounded far beyond the village and port. In Jacques Colinet's meadow they heard it.

'That's a Sten,' said Jeanne. 'Meslin has a Sten. Who else does?'

Heads shook.

'It's Meslin,' said Colinet softly. 'God knows what he's done. If he's been caught, do we abort? We could be bringing the aircraft into the hands of the Boche.'

Jeanne shook her head. 'Whoever's on board knows the risks. We see this through.'

At their position above the railway line, Luc Clavier and Gérard Leroux also heard the gunfire.

'Doesn't sound good,' said Clavier. 'Where do you think it was?'

'In the village,' suggested Gérard Leroux. 'Maybe the port.'

'Not the plain, where Charles and your Paul are?'

'No, not there.'

'Maybe some drunk settling a score.'

'With a submachine gun?'

Alone of all of them, Paul Leroux knew that the gunfire had to be something to do with Charles Meslin. Like Jeanne, he also saw that there was nothing he could do about it. Meanwhile there was a job to be done; one man could do it as readily as two; he was here, so he was that man.

He resumed watching the sky and listening.

Graf bent over Meslin's body. There was one piece of information the Frenchman had left as his legacy – his smell. Graf had first caught it when one of those filthy hands had clamped itself over his mouth and then again when it seized his cigarette.

He waved the unit's obergefreiter over.

'Issue an immediate alert. Full emergency deployment. Get every man and vehicle armed and out of barracks. Patrols and checkpoints on every road, bridge, railway line, every building we hold.' For a second time he kicked Meslin's body. 'This bastard was handling explosive. He might only have been transporting it. Or something might be about to happen. We're not waiting to find out which.' He kicked Meslin again. 'And take this garbage to the barracks. I have plans for it.'

He climbed into the Citroën, gunned the six cylinders into life and skidded away.

Luc Clavier caught Gérard Leroux's arm and pointed. Almost due north of them a tiny smudge seemed to hang above the horizon, motionless and so indistinct that the only way to confirm its existence was by not looking directly at it; it vanished then. As it slowly grew in size they raised their field glasses and watched until there was no question; it was an aircraft.

'How do we know it's the one we're waiting for?' said Leroux. 'What if it's German?'

'Coming from England?'

'Maybe returning from a raid.'

'Life is full of uncertainty,' said Clavier. 'Get down.'

As they flattened themselves against the hillside, he rammed the plunger home.

* * *

151

On the plain of Le Manoir, Paul Leroux knew something big was happening. Every light in the courtyard of the château had come on. Even at this distance he heard the powdery click of electrical power as the floodlights in the watchtowers also burst into life, their beams washing over the killing strip and the plain. The gates opened, revealing a fury of activity. Then from behind him the long black car that had driven away from the château earlier roared back at speed and disappeared inside.

He had no time to figure out what it was all about. Meslin's guidance proved right: first came a vivid orange light in the sky over towards the coast where the railway line ran and his brother and Luc Clavier were stationed, then he heard the crump of an explosion.

He paid Charles Meslin a silent compliment, flicked open the catch on the magneto box and cranked the handle for all he was worth.

The hurricane lamps had been lit for the last ten minutes, their wicks set to the lowest level, the glasses hooded so that no light showed. Now as the two explosions flashed in the sky to east and west and their dull thuds followed, Jeanne and the others dashed along the lines of lamps, removed the metal hoods and turned the wicks to maximum.

Even before they had returned to their ditch, they heard the soft drone of the approaching aircraft.

Le Manoir was in a state of barely controlled chaos when Graf arrived, a tornado of revving trucks and armoured vehicles, of weaponry and munitions being loaded, of shouting, running men, each with his task, every individual focused and determined. The place was as bright as day, the blackout order suspended. Both sets of gates stood wide open in readiness for patrol units to tear through them and into the night.

Then came the first explosion, distant but powerful. Graf had time to realise he was too late, that the action in which Meslin had been engaged was already in hand, then the second blast shook the ground beneath him. This one was close, very close. All activity ceased. Troopers stopped in their tracks, their faces turned in the direction of the main gate. He followed their gaze and saw the plume of smoke and dust that was rising from the hole in the ground that had been the lane to the barracks.

Two blasts. Two scenes of sabotage that demanded his attention. Actual now, facts in their own right, actions carried out, no longer merely theoretical possibilities premised on nothing more than the stink that clung to Charles Meslin.

Humiliatingly, two events that Jürgen Graf had failed to prevent.

His mind raced. Two blasts within a breath of one another. Coordinated, therefore. Why two on the same night? Not only the same night but the same moment. So two scenes that demanded his simultaneous attention, that sought to turn him into the proverbial starving donkey caught between two bales of hay.

Then he saw the truth. Neither was the real event. His spirits lifted. There was no humiliation. The real event was something else; and it was somewhere else. That was the prize tonight. That was what he had to find.

There was movement in the forward cockpit. Smith opened his side panel and positioned the machine guns. Tillman raised his gauntleted hand, two fingers extended. Benedict's headphones crackled.

'Landfall two minutes.'

There was still the dark sea beneath them but Benedict looked to port in time to see a bright orange flash on the coast, somewhere north of their destination. He pictured the map he had studied on those blustery days on Lewis. The railway line ran along that stretch of coast, the line the convoys used for the work on the Atlantic Wall. The flash could only be an explosion on the line. Either a genuine action or a diversion to distract from their arrival. Maybe an opportunistic bit of both.

A second flash appeared to starboard, close to a brilliant cluster of white light in the otherwise dark landscape. Unlike the orange flashes, the blaze of white held steady and continuous. It had to be Le Manoir, the old château, now the garrison barracks. Someone there was breaking blackout regulations on a grand scale. And someone else was setting off bangs on their doorstep.

All in all, a brisk night. Evidently Tillman thought the same. The headphones crackled again.

'Watch yourself down there.'

The Lysander's nose dipped, the note of the engine eased. Benedict caught a glimpse of a tall shadow to port, then it vanished – the old lighthouse. Beneath him the delicate tracery of the waves yielded to long curls of breaking surf, in the moonlight white lace on dark velvet, so close that he felt he could stretch down and run his fingers through them. Directly ahead stretched two parallel lines of flickering lamplight and a pair of marker lights to signify the end of a makeshift landing strip.

Now the strip was under them. The lights in the Lysander's wheel spats came on. He saw grass, a meadow, and caught flashes of white nearby, probably an audience of very bewildered sheep or cows; he hoped they were the only outsiders present.

At the last moment the nose of the little plane lifted, the

wheels bounced gently in a flawless touchdown, the aircraft taxied in a tight circle ready for departure and slowed to a halt.

As far as Baker Street was concerned, Benedict was in the field. But the way he saw it, he was home.

9

He flipped open the cockpit and took in his surroundings. His reception committee comprised three dark-clad figures, almost invisible in the shadows at the edge of the meadow. They kept their distance, like shy children arriving at someone's party. He knew they would stay there until the Lysander departed, leaving him safely outnumbered. No Lysander had ever fallen into enemy hands but there was a first time for everything; for all his hosts knew, this might be it. They were right to be cautious.

For his part, there was just as much risk: they might not be who they purported to be; or there might be other welcomers waiting for him in those deep shadows.

Either way, it was not a time to hang about. He unclipped his parachute harness, tucked the leather flying helmet away, grabbed the bedroll that was his only baggage, clapped Smith on the shoulder and called his thanks to Tillman, then clambered down the narrow ladder fixed to the aircraft's port side and stepped quickly away to be clear of the tailplane. As soon as his feet touched French soil the Lysander was on the move again. The tail zipped past him and the plane's landing lights came back on, this time to illuminate its take-off run. Seconds later it was back in the air.

He was on his own.

The shadowy figures came forward. He saw now that one of them was a woman, small and slightly built. She walked a pace ahead of her companions. So she was the leader. She stopped about four paces from him. He was able to make out her features in the moonlight. He saw dark watchful eyes, a face that was thinner than it should have been, but strong. A set to her jaw. No nonsense. Age somewhere in her thirties, impossible to be more precise; hard times blurred a person's age.

The older man had the solid build and weathered face and hands of a woodsman or a seaman. Or a farmer. The younger man was as tall as Benedict. Untanned skin, so an indoor worker.

He knew that they were assessing him too, with the difference that he was the one with three submachine guns trained on him.

'Weapons and bedroll on the ground,' said the woman. Her voice was quiet but assured, accustomed to command. 'Move slowly, one hand at a time. Raise the other hand. When you finish, raise both.'

He dropped the bedroll, raised his left hand in the air and with his right withdrew the 9mm Browning from his waistband. He held it high for a moment, pointing skywards, to let them see that all fingers were well away from the trigger, then set it carefully on the grass. Then he raised the other hand and took the dagger from his boot, placing it beside the pistol. He raised his left hand again and laced his fingers together behind his head.

She nodded to the farmer. He stepped forward and searched Benedict quickly and expertly. Benedict caught a whiff of earthy aroma from him, the unmistakable bouquet of piggery.

The pig farmer went for the bedroll. Benedict planted his foot firmly on it.

'No,' he said.

The pig farmer straightened up and looked at Benedict, a hint of amusement in his eyes. He lodged the muzzle of the submachine gun in Benedict's stomach and began to bend down again.

Benedict pressed his boot harder on the bedroll.

'Leave it,' he said. He lowered his hands slowly and pushed the submachine gun away.

The pig farmer turned questioningly to the woman. She shrugged, shook her head, and he resumed his place beside her.

'Your name?' she demanded of Benedict.

'Avignon. Yours?'

'Lisieux. Where's Béthune tonight?'

The question was the opening password phrase.

'He injured his ankle,' Benedict replied.

'I hope he makes a quick recovery.'

'Danton assures me he's in good hands.'

Suddenly an unwanted sound cut through the night: the roar of motor vehicles approaching from a distance but at high speed. No headlights were yet visible.

Introductions were over. The woman Lisieux and her companions ran to extinguish the hurricane lamps. Benedict calculated, again calling the local geography to mind. Two lanes led here, converging on the west side of the meadow. That was the only direction from which the Germans could appear unless they were also on foot and simultaneously approached from behind. But that was unlikely; it would call for advance intelligence – an informer – and if they had that, they would have taken up position before the Lysander arrived.

He remembered the blaze of light at the barracks. Whatever its reason, he suspected that the result was a major scurry of troops across the countryside. Hence these uninvited guests. So, not a planned intervention. Not the handiwork of what Pascal of the neat little beard called a cuckoo in the nest.

To the north, the direction he had come from, lay only the shore and the sea. Escape was possible only to the south or east. But to choose between these he needed his hosts to guide him. He recovered the Browning and the dagger. A hand seized his arm. It was Lisieux, answering his unvoiced question.

'This way,' she said, indicating the south side of the meadow.

But it was too late. Narrow beams of light on the other side of the hedgerow and a concerto of squealing tyres confirmed that company had arrived. German voices shouted, searchlights hummed into life and began to sweep the meadow from side to side.

He hit the ground, pulling Lisieux down with him. The pig farmer and the youth were also down. Good fortune put all of them in the cover provided by a slight rise in the lie of the ground. Over the shouting he heard the crackle of RT exchanges. Reinforcements were being called in.

Even though the searchlights had located no targets, a submachine gun rattled into life. It was soon followed by others and the deeper snore of a heavy machine gun. Either the squad's leaders had lost control or they were letting things rip on the basis that if they put enough metal into the meadow they would hit something sooner or later.

'Be ready to run,' he told Lisieux. 'All of you. I'll catch up.'

He had continued watching the searchlights. There were three of them. Judging from their elevation, they were mounted on the roofs of vehicles. A trooper would be standing behind or beside each one to operate it. They had been trained to sweep randomly, avoiding any obvious pattern, but all the sweeps were long: novices' instinctive response to the width of the meadow, with no sudden surprise jerks in a contrary direction.

The moment came when all the beams were at their furthest from where he lay. He rolled quickly away, forsaking the reassuring rise of land. By the time the beams swept back he had travelled a good ten metres. His first shot went home. The searchlight died. Its casing would be light aluminium, which the round would penetrate. Too bad for anyone standing directly behind.

He rolled away again in case his pistol flash had been seen. This time he covered only a couple of metres before one of the two remaining beams returned. He ducked in time but what he saw when he looked up was bad: a series of white headlamp slits approaching rapidly along the lanes. Reinforcements. He planted his elbows square on the ground and selected the next searchlight.

At first he thought the heavy rumble was from something the new arrivals had brought. His ear had registered all the signatures of the weapons in use, and this was a new addition, another machine gun of some kind. He saw a dancing trail of sparks travel along the hedge as a volley of rounds stitched a path along the German vehicles. Judging from the screams, it was stitching more than vehicles.

The slipstream of the Lysander passing at zero altitude pressed him to the ground. The aircraft swept beyond the meadow, lifting abruptly to clear the dark silhouettes of the trees along the south perimeter. It swung into a tight roll and he realised that Tillman was going to level out and approach again for a second pass.

The Germans were in disarray. Smith had knocked out a second searchlight. The scale and volume of gunfire diminished. The shouting in the lane took on a different resonance, that of fear.

While the Lysander manoeuvred, he settled himself again, gathered his concentration and made the shot. The third and final searchlight died. Even if the reinforcements had brought more, it would take a very brave trooper to switch one on.

He hugged the ground as the Lysander passed above him again. More heavy rounds peppered the Germans. He kept his head down. A wave rippled through the earth. His entire body lifted clear of the ground and fell back again, as if the meadow was a carpet that giant hands had shaken. A blinding flash and the roar of an explosion came at the same time. When he raised his head he saw that an armoured car had exploded and was burning like a funeral pyre, which was exactly what it had become. More shouts had become screams.

He looked seaward, where the Lysander's wheels were skimming the surf on its homeward run, which it would have to stick to this time. Unless Smith had taken out the RT vehicle, an alert would be raised and Luftwaffe fighters would be scrambled to bring the Lysander down. As he watched, the little aircraft climbed high enough to dip first one wing and then the other in farewell, then dropped towards the waves again and ploughed off into the night.

A second explosion rippled the earth, signalling that the blaze had found its way to another vehicle and its fuel. That would not be all. As each fuel tank burst, burning fuel would spew over the lane, setting tyres alight and making the roadway impassable. Now the Germans would discover that part of their misfortune lay in the very reinforcements they had summoned – all the more vehicles to turn into bombs, all the more to block the lanes and lock their human cargo into the furnace, all the more reserves of explosive ammunition to add to the lethal mix.

There was no gunfire at all now. The swirls of movement he could make out were men dying or trying to flee. Even their boots were on fire.

He covered the ground at a crouch, back to where he had

parted from Lisieux and the others, snatched up the bedroll and carried on towards the south side of the meadow. They were waiting for him in a shallow ditch. They called quietly to let him know where they were, though they could have used a foghorn and the Germans would never have heard. He slid down to join them.

'Welcome to France,' said Lisieux. 'Welcome to Caillons.' The words were hospitable but her tone was not. 'Don't do that again, Avignon.'

'Don't do what?'

'Take over. Give orders.'

'Why? Will you court-martial me?'

'No. We've cut out the middleman. We'll simply shoot you.'

There was a snort from the pig farmer but he might only have been clearing his sinuses.

Caillons had never known a night like it. There was not a man or woman still asleep in the village, the port or the surrounding countryside for many kilometres around. Some smiled in satisfaction, knowing that such a barrage of explosions at all points of the compass and such a gun battle were bound to be costing the Germans dear, even if they also took a toll in French lives. Some fretted that it was themselves who would pay dearly, or their neighbours or their loved ones, once the reprisals followed as they were sure to do.

Père François Lachanau peeled the bandage from his head, heaved a sigh of relief and scratched every square millimetre of his scalp. He picked up the small black briefcase that was always kept ready, kissed his wooden crucifix, retrieved the parcel for which he had traded his sack of mussels on the night of Jeanne Dupré's detention, slipped his folded biretta into a pocket, mounted his pushbike and set out to seek Armageddon.

With one small task along the way.

Like François Lachanau, Major Klaus Ebermann was awake because he had never been asleep. Sleep had rarely been much of a friend to him these last few years.

He was standing on the open gallery of the Villa Normandie when he saw the bright orange flash of the first explosion in the night sky and heard its dull crump a second or so afterwards. He judged it might be the railway line along the coast. Then came the second blast, well inland. Perhaps the plain of Le Manoir; perhaps even the barracks themselves.

He was the senior Wehrmacht officer. He was Berlin's representative, its authority, its strong fist, what the ancient Romans had called *rector provinciae*. Graf would organise investigation, response, troops on the ground, capture or termination of the perpetrators if at all possible and reprisals in cold blood if not – God help Caillons, for what Graf would require would be fearsome – but it was he, Klaus Ebermann, who remained responsible for all these things in the eyes of Berlin.

But he remained responsible in the eyes of God too – God who watched all, including whatever Klaus Ebermann gave Graf rein to do.

Now he heard gunfire and further explosions – somewhere on the coast again, startling flashes along the horizon that did not fade with the blasts this time but persisted beyond them. So fires were blazing. Something was burning. The gunfire ended with another cluster of explosions.

In the bedroom his suitcase was packed and ready. He was to depart before first light. His driver was to deliver him to Paris and the military flight that would take him to

163

Germany for the few days Berlin permitted for the funerals and the tidying up of family affairs.

A man must be there for the funerals of his own and only family. That was his priority. If a man had so rarely been there for them in life, the least he could do was be there for them in death.

He returned inside, shutting out the night and the sounds of racing vehicles crossing the countryside. On the other side of the room the door opened and Leutnant Neiss entered. His uniform and shirt were yesterday's, donned again in haste, his face was crumpled and stiff with sleep, his eyes blinking slowly and still only half open.

'Herr Major.' No Hitler salute but a proper military one, even if blunted by sleep. He settled his spectacles in place.

'Cancel my flight,' Ebermann said.

The leutnant, who had known as much already, saluted again and left.

Gaspard Baignères sat at his table beneath the cottage's single weak bulb. Smoke curled from the Gitane held loosely between his lips, adding a little more yellow stain to the grey in his moustaches. His notebook was open on the table, his left hand holding it flat. In the fingers of his right hand was a pencil. Not the short stub that was usually all he had and that always needed licking but a brand-new Swiss Prismalo, full length, beautiful fine point. No licking necessary.

Opposite him sat the man who had brought the pencil as a gift tonight, one Maître Aristide Péringuey, schoolmaster of Caillons these last thirty years and recently as naked as a fish in place de l'Église. His pushbike stood against Gaspard's in the corner. He was hunched in his chair, his damaged shoulder blade tightly bound and strapped beneath his shirt. Every movement was still agony for him; the ride to Gaspard's cottage had been murder.

'Why couldn't we meet down in the village?' he complained. 'You're like a hermit, all the way up here. Why do I have to come here?'

'Because I said so.'

'Why at this hour? Decent people are in their beds at this hour.'

'We're not decent people. Not many decent people left in Caillons. Not that many left in France.'

The two explosions rumbled through the night and up to the cottage. The animal snares and traps hanging on the wall rattled, the light bulb shook, making the shadows quiver.

'Sounds like somebody else isn't in bed,' Gaspard added. 'See what I mean?'

Maître Péringuey looked as if he might faint. 'My God.' His eyes rolled in their sockets, reminding Gaspard of the terrified horses that had drawn the wagons at Verdun. 'How do I get home now? The Germans will close the roads. What have you got me into?'

Then came the sound of the gun battle. Péringuey fell silent, taking his anxiety out on a fingernail, and the two men listened together without comment, each guarding his own thoughts. The schoolmaster jumped with each boom or burst of gunfire, his long face growing even longer, his expression strained with the pain each twitch inflicted as much as by fear. Gaspard sat as still as a toad.

As a grand finale there came several more explosions that rattled the cottage again, then a rapid series of sharper blasts, higher in pitch. Gaspard nodded slowly, as if a hypothesis of some kind had been confirmed, and drew on the cigarette. Smoke ascended in a lazy ring towards the light bulb.

'Ammunition,' he observed with the air of a man

assessing a bill of goods, tallying and analysing. 'Exploding. Boxes of ammo going up. That means vehicles. They had time to send out vehicles. The other bangs – the vehicles going up. Ammunition's usually the last thing to go, so that'll be the end of it now.'

Péringuey looked unsure but Gaspard was right. The night returned to comparative silence. From time to time there was the whine of vehicle engines far below in the distance, their sound moving across the countryside, or a faint chorus of shouts, brief and urgent; but no more explosions or shooting.

Gaspard grunted to himself, looked at the shiny red pencil, raised it to his lips without thinking but remembered himself in time, and returned his attention to the notebook.

'Rousselot,' he said with a sigh. 'You told me the family Rousselot. Come on, Aristide, get a grip.'

Péringuey rubbed his eyes with his bony fingertips and nodded. Gaspard noted the name.

'André and Estelle. Yes?'

Péringuey nodded again. The names were duly recorded. Gaspard kept the book well away from him.

'And Jean-Marie, André's brother. Good sort, always paid what he owed, never a day late. Good customer. So that's all three of them. Yes?'

Another nod. The name of Jean-Marie Rousselot went in the book.

'The family Rousselot had only one Jewish child. This one?' He pointed at a name already written on the page, positioning his other hand so that Péringuey could see only what he was meant to see.

Another nod.

'And the other family – Lanery?'

'There's only Agathe now. Fernand's on STO.'

'Another good customer I won't be seeing again.'

Péringuey's expression was funereal. 'We won't be seeing Agathe either. Everybody's a customer to you.'

'I don't force anybody to do business with me. Did I force you? The family Lanery, how many children? Two, brother and sister?' He indicated the two names in the book.

'That's them.'

Gaspard completed his notes. He closed the book, opened the door of the stove and dropped his cigarette butt into the glowing embers.

'You can go now,' he told Péringuey as he watched the butt burn. 'Say hello to those German patrols.'

'Why do you keep these lists? What's the point? Why does any of it matter?'

Gaspard set the book on end and stood it on the table between his hands. He tipped his head and squinted at it as at a target. 'Because someone should. Because it does matter. Because the Germans won't be here forever and –'

'You really think that?'

'And afterwards we'll need to remember. You're an educated man, I'd expect you to know that.' He raised the Prismalo and sighted the book through one eye like a sniper. 'We are what we remember. That's why it matters.'

'There are things that not everyone will want to remember.'

'All the more reason why the rest of us should.'

Péringuey tried to find a comfortable position on the chair, not much liking what the words implied.

'What happened at the school wasn't my fault. Or Maîtresse Lavisse's. There was nothing we could do. You see that, don't you?'

Gaspard's moustaches drooped a little lower as he pursed his lips. 'Maybe. Or maybe you could have lied.'

'How could we? He saw them naked.'

'Who are this "we"? Leave Maîtresse Lavisse out of it.

167

This is about you. You spoke up for Hervé Meslin.'

'Much good it did.'

'At least you tried. You didn't try for the little Jews. So I heard. You should get home now.'

Péringuey made no move. 'You like that pencil?'

Gaspard shrugged. 'It writes.'

The schoolmaster looked speculatively at the notebook. 'You'll cancel what I owe? I did what you wanted, I took them into the school. I risked my life. He could have shot me on the spot. And this shoulder ...'

Gaspard picked a shred of loose tobacco from his lip. He placed it on his tongue and bit into it. The bitter flavour filled his mouth.

'I'll reduce your debt by a quarter. That's generous, considering you didn't complete the contract. I'll let you know if another opportunity arises for you. Maybe you'll have better luck next time.'

Péringuey began to protest.

'Aristide, Aristide,' Gaspard interrupted him wearily. 'Give it a rest. Go home.' He took the Star semi-automatic from beneath his shirt and placed it on the table. Péringuey's eyes became round orbs of terror.

'You wouldn't,' he said.

'I might.'

After the schoolmaster had finally departed, Gaspard stood in his open doorway, the cottage now in darkness. He gazed over the landscape below, towards an orange glow where fires still raged. Vehicles. The Germans had sent out their vehicles. A lot of vehicles. They had time to do that.

All was quiet now. At this distance anyway. Quiet, yes, but not at rest, not settled, for every transaction came at a price.

He lit another Gitane and wondered about that price.

* * *

168

Isabelle knew it was Hélène downstairs. She knew her sister's shuffle, the scrape of her left foot as it dragged behind her, as familiar a sound as her elder sister's voice. She heard the rush of the tap as Hélène washed at the deep sink. It sounded as if clothes were being rinsed through as well. Some minutes later she heard Hélène climb slowly upstairs, step by awkward step. She seemed to ascend even more slowly than usual. Isabelle was lying on her side, facing the curtain, but felt the bed move as her sister sat down behind her to unbuckle the leg brace. She heard the steel and stiff leather scrape on the bare boards of the floor, then the bed moved again as Hélène slid in behind her.

When the sobs began, no more than soft gasps and felt through the thin mattress as much as heard, Isabelle turned without a word and put her arms about her sister. There was no response but no resistance either. It was like grasping the cloth doll Isabelle had clung to as a child, something limp and lifeless. She drew Hélène close and stroked her hair. When she felt the chill of her sister's body, still damp from the cold water, she drew her even closer. She murmured quietly to her, no words, only gentle susurrations of comfort.

Then from far away she heard the first two explosions.

'Where are you, Maman?' she wondered silently. 'What have you done?'

Though she feared she knew.

Then she returned to comforting her trembling sister. She feared she might also know what Hélène had done.

Oberleutnant Jürgen Graf stood in the hatch of the armoured vehicle and surveyed the dreadful scene of destruction before him.

He had counted fifteen dead. At least as many again wounded. And at least three of those were unlikely to last the night.

The fires were almost extinguished now, and a triage station had been set up along the lane. Medics moved between the stretchers, assessing the wounded while ambulances waited or reversed from the lane to make their way back to the barracks.

In the meadow the hurricane lamps had been left in situ for his inspection – unnecessarily so: that the field had served as a landing strip was hardly in any doubt. Even so, he had walked the field. A flashlight and the light of the moon, sinking now but still bright, had shown him the tracks of undercarriage wheels in the cropped grass, and he had kicked the toe of his boot in the strips of sandy earth where the aircraft's two forward wheels had bitten as the brakes were applied. He had also come upon the corpses of two sheep that had been caught in the crossfire. He had ordered that they be taken to the barracks butchery. No point in wasting good mutton or leaving it for the local savages.

His men said the aircraft was a Lysander and he trusted their skills of recognition. What its pilot had done was bold and valiant – he gave the man his due as one warrior to another – and he might get away with it: although a bevy of Messerschmitts was already in pursuit and was well able to outrun the Lysander, the ocean was wide and the English plane would be showing no lights and skimming the waves. The further ahead the Messerschmitts wanted to see, the higher they had to fly, exposing them to English radar; and the closer to England they ventured, the greater the risk from enemy aircraft.

So the reality was that retribution was unlikely to be delivered in the skies or above the ocean. Retribution had to be doled out here, on dry land, where the act that made it necessary had taken place.

An eager desk clerk at the barracks, hastily second-guessing him, had checked the local land records and established that the meadow belonged to a farmer called Jacques Colinet. Graf recognised the name. He also knew that the clerk's information was probably quite useless – ownership of the meadow was irrelevant, it proved nothing – but the young man had shown good initiative, so the oberleutnant praised his efforts and promised to pay the farmer a visit.

Everything boiled down to the two simple questions to which he kept returning. First, why was the Lysander here; what had been delivered tonight at the cost of so many German lives, the lives of his fine young men? Second, what was so important that it justified the Lysander's return to protect it?

Or was it a question of who?

The village was hushed and still, even more so than if it had been asleep. It had drawn in upon itself, coiled and holding its breath, but François Lachanau knew that every soul behind every shutter was wide awake. Some would be whispering together. Some would be praying – he knew which ones they would be; and pitifully few of them too. Some would be peering around the edges of their shutters. All would be waiting for what might happen next. Some would be waiting for what they could pass on as information to their German masters. They were the ones who would see him and report him.

No matter. What priest would not be expected to be out this night, curfew notwithstanding?

The small briefcase swung from a handlebar. He had wrapped the parcel in a ratty old piece of curtain and tied it tightly to the saddle. Now his backside rested squarely on it. The covering power of the backside was beyond question; the parcel was well and truly concealed. The watchers behind the shutters would have to seek other titbits.

From place de l'Église he cut along rue du Verger and freewheeled part of the way downhill along rue du Port, then swung left and pedalled hard to make the most of his momentum as the road began to rise again. There was not a German to be seen anywhere, no roadblocks, no patrols lurking in hedgerows or behind gable ends. That would shortly change, but for the moment the garrison's priority would be to gather its dead and wounded.

Gradually the houses began to thin out, narrow, pinched frontages that kept themselves to themselves, and now every dwelling he passed alternated with two or three vacant plots overgrown with ragwort and weedy grass and tall clumps of thistle, ugly gaps that were evidence of the community's reduced population. War and STO took their toll. The Germans knew that; devour the men and you devour the future.

Rue du Phare was deserted, not even a dog or a cat in sight. The surface of the road was pitted and rough; he took it slowly and carefully, watching where the wheels traced their route, not wanting a bent spoke or a punctured tyre. Beyond the kerbstone edging the expanse of open ground was a mix of hard sandy earth, rubble and coarse gravel bound together by nettles and groundweeds. There was no shortage of rubbish – old car batteries white with crusts of spilt acid, tin basins rusted through, festering bits of a broken harrow, rusting discs that might be the tines of a cultivator, a mouldering lichen-covered mattress alive with rats. The rats were the only things moving; they scurried away as he approached.

No one knew where the car, an ancient Peugeot, had come from or who had owned it. One December night

172

many years before, flames lit the sky and there it was, a bonfire for a cold winter night. The thing was such a rusty, ashy heap that even the village children and the rats left it alone. It squatted there, sunk down on its collapsed springs and disregarded by the world.

Lachanau propped the pushbike against the side of the vehicle and stood looking at nothing in particular, as would a man catching his breath. He looked at nothing but he watched every shadow, every corner and mound of rubble.

Once the parcel was freed from the saddle, one quick movement slipped it beneath the wheel arch and behind the charred remains of the wheel. A moment later he was on his way again, briefcase swinging from the handlebar, his backside resuming its normal elevation.

At first Graf thought he was seeing things.

He had spent some time in the triage area, talking quietly with the wounded, and now he was back in the hatch of the armoured car, indicating on a map the zone to be cordoned and searched and spelling out his orders to the obergefreiter standing below him on the lane. The rest of the troopers, those who were uninjured in the Lysander attack and those who had helped to extinguish the fires, stood or sat in anxious groups, smoking and waiting for their next orders.

Graf glanced up at the precise moment when something black moved across the white form of one of the stretchered troopers in the triage station. He narrowed his eyes and looked again. Perhaps it was a trick of the light: the emergency lighting set up for the medics was adequate for close-quarters work but poor at a distance. The shadow moved again. It was no trick of the light. It was a man, a large man, and he was dressed in black. The medics wore white, not black.

The man bent down and seemed to be conversing with the

173

wounded trooper. Then he straightened up and turned slightly, and Graf's eyes popped. He caught a flash of white and gold from the embroidered stole that hung about the man's neck and chest. He saw the unmistakable gleam of gold in his left hand, a shovel of a hand, and the small white disc that the other hand was placing, so delicately despite the size of the hand, on the injured trooper's tongue.

Lachanau. The holy bastard Lachanau, flapping his black skirts over these good German boys like an old crow that could hardly wait to peck their eyes out.

'Unbelievable,' rasped Graf.

'Herr Oberleutnant?' said the obergefreiter.

Graf ignored him.

'Priester!' he roared at the top of his voice.

Every medic in the triage enclosure stopped in his work and turned to stare at Graf. There was a stir of movement among the white stretchers as those injured men who were conscious tried to see what was going on. Among the rest, heads turned and conversations ceased, cigarettes burned unattended.

Lachanau paused briefly, as if a trivial distraction such as a buzzing insect had seized his attention for a moment, then moved on to the next stretchered trooper.

Graf swung the armoured car's MG34 machine gun towards the priest, tilted it high and loosed off a burst. The muzzle spat fire, the heavy rounds flared yellow against the night sky. Alarmed medics and troopers ducked or flattened themselves on the ground. The stretchered men, who had had enough for one night if not for a lifetime, quaked beneath their sheets. Only Lachanau held his position, upright and serene.

'Get out of the triage area,' bellowed Graf.

The confused medics began to rise to their feet.

'Not you – the priest,' yelled Graf, becoming shrill in his

frustration. 'You, Lachanau, out of the triage.'

Finally Lachanau turned to face him. 'You want a clear shot, Oberleutnant?' he called. 'Let me oblige.'

He marched clear of the triage area and crossed to the other side of the lane. He was still holding the gold chalice, a warm glow in the moonlight, and in his other hand the black briefcase, his portable mass kit, in which the chalice and other communion items had travelled. He raised the chalice to his lips and kissed it. Then he set the briefcase down and stretched his arms wide, the chalice still in his left hand.

'Go on, Oberleutnant,' he called. 'Complete your journey to perdition. God will forgive me for helping you.'

All watched the performance. It would be interesting to see what the heavy gun would do to a man at such close quarters. Some of the injured men managed to raise themselves on elbows or crane their necks.

Lights flashed through the hedgerow along one of the lanes. A pair of narrowed headlight beams rounded the corner. The staff car pulled in behind Graf's armoured vehicle and Klaus Ebermann climbed out, his attention on the priest. He took up position alongside Graf but seemed not to notice him. He looked slowly from side to side, assessing the scene, then returned his gaze to the priest.

'Père Lachanau,' he called. 'I'm glad to see you consider my men part of your ministry.'

Lachanau grinned, like a schoolboy who had been found out. 'All souls are equally worthy of my saviour's love.'

Ebermann translated their exchange for the benefit of the audience, adding, 'But of course Père Lachanau will only minister to those who ask for him.'

Then in French to the priest: 'Not all here share your faith, Monsieur.'

'Christ's love is there for all. He judges by need, not by

the foolish divisions of man's invention. His forgiveness and his succour are for all. Then again, I think you know this.'

'Thank you for reminding me, Monsieur le Curé. Please resume your ministrations.'

Now Ebermann acknowledged the presence of Graf and the young trooper.

'Please excuse us, Obergefreiter,' he said.

The soldier glanced up at Graf, then raised a Hitler salute in Ebermann's direction and marched obediently away.

Ebermann now turned his back completely on Graf. He looked again at the wreckage and carnage at the intersection of the two lanes.

'You know what your duties are, Oberleutnant. I expect you to perform them to perfection – by which I mean establish what happened here tonight and apprehend the perpetrators. I hold you personally responsible for the fact that tonight's attacks were allowed to happen and for the lives lost and the property destroyed. My report to Paris and Berlin will make that clear. I understand that you were actually in the barracks at Le Manoir when the explosion close by occurred. I look forward to receiving your explanation of how such an assault could take place under your nose and yet you failed to prevent it. You've made the Reich and the Wehrmacht look incompetent and Berlin will not be happy. I also understand that your investigation of the scene at Le Manoir was only cursory, and that you sent only a limited force to investigate the destruction of the railway line at La Vierge and in fact didn't even go there yourself. I look forward to receiving your explanation of that as well. All these things strike me as dereliction of duty among other possible charges, but of course I will leave that for Berlin to decide.'

Graf stuttered the beginnings of a defence. Ebermann,

still looking away, raised a hand to silence him.

'I haven't finished. I spoke of your duties. They are not to include reprisals against the civilian population. Is that clear?'

'Herr Major –'

'No reprisals, Oberleutnant. You understand? I'm not asking if you agree. I'm asking if my orders are clear. Only that.'

'They're clear, Herr Major, but –'

Ebermann had never bothered to look at Graf and now he was already climbing back into the car. Graf passed a hand across his face, feeling a great weariness come upon him.

Unjust, what Ebermann had done, undermining him by colluding with the priest. Unjust too, the accusations and threats. And done in such a way that his own men had witnessed everything. That was no accident. What was filthier to a soldier than injustice?

He saw that Lachanau was watching him from the corner of the triage area. He waited for the insult the priest would throw at him or the sarcastic gesture – a mock salute, at the very least a triumphant raised finger.

But the priest merely nodded soberly and crouched down beside a stretchered trooper.

10

Their descent of the treacherous cliff-face path to somewhere that Lisieux referred to as the icehouse was interrupted by a distant burst of heavy machine-gun fire. With the distorting effect of the cliff on one side and the open ocean on the other, it was impossible to say where it originated. Benedict thought it came from the direction of the meadow.

They halted and listened, waiting for more. But there was only the rise and fall of the surf and the whisper of an onshore breeze ruffling the dense maquis. Even the sounds of vehicle engines at full throttle that had been the backdrop to their trek through fields and woods had now ceased.

Lisieux had warned him to follow her exactly along the path down the cliff. There was an emphasis in that 'exactly' and he soon saw why – one misplaced step in the darkness, one trip or snag on the unyielding sprigs of woody vegetation and a hundred-metre drop awaited him. But it was like chasing a mountain goat. She suddenly disappeared from view about halfway down. The pig farmer pulled a curtain of undergrowth aside and guided him into the hidden opening. He found himself in a low tunnel and with no choice but to go forward. He heard the squeak of hinges, saw a glimmer of light and realised that he was approaching a door. He heard her voice, then the door opened to admit him to a chamber – the place seemed too regular in shape to be called a cave – in which a single hurricane lamp was burning on an upended crate. At last he was able to stand upright again.

In the shadows beyond the weak flame three men were waiting. They set their weapons aside and embraced their companions. There was a nervousness about them but he sensed that it was not the result of his presence or the natural jumpiness of résistants after an action. He was presented to them as Avignon but, as with Lisieux's other companions in the meadow, was given no names in return, not even assumed ones.

'You're not here to work with us,' she pointed out. 'You're merely passing through. The less you know about us, the better.'

His instinct about the three men turned out to be right. As they made their report to Lisieux, he gathered that there were originally four of them, two teams of two, but one man had absconded in mid action.

'I knew it,' said the pig farmer. 'I knew something was wrong as soon as we heard the Sten.'

'We had difficulties of our own, those who met the aircraft,' said Lisieux. She gave an account of what had happened.

'Have we been betrayed again?' said someone. 'Why were the Germans at the landing area?'

'Surely it couldn't have been –' said the youth from the meadow. Lisieux flashed him a warning glance before he could speak the missing man's name. 'What if he's been captured? The Boche have their ways of extracting information when they get their hands on someone.'

The pig farmer grunted dismissively. 'If a man can't be sure of holding his tongue, he should make arrangements. He should have his escape prepared in advance. And always available.'

'Escape? Like a bullet, you mean?'

'Each to his own taste.'

179

'Enough,' said Lisieux. 'Go back to your homes now, all of you. It sounds like the whole garrison is out, so take special care. We did well tonight. We did all that was demanded of us.' Her gaze fell on Benedict. 'Let's hope it was worthwhile.'

'Avignon, I don't need to know what your mission is. And I don't want to know. No doubt it's important, but I don't want you here in Caillons a minute longer than necessary.'

She was showing him the small stock of food she had laid aside for him in the icehouse: some strips of cooked meat, dry bread, boiled eggs, all packed in a tin box.

She was full of instructions. He was to leave the tin behind; such things were scarce. There was a bottle of water. He could take the bottle with him when he departed, in order to refill it where and when he could; she had plenty of bottles. He was not to smoke in the icehouse; the smoke would leak outside and be detected. He was to keep the wick as low as possible in the hurricane lamp and in fact use the lamp as little as possible; paraffin was also in short supply, and, besides, they had lost several lamps tonight. She made this last sound as if it was directly his fault.

'You've brought us nothing,' she went on, becoming explicit. 'No munitions, no supplies. Your arrival endangered my cell and you continue to endanger it as long as you stay here. The Germans will figure your aircraft wouldn't have returned to attack them if it had brought only supplies. It might as well have dropped leaflets announcing an agent was being landed.'

'Your other actions tonight told them that anyway.'

'We had no choice. The Germans will be looking for you – that puts everyone in danger. And there may be reprisals for the aircraft's attack.' He tried to speak but she raised a hand to stop him. 'I have to leave. I must get home before first light. If you haven't got everything you need, you'll have to make do – I can give you nothing more.'

'Where is your home?' He had the map in his mind, every detail.

She frowned. 'You don't need to know.'

'As for endangering your cell, the man who ran away may have done that without any help from me.'

That angered her. 'He didn't run away in the sense you imply. He's not a coward. It's you who's the problem. We're not a halfway house at London's beck and call. We don't like London treating us like that.'

'You don't like London. You don't like SOE. You certainly don't like working with us. You think we should keep to our own networks and stay out of your Free French ones. No crossing over. But you don't mind when we send ammunition and weapons. You don't turn them down. You've admitted as much.'

'That doesn't make us SOE's lapdog, waiting for its instructions.'

'Well, there's no point waiting for instructions from de Gaulle.'

'What do you mean by that?'

'He can do nothing without London. All he does is talk – "France has lost a battle, but France hasn't lost the war." Stirring words but a leader should offer more than talk.'

'This is a stupid conversation. You English are all the same.'

He could not help but smile. 'Are we?'

'Full of stupid ideas.'

'Perhaps you should leave resistance to the communists.'

'There are no communist cells here.'

'There will be. You'll see. They're infiltrating your networks already. Hasn't your great leader warned you?'

Suddenly her eyes blazed. 'I'll tell you what no one

warned us about – that our so-called friends would be as dangerous as the Nazis, that thousands of innocent French people would perish in bombing raids by those who claim to save us. What kind of allies are those, Avignon? We can survive our enemies, but can we survive our friends? I've heard enough. When will you be gone from here?'

'Within twenty-four hours, I hope.'

'I regard that as a promise. This place, this icehouse, belongs to my family. Most Caillonais have forgotten it exists, but if the Germans find you there'll be people in Caillons quick enough to remember whose it is. Some of them would be happy to see the end of me. My family too.'

'What family do you have?'

'That's something else you don't need to know.'

'Tell me.'

She took a moment. 'Two daughters.' She looked at the floor. 'That's all. Two daughters.'

'How old?'

'Fifteen and thirteen.'

'Not good times to raise children.'

'We manage.' She hefted her submachine gun and checked the bolt. 'No more questions.'

But at the door it was she who asked, her back still turned to him, 'You have a family?'

'Am I married? No.'

'But you have other family?'

'My mother and father are dead.'

'Brothers, sisters?'

'No.'

'You should marry. A man should be married.'

He smiled again. 'Perhaps. When the war's over.'

She swung around to face him. Her expression was solemn. 'Another stupid thing to say. People can't stop living simply because of an idiotic war. Have the birds stopped singing or the flowers growing? People have to keep living.'

She unlocked the door, hauled it open and slipped away.

His gaze remained on the closed door. She had never sat down or stopped moving throughout their exchange. One moment she was by the crate, the chamber's table, rubbing its coarse surface or picking at a splinter of wood or fiddling with the lamp for fear a millilitre of paraffin might be wastefully consumed, the next she would flit to the door and check that it was locked for a fourth or fifth time.

She never let her gaze light on him for more than an instant, then it flicked away – anywhere, the rock floor, the lamp, anywhere but rest on him. Her irises were as dark as the chamber's deepest shadows, and when he did catch her gaze on him – she only ever looked at him when his attention was elsewhere – he sensed he had been inspected, assessed, evaluated, all at high speed, then her gaze had moved on again.

Such gravity, such intensity. Her declaration that a man should be married was straight from another century. Aspects of her were French to the point of parody.

She seemed to be well educated; her speech retained traces of hard Norman consonants but she used none of the old vocabulary, unlike the pig farmer and the others. And this icehouse – what kind of family would have a place like this? Certainly not labourers or fishermen living from day to day. And evidently it was a family that had been in Caillons long enough to be the target of local resentments.

The oversized leather blouson and the work boots – certainly not hers, no more than were the ill-fitting trousers. Yet there was no mention of a husband, present or past, who might once have owned these things or still did. Her outburst about Allied bombing – what lay behind that? Then there was her firm emphasis, perhaps too firm, on her daughters as the entirety of her family: 'That's all.' Perhaps what she called this idiotic war had taken more from her than food and paraffin.

He locked the door, unfurled the bedroll and extinguished the lamp. But she was there, standing by the door and fixing him with that fierce gaze or moving about the chamber, every time he tried to turn his thoughts to what had brought him here.

Dawn was blossoming in the trees as Jeanne hurried through the bois de Caillons and towards La Croisette. The woods were carpeted with bluebells so densely that their colour seemed to hang in the air, staining the morning mist.

As she left the cover of the woods she kept close to the weathered stone walls and the tall bocage, the high hedges, exactly as she always did. She slipped unseen and unheard past a pair of deer grazing not many metres distant; only when a shifting breeze brought her scent to them did they lift their startled heads towards her and flee for the safety of the trees.

The whitewashed walls and ochre roof tiles of La Croisette came in view. By the time she reached the march of pine trees along the border of the third field she was worried that she had lingered too long with the Englishman, for now the light was rapidly spreading higher above the horizon.

But it was the hastening light that saved her. It glinted on the helmets and weapons of the German troopers as they plodded up from ruelle de la Baie and along the footpath to La Croisette.

'No. Absolutely no.'

Isabelle stood her ground, unfazed by the submachine guns and uniforms. She had flung a coat over her nightdress and was arguing with the troopers in the doorway. Hélène strapped the leg brace on and hobbled down the stairs to join her.

'You've already searched here,' Isabelle told the trooper in charge; it was the same obergefreiter who had brought Hélène home after her encounter with Graf by the harbour. 'Don't you remember? Don't you remember my sister?'

The obergefreiter glanced at Hélène, then back at the younger sister.

'Yes, Mademoiselle, but we have to search again.'

'You'll regret it.' She squeezed Hélène's hand.

Suddenly Hélène saw where Isabelle was going.

'Not until Jürgen gets here,' she said.

'Jürgen?' said the obergefreiter.

'Oberleutnant Jürgen Graf. I advise you to fetch him before you do something you might regret.'

Isabelle leant forward. The obergefreiter stepped back in alarm. She closed the gap. She stretched up and put her cheek close to his so that her lips were by his ear. She let her hair brush against his face. She knew he would smell her body and feel her warmth, fresh from bed. She knew the ache a lonely farm boy far from home would suffer.

'We don't want you to get into trouble,' she whispered. 'There are things here that belong to Oberleutnant Graf. If your men found them …'

The other troopers watched with interest. They heard Graf's name. What was going on?

They never found out. Jeanne rounded the corner of the cottage and lunged at one of the troopers standing in her kitchen garden.

'Get your feet out of there.'

She had shed the leather jacket, concealing it beneath a clump of ferns along with the MP40 and the spare magazines. In her old jumper and Michel's trousers and boots she could have been any Norman countrywoman who had thrown on whatever fell to hand for her dawn forage through the fields for fruit and berries for her breakfast table. Dark soil clung to her hands, the loamy soil from beneath the pine trees that edged the third field and at whose base the fat white mushrooms grew. She carried a wicker pannier filled with champignons de couche.

She pushed the trooper back, dismissive of his submachine gun. Soil transferred from her fists to his tunic. Other troopers who had strayed onto the vegetable patch shuffled back to the narrow path. She glared at the damage and harangued them. Then she harangued the obergefreiter.

The cottage was still searched, but half-heartedly; again the henhouse was omitted, though this time there was nothing incriminating there. Isabelle and Hélène were allowed a minute to assemble the oberleutnant's mysterious 'things': one of their father's shirts, an old shaving brush and folding razor sufficed; these they showed fleetingly to the obergefreiter.

When the troopers were gone, Jeanne took her daughters in her arms.

'What would you have done if I hadn't got back in time?'

'But you did,' said the logical Isabelle.

Jeanne drew the girls closer. The shirt still lay on the table. If she picked it up she would smell Michel. If she lifted the shaving brush she would smell his morning smell.

'I have something to tell you,' she said softly. 'Something terrible.'

Isabelle sighed. 'We already know, Maman.'

'It's Papa,' said Hélène, her tone dull. 'He's dead.'

'How could you know that?'

'We guessed for ourselves.'

'Did you? How could you?'

Neither daughter answered. Their silence was like an

accusation. Jeanne closed her eyes. A leaden sorrow filled her. So now her own children had secrets.

Like mother, like daughters.

Despite Père François Lachanau's scepticism about German promises, Jürgen Graf kept three promises that day. The first was the one he had made to Klaus Ebermann and Hélène Dupré concerning the release of Hortense and little Hervé Meslin.

Without explanation, they were marched from their cell to the main gate of Le Manoir and ushered out at gunpoint. Hortense feared that they were being taken to be shot. Instead, like Jeanne, she found herself anxiously crossing the killing strip. At every step she expected bullets to tear Hervé and her to shreds. As soon as she reached the end of the ploughed strip of earth she began running, pulling Hervé along, slowing to a breathless walk only when they came to the huge crater in the approach lane. It was already being repaired. She recognised and acknowledged with a nod each of the village men who were working there under the supervision of armed troopers. She had been frightened by the blast during the night, had felt its shock wave in the underground cell where she lay awake while Hervé slept or sobbed, and fretted that they would be buried alive if the building was under attack.

Then she had listened to the commotion as the garrison emptied itself of troops and vehicles. She knew nothing of the night's other events, and although she saw now that the blast was not the château falling in on Hervé and her but merely this deep hole, she still had no idea that it was her husband's doing.

Nor did she understand why the men working there this morning exchanged glances as she and her son passed, or why they returned her nod of recognition with uncharacteristic restraint. Not one of them had a word or a wink for Hervé, who wanted to stay to watch them. She put it down to their caution while under the gaze of their Wehrmacht guards.

On she trudged through the rising heat of the morning, sometimes stopping to let Hervé rest, until at long last they were descending the steep road to the harbour. For the first time since her ordeal began, she smiled, because there at the foot of the hill was her little cottage waiting for her.

But outside the cottage stood a knot of half a dozen of her neighbours. Why were they there?

Then Audrey Sablière, her cousin and closest neighbour, glanced around and saw Hervé skipping excitedly down the hill. He waved, a two-armed wave to express his joy, and called to her. The others heard and swung around. Audrey ran to the boy and snatched him up in her arms in the way that she, the childless one, always did. But today the expression on her face as she met her cousin's gaze filled Hortense with dread.

Now Hortense looked more closely at the little group of people. The tall figure in black turning towards her – why was Père Lachanau here? And what was concealed beneath that heavy tarpaulin spread on the ground? Why were Monsieur le Curé and the others hurrying towards her, their arms outstretched as if to keep her away from it?

The gulls wheeled and cried through the clear sky above the headland, the sun sparkled on the surf foaming in the bay as Hervé raised his head from Audrey Sablière's arms and felt the cool spray from the ocean on his cheeks. He was home at last. He was happy.

Jacques Colinet was lugging a bucket of cabbage for Pompadour across the yard when he heard the roar of engines. He and Pompadour watched as an armoured

188

vehicle rounded the corner and came to a halt in a cloud of dust. Colinet recognised the man standing in the hatch as Oberleutnant Jürgen Graf, despite the dark glasses and battledress and helmet. A moment later a truck roared in and disgorged half a dozen heavily armed troopers. More dust flew around the yard. Pompadour became restless. The troopers vaulted to the ground, followed by Graf himself. He grinned at Colinet. Pompadour grunted anxiously.

After half an hour of searching, one of the troopers presented Graf with a small folded document made of thick, cloth-like card. The oberleutnant flipped it open and gazed for a time at the photograph on its inner panel. Colinet knew what it showed: a German boy of nineteen or so, fair hair, light-coloured eyes that in life had been blue, a serious expression as was required in such an important document but with the hint of a smile not far away.

Graf peeled off his dark glasses, as if to see the photograph more clearly. He turned the card around so that Colinet could see it.

'Monsieur Colinet, please tell me why you have the Kennkarte of one of my men who was recently murdered by criminals who glorify themselves as résistants.'

He spoke gently, as if not to cause offence. He leant close, searching Colinet's face. Colinet caught a whiff of cologne, a change from Pompadour's heavy must.

'You see, Monsieur, I'm puzzled. You're an honest, well-behaved citizen. You help my men, you take away the bodies of our enemies and dispose of them on your own land. A valuable service to the Reich. But this is the identity card of Gefreiter Wilfried Hermann Wiedemuth. Why do you have it in your possession? Perhaps you found it. Perhaps you were about to hand it over.'

Jacques Colinet turned instinctively towards his house. A familiar shadow told him that his mother was in her

189

accustomed place in the kitchen from which she could see everyone and everything. Not even a Wehrmacht squad could dislodge her. He thought of his Delphine, weaker than ever this morning. He shifted his gaze to take in the rest of the yard and saw his two daughters enter from the direction of the east field and stop in their tracks when they saw the truck and the armoured car and the German officer staring into their father's frightened face.

'Monsieur Colinet? Please explain these things.'

The scene blurred as Colinet sought to fix it in his mind. So much to remember, so much that he would never see again.

'Monsieur?'

Graf sighed and closed the Kennkarte. In time, when the proper procedures had been followed and the card was no longer required by the Wehrmacht, he would dictate another letter and send the card to a grieving German mother. It was a fine photograph; it did the boy justice. She would rightly treasure it. It would pass down the generations.

He motioned a trooper to take charge of the prisoner.

His second promise had been honoured, the one to the desk clerk who had checked the local land records.

As he climbed into the armoured vehicle, Pompadour caught his eye. The creature was truly enormous. Hideously so. Was it pregnant? It was flinging itself against its pen, trying to get to the spilled bucket of cabbage that Colinet had dropped.

Graf paused, one boot on the steel steps. He saw bacon, chops, gammon steak, hams, Bratwurst, all in vast quantities. If the animal was indeed pregnant, in time there would be tender suckling pig as well.

'Bring the pig,' he called to the troopers.

* * *

190

The memorial was in grey granite as brutally cold as the dead it commemorated. An obelisk a good three metres tall, it dominated place du Maréchal Joffre. At its base a mother was taking leave of her son. Her words were carved above them: 'Tu es français; souviens t'en' – 'You're French; remember that.' The legend beneath their feet dedicated the monument to the Caillonais, the 'enfants de Caillons', who had died in the conflict of 1914–18. Same old enemy, different war.

The roll call on the sides of the obelisk listed the dead by year, family names that still abounded in the village and the port. With the hurt of loss still raw in many families, the flowers and wreaths of evergreens at the foot of the monument were always fresh according to season. There was no system by which this happened, nothing as mechanical as a rota or plan. It simply happened. Nor did anyone ever notice flowers being placed, because there was no fuss, no ceremony about that act. It happened because the people of Caillons wanted it to happen.

Each year on the day and at the time prescribed, of course, there was an actual ceremony. First, in the weeks before, as October turned and the cider apples ripened, little blue cornflowers made of tissue paper, the bleuets de France, began to appear on the jackets and dresses of the Caillonais. They symbolised the cornflower-blue uniform worn by the French in that war that had failed to end all wars. By common consent, Delalande the one-armed tinker had the right to make and sell these bleuets in the villages through which he passed. He had fought; he had earned the right. As the month matured, more bleuets appeared on coats and hats, more memories were jogged and more bleuets were required, until every man, woman and child wore the memento of lives wasted.

Then would come the Sunday morning in early

November when Père Lachanau would find his church full to overflowing. His procession through the streets of Caillons from place de l'Église to place du Maréchal Joffre would be so well attended that he would arrive at the memorial while those at the other end of the line were still leaving the church. He would pad out his prayers and keep the incense burning until they caught up and the memorial square was packed.

In these ways did Caillons honour its war dead, with the memorial at the chill heart of its loss.

On that morning in May the sound of the Wehrmacht half-track approaching was like a rumbling drumbeat. Its caterpillar tracks left indentations in the road surface softened by the early summer heat as it rolled into the square. It carried four troopers inside and another four atop its armoured flanks. It swung around and reversed up to the memorial.

A small crowd began to assemble, observing and whispering but keeping their distance. Other villagers hurried past, wanting no part of whatever was about to happen, knowing that whatever it was, it would not be good. The eight troopers climbed down and marched towards the centre of the village. At rue du Phare they split into two units, one carrying on to the village, the other detouring down to the harbour. Between them they rounded up a dozen men and marched them back at gunpoint to the memorial square.

The driver of the half-track opened the vehicle's rear doors. He dragged out a long heavy chain, every link the size of a man's fist, and dumped it on the ground. Under the supervision of the troopers, four of the village men looped it around the base of the monument.

Now there was a period of measurement and calculation by the driver, involving the chain, the height of the monument and the distance between it and his vehicle. The troopers became impatient. Tempers frayed, voices were raised. A couple of the press-ganged village men edged away and made good their escape. Tempers frayed further. Everyone sweated in the heat. At last the calculations were settled and the two ends of the chain were hooked to the rear of the half-track.

It took a quarter of an hour to bring the memorial down, the half-track shunting back and forth to loosen the thing from its base while the square filled with exhaust fumes. Finally the monument tipped forward a fraction more, tottered and then tumbled with a fearsome crash, sending up a huge plume of dust.

The driver opened the vehicle's doors again. Under the orders of the troopers, the village men hauled out pickaxes and sledgehammers.

Graf arrived. He nodded the signal to the troopers, who levelled their submachine guns at the village men and shouted for them to begin work. Blow by blow, name by name, the destruction of the memorial to the war dead of Caillons got under way.

Graf tapped an Eckstein against its packet and lit up. Third promise fulfilled: no reprisals against the civilian population. That was what the major had ordered. And that was what he was getting.

Musset the postman, his morning deliveries all done, had stopped to watch the proceedings, leaning comfortably against his faithful old pushbike.

Occasionally he scratched his beard or yawned. He seemed half asleep, which, as everyone in Caillons knew, was his usual state. He rolled a cigarette, lit it and then let it dangle in place on his lip when it went out a minute later, as if relighting it would have called for too much effort. He peeled off his cap and let the sun warm his balding cranium, much as that new oberleutnant was enjoying the very same sunshine – German, French, it made no difference to the sun who its beneficiaries were.

There had been few letters in Musset's satchel today. For that matter, there were few enough any day. So standing here in this nice sunshine was as good a way as any to pass a bit of time. Why would a man work himself to death on a day like this?

Only when the obelisk finally came smashing to the ground did Musset find the energy to hitch his leg over the pushbike and cycle majestically away.

At the old stone building that housed La Poste he unlocked the side gate and let himself into the yard. Then he unlocked one of the big doors to the sorting office and wheeled his pushbike inside. There were three or four other bikes leaning against the wall by the sorting rack, all of them even older than his own but all still serviceable enough. Once upon a time Caillons had boasted two postmen, himself and his younger brother, Antoine. Now there was only Musset the elder. And surplus pushbikes.

There was no one around. It was past noon and Madame Caron the postmistress would be lunching upstairs with Roulier, her regional manager and lover. Such lunches could take a long time; more important, their non-food element demanded Madame Caron's full attention, which she was happy to give. Certainly they were not the kind of encounter in which she would be gazing idly from a window, watching the world go by; or counting the pushbikes in her sorting office.

Musset chose one of the bikes – it was out of the question that he should part with his own faithful steed – unscrewed the battered metal plate that said 'La Poste' and the mail panniers, and returned with the machine to the quiet lane outside, locking up again as he went.

Just as François Lachanau had done on the previous night, he slowed to a cautious pace when he reached rue du Phare, avoiding the sharp rubble and broken glass and the deep potholes. Unlike the priest, he had the advantage of daylight. He dismounted when he came to the burnt-out Peugeot and walked the pushbike to the far side of the wreck, the side that was not visible from the road. He dropped the bike on its side and slid it quickly beneath the blackened chassis. There was enough space; only the handlebars stuck out, but hidden from the view of anyone passing along rue du Phare.

Now at last, as he walked home, he bothered to relight the wire-thin cigarette, reflecting while he smoked on what he had seen in place du Maréchal Joffre. By this time, he supposed, all the names of the glorious dead would have been obliterated. Crushed to nothing. Including the name of Antoine Musset, his cherished brother and former postman of Caillons.

11

Benedict spent his day in the icehouse going over the details he carried in his mind of the roads and lanes he would use on the journey that lay ahead. He saw each of these mental maps as clearly as if he held them in his hand. Things he looked at in his mind had always been like this from as far back as he could remember.

The maps were based on those produced by the French company Michelin, whose 1939 edition for France, the last before the arrival of the Nazis, had been quietly reprinted in the United States for military and intelligence use with the discreet agreement of Michelin in Paris. They were updated by SOE operatives across France and by French citizens in exile, including some who frequented Le Singe Rouge.

The accuracy of the maps was vital. It was also vital for Benedict to have them embedded in his memory. In much of rural France, local people had torn down road signs or moved them to wrong locations, to confuse the German occupier. Benedict needed a reliable picture of the lanes and back roads that only locals would be familiar with, the shortcuts and detours they would use and that outsiders would not know – and these were the routes where accurate signage might no longer exist.

In addition, roadblocks and patrols were more likely on the larger roads. Staying out of the Germans' way made sense in itself but it was also what locals aimed for; and the less he stuck out as a stranger and an outsider, the better. This meant carrying knowledge of routes exactly as a local would carry it: in his head, as second nature.

When he was satisfied with this part of his preparation, he turned his attention to the items he had brought with him in the bedroll, the things he had refused to let the pig farmer paw over. These included changes of underwear and socks. The vest and underpants bore French labels and were suitably shabby. The socks had been darned numerous times. There were also two collarless shirts. Like the shirt and clothes he was already wearing, these were black and far from new.

There were also three detachable collars, one of which he now fitted in place. The collars were white.

There were some French franc notes and loose change, a roll of Reichsmarks, identity papers, an envelope of laid paper and a longer, white envelope, all of which he now transferred to his pockets.

The final items were a small wooden case and a book bound in black leather. Both showed signs of many years' use. He checked that the contents of the case had not been damaged during the flight or the night's activity, then slipped the book into the case and snapped the lid shut.

From time to time as he waited for nightfall he ventured briefly beyond the door and along the cramped tunnel to keep an eye on the weather and what little he could see of the world through the curtain of undergrowth. He watched the sky, which remained clear, and the small fishing boats that made their way from the port to cross this part of the bay.

The day passed without incident. He heard no sounds but the crashing surf and the cries of seagulls. He saw no one on the beach below or up on the northern sweep of the headland where it curved across his view, no boats entered the inlet beneath the headland and no one came to disturb him. Nothing troubled the steady, almost meditative, state

197

of concentration that was his habitual prelude to a mission.

Nothing except one thing. When he ate the food that Lisieux had left for him, when he gazed about the rocky chamber and his glance fell on the old crates and barrels that furnished the place, he still saw again that slight figure in its oversized clothes prowling restlessly back and forth and remembered how her eyes had measured and weighed him.

The cell to which Jacques Colinet had been consigned was deeper below ground than Jeanne Dupré's, well below the water table. The water was as high as his ankles and icy cold despite the warmth of the day he had left behind. That wonderful sky up there, in the world outside this dungeon, he would never see it again. Never see God's daylight again.

His whole body shivered, uncontrollable tremors that coursed in waves through his shoulders, arms and legs. He wrapped his arms about himself, clutching his body to try and stop the shaking. But it could not be stopped. It came from fear as much as from cold. But not fear of Jürgen Graf; it was fear of himself that rattled his teeth and bones, fear of his own weakness.

He had known many courageous people. Such as men who had served alongside him in that earlier war. There was Gaspard Baignères for one, scoundrel that he was now. On that August day thirty years ago the fog had been as thick as soured milk in the forests of the high Ardennes when he and Gaspard and the rest of the unit, all of them only youngsters, stumbled into the Germans, as blind and lost and surprised as themselves – two frightened armies searching for each other, each secretly hoping they would find nothing and to hell with what the generals wanted.

They stared at each other, dripping in the fog that had

drained all colour from their uniforms so that both sides were as grey as the fog itself, then the French saw the spikes on the German helmets and the Germans saw the French helmets with no spikes, and the shooting began. God, the noise of those guns, bottled within the fog. Gaspard charged on when every man around him except Colinet and a handful of others had been sliced to ribbons by the German machine guns. All that Colinet and the rest could do was follow him, for there was nowhere else to go. When Gaspard ran out of bullets he used his bayonet, slashing and jabbing until all was still beneath the trees.

Afterwards he was the only one who knew about the mess in young Jacques Colinet's trousers. All these years since then and he had told no one – in the same way as he never spoke about his later days as a sniper, always trying to even the score for that day; Colonel Mauser, they nicknamed him, after the captured German rifle he favoured, far superior to any French weapon. How many did he kill? He would never say. But it was all there in that notebook of his.

A man who knew how to keep his trap shut, that was Gaspard Baignères.

Pierre Rochard, another courageous one. So too Guillaume Raynal and Louis Fougeret, who gave their lives with him. They had held their tongues, had taken whatever the Boche had done to them rather than name names or tell tales. As Jeanne Dupré had pointed out, that was why the rest of them remained free. Remained *alive*. Pierre and the others had given Jacques Colinet these last few weeks of life since their capture. That was their gift to him, given as ungrudgingly as Christ had given himself on the cross. Without their courage Jacques Colinet would already be dead.

Then there was Jeanne Dupré herself. She too was the

sort that would never talk.

And there was Charles Meslin.

But here Jacques Colinet's thoughts stumbled. Poor Charles, had he betrayed them after all? Well, if he had, it was not the real Charles. It was whoever a man became when his mind slipped away from him.

And that was the point. He, Jacques Colinet, he was in his right mind. At present. But unlike Gaspard Baignères and Pierre Rochard and Jeanne Dupré, he was not courageous. He knew this in his heart, had known it ever since that day in the high woods of the Ardennes. So now was the time to make his decision, his last chance before Graf got to work on him and his mind slipped away. Because once that happened he could not be sure of himself. He could not be sure of holding his tongue.

It was not only a question of protecting Jeanne and the cell. Now there was the Englishman too. For Jacques Colinet could size up more than livestock. Gauge the worth of a man and you had the worth of his intent. Whatever the Englishman's purpose, it had to be a matter of great worth. Jacques Colinet had a duty to protect that as well. It was his turn to give.

It was not such a big thing, what he had to do. He was a farmer, he knew that all lives had to end their course. It was the way of nature.

Not such a big thing but oh, it was hard. His beloved Delphine – who would care for her when he was no longer around? He prayed every day for her release, a prayer that flowed from love, for his greatest fear had always been that he would be taken from her. What was to become of her now? And his old mother. It was a lot for his daughters to take on.

His daughters. Thinking of them was hard too. And dangerous, because that was how a man could twist himself around in his noose, could come to tell himself that there *was* a way, that all he had to do was give his inquisitor what he wanted and then he would go free.

Which was as likely as charity from a rich man. No, Jacques Colinet would not be strolling free from here. Whatever Graf might promise, Jacques Colinet's course was done and the only place he was going was beneath a layer of quicklime in the pit behind his own barn.

So now it was time. God would understand what he had to do. God in his mercy, who gave his only son and understood sacrifice.

Jacques Colinet pulled up his right trouser leg, raising it clear of the filthy water. The razor blade was stitched into the double fold of the turn-up. He pressed the cloth against it so that it severed the clumsy stitching, his own handiwork. There was another blade in the turn-up of his other working trousers, and one in his only suit, the one he wore for mass and funerals. A simple matter of preparation, of escape, as he had remarked last night, for there was no knowing the hour when the thief would come.

The thin blade was made of ordinary carbon steel and was rusty after its months of concealment but the rust had not eaten through the metal or pitted the edge, so it would still be keen enough, still be up to the task. He ran it along a fingertip and watched the clean line of blood that formed. Then he knelt down in the water, crossed himself and began to pray, bending right down until his forearms were flat on the floor of the cell and both his wrists were immersed in the numbingly cold water.

This would not take long; not if he got it right.

No reprisals against the civilian population? So far, so good, reckoned Jürgen Graf; blocks of granite were not civilians.

Apprehend the perpetrators of last night's massacre? Good again, Herr Major, for Jürgen Graf had made a fine start. A man in possession of the identity card of a loyal Wehrmacht trooper who had been brutally murdered would know a good deal about that murder. More than likely had a hand in it himself. That man would also know about last night's massacre because there could be no doubting that both despicable events were the work of the same scum; and surely that man, the farmer Jacques Colinet, was one of them. Which meant he knew who the others were.

Most important of all, he would know why the Lysander had returned to protect the cargo it delivered. Which had to be human cargo.

All these things he would very soon tell Jürgen Graf.

Two armed troopers preceded Graf and the medic down the stone staircase. The walls ran with condensation, the water that streamed down them mingling with water seeping in from the earth, making the steps mossy and treacherous. The deeper they descended, the colder and more poisonous became the air. The medic produced a little gauze mask and pressed it over his mouth and nose for protection. Graf paused to light an Eckstein. The flame of the lighter struggled to hold.

They reached Colinet's cell. Graf unlocked the door and nodded for the troopers to enter. There were more steps down to the cell floor and he knew that the water there would be deep; he had no intention of venturing his battledress boots and clean gaiters into that muck.

But he saw more than only muck in the water. The light was dim but there could be no mistaking the swirls of dark fluid that curled across the flooded floor and up to the steps beneath the raised doorway. Nor did he need the medic to tell him that life had departed the body that lay face down in the cell, arms outstretched, the foul water and Jacques

Colinet's own blood lapping gently against it.

All day and into the evening the people of Caillons came to rue du Phare in mute twos and threes, to the corner where the broken pieces of the war memorial had been dumped. They brought with them old cardboard valises, baskets, bedspreads. They rummaged through the chunks of shattered granite, making whatever choices they could. There was no chit-chat; they worked in respectful silence. Some sought fragments bearing the name, or part of the name, of a loved one, though in such a vast heap of rubble this was usually a hopeless quest; some wanted a section of the memorial's legend; some were content with any random piece.

When they had made their selection, they secreted it in their valise or wrapped it in the bedspread or hid it beneath a cloth in their basket and carried it home.

Gaspard Baignères had his notebook but Père François Lachanau had his registers: for births, for deaths, for marriages. The priest worked his way patiently through the deaths registers for the years in question – completed by his own hand: a younger, more flowing hand back then – extracting the names that he himself was sure of. As often as not they had been a name without a body, a mass with no coffin, sad facts that aided his memory now.

He did not labour alone. Occasionally a shy knock came to his door. A name and a year would be given. Tightly folded scraps of paper were passed through the grill of his confessional. Delalande the one-armed tinker showed up in the evening, bringing a dozen names.

Often the information simply confirmed the priest's own research, but sometimes an additional name emerged, such as a son of Caillons who had moved to another village before going to war: his death therefore recorded in the

203

register of that other parish, it was to be hoped, but still a lost child of Caillons.

And here on François Lachanau's doormat was what appeared at first to be a late delivery of post but turned out to be a folded piece of paper bearing another name, one that he had already listed; but he was glad to see it still remembered and the restoration of its honour sought.

The name was that of Antoine Musset, erstwhile postman of Caillons.

That afternoon Hélène told Jeanne the whole story of her offer to Graf and his acceptance of the arrangement. So calmly and quietly that she could have been describing a trip to the market. Which was perhaps exactly what it was: a business transaction.

Jeanne closed her eyes and was silent for a long time. They had come to this, her daughter nothing more than a trade, a barter that made the dealings of Gaspard Baignères look honourable. She had allowed her beautiful Hélène to sink to this.

'Maman? Maman?'

Jeanne opened her eyes. It was an effort. She looked at Hélène. Isabelle sat watching them both fearfully. She reached for her elder sister's hand. Hélène's eyes pleaded.

'Maman?'

'You've made a pact with the devil,' Jeanne told her.

'I did it for Hortense and Hervé. I haven't given Graf anything he hasn't already taken.'

'Your heart?'

'Give my heart to Jürgen Graf? Don't be ridiculous, Maman. That'll never happen.'

No more was said. There was no more to say. What right did either have to judge the other now?

That evening Jeanne sat alone with her thoughts. There

was a movement beyond the open window. Hélène and Isabelle were returning from the village. For once Isabelle was not rushing ahead but was patiently keeping step with her sister's pace. Their hands touched, clasped for a moment. There was news, something had happened; Jeanne saw it in her daughters' faces and those clasped hands.

The latch of the door scraped and clattered. Hélène entered first.

'Hortense and Hervé have been released,' she announced. 'They're home.'

The news was good but her tone was restrained and nervous. It was Isabelle's words that explained why.

'Charles Meslin and Jacques Colinet are dead.'

Jeanne drew back in her chair, as if evading a blow. So many dead for France.

'The Boche dumped Charles Meslin's body outside his house just before Hortense and Hervé got there,' added Isabelle quietly. 'It was waiting for them. It was in a terrible state. His injuries ... he hadn't just been shot, he hadn't been shot at all –' Her voice trailed away.

Jeanne understood. Hélène's bargain had been fulfilled, yet still Graf had found a way to spoil the goods. She looked at her elder daughter; yes, Hélène understood too.

'And Jacques?'

'Arrested this morning but no one knows how he died. Delphine's dead too. Old Mother Colinet says the shock was too much for her.' Isabelle crouched down beside Jeanne. 'Maman, were Charles Meslin and Jacques Colinet résistants? You know why this matters.'

Which Jeanne did. With as much certainty as she knew what was in Isabelle's mind.

'Yes, they were.'

'Will they have told the Boche anything about you?'

'Not them. Not Charles or Jacques. Never.'

205

'Can you be sure? Maybe you should go to the hills or the woods. Or the icehouse.'

Jeanne shook her head. 'If I disappear, what do you think the Germans will do? You'll be arrested, interrogated, tortured. Graf won't save you, Hélène, neither of you. You'll be executed or sent to a camp, which comes to the same thing.'

'Then we should all get away from here,' said Hélène.

'Where to? No, you two will go to Père Lachanau. I'll stay here.'

'Until when?'

'Until the Germans come for me. Or until we know they're not coming.'

'How will we know that?'

'We'll know. Now you must go.'

The girls argued but gave in. One brief embrace and they were gone. Too brief for Jeanne, that embrace. No embrace would have been long enough. Emptiness ached inside her as she saw them go.

She fetched the MP40 and all the ammunition she had. If the Germans did come, she would not survive, of course. That was not her purpose, still less her hope. But before dying she would simply kill as many as she could.

She did not fear dying. Her fear was of not being alive. Of not seeing Hélène and Isabelle grow and marry. Never holding their children.

She feared not seeing France free.

As for the icehouse, it was the last place on earth she wanted to be. She wanted nothing more to do with Monsieur high and mighty Avignon. She had enough to fear from God's judgement on her.

Graf had a small room to himself on the top floor of Le Manoir. A tiny place but well away from the wing in which his troopers were barracked and with its own window and bathroom. He had the only key to the room; he had made sure of that.

The room contained a narrow bed, a cabinet, a shallow wardrobe, a small table and a single stick-back chair, a washbasin with running water, and some shelves. On the shelves were ranged his modest library, including works on psychology by Alfred Adler, Sigmund Freud and Wilhelm Reich – all Jews, of course, as he had pointed out to Neiss, but that was exactly what equipped them to explore the dark things that lay deep beneath the waters of the mind, because the Jews were themselves the darkness within.

Here too were various papers by Carl Gustav Jung, assuredly no Jew, cleverer than all the others put together and one who knew what it was to have a mother cursed by madness.

The room was as spotlessly clean as a hospital ward. In the cabinet, which was always locked – again Graf had the only key – reposed his treasures: his father's watches and watchmaking tools. There were a dozen watches, all built by Erich Graf, all bearing his name. They were what was in stock in the little shop on the day Erich died. The day of his murder. The tools were older than Jürgen Graf himself, the finest that money could buy in their time: ranks of precision screwdrivers, tiny pliers with delicate jaws, loupes and other magnifiers, closing presses and dies, tweezers in various numbered sizes, devices for removing watch hands and reseating them, and an array of other exquisitely machined implements; and he still remembered standing by the bench as his father worked and explained patiently what each tool did and the right and wrong ways to use it.

Sometimes as he picked up a tool he would have a sudden flash of that same tool in his father's hand and the watch on which he was working that day. These moments were startling in their vividness; he would recall the weather or the meal they ate that night or an item of clothing he had been wearing or an event from his day that he was recounting as his father worked.

The father had built the watches but the son had taught himself to disassemble and reassemble them. It was a tribute to his lost father, a way of being with him again, but it was also his refuge and comforter, and the zone to which he retreated to think things through, an escape to a world of precision and order in which every cog and spring had its purpose and fulfilled it with unerring accuracy, a world of perfect tiny events that processed along their set path with no departure from their given pattern, never a failure. It was proof that chaos and disorder could be overcome, that they were not man's inevitable condition but only what waited for him if he let go the reins of command. The Jew's limbs twitched when the spinal cord was severed but it was the technician introducing the electrical current who was in control, not the Jew.

Graf unlocked the cabinet and chose a watch. He set it on the table and unrolled the three velvet cloths of tools. He switched on the Stocker Yale, the American-made light under which his father had always worked, angled its arm and set to work.

Colinet and Meslin had been his best chances. Wasted. Rochard and the others too. So far all he had for his labours was one fat pig. And the services of the little cripple Dupré.

Thinking of her brought the mother to mind. The images paraded before him: Jeanne Dupré warming Ebermann's bed, placing her bunch of weeds on her brother's body, thinking she was so clever with her evasive answers when he had her under lock and key. Sister of an executed criminal. The death of her husband – no doubt she would blame that on the Reich.

He removed the loupe from his eye and stared at the open watch. Where was Jeanne Dupré when the Lysander aircraft was butchering his men, when the enemy agent – for he was certain there was one – was being brought here? Where was she on the night of the ambush that killed young Wiedemuth and Schmidt and Prausmüller and his other fine troopers?

No point asking Jeanne Dupré herself. She would lie and evade. With no hard evidence against her, Ebermann would order her release.

He tapped a cigarette and lit it, inhaling deeply. He went to the window and gazed over the plain of Le Manoir, over the repaired lane and beyond the woods, towards Caillons. The afternoon burned towards its end, the sun still hot. Still Hitler weather.

He gathered the half-disassembled watch together, folded it carefully in a velvet cloth and put it back in the cabinet. He wrapped the tools and put them away. He switched off the Stocker Yale and closed the window. He took a small bottle from the cabinet, set it on the table and relocked the cabinet.

He would shower. He would shave. He would dress in fresh Feldbluse and polished jackboots. He would take the Citroën. No need for a driver. He would drive himself.

The dusk drew Hélène as light drew a moth. The priest's house was a cage to her, its bars drawing closer as the light faded from the sky outside. She watched her sister, who seemed content to leaf forever through the books and pamphlets that Père Lachanau had suggested might be suitable to amuse them. The priest had an Ausweiss so that he could visit Hortense Meslin and Jacques Colinet's mother and daughters; he would not return home for many hours.

'If the Boche haven't come for Maman by morning, we'll know she's safe,' Isabelle declared as Hélène sighed her hundredth sigh. Then the younger sister rose and closed the shutters. There was a moment of darkness before she switched on the dim light.

In that darkness Hélène made her decision.

'I'm going for a walk.'

'It's long past curfew.'

'I'll suffocate if I stay here.'

She crossed place de l'Église and stood out of sight in a bricked-up doorway at the top of rue du Verger, listening and watching. Off to the left she heard German voices and the growl of a patrol vehicle. French voices drifted up to her from the port: fishermen with permits for night fishing, setting out or returning.

Halfway along rue du Maréchal Pétain she saw a patrol ahead, but she kept out of sight and turned down the side of an old warehouse.

It was only at the beginning of rue du Phare that she stopped. For a moment whatever impelled her eased its hold. This was insane, to come here. Her leg was hurting and growing weaker. She should rest, she should return to the priest's house.

But whatever held her tightened its grip; she began to walk again.

Full night had come but the moon had risen. It was still low in the sky but was bright enough to help her over the broken surface of the road and pavement. Everything in this decrepit part of the village was broken or discarded or in a state of decay, made even bleaker by the moonlight. The forlorn houses, the waste ground, that old burnt-out carcass of a car. She was right to be here after all, she understood now what had brought her; this was where she belonged with her broken and wasted body, here where she had sold herself and discovered who she really was.

She saw the play of headlights on the road and her heart missed a beat. He was here too. An omen, surely, that she had been right to come. They were both meant to be here.

The long black Citroën drew alongside her. The window was open.

'Good evening, my alley cat. Can't stay away, I see, can't help yourself.'

The words were his usual mocking style but their tone was gentler tonight. He stretched across and opened the door.

'Be quick. Last time I was here I ran into a little trouble.'

She climbed in and closed the door. There was the smell of leather that she remembered. There was the scent of him again. She was floating in a bubble far away from Caillons and the broken road and the waste ground. All pain had vanished from her leg.

'This is for you,' he said. He placed something in her lap. 'French perfume for my French alley cat.'

She uncapped the tiny bottle and pressed it against the inner surface of her wrist, where the warm veins ran. She rubbed her other wrist against it in the way she remembered her mother doing a lifetime ago. She raised the wrist to her nose and caught the scent of heaven.

On the far side of the waste ground a thin figure pressed itself out of sight behind the broad trunk of a plane tree. Adalard Fougeret was dry-mouthed with shock and anger. The inexplicable had been explained.

'Collabo,' he hissed between clenched teeth as the long black car swept Hélène Dupré off into the night.

It was approaching midnight when Benedict extinguished the lamp and left the icehouse. The bedroll was strapped across his back, the small wooden case secured safely inside it.

The night was warm, the sky as cloudless as it had been all day, and the moon that had escorted him safely to France was still gibbous and bright. A friend last night but it could betray him now.

Before stepping beyond the tunnel he studied the shoreline beneath the cliff until he was sure it was still deserted. He remembered balmy nights like this in his boyhood, a pure white moon drifting like a lantern to light the fields all the way to the horizon. That was a different France from the land he was venturing into now. But it was a France he had come to reclaim.

Or perhaps that was something Lisieux would dismiss as another of his stupid ideas.

As he climbed the path to the top of the headland he heard her crisp directions. 'Keep going up,' she had said. 'Even an Englishman knows which way is up.'

Near the top he paused where he could see over the thick maquis. The piney scent of juniper filled his nostrils, a gentle breeze brought the tang of the ocean. Nothing was stirring, he heard no sound but the surf. He pressed on, retracing some of last night's route, then turned towards the harbour and took the lane behind the row of cottages that brought him to rue du Port near the top of the hill.

He was in the village proper. A hundred things could endanger him. Curfew was in place and security was bound to be heightened. His ears strained for the sound of an engine, the strike of a boot on cobbles, a German voice, the rustle of clothing, clink of metal.

But there was nothing. Only the chimes of midnight from the mairie clock. The place was pitch black, not a light showing, bathed in a silence that was almost solid, as profound as the deep heart of France, pressing itself against him. It was a sensation he knew well – something conjured by fear, the awareness that at any instant a bullet might tear through the silence.

On the outskirts of the village the streets opened out and the moonlight fell on small houses interspersed with stretches of rough ground. He was in rue du Phare now, his destination. Among the broken carts and rusting lumps of machinery he picked out the silhouette of the burnt-out Peugeot but did not approach it immediately. He waited beneath a plane tree from which he could view the whole area. The moon was high and the shadows had shortened, making movement harder to discern. The rubble and garbage littering the ground added to the difficulty, creating a terrain in which irregularities and dark shapes were the norm. A sudden movement caught his eye but it was only a pair of rats. He watched as they disappeared into the distance, heard their claws rustle over the ground, then the place settled back to silence.

He edged his way beneath the broken wall. When the wall ended, he covered the final yards at a crouch, sidestepping rocks and broken bottles, and slipped out of sight behind the Peugeot.

Immediately beside him was a pair of handlebars, poking up at right angles. He counted the seconds away through two minutes, watching and listening, then he dragged the pushbike out.

Next came the package. It too was where he had been told it would be, on top of what was left of the front wheel. It consisted of a musty-smelling piece of heavy fabric, rough and patterned under his fingers. He unwound it and took out the items inside: two priest's stoles, one green and one purple, both richly and intricately embroidered. They were items that SOE had been unable to obtain or replicate. He checked the manufacturer's label in the moonlight: Les Fils

213

d'Adrien Fournier. Authentic, perfect.

He refolded the stoles, extracted the wooden case from the bedroll and placed them inside, strapping the bedroll securely afterwards. Then he slid the hank of fabric back beneath the wheel arch. A minute later he was pedalling along rue du Phare and away from Caillons.

In his dog collar and priestly black, Daniel Benedict, who had become Avignon but was known to all at Le Singe Rouge as Georges, had now become Père Nicolas Marot, complete with breviary, holy stoles and portable travelling mass kit.

Gaspard Baignères lowered the field glasses. He wondered if it was true that the Germans had glasses that enabled a man to see as clearly at night as in daytime. No matter; in the moonlight he had seen well enough.

Ah, how long it was since the circus had come to rue du Phare, and how far away those times seemed now. But tonight's little performances down there on the waste ground had as magical a sense of theatre, as much mystery and intrigue. The little professor would do well if his dramas were half as good.

First act, enter the girl. With that limp there was no question who she was.

Second act, the car. No need to see the driver; the audience knew this vehicle. An assignation or a chance encounter? Or a mutual wish fulfilled? Who could say; indeed, what did it matter? The outcome was the same: third act, she climbed aboard, the car drove off.

All observed by that bent figure lurking in the wings. No question who that was either. Gaspard tut-tutted softly to himself as the figure melted away: 'Behave, Adalard. Nothing rash, please.'

And then the interval, a very lengthy one. He smoked a

few Gitanes to pass the time, ducking down to hide the flame and the glowing tip of the cigarette.

At last the dark figure entered rue du Phare, moving so skilfully within the shadows that the audience could easily have missed it. A subtle performance for the drama's final act.

The intruder did not overplay his role but simply did what he had come to do and departed. Might never have existed, might only have been a figment of the audience's imagination.

Gaspard lit another Gitane and waited a while to make sure there were no more entrances or exits, no encores.

But the show was truly over. He made the long winding descent down the staircase of the lighthouse, padlocked the arched door and cycled for home, his oilcloth cap pressed firmly in place.

As the night melted into dawn, Jeanne heard the sounds she had known all her life: gulls crying above the bay, the delicate notes of a blackbird. A wood pigeon started up, crickets gave way to the tireless bees.

Her land. Her fields and woods and forgotten lanes. Her France.

She made the submachine gun safe. No Germans had come for her. None would come now. She would fight on for France. And to save her daughters.

12

It was slow going for Benedict, for the old pushbike had only one gear. He stuck to the smallest lanes and tracks, weaving his way beside fields, through patches of woodland and small cider orchards, over pastures where cattle and sheep lifted their heads to observe him, and along the margins of coastal dunes where the hard dry earth and rough gravel gave way to sudden pockets of sand that swallowed his wheels.

These winding detours to avoid the main highways lengthened his journey but the reward was the absence of German patrols. He encountered no other travellers. Either the locals were punctilious in their observance of the curfew or they caught wind of his approach before he could be aware of them and were keeping a prudent distance. He suspected the latter, for now and then he heard a rustle in bushes or undergrowth as he passed, or glimpsed the movement of a shadow among the trees: poachers at work, lovers trysting, perhaps even résistants or maquisards on the move. But whoever and whatever they were, they left him alone.

The moon was now his friend again, providing light not only to show him the way but also to help him avoid the worst ruts and fissures in the tracks and lanes. Sometimes his route took him inland for a time but eventually he would work his way back towards the coast. He would reach the edge of a field or emerge from the passage between a pair of barns and stop to take his bearings and check for danger ahead. In the stillness he would hear again the rush of the surf, still faint in the distance, then the salt savour of the ocean would reach him. When he looked up at the sky, every star in the universe seemed to be out, white mists of galaxies trailing across the sky. These moments held great power for him, as if, like the poachers and lovers who had watched him pass, they were confirmation that the old France still lived and breathed.

The man in the rowing boat was asleep, as evidenced by his snoring. He was young, perhaps in his twenties. An empty wine bottle lay in his lap.

Benedict levelled the Browning at the man's head. He released the safety and the young man woke with a start. His eyes swivelled towards the sound and widened with alarm as he saw Benedict and felt the muzzle of the gun brush his hair.

'Don't move,' cautioned Benedict quietly. 'Be calm. Your name?'

'Jean-Paul Loffet.'

That much was correct. First staging post.

'Your papers. Slowly.'

Jean-Paul tugged the folded identity card from his back pocket and handed it over.

'Not wise to fall asleep on the job, Jean-Paul. Not wise to drink, tonight of all nights.'

'You're the priest?'

Benedict raised his chin so that the moonlight caught his white collar.

'I'm your passenger. I'm the priest.'

They were seven or eight of his winding kilometres inland from Trouville. He had an obstacle to cross, and London had known he could not wait until daylight to cross it: La Touques, the river that flowed into the estuary between Trouville and Deauville. South of the estuary there were various small road bridges and a railway bridge, but all would be patrolled and guarded and were out of the question for him during curfew. Worse was pont de l'Union, the stone bridge linking Deauville and Trouville across the estuary, its main crossing point. In once-graceful Deauville, with its casino and hotels, there were now as least as many Germans as French, following the evacuation of the town's children and older inhabitants when the Germans arrived. The casino, the elegant villas, the hotels – all now accommodated or had been commandeered by the occupier. Even if there had been a way to cross from Trouville to Deauville at night without using pont de l'Union, moving safely through Deauville after curfew would have been well-nigh impossible.

But here, where the waters of La Touques curled lazily over their floodplain west of the tiny hamlet of Bonneville, where the nearest house was several hundred metres distant, no German vehicle or squad could move without making its presence known. And here the river was less than twenty metres wide. A boat could cross with ease. So a boat had been arranged.

'I was told you'd have a vélo,' said Jean-Paul.

'It's here.'

'Bring it on board, mon père. Let's get this done.'

'Good idea.' Benedict took a step back, making room for Jean-Paul to pass. For a moment the man looked as if he might argue. But only for a moment as his gaze went to the Browning.

While Jean-Paul fetched the pushbike, Benedict settled himself in the bow where he could watch both Jean-Paul and the riverbank.

'I'm not your enemy,' said the young man as he laid the pushbike down between them. 'I'm helping you. You can put the gun away.'

'If you're not my enemy, you needn't worry about the gun.'

'Some priest, that carries a gun.'

'Some résistant, that drinks himself comatose.'

In two or three minutes they were across and Benedict was walking the pushbike over the marshy ground in search of the path that would lead him back to his route.

Dawn was lighting the ocean behind him when he rapped softly on the door of a small white cottage in a cluster of half a dozen similar homes north-east of Houlgate. A tiny church stood nearby, in the lee of a stand of trees.

The door opened immediately. Light from the single ground-floor room fell briefly on him before being switched off.

'Père Mathieu?' he asked.

The man nodded and stood aside to let him enter. 'Welcome, Père Nicolas.'

Second staging post. They shook hands. Mathieu was short and slightly stooped, as though too many hours had been spent over books or in prayer. He looked ten years older than Benedict but in fact the two were of an age. Benedict knew this because he knew when and where Mathieu had been born. He knew where he had been educated. He knew a great deal about Père Mathieu.

The priest opened the shutters of the room's one window.

'May I help you with that?' he asked, indicating the bedroll.

Benedict let him take it but shook his head when the priest invited him to remove his jacket. There was the small matter of the Browning. Mathieu nodded slowly, perhaps guessing the reason for the refusal. He looked anxious.

'Please make yourself comfortable,' he said.

On the table were waiting a jar of rough cider and a platter of bread. Mathieu said a brief grace, then watched as Benedict ate; he took no portion for himself.

'Communion?' said Benedict.

Mathieu nodded. 'Nothing to break my fast before mass.' He frowned. 'I assume you're not really a priest, Nicolas.'

'Did you think I was?'

'No.'

Benedict drew the small envelope from his pocket and passed it across the table. Mathieu examined it with interest, recognising the crest in the corner.

'From the archbishop?' he said, intrigued.

The letter inside consisted of two brief paragraphs. The first was in French, the second was a German version of the same text. Two different typewriters had been used, the usual procedure in such cases. In each paragraph the archbishop of Rouen requested that unimpeded passage be granted to Père Nicolas Marot as he travelled to assume his new appointment in the parish of Quinéville in north-western Normandy. The archbishop named a member of the HQ administrative staff of General Karl Kitzinger of the Militärbefehlshaber in Frankreich, the MBF, the military command that controlled France, who had approved the travel arrangement.

'Is this genuine?' Mathieu asked.

'Of course.'

'Including the MBF approval?'

Benedict took the letter back and replaced it in the envelope. He passed the second envelope across, the long one. It was emblazoned with the Reich eagle and swastika set over the MBF address at the Hotel Majestic on avenue Kléber in central Paris.

Mathieu opened it and read the letter. It was from the official named by the archbishop, confirming the grant of passage. Only one paragraph this time, in German.

'Not so real, this one?' said the priest.

Benedict shrugged.

'Quinéville,' said Mathieu. 'You have a long way to go.'

'I need three things, Mathieu. I can't get food in the usual way. I don't have local contacts. I have coupons in case I'm searched, since no one travels without and it would raise suspicion to have none, but I'd be a stranger in any shop and draw attention if I used them. Best to avoid that.'

'You can share whatever I have.'

'I need shelter this morning until you return from mass.'

'I don't have a housekeeper. You're safe here in my absence. The third thing?'

'You.'

The priest frowned. 'I don't follow.'

'There are places I need to see but I can't go to them alone. I need a pretext. You must accompany me. You have a vélo?'

'Of course. What places?'

'We'll be two priests walking together, deep in conversation. A real conversation in case we're asked to recount it later.'

'My God – you mean interrogated?'

'We'll be out for a stroll, talking about whatever priests talk about when they haven't seen each other in years. Two friends who lost touch.'

He rattled off the facts, all of them consistent with Mathieu's own history: the small seminary in Plombières-lès-Dijon where they had trained, the names of other students, their year of ordination.

'After ordination I went to North Africa. That's how we lost touch. So you know nothing about me during those years. When war came I was recalled to France and now I've come to renew our acquaintance since we both serve in

221

the same archdiocese.'

The priest sat in silence for a time. Benedict said nothing to interrupt his thoughts. Eventually Mathieu stood up and began to pace the small room.

'These places you want to see – where are they?'

'On the coast. In Houlgate.' Benedict watched the priest's face. 'Les Falaises – the cliffs.'

The fear in Mathieu's eyes was beyond doubt. 'The Atlantic Wall? Do you realise how dangerous that is? You're asking me to put my life in your hands.'

'And mine is in yours as soon as you're out of my sight this morning.'

He turned back to the table to help himself to more bread and cider. After a moment he heard the door open and close as the priest departed.

Like Père François Lachanau's black briefcase, Benedict's portable mass kit comprised a chalice, paten, cruets and other items embedded in a shaped velvet base on a rubber backing. There the resemblance ended, for the hollowed-out base beneath the rubber shell was shaped to accommodate the dagger, the Browning and a magazine of 9mm rounds. With Mathieu out of the way, Benedict lodged these items in place and repacked the other contents of the wooden case, including the two stoles but not the breviary, which he slipped into his pocket. He wrapped the case in the bedroll.

On Mathieu's return after mass they bundled the remains of the bread and some slices of sausage in a cloth, and set off. A few hundred metres from the cottage they came to an avenue of beech trees that Benedict had noted earlier. He stopped and dismounted. The root of one of the trees had pushed itself above the earth, on the field side. He secreted the bedroll and case beneath it and covered them thoroughly with moss, stones and leafy twigs. He positioned the final few twigs and a squarish-shaped stone with particular care.

'Better here than in your cottage,' he told Mathieu. 'In case the place is searched.'

He was now unarmed. But if he and Mathieu were challenged and weapons found on him, it would not be only Benedict who would pay with his life; the little priest would pay that price as well.

The day was bright, the sun hot, with not a breath of wind. By the time they reached the wooded rise of land known as the Butte on the edge of Houlgate they were both perspiring. The sea was on their right now, beyond the trees and the steep fall of the cliffs. Benedict led them straight into the woodland rather than turning south to skirt it. The road had become a lane. Gradually it petered out and became a track of sun-hardened sandy earth. There was the occasional villa now on their left, the landward side. Here, as they approached the end of the track, Benedict stopped. Pushbikes, even ones like his, were valuable machines, so he and Mathieu wheeled them into the woodland and pushed them deep into a thicket.

He gave Mathieu his briefing as they walked back to the track.

'Take your breviary from your pocket and carry it – it looks more priestly.' He produced his own breviary. 'You'll monopolise our conversation. You'll tell me all about your life since ordination. No detail is too small. Just keep talking, I'll hear it all. I'll tell you nothing of my life in Africa. That way, you don't have to remember anything except what you've told me. You understand?'

Mathieu nodded; this was a brief he could master.

'When should I start?'

Directly ahead, beyond the end of the track, two armed Wehrmacht troopers had appeared.

'Now would be good.'

The troopers paid the two priests no heed but walked straight into a small road that ran off at right angles from where the track met a second road. Benedict studied them as Mathieu prattled. There was no bravado about them, only an air of exhaustion. They were not strutting like conquering occupiers. They clomped wearily along in their heavy boots, gaiters and full kit, heads down and drained of energy, their thick serge uniforms dark with sweat, their belts and webbing sagging with water flasks, ammunition packs, field glasses and other paraphernalia. One unstrapped his helmet and swept a torrent of sweat from his head and neck, the fat droplets sparkling in the sun. Their submachine guns were a burden to them, not insignias of power. These were men who were off duty, and glad of it. More than that, they were men who had been standing for a couple of hours in the full glare of the hot morning sun.

'Turn down here, Mathieu.'

The troopers had appeared so suddenly because they had emerged from a flight of steps that ascended to the road and track. Benedict took Mathieu's elbow and steered him towards the steps.

'Keep talking.'

He could see now that the steps led all the way down to the shore, a vertical distance of at least a hundred and twenty metres but more than that given the angle of the slope. They were primitive in construction, slats of timber set at intervals to retain the treads.

'We can't,' said Mathieu. He was staring at the large warning signs erected at the top of the steps. Their message was in French and German. Verboten. Interdit.

'We can.' Benedict pushed him onwards.

The gun enclosure or casemate, a massive bunker of

dazzling white concrete, was visible after the first few steps down. A path ran to it from the steps. Only one side of the structure, with a low doorway, was visible to Benedict and Mathieu. Its top was shaped into a rough curve, flattening into a roof that disappeared into the surrounding undergrowth. The depth of the doorway suggested walls a metre thick. Two troopers, replacements for the two whose watch had ended, stood smoking and chatting in its shade. Here at the top of the cliff, the sun would be merciless from dawn to dusk and the vegetation that bordered the path was too low to provide any other protection. Soon the men would be as drained as their predecessors, which was why they were taking this last opportunity for some respite – and neglecting their duty as a result, for Benedict and Mathieu passed them unnoticed.

A few levels further down, Benedict turned as if responding to Mathieu's tale of mysteriously diminishing stocks of altar wine in his first parish. He faced the priest but his gaze went up to the slit opening in the front face of the casemate. Three large gun muzzles peered out from the darkness within, 155mm French GPF418s by his reckoning; the Germans had captured several hundred such artillery pieces when France fell.

'It was the sacristan,' concluded Mathieu. 'Can you believe that?'

From here Benedict could make out the shape of the casemate more clearly. It was a brute of a thing, a type H679 – one of the structures represented by its code on the clifftop tarpaulins on Lewis. In this real version, as he knew from the architectural drawings, there would be several rooms linked together by internal corridors. He gauged that he and Mathieu were now beneath the eyeline of the gunners. The guns' traverse angles were limited to sixty degrees on either side. So craft approaching by sea – the guns had a range of twenty kilometres – and men being landed on the beach would be squarely in the line of fire, but there would come a point when an assault unit approaching from either side would disappear from view and be beyond the sweep of the guns.

He shook his head in despair at the thought of the perfidious sacristan and noted a second casemate further along the cliff: another H679 with more heavy guns, no doubt also 155mm. In all likelihood there were underground tunnels connecting the bunkers.

He nudged Mathieu on and they descended once more. A series of semicircular gun emplacements had been built into the cliff beneath the level of the bunkers. He saw 37mm flak cannon, 105mm howitzers and heavy machine guns. He also saw the gunner who was pausing in his cleaning work to stare at the two priests.

Mathieu's thoughts and talk had turned to a young widow in Oissel.

'Hurry, Mathieu.'

'With the widow?'

'No. Down the steps.'

The gunner had gone. They reached the bottom of the steps.

'Now tell me about the widow.'

Giant coils of barbed wire stretched along the beach as far as the eye could see. There were lines of three-legged structures made of slabs of concrete anchored deep in the sand, perhaps three metres tall above ground, others that were simple inverted Vs, and rows of six-armed constructions two metres tall and fashioned from iron girders: so-called hedgehogs. All of these were designed to block tanks and landing craft. The longer the craft and tanks were delayed, the more they would be exposed to the guns on the clifftop and the longer it would take the ships to unload them, thereby also leaving the ships exposed to prolonged attack from the cliff. The further away the craft were halted in their eventual approach, the greater the distance over which the invading troops would be exposed to the heavy machine guns above them. When the troops passed beyond the tank barriers, for men could pass where tanks could not, they would lose the cover that the tanks provided, rendering them even more vulnerable to the heavy guns and also now to closer-range submachine-gun and rifle fire.

The barbed wire was the final trap. There was no fast way through it; the troops would be pinned to the ground, sitting targets, while the machine guns raked them at leisure.

All of this he saw. All of it he filed away.

'Are there mines?' he asked Mathieu.

The priest broke off his monologue. He looked puzzled.

'Have they mined the beach, Mathieu?'

'I don't know.'

'Let's get back to the widow. How often did she send for you?'

He knew they had only seconds left if the gunner who had stared at them and disappeared was up to the mark. Benedict scanned the cliff face once more, registering distances and heights. Now, at last, he made out the feature he was seeking: the battery's observation post. It was located at the highest point, roughly in line with where they had left the pushbikes, and enclosed within a wide semicircular ring of concrete four metres across. That too he logged. Only one thing remained now.

First they heard the shouts, then the clatter of boots as four troopers closed on them. There was no time to tell Mathieu to look frightened but it would have been a superfluous instruction; the priest could not have looked more petrified.

Both of them raised their hands over their heads. Mathieu's breviary fell to the ground, prayer cards and palm crucifixes spilling out from between the pages.

The obergefreiter's French was basic and to the point. What were they doing? How did they get here? This area was verboten. There were signs saying so.

Benedict apologised. It was all his fault. He had been so caught up in listening to his brother priest that he had led them down here, down this convenient flight of steps, entirely without thinking. Such a charming view of the sea, how could anyone resist? There were signs? Where were they? He had missed them. He was not familiar with the area and was unaware this place was off limits.

By now Mathieu had gathered his thoughts, though he still trembled and beads of perspiration ran from his forehead. In quivering tones he begged to differ with his friend. No, it was all his fault. He did know the area, he should never have let this happen. He had been selfish and thoughtless, doing all the talking instead of paying attention to where they were wandering. He was sorry for the disruption he had caused the obergefreiter and his men, who had more important things to do than this.

The obergefreiter looked bored by the gibbering priests but mollified, his status and power confirmed. And besides, the day was too hot. He waved their arms down. Mathieu hurriedly picked up his breviary and its contents.

'Papers,' the German said mechanically.

They handed over their identity cards. Benedict held his two envelopes in readiness. Mathieu's card had nothing to interest the obergefreiter and was quickly returned. Benedict's was marginally more interesting. The section for change of domicile address had been filled in. The old address was in Rouen, the new one in Quinéville.

'Why are you here, Priester?'

Benedict handed him the two letters. 'I'm on the way to my new parish. I stopped here to look up my old friend. I'll be on my way again this afternoon.'

The obergefreiter returned the letters, unopened and unread, and the identity card.

'Don't let me find you here again.'

They were not allowed to return up the steps but had to go along the narrow street parallel to the sea and take a roundabout route back to the pushbikes. The obergefreiter stood yawning but the troopers watched them until they turned out of sight. The detour allowed Benedict a further view of the beach defences below them.

'You did well, Mathieu.'

The priest wiped sweat from his eyes. 'I've never been so afraid.'

'Not even of the young widow of Oissel?'

They retrieved the pushbikes and brought them back to the track. Only that final task remained now. It was one from which Mathieu could be spared.

'Wait here,' Benedict told him. 'Call of nature.' He disappeared back into the shadows of the close-growing conifers before the priest could argue.

Somewhere in this, the northern section of the Butte, was the highest point. Time was short, but Benedict advanced with care. There would be guards, possibly also dogs, and neither the men nor the animals were likely to be as inattentive as their comrades down below. He dared not stumble about in here for too long.

But he need not have worried. He found what he was looking for within seconds. He could hardly have missed it. The building was new and, like the recently built casemates, blindingly white in the sunshine. Rising taller than the conifers, it shone through the trees like the mirage of a gleaming palace. On the flat roof was a forest of aerials

229

and masts. On the seaward side was the huge open-mesh radar dish, turning slowly from side to side, its angle of elevation shifting with each pass, scanning the ocean and the skyline.

There was no need for him to approach any closer, no need to risk the guards or dogs. The radar station was there, that was all he had to know, that and to file its exact location away with everything else he had gathered so far.

His work in Houlgate was done.

The twigs and moss and the squarish stone were as he had left them. He strapped the bedroll over his back and went to retrieve his pushbike.

'No, wait, take this,' said Mathieu. He wheeled his own machine over to Benedict. 'Three speeds. What do I need three speeds for? I never go far. Take this too.' He handed Benedict the cloth with the bread and sausage wrapped inside.

The pushbike had a rack above the rear wheel; Benedict unstrapped the bedroll and transferred it.

The priest thrust his hands into his pockets and turned aside. He frowned into the distance and cleared his throat. 'You know, I've never told anyone else those things.'

'What things?'

'The things I told you, about the widow in Oissel.'

'You didn't tell me anything. You told Père Nicolas. Goodbye, Mathieu. Dominus tecum.'

When he looked back, the priest was still standing there.

Benedict crossed the bridge from Dives into Cabourg without incident. There were some troopers watching the dispirited procession of people who trailed past – shop girls, waiters, labourers, delivery boys, a few cyclists like himself – but no one challenged the black-suited priest who made no eye contact and seemed absorbed in prayer or contemplation as he cruised unhurriedly along.

Père Gilbert Trèves, in his late seventies according to the file Benedict had seen, was tall and with not a pick of fat on his bones. His movements were small and jerky, as if his joints were screwed together a little too tightly and each movement was a sudden victory of will. He stared at Benedict through heavy black-framed spectacles.

'At last,' he said. His voice was dry and faint, little more than a whisper.

'At last?' queried Benedict.

'You're here. So they must be planning something.'

'They?'

'Get inside. It's a miracle you haven't been shot already.'

The small church and Père Gilbert's double-fronted house stood one on each side of allée Saint-Joseph in the village of Varaville, about four kilometres west of Cabourg. Until now all that Varaville had meant to Benedict was the battle it had witnessed between the king of France and William of Normandy – the same William who would later invade England, as recalled by a certain colonel in London's Baker Street.

But now Varaville once again bore the scars of war. The land had been cleared, houses flattened and their inhabitants sent away, all of it the doing of the German occupier who wanted clear access and surveillance towards the sea, whence a more modern invasion was feared. Benedict had seen the evidence of the preparations as he drew near. Almost every tree had been felled in order to construct the defence system nicknamed Rommel's asparagus: the clusters of pointed stakes that marched along the coast, sometimes laced together by cables and barbed wire, to impale or slice paratroopers and prevent gliders landing.

In the midst of this savage landscape stood Père Gilbert's

house and church, as stripped of parishioners as the land was stripped of trees.

'Why are you still here?' Benedict asked the priest.

'Who else would keep the church standing? If I go, the church goes. My church is a consecrated house of God and Christ is still there. I cycle the lanes, I walk the fields, I let it be known I'm here if anyone needs me. I even talk to the Germans. I'm Christ's last flicker of light in this wilderness.'

Benedict studied the frail old man. 'You still cycle?'

The rheumy eyes behind the thick-rimmed spectacles glared defiantly at him. 'I'm tougher than I look.'

Benedict noted the black telephone in the corner as he followed Gilbert into the small back room. Through the open window he could hear the sea, at most three hundred metres distant.

'Tell me how I can help you, Père Nicolas. I was told you'd explain when you got here.'

Unlike Mathieu, the old man turned not a hair at the mention of accompanying Benedict.

'You're talking about the Atlantic Wall,' he said with satisfaction. He rubbed his bony hands together. 'So it's here they're coming.'

'Who?'

'You British. The Americans. Many others too, I hope and pray. I'm old but I'm not an imbecile. We have a splendid communication network in the priesthood. The Boche have been fortifying the entire Atlantic coast all the way south from Scandinavia for years now – Norway, Denmark, the Low Countries, as well as here. What they know, what we all know, is that an invasion is coming – but they don't know when or where. And then one day I get the message to expect a visitor – you. So unless London is despatching agents to every bit of coast from Norway down, this is where it's going to happen. And it's imminent. You're here to make an up-to-date assessment – what exactly the defences are, where they're placed, how extensive they are, how much of a threat. A last recce before the big push.'

He rose to his feet in a series of brittle little movements and left the room. Benedict listened as the priest ascended the stairs; then came the sound of furniture being moved. The stairs creaked again and Gilbert returned. There were smears of spiderweb across his soutane. He was carrying a sheaf of papers.

'These are for you.' He shoved the papers at Benedict and lowered himself back onto his chair.

Benedict leafed through the sheets of drawings. They were thorough and detailed. He looked up at the priest.

'You did these?'

Gilbert nodded. 'Before the priesthood I was an engineer. This is every metre of my section of the Wall, from Cabourg to Merville. The drawings are roughly to scale but I've marked in critical distances and dimensions. It's all there – gun emplacements, radar units, symbols for different types of weaponry, anti-invasion devices, minefields. I've been making these drawings since the Boche started this nonsense. God listens to our prayers but he expects us to do our bit too. He's not one for the lackadaisical man. I go around the locations in sequence and update the drawings as needed.'

'No one stops you?'

'Why would they? I'm just a senile old priest. The more the Germans see me, the less they suspect me.'

'I still need to see everything for myself.'

'I'd expect no less.'

Benedict took his chair to the table beneath the window. He arranged the pages in their correct sequence, then set each page on its own to study it. Thirty-odd drawings, one minute for each. When he finished he returned the pages to Gilbert with an instruction to destroy them.

'Shall we take a breath of sea air now, Père Gilbert?'

'That would be very agreeable. By vélo?'

'Anything else would be lackadaisical.'

Père Vincent was his next staging post, outside the town of Douvres-la-Délivrande, which took its name from its church dedicated to Our Lady of Deliverance, itself named after Normandy's ancient custom of the pilgrimage of deliverance. As well as the nearby coastal defences, there was a massive radar station spread across what had once been farmland between Douvres and the village of Bény-sur-Mer. Benedict recognised a long-range Siemens dish plus medium-range and short-range apparatus. Elimination or jamming of radar stations would be as important as destruction of bunkers and artillery casemates. Many lives would be in the hands of the boffins and the Allied bombers. Our Lady of Deliverance, like Père Gilbert's God, would need a helping hand.

And so, all the way to Quinéville, Benedict's own pilgrimage progressed. At every village and stretch of coastline that the Germans had desecrated with their fortifications and concrete, willing priests were his staging posts, his hosts and guardian angels. Not one of them considered or called himself a résistant but they sheltered him and risked their lives for what he had come to Normandy to see and store in his memory.

13

'Give my heart to Jürgen Graf?' Hélène had scoffed. 'That'll never happen.'

But it had. Piece by piece.

She now thought of what they did as making love. She repeated the phrase to herself when she was alone, thrilled by its sound, with no Isabelle within earshot to mock her and no mother to crush her dreams. What she and Jürgen did now was not how it had been before. They had never been completely naked then, in the long black car. But out here in this abandoned cottage that he had found for them at the far end of chemin des Mesliers, well away from Caillons, there was a proper bed. Being completely naked was part of making love, rather than the other thing. The most naked moment of all for her was when she removed the brace from her leg. Then she was truly as God made her. This was finally everything she had to give.

Jürgen gave too, in his fashion. He brought her gifts. She feared for him, she worried about the risks he might be taking to obtain them. There was the perfume. A fine gold chain. Soap. Chocolate. Silk underwear as fine and soft as her own skin. Things she had to hide when she took them home.

He showed her books and other publications, strange texts by strange foreign doctors about people who were not right in their minds. The books were in German, so he translated passages here and there for her and explained what they meant. He was at his most focused at these times and she saw how important it was to him that she should understand and share his passion, so she tried as hard as she could. And gradually she did begin to grasp the ideas that lay behind the stories and the things the doctors had written. Sometimes after these readings his lovemaking was very fierce, as though the haunted people in the books transmitted an energy to him. Soon the energy flowed through her too, and she became his equal in the demands she made when their bodies locked together.

They had to be secret, of course. She knew and accepted that. No one in Caillons could possibly understand the richness and beauty of what they had and what they meant to each other. The old cottage was their refuge, their safe place. For Hélène it was like having their own little home. And the secrecy made their time together all the more delicious, for their love was something to be protected, like a child they had conceived. How infinitely blessed she was.

And how they talked. That too made it love rather than the other thing. They talked about the books, of course. About their feelings for each other. He described the world as it would be after the war, how the Reich would change everything forever. It sounded exciting. He had such fervour. He spoke of his loyal Wehrmacht troopers with pride.

But most of all, he listened. He drank in her words when she talked about herself, her family. It seemed as if he could listen to her forever. She had never been listened to in such a way before. At these times nothing else in the universe existed for him but her; she saw it in his eyes.

'Tell me about your mother,' he said. 'I think she must be a very strong person.'

'She is.' A door slammed shut in Hélène's head. 'Was your mother strong?'

'She had the strength of the insane.'

Hélène smiled at what she took to be a figure of speech.

'It's true,' he said. 'She was insane. I have a secret for you.'

Another secret. She held her breath.

'What?'

'She murdered my father. I was there. I saw her do it.'

She gasped.

'Now perhaps you understand,' he said. 'You see, you can tell me anything – anything at all. Nothing will ever shock me, no matter what.'

She folded herself about him.

'Make love to me again,' she whispered. 'Don't be gentle.'

He asked questions, she answered them. Her answers led to more questions. She answered these too. She told him about her childhood, about growing up in the Villa Normandie, about her grandparents, about how wonderful her father had been, about her fear when war came, her distress when her father was called up for STO. She told him everything a first love should be told.

But nothing about her mother.

These were busy days for Gaspard Baignères. The isolation of his cottage deep among the fir trees protected him from Graf's heightened security measures and the search for the mysterious foreign agent rumoured to have been landed in Caillons; but there were more patrols than usual for him to dodge on roads and lanes, more troopers getting in his way with whom he had not yet got around to forming friendships. Still, business was business and it had to carry on. Money disliked neglect. So one morning he cycled inland where things were less fraught. His destination was a small farm where the owners, two brothers, knew him on sight and to do business with but not by name or where he came from. On his back was a mussel basket.

He found the brothers at work in their creamery. Butter was what they were best at. It had been their family's speciality for generations. Butter ran in their veins, they liked to remark. They were no different from a hundred other Norman farmers except for one thing: they knew how to make butter the way the Germans liked it. And the Germans paid in Reichsmarks.

Gaspard called out a greeting as he propped the pushbike by the creamery door and entered the shaded interior. He swung the mussel basket down from his back. There were handshakes and the usual chat over comradely cigarettes lit from a shared match. Then a silence fell that said it was time for the visitor to account for his presence.

'Something for you,' Gaspard said. He removed the lid of the basket and shoved his hand down through the shiny blue-black mussels. When it emerged it was holding a large leather boot: Wilfried Hermann Wiedemuth's boot, one of the pair provided by the late Jacques Colinet. Gaspard pulled the tongue wide and tipped the boot upside down. Mussels tumbled back into the basket. He produced the other boot.

'Good thick leather – see,' he said. 'Well dubbined, hardly worn, steel insets all the way around the soles and heels. Brand-new laces. Great boots. Last a lifetime.'

'They stink,' said a brother, wrinkling his nose at the fishy aroma.

'They'll be worse after a day on your feet.'

A respectable bout of haggling followed, then finally palms were spat upon and handshakes exchanged, and Gaspard was on his way again, the basket empty, the mussels being his goodwill bonus to the brothers, and his wallet full.

It took him a couple of hours to get to Honfleur. The

notaire's office was in a courtyard approached through a short passageway off rue Saint Léonard. The notaire was pleased to see him. He was always pleased to see a good client. He detected the briny odour that accompanied Gaspard on this occasion but was too polite to mention it.

'Well,' he said as Gaspard laid the crinkled stacks of Reichsmarks on his desk and smoothed them out: not only the brothers' contribution but the proceeds of the month that had passed since their last meeting. Together they counted the notes twice.

'That's it,' the notaire concluded. 'It's all there. Every sou. Well, better than sous.'

'So the parcel of land is mine?'

'It's yours, Gaspard. This is the vendor's price and here it all is. I'll read the deed through to you and get the cash banked. Then our business is concluded.'

'Until next time.'

'If you have more purchases in mind.'

The notaire looked sideways at his client, who was busily writing in that notebook of his. Never a visit passed without the notebook making its appearance.

'All this land you keep buying, Gaspard – what are you going to do with it, what do you want it for? A parcel here, another bit there.'

'There's a war. Buildings fall down. Land doesn't.'

'You could hang on to the cash – good Reichsmarks.'

'They won't be good forever.'

The deed was read aloud as the law required, a glass of wine was drunk, and Gaspard was on his way once more, oilcloth cap at an angle and the empty mussel basket bouncing at his back.

Jürgen Graf knew it was time to face the truth.

He bent over the table in his room. The velvet cloth was

239

unrolled, the components of the disassembled watch were spread out before him in the glare of the powerful lamp.

Hélène Dupré was sharper than he had expected. She took every gift he threw her way, she wove stories like a French Scheherazade, telling him every detail of her life and dreams, always with more to come.

And always, like Scheherazade's bemused king, he wanted to hear more.

But concerning Jeanne Dupré he had learnt nothing. That alone was a hard enough truth, but there was another. And it was worse. He had learnt nothing about the mother but something was happening with the daughter. No, had already happened. The alley cat had claws; she had sunk them deep and there was no getting them out. Here was the evidence before his eyes. It needed no magnifying glass to reveal it.

He set down the tiny screwdriver. His hands were trembling; that was the evidence: a watchmaker's son with trembling hands. The worst of it was, he knew beyond any sliver of doubt why they were trembling. The impossible had happened, the unimaginable. Something had taken root within him and grown until it held Jürgen Graf, the uncompromising ideologue and leader of men, utterly in its control.

That something was his feelings for Hélène Dupré.

Marcel Voinet, the pale youth who had met Daniel Benedict in Jacques Colinet's meadow, looked up as the shadow of a patrol vehicle darkened the window of his father's charcuterie. The armoured car passed from the square into rue du Centre. A minute later another shadow darkened the shop, one not quite as hefty as the German vehicle but just as unwelcome. Joséphine Sulot, one of the five sisters of the proprietor of Café du Marché, entered. As usual, she scowled by way of greeting. As usual, she took a look around to see what she could complain about. As usual, she had a gang of squalling children in tow. And as usual, Marcel retreated to the back of the shop. He had refused to serve Sulot or any of his sisters since the day the man started putting German posters in the windows of his café and serving Oberleutnant Jürgen Graf his morning coffee. Sulot swore the posters were there to fool the Boche and he always spat in the coffee but Marcel remained unconvinced.

As he reached the side entrance to the shop, the door burst open and a plainly panic-stricken Luc Clavier stumbled in from allée de l'Église. Marcel stared in shock at his fellow résistant for an instant, unable to believe the man's stupidity in showing himself in Caillons. Without a word he pushed him behind a tall weighing scale. The circular face of the scale was at head height. Scant cover, but there was nothing else.

Joséphine and old Voinet were arguing over prices. She had not seen Luc Clavier. Not yet.

'You can't come here,' whispered Marcel. 'My God, you know that. And in broad daylight. Are you crazy? Are you trying to get us all killed, my father too? You'll be recognised. You're a wanted man.'

The railwayman was round-eyed with terror. He was breathless and almost steaming with sweat.

'I think I've got rid of them, Marcel.'

Them? Meaning the Boche? It was the worst news.

'I need to rest for a while. They were combing the woods. I was keeping well ahead and out of their way. I was moving ahead of them. I was doing well, it was working. Then reinforcements arrived with dogs –'

'Dogs? My God. You'll bring them here. Dogs?'

'I've shaken them off now. I swear.'

241

'You don't shake off tracker dogs. You can't stay here.'

Marcel thought quickly. There was one chance. There was a time when his father had sold real pork. Pork from corn-fed pigs. Corn fertilised with marl.

'I know of an old marl pit. It isn't worked any longer.'

'How do I get there?'

Marcel was already untying his apron. 'You'll never find it. The way in is just a hole in the ground. I'll have to take you.'

Olivier Sulot, seven years old, was small for his age, small enough to be hidden by the counter where meat was boned. He was no genius but he was devious enough to recognise deviousness in others. And to know when he might profit from his observation.

He was at his mother's side and pummelling her ample hip before Marcel and Luc knew they had been seen and overheard. He blurted out all, she listened, glanced up in time to see Marcel shoving Luc back towards the side door, recognised Luc instantly, and sent Olivier sprinting from the shop. The boy now had a mission and he acquitted himself admirably. He caught up with the patrol, cried out the only word that mattered, whether it was accurate or not – 'Résistants!' – and led four Wehrmacht troopers charging back to the charcuterie.

Here they found the boy's mother pointing them towards the side door. Three skidded into the alleyway while the fourth slammed the butt of his weapon into old Voinet's skull when the butcher ran at him, hands flapping in protest. The charcutier crumpled to the sawdust floor, dead.

Marcel Voinet was unarmed but Luc Clavier produced an old Ruby pistol and opened fire as soon as the three troopers rounded the corner into the alleyway. He stood no chance. Three submachine guns delivered a hail of bullets that brought him and Marcel down. They were both dead before they hit the cobblestones.

So was Olivier Sulot, caught by one of Luc Clavier's rounds as he gawped at the action.

In his first-floor office in the mairie, Leutnant Ernst Neiss heard the shouts and pounding feet and gunfire and looked up in alarm from his paperwork. The shooting sounded as if it was right outside. He hurried to the window. What he saw horrified him.

A small boy lay face down in a pool of blood at the foot of allée de l'Église. He was clearly dead. Three Wehrmacht troopers armed with submachine guns stood over the body. They were arguing loudly. There seemed also to be something in the alleyway that was taking their attention; the high wall of the churchyard blocked it from the leutnant's view. Between the charcuterie and the alleyway a large woman surrounded by several children – they were milling about so much that Neiss was not sure how many there were – had either collapsed or flung herself to her knees and was wailing like a lost soul. Each time she tried to crawl towards the dead boy a fourth trooper pushed her back at gunpoint, provoking her and the other children to wail even more pitifully.

Along rue du Centre people were peering fearfully from doorways and windows. Here and there a window opened, a head appeared, then was quickly withdrawn. The door of Hodin's boulangerie flew open and Marguerite Voinet, the old charcutier's young wife, ran into the street. There was a commotion outside Café du Marché. As Neiss watched, the man called Sulot who owned the café burst through the little knot of villagers clustered around his doorway and waddled as fast as his short legs could carry him towards place de l'Église. His hands flew to his head and tore at his few strands of hair, he wailed as loudly as the fat woman,

243

whom Neiss now recognised as his sister, and he was pursued by his four other sisters and a posse of children, all wailing and screaming.

In place de l'Église a tall black-clad figure raced along the pavement from the church to the alleyway, the skirts of his soutane spreading like wings. Père François Lachanau covered the distance in half a dozen of his long strides. His biretta flew from his head and spun to the ground, ignored. He knelt over the boy. Neiss saw him raise the child's wrist and feel for a pulse, then he placed his fingers against the boy's neck. He shook his head. A trooper tried to move him but the priest glanced up angrily and said something that made the trooper back away.

But in looking up, Lachanau seemed to see something else deeper in the alleyway, the same thing that was preoccupying the troopers and which Neiss could not see. The priest stared for a moment, then drew a long band of cloth from his pocket, kissed it and draped it about his neck. He made the sign of the cross and bowed his head over the dead boy.

Neiss turned away from the window. Whatever had happened in allée de l'Église, it needed the major's attention. But at this moment Major Klaus Ebermann was somewhere in the skies between France and Germany. He was at last, and belatedly, on the way home to bury his family. Oberleutnant Jürgen Graf was in charge of Caillons.

Neiss groaned. Graf in charge. And there was the long black Citroën already skidding into the square.

The leutnant fetched his jacket and hurried down the stairs. Death made him feel sick. But the thought of Graf in charge today, with this to deal with, whatever it was, made him feel even sicker.

Graf looked at the sorry mess that was the remains of

Marcel Voinet and Luc Clavier. He was indifferent to the dead child. Then he looked at the sorry mess that was Ernst Neiss. The leutnant was as white as the corpses in the alleyway; he looked like he might keel over at any moment.

'You're in the way here,' Graf told him.

Place de l'Église had now been cleared of civilians, including the Sulot clan, the priest and the wife, now widow, of old Voinet. The armoured car had returned. Order had been restored. Troopers were stationed around the square to keep prying eyes away. The only fly in the ointment was Neiss, who had inveigled himself here and seemed to think he had a right to interfere.

'I apologise, Herr Oberleutnant, but I have to make a full report to Major Ebermann.'

'No, you don't. I'm handling the situation. I have full authority in his absence.'

'Of course, Herr Oberleutnant. We both have our responsibilities. Mine is to keep the major informed of all significant developments in his absence. I think this qualifies as a significant development.'

'Suit yourself.'

'Then my report, which is based on the information I've gathered –'

Graf closed in on him. 'What do you mean, gathered? Have you been pestering my men behind my back? You had no permission from me to do that.'

'I apologise again, Herr Oberleutnant, but you were busy, I didn't want to distract you. Regulations state that in cases of emergency –'

Graf waved the explanation away. 'Let's hear this report you're cooking up.'

'Four civilians are dead, Herr Oberleutnant. Three were killed by men under your command –'

'The old charcutier was an accident.'

Neiss blinked slowly, then continued as if Graf had never spoken. 'Three of the civilians were killed by men under your command. The fourth, a child, was killed in the crossfire of the gun battle in which your men were engaged.'

'He was shot by one of the résistants.'

'I understand he was shot by one of the French civilians who died, a Monsieur Luc Clavier, who was being sought by Reich authorities for evasion of STO. But I'm not aware of any evidence that Monsieur Clavier was a résistant.'

'Of course there's no evidence. There never is. But why else did he open fire? Why was he armed, in contravention of Reich law?'

'I can't answer those questions, Herr Oberleutnant.' The slow blink again. 'Unfortunately neither can Monsieur Clavier, since he's dead. Meanwhile, his companion –'

'His accomplice.'

'The man who died with him, a Monsieur Marcel Voinet, son of the dead charcutier, was not suspected of any criminal activity.'

'He was suspected by me.'

Concern creased Neiss's face. 'Herr Oberleutnant, I found nothing on file. I checked as soon as I established the men's identities. I apologise yet again – this must be an error on my part. I'll check more thoroughly.'

Graf looked away. 'You won't find anything. There's nothing on file about Voinet.'

'I see. Then in summary we have four civilian fatalities – one a child, one an elderly shopkeeper, unarmed and in his own shop, one an unarmed man with no charges against him, and the fourth an STO evader armed with a pistol. So we have four fatalities but the STO evader was the only person breaking any laws. That will be the essence of my report, Herr Oberleutnant. I'll send it with the day's other communications traffic to Paris. Major Ebermann will receive it tomorrow in Germany, with the rest of today's updates. One question, if I may, Herr Oberleutnant?'

'What question?'

'Have you made any progress regarding the suspected foreign agent? The major specifically asked to be kept informed.'

Graf shook his head but could not bring himself to say the word. Nor to meet the leutnant's gaze.

'Then I'll tell Major Ebermann the matter is still in hand,' said Neiss. At last he turned to go but then paused. 'I wonder if the dead men knew anything about the foreign agent. Sadly, we'll never know now.'

The bed in the old cottage on chemin des Mesliers was narrow. Graf felt every centimetre of Hélène's body clasped tightly against his own. They had drained each other to the core, he as if to banish the memory of another day with nothing achieved, she sensing his need to drive and punish, offering her body as hostage to his demands, however harsh, however brutal. That was her way; just as she had promised at the outset.

'What happened today?' she asked, sleepy and exhausted. 'I waited for you here. I thought I heard shooting from the direction of the village.'

'It doesn't matter.'

Not true. These days with no result did matter. All he had to show for today was an inconsequential death or two; despite all his efforts there was still neither head nor hair of any enemy agent. Only Neiss making the customary nuisance of himself. This Scheisshaus of a country could grind a man down.

He tapped an Eckstein against a thumbnail and lit up.

'You must leave Caillons,' he told Hélène. 'Get out of

this place. Out of France.'

She raised her head from his chest. 'What do you mean?'

'I've thought it through. It's the best thing. I can send you to Germany. I can arrange it, there are special exemptions I can obtain. When this war is over and the Reich has triumphed, we'll be together in the Fatherland. We'll have everything – all of Europe will be the Reich's, which means it will be ours. You'll be the wife of a fighting man who helped the Führer to achieve this. We'll make a home, we'll travel, we'll have the world at our feet.'

'Your wife?' The springs of the bed squealed as she pushed herself up on an elbow to look directly at him. She was fully awake now. 'I'll be your wife?'

'You'll have babies, perfect German babies.'

Her gaze shifted; he knew she was looking at the leg brace where she had left it on the floor.

'How can our babies ever be perfect? With me as their mother?'

'Your condition isn't congenital. Your suitability to breed isn't in any doubt. Our babies will be perfect.'

'But how can I leave France? It's impossible. I can't abandon my family.'

'Ah yes, your family.'

The hardest truth of all.

Nothing achieved there either.

'We're in love, Maman.'

Jeanne froze at the words. A cold terror flooded through her.

Hélène had come home. It was her pattern nowadays: to disappear for hours at a time, sometimes overnight, returning only when it suited her. No apologies, no explanations. Where she went during her absences, neither Jeanne nor Isabelle knew; certainly it was nowhere within their gaze. But wherever it was, they both knew who was there with her.

'I love Jürgen, Maman. He loves me.'

Jeanne left the dishes she was rinsing and dried her hands.

'You don't know what you're talking about, my child. You're not in love with him.'

'Because he's a German? So you and your major, you can't be in love?'

'That's over. Besides, I was never in love with him.'

'And you think that makes you better than me?'

Isabelle stepped between them.

'Hélène, have you told Graf anything about Maman?'

Hélène glared at her. 'You dare ask me that? You would *dare*?' She shook her head. 'Jürgen's right.'

Jeanne tensed. 'Right about what?'

'I don't belong here.'

'This is your home. Where else would you belong?'

The reply chilled Jeanne's blood even further.

'In Germany.'

It was too much even for Isabelle. Tears spilled from her eyes.

'How can you say that, Hélène? How can you even think it? What's become of you? How has he done this to you? Maman – what are we to do?'

Jeanne stood there trembling, at a loss.

What indeed.

Gaspard turned down the track that led to his cottage. As he dismounted from the pushbike he heard a small sound off to one side, as of a twig crushed underfoot. Probably nothing more than a deer passing by.

Probably.

He showed no reaction as he let himself in and closed the door. He retrieved the Star semi-automatic from the hollowed-out roof beam, primed the weapon and slipped his hand and the gun inside the empty mussel basket. He returned to the door and opened it.

The woman was waiting for him on the overgrown path. She inclined her head in greeting.

'Shalom.'

Just as the butter brothers did not know his name, so he did not know hers. She was short, strongly built, with olive skin and black hair. The hair had a thick streak of grey, even though he guessed she was no more than forty.

'We lost the children,' he told her. 'All of them. I'm sorry.'

She nodded. 'I heard. HaShem has them in his care.'

'If you say so. Come inside.'

But she returned to the shadows of the undergrowth. He heard her speaking in an undertone. A moment later she emerged again. Half hidden behind her and clutching her hand was a small girl, about three years old. Large frightened eyes as black as jet stared up at him.

The woman was carrying what he took at first to be a bundle of clothing, perhaps the girl's. But there was a tiny face deep within the bundle, its eyes clamped shut. He was no expert, but the baby seemed to be no more than a few weeks old.

'No.' He shook his head. 'No more. Not after the others.'

'Please.'

'You don't understand. We didn't lose only the children, we lost the families too. Caillons families. Good people.'

'And how many families are *we* losing? They're good people too.'

'Things are different here now. Someone informed.'

'Please. We have nowhere else, no one else.'

He looked again at the little girl. A mistake. He looked away but the damage was done.

He stepped back from the door.

'Inside quickly,' he said.

Père François Lachanau sighed as he entered the empty church and went through to the sacristy. What was happening to his flock? So many souls tumbling over the precipice of life and into eternity, even little innocents like the Sulot child. Truly a vale of tears.

He was tidying away some candles when he thought he heard a noise outside the sacristy door. Not the racket of heavy-booted Germans but a furtive noise, as if someone was trying to be as quiet as possible. The handle turned, the door opened. In came Gaspard Baignères.

'Ah, you're here, François,' he said.

He was carrying a mussel basket. Its lid was moving. By his side and holding his hand was a small black-eyed girl clutching a cloth doll. Her clothes were ragged and stained, as if she had worn them for many days, as if they were the only garments she had. She looked around the room anxiously, her gaze settling on the priest, then she took refuge behind Gaspard's legs.

Lachanau crouched down and gave her his friendliest smile. He had never seen her before; this was no Caillons child. He kept the smile going but his heart sank.

'The family Cuisson,' Gaspard was saying. 'I was thinking, they're well outside the village, well out of harm's way. They rarely even see a German. Twin daughters already, so they'll never notice another. And the baby –'

'A baby?' Lachanau stared apprehensively at the mussel basket.

Gaspard nodded. 'Hortense Meslin, perhaps. Don't you agree? Hervé will be overjoyed to have a little brother. And what better to prise the grief from Hortense's heart after losing Charles? The Germans are no longer interested in her

251

and the child is young enough to be his.'

'But Gaspard, our informer, we don't know who –'

'They've come a long way, these two,' said Gaspard. 'They need shelter and food. And you can see she needs clothes, François.'

'They always do.'

Gaspard smiled grimly. 'Precisely. That's the other thing I want to talk to you about. They always need clothes. And you never let them down.'

14

Jeanne dressed for her cleaning work at the Villa Normandie, choosing an old belted skirt of her mother's and a loose, long-bodied blouse. She replaced the skirt's fabric belt with a strong leather one. She searched the trunk in her portion of the loft and found the blue cape that her mother Colette Rochard used to wear on high days and for travel. She shook it out and settled it on her shoulders. She slipped Wilfried Hermann Wiedemuth's Luger inside the belt at the back of the skirt and pulled the blouse down over it, then resettled the cape. From what she could see in the square of mirror by the sink, it looked fine.

She took a last look around La Croisette. The fire was damped down; it would still have life when her daughters got home – assuming Hélène came home. In the larder there was baguette from yesterday, cheese and a cabbage. The girls would not go hungry: there was the kitchen garden, if they tended it with care. The cottage was clean; she would not have it said that Jeanne Dupré had let things go. The chickens had been fed and they had water. And she had removed the MP40 and its ammunition and slid them into the cleft of the beech tree split by lightning in the second field, where they would probably rest for eternity.

She could do no more. It was time to go. She put on her sabots, locked up and stepped firmly down the path. She did not look back.

Even in Caillons, where diets left something to be desired,

children outgrew their clothes. Their mothers made and mended as best they could with hand-me-downs, alterations, garments borrowed from neighbours and friends and other branches of the family. But sooner or later these sources failed; there was a limit to how often a trouser leg could be lengthened or how many wearers the same coat could survive. So sooner or later every Caillonaise mother climbed the stairs from Pauthier's greengrocer shop to Mathilde Pauthier's garment room.

When she did, she could buy outright with cash or she could barter a garment of the family's own and pay the balance in cash, always francs since they were the only currency ordinary folk ever got their hands on. The one thing she could not do, not ever, was barter without cash.

'No,' Mathilde would say firmly if the suggestion was made, lips thinning to nothing and eyebrows gathering together. 'We have to eat, Pauthier and me. Exactly like you, Madame. I can let you have this good coat for cash alone or a little less cash plus that moth-eaten old skirt you're bringing me – but there has to be cash. Didn't you see that deserted shop of Pauthier's downstairs? Never a soul in the place. We'd starve if it wasn't for me. Away with you now, I'm busy.'

And she would begin to fold up the coat or whatever the garment was, knowing that its imminent removal from view was more than the desperate mother could endure.

Madame Guinard was her best customer as well as her friend. The Pauthiers' best customer, to be precise, Mathilde and Pauthier together. Major Klaus Ebermann felt it his duty to support what was left of the lawful local economy, as did Père François Lachanau. So good Madame Guinard purchased from Pauthier downstairs what she needed for the unfathomable dishes that graced the major's and the priest's tables, which usually meant little more than a few carrots or onions in the major's case since the Reich maintained an impressively stocked sous-sol at the Villa Normandie, while from Mathilde upstairs she purchased the clothes that the priest from time to time paid for from his own pocket for this or that family whose needs exceeded their means.

And here was the nub. More than once, Mathilde Pauthier suspected, the priest had sent old Marie Guinard – quite unwitting, heaven bless her in her innocence – to purchase garments for those Jewish children that thankfully the village was now rid of. A Catholic priest squandering Catholic money on the killers of Jesus? The thought appalled Mathilde Pauthier, but this was the conclusion she had arrived at after a deal of thought and observation. For Mathilde's eyes were sharp not only when it came to her craft but also when she lifted them from her busy needle and pattern sheets and chalk and directed them through her window to the vista below. Directly beneath her were rue du Centre and place de l'Église, to her left Café du Marché with its reprobates, while straight ahead was rue du Port, all the way downhill to the port itself.

Mathilde saw a great deal from that window as Caillons went about its daily goings-on. She knew which children were whose; she knew which families had no children at all. She could also tell at a hundred metres and without a second glance every garment she had made. So naturally she had noticed when a small boy was to be seen wandering in and out of the cottage of childless André and Estelle Rousselot – a boy who seemed to have materialised from nowhere, whole and complete. And wearing jacket and trousers of her own manufacture. Jacket and trousers lately chosen and paid for by Madame Guinard on the say-so of Père François Lachanau.

The same with Agathe Lanery. Where on earth had

255

Agathe found that little boy and girl – under a bush? Again, there were Mathilde's trousers and skirt and coats, walking about for all the world to see. And, like the garments worn by the boy living with the family Rousselot – she could not bring herself to think of him as the Rousselot boy – paid for by the priest without barter, hard cash only. Lucrative trade for Mathilde, but galling to see those good clothes tailored and stitched by her own Catholic hands sheltering the backs of Jews.

So as a loyal citizen of France and its new masters, what could Mathilde do but mention her suspicions to Oberleutnant Graf? Naming no names, of course. She had her standards. It was for the authorities, meaning him, to do the rest. She was no informer. And her public-spirited action may have caused a little temporary inconvenience to Hortense Meslin and her child – one coat for the child, one pair of trousers, one dress for the mother over the years, never anything for the father: hardly what one could call regular custom – but those Meslins were no loyal citizens, were they? Not with Charles Meslin slinking off into the maquis instead of doing the decent thing and facing his STO duties like a man. And just look where that had got him.

At Quinéville Benedict crossed the river over pont de la Sinope. The river was a thin ribbon here and the tiny single-track bridge was unguarded and unpatrolled, as he had been told it would be, though in the silence of the day the wheels of his pushbike rattled the warped wooden boards with a racket that seemed guaranteed to draw every German trooper in the region. He skirted the river basin, more mud than water in the heat, and passed through a run-down sprawl of abandoned and desolate buildings that he guessed had once accommodated boatbuilders and chandlers. In the distance rose the spire of the church.

Despite his din on the little bridge, no Wehrmacht troopers or vehicles appeared. He turned inland and soon the countryside opened out to an expanse of flat fields and the huge azure bowl of the sky. It was as if all of France stretched before him.

Only now did he breathe freely. Not only because he had left the zone of most immediate threat but also because his work was done. This was the homeward leg of his mission. Returning safely was the objective now, bringing with him the information for which the colonel and the thin man in Baker Street were waiting.

He never let his attention slip from the physical landscape, watching for patrols and checkpoints in the distance and listening for the faint buzz of engines that could signal the approach of German vehicles, but his mind also had its own internal landscape. Every location he had been to, every fortification he had seen, all were imprinted and safely preserved in his memory. He ran through their details, over and over, every image as clear as a photograph. Each was there in front of him as he pushed through the kilometres, presenting itself to him with a reality that paralleled the endless fields and banked hedgerows around him.

But there were other images too. These were the ones that came unbidden. He tried to shake them away but they always returned, seeping through the foreground like portraits on a repainted canvas. Images of someone he knew only as Lisieux.

Every sniper needed his observation man. That Gaspard Baignères had once been the best sniper in the French lines was partly because Mirabaud, before the Somme took his sanity from him, was the best observer, the best spotter. Did

257

that tussock look different today? Was that a movement in the north-east quadrant? Was there a glint of metal when the sun broke through the cloud?

Together the two comrades had made a formidable team. And bonds forged in the blood and mayhem of that earlier war did not dissolve.

Eyes straight ahead, bare feet slapping on the floorboards, Mirabaud came briskly to attention before Gaspard and François Lachanau in the priest's house and snapped a salute that was as sharp today as thirty years ago.

'Reporting for duty as commanded, mon colonel,' he announced, loud and clear.

'Summarise enemy movements and all civilian contact with said enemy, soldier. The last two weeks will suffice.'

Mirabaud obligingly rattled off dates, times, names and places. He needed no notebook; for when it came to this and his other military duties – duties that would never end, for that other war would rage forever in Mirabaud's world – his brain was crystal clear, not sullied by any speck of Somme mud.

'You were right,' Lachanau told Gaspard when the man had finished.

'Time spent on reconnaissance is rarely wasted, François. The pity is, we didn't do our reconnaissance earlier. I curse myself for that.'

He delivered a crisp salute to Mirabaud. 'Thank you, soldier – you're dismissed. You may eat now. Monsieur le Curé has one of Madame Guinard's finest dishes for you.'

Best not to try to name the dish, the priest had warned. But it was all the same to Mirabaud.

'Lucky Mirabaud,' he chirruped. 'Good Colonel Mauser.'

While he ate, Gaspard and Lachanau withdrew to the other side of the room. Gaspard produced his notebook and the fine Prismalo pencil. He found the page of names he

258

had confirmed with schoolmaster Aristide Péringuey: the three Rousselots and Agathe Lanery, none of them seen since their arrests and all by now in the hands of the Gestapo in Le Havre.

Lachanau watched him.

'Who owes you money now?' he asked.

'Debts come in many forms, François. Not always cash. Whatever is done, whatever is owed, we must remember. France must always remember.'

He inscribed the name of Mathilde Pauthier at the top of the page.

Jeanne met no one on ruelle de la Baie and there were few people in place de l'Église. The morning was warm, the shadows long and sharp. The Luger pressed itself awkwardly into her back, chafing her flesh, but she tolerated the discomfort.

Down in the port the fishing boats were hard at work. Gulls swooped as the night-time nets were landed. Sunlight sparkled on the waters of the bay and the little rills of surf around the mussel bouchots, and made the dense maquis on the headland gleam like a cascade of emeralds. Where the vegetation had left the cliff uncovered, the falls of limestone were as white as sun-bleached bone.

Her eye was drawn to where she knew the icehouse was hidden. She thought of the Englishman and heard his voice and the laughter she had provoked from him. Foolish man, foolish ideas. As foolish as the notions he had stirred in her. For all she knew, he was dead by now. The confident ones fell first. But if he was dead, had he endangered her cell before dying? She had tried to be careful but it was impossible for him to know nothing; there was the icehouse for a start, the fact of its existence and the description he could provide of its location. He could also describe her and the others. The unforgivable thing was that she had allowed him to draw her out: two daughters, she had admitted, even giving their ages. Stupid, stupid. And yet it was she who had lectured him about endangering her cell and her family.

She sighed. What was done was done. She could only pray that Hélène and Isabelle were kept safe. As for the cell, it hardly mattered now. So many lost, so many dead for France, so few left. Danton had a great deal to do. She regretted adding to his burden today.

As she crossed the square she saw that her timing was good. Outside the mairie the Wehrmacht motorcycle messenger was climbing off his machine and unloading the panniers that contained the overnight communications pouches from Paris. He would deliver these to Leutnant Ernst Neiss in his upstairs office. Little Neiss would sign for them, then sift through the material. Some would be for Major Klaus Ebermann, and Neiss would deal with these in the major's absence, but some would be for Graf. The oberleutnant would arrive to deal with these himself.

She slowed her pace and looked from the messenger towards rue du Centre. She found what she was looking for. As always at this hour, unless unforeseen events had intervened, the long black Citroën saloon was parked outside Café du Marché. The hood was down. Graf sat alone in the rear seat, drinking his morning coffee – real coffee, which Sulot kept for him and him alone. The sunlight glinted on the visor of his uniform cap and the silver oakleaf insignia and Reich eagle.

She could continue down rue du Centre and resolve matters there and be done; but Graf would see her coming from far distant. No, her original plan was better; she would stick with it.

She turned away so as not to catch the oberleutnant's eye. Her gaze fell on old Voinet's charcuterie. The Germans had lost no time. Already the doors and windows had been boarded up and covered with their propaganda posters. Like France itself, the venerable old shop had become the occupier's plaything.

Like Hélène.

Adalard Fougeret stood on the corner of rue du Centre and allée de l'Église. He was reading the posters on the charcuterie windows. Merely an insignificant old man to whom no one paid any attention. Some people, such as those with important things on their mind, would not even see him. People such as Jeanne Dupré. Or Jürgen Graf.

He read on.

Put your trust in the German soldier!

Behind everything – the Jew!

Free the prisoners by working in Germany!

He knew the black Citroën would be here any minute. His mind became as clear as it had been on the day he married his sweet Adie, as clear as the morning he had taken their newborn son Louis in his arms and kissed him for the first time.

He clutched the folds of his old gaberdine coat close about him.

Gaspard was whistling something tuneless as he cycled along rue du Centre, the melody fracturing all the more with each bump of the cobbles. He passed the black Citroën but paid it little heed; it was a common sight these days, unfortunately. And provided the oberleutnant kept his nose out of Gaspard's business, Gaspard had no particular bone to pick with him.

He whistled louder as he reached Pauthier's greengrocer shop, where Mathilde was no doubt monitoring everything from that upstairs window of hers.

261

Ah, Mathilde, to see so much but love so little.

Poor henpecked Pauthier was mooning about aimlessly inside the store when Gaspard entered. As usual there were no customers. He looked distrustfully at Gaspard.

'I'm buying nothing from you, Gaspard Baignères.'

'Then we're of a mind,' said Gaspard. 'I'm not here to sell you anything. What I have is free today. Because it's priceless. Life-transforming, even. It's advice for Mathilde.'

'Good luck, then. She doesn't take advice.'

'I don't plan to give it to her. You'll do that.'

Pauthier's suspicion became nervousness. 'Not sure I'd want to risk that.'

'No risk. Only once in a lifetime does a man get an opportunity like this. Well, only once in your lifetime. It's advice about the company your Mathilde keeps. And her mouth.'

'Her mouth?'

'She should keep it shut. Or someone will shut it for her.' Gaspard tilted his head and mimed a hanging. 'To bring that about you need only say the word, Pauthier, because from now on you'll be watching her every move. And the pleasure of telling her this will be all yours. How's that for a business proposition? Interested now? Then allow me to explain.'

By the time they parted a few minutes later, Pauthier was a changed man. And Mathilde Pauthier would cause no more trouble.

As Gaspard remounted his pushbike he glanced over his shoulder in time to see Sulot retrieving the empty coffee cup from Graf, nodding obsequiously to the oberleutnant. The German ignored him. He issued a curt order to his driver. The Citroën's engine growled into life and the vehicle moved away.

Gaspard pushed off along the cobbles and resumed his tuneless whistle. But the notes died on his lips as he took in the tableau in the square ahead, into which the Citroën was driving.

Adalard Fougeret was there, his body twisting restlessly to and fro. And here too was Jeanne Dupré. Since when had she taken to that cape of Colette Rochard's? Gaspard remembered the cape. No one in Caillons had ever owned anything as grand. Typical Colette. But Jeanne Dupré wearing it? To show up in a headscarf of fine lace on that black day of her brother's execution, that was one thing, a sombre garment suited to that black occasion. But where was the need for a cape today?

And that old gaberdine of Adalard's, why was he drowning himself in that on this sweltering morning?

Or was clothing just too much on Gaspard's mind today, his imagination running away with him?

The Citroën drew up outside the mairie. The driver hopped smartly out and opened the rear door. Graf began to climb out. There was movement in allée de l'Église. Carefully skirting the still-visible bloodstains where Luc Clavier and Marcel Voinet had fallen, Hélène Dupré stepped from the alley and into the square. A few metres away Jeanne Dupré stepped forward. Adalard sidled closer towards Graf – or was it towards Hélène? – in that sideways slur of his.

In that instant Gaspard realised what was coming.

Jeanne saw the fleeting look that passed between Graf and her daughter as Hélène turned the corner and the two found themselves alongside one another. She could tell that the encounter was accidental, but the conspiratorial ease with which they handled it sickened her.

Neither of them noticed her. Beneath the cape she reached

for the Luger.

Adalard, not distracted as she had been, was faster. An ancient shotgun swung up from the folds of his coat.

Hélène turned, startled by the unexpected movement. She saw the gun and screamed. Graf saw it too and lunged forward, placing himself squarely between Hélène and the shotgun. Already his pistol was in his hand. He fired. An empty casing spun through the air and landed at Jeanne's feet. The old man's body bent almost double as the force of the bullet drove him backwards. The shotgun dipped towards the ground but Adalard still held it, his finger still in the trigger guard. He stepped backwards, fighting to hold his balance and raise the weapon again. His eyes were wild. Graf fired again, at the same time pressing Hélène further behind him. Then a third shot. At last Adalard went down, the shotgun, never fired, clattering to the pavement beside him. Graf slammed his boot down on it. He bent over Adalard's prone body and bunched the coat into a thick bundle behind the old man's head, raised the Luger and delivered the coup de grâce. The cloth absorbed the round as it passed through the skull, so that there was no ricochet from the pavement.

Jeanne was suddenly aware of someone very close behind her. Before she could turn to see who it was, a strong hand gripped her right arm. She could not move. Another hand slipped under her cape and grasped the Luger. Gaspard Baignères leant forward, his moustaches scratching her cheek, and put his mouth to her ear.

'If Graf sees that gun, you're dead,' he whispered.

'So? Maybe I came here to die.'

'Maybe. But I think you came here to kill first. Believe me, that can't happen, Jeanne. Graf's too fast, he has eyes in the back of his head. Look at Adalard. What a waste of Jeanne Dupré that would be. A death with no purpose. You should go home, Jeanne.'

'This is none of your business, Gaspard.'

'You'd be surprised how many things are my business. Go home, I said. You have work to do. Important work – and soon.' His grip on her arm tightened. 'Danton's orders. Which is to say, my orders.'

She tried to turn to look at him but he held her fast. His grip tightened again.

'Do we understand one another, Lisieux?'

She expelled the breath she was holding and nodded slowly. He released her arm and let go of the Luger. She felt him move away. She continued to look straight ahead, where Hélène and Graf stood together, the German's hand resting reassuringly on her daughter's shoulder.

The square, empty a minute ago, was beginning to fill with activity. Leutnant Neiss, paler and more worried than ever, had appeared at the mairie door. With him was the Wehrmacht motorcyclist, gun in hand. An armoured car lurched in from rue du Port, its troopers leaping to the ground even before it stopped.

Père François Lachanau bounded down the steps of his church, death calling him yet again. Villagers edged their way along rue du Centre and up from rue du Port, torn between curiosity and caution. Mirabaud skipped alongside them, singing as though on the way to a carnival. Outside the Villa Normandie, Musset the postman was picking himself up from the ground, the gunfire having sent him diving for cover.

One tiny figure seemed unconcerned with safety. Elbows pistoning, her shawl falling disregarded from her shoulders, Adeline Fougeret puffed at full speed along rue du Centre in search of her dear Adalard.

The only person backing away from the scene, pausing to lean his pushbike against a hip while he lit a cigarette, was

Gaspard Baignères.

Graf had disappeared into the mairie. Jeanne saw that Hélène was now looking directly at her. There was understanding as well as fear in the girl's eyes. She knew it was not cleaning duties that had brought her mother here; just as she knew the decision she had made, if not the reason. She inclined her head a fraction, just once; as if she might be thanking her mother.

Jeanne held her daughter's gaze until a warm hand grasped her own trembling hand.

'Come home, Maman,' said Isabelle.

Half an hour later the body had been cleared away. These days bald Coeffeteau the stonemason had taken over Jacques Colinet's wagon and bony horse and with them his grisly task, hoping for favour one day from the Reich if it ever got around to rebuilding or repairing what it had ruined. His dreams were of staircases and crenellations and repairs that could be put in hand, and perhaps, if he was lucky and canny enough, of fees and inflated estimates of cost.

Meanwhile, all that was left of Adalard Fougeret was another bloodstain on the streets of Caillons. François Lachanau shook his head sadly as he passed it and climbed the steps to the mairie. Another dead parishioner, another batch of paperwork to fill in for Leutnant Neiss.

'Adalard was an old man whose heart was broken,' the priest told Graf angrily as he completed the forms. 'You broke that heart, Graf, you and your kind. You broke his mind too. That shotgun was even older than him. It would have blown him to eternity.'

'He was the father of one of the three criminals we despatched the other week. When the blood's bad, it's bad from father to son.'

'What about from mother to daughter?' replied Lachanau. He had seen Graf and Hélène after the shooting; he had seen her clinging like ivy to the oberleutnant. He had seen her compliant nods and trusting glances in response to whatever the oberleutnant was whispering to her, the gap so slight between their bodies.

Graf's face darkened. He looked like he might throttle the priest on the spot or give the Luger another airing. But at that moment Neiss looked up from his typing.

'I'll have the report ready in an hour, Herr Oberleutnant,' he announced. 'You can sign it off if you wish.'

Graf tore his blistering gaze from the priest.

'What report? What is it this time?'

'My report for the major about this morning's incident.'

'You and your damned reports. There's nothing to report. The old man tried to shoot me. I shot him first. Report ends.'

'I must beg to differ, Herr Oberleutnant. I saw everything from my office. So did the motorcycle messenger and he has agreed that I may include his account. We both saw the same thing – Monsieur Fougeret was pointing his gun at Hélène Dupré, not you.'

'Rubbish. Why would he want to kill her?'

'I don't know, Herr Oberleutnant. Do you? Is there anything special about her?' he asked innocently.

Graf bristled but managed to rein himself in. 'The old man knew I'd be there. He was lying in wait to ambush me.'

'With respect, Herr Oberleutnant, the gun was pointing at Mademoiselle Dupré until your intervention. The messenger and I could see that. This was in fact a dispute between two civilians. Monsieur Fougeret has been seen hanging about the streets for no good reason in the last few days, so it's likely he was waiting for his opportunity to

267

attack her. Your life was not in immediate danger until you placed yourself, of your own volition, in the line of fire. The correct response would have been to require the armed civilian to put his weapon down, warning him that you would take any necessary measures including lethal force if he did not. If he failed to comply, you would then have been at liberty to open fire. Unfortunately you didn't issue such a caution. Instead you intervened in a way that could have drawn his fire on your own person.'

'What's your point, Neiss?'

'No point, Herr Oberleutnant. Only to advise you that it might be viewed that as a representative of the Reich you involved the Reich inappropriately in a civilian matter and then concluded that matter in an incorrect manner. Which will be in my report for the major to consider. So, no point at all, Herr Oberleutnant, only that – and of course to let you know that you have the option of signing the report off if you wish and adding any comments of your own. But naturally I have to send the report anyway. The major's instructions were perfectly clear.'

'Type the damned thing in quintuplicate and a dozen colours, for all I care. I won't be signing it.'

'Maybe Adalard had you both in his sights,' suggested Lachanau. 'Two birds with one stone.'

Graf glowered at him, then turned on his heel and strode off.

15

Under cover of night, in the countryside to the north-east of Houlgate a solitary Wehrmacht truck was moving along the narrow roads that followed the coastline. It progressed slowly in order to minimise its engine noise. It passed cottages and isolated farmhouses where nothing stirred, where no lights were to be seen and the occupants, hopefully sensible law-abiding citizens, would be fast asleep. The intention of the fresh-faced young leutnant in the front of the truck was that they should stay that way; and if they were not asleep and especially if they were not law-abiding, that they should not be drawn to their windows or an alarm raised.

The vehicle passed along an avenue of beech trees and shortly afterwards turned inland towards a small cluster of white-painted cottages. Near them stood a little church, not much bigger than any one of the cottages. Behind the church was a thicket of trees, dark against the night sky.

The leutnant's information was imperfect. He understood and accepted this. A stranger had been observed; the stranger had come and gone; he might have come back again; he might still be present in one of the cottages; he might equally well be in any of the other houses in the vicinity that the truck had passed, for there was no telling whether an entire network was involved or how extensive its tentacles might be.

These questions were the first imperfect part of the leutnant's information. The perfect part was the testimony extracted from a certain obergefreiter who had been on duty some days earlier in a section of the coastal defence structures in Houlgate. Yes, he admitted before losing consciousness, there were two priests, one of them the priest who lived here, in one of these white cottages. And that was as far as the obergefreiter could go, however many of his bones his interrogators broke, for he had not recorded and could not recall the name of the second priest. Only that he had claimed to be on his way to … oh, somewhere else entirely; French place names were confusing.

These woeful omissions were the second imperfect part of the leutnant's information, an imperfection for which the obergefreiter would pay with three years' hard labour in an STO camp; which in effect meant that he would pay with his life long before he got to three years. All because the sun had been too hot that morning and he had been too lazy; thus recalled the gunner who had raised the alert about the two priests and the troopers who had reported their indolent obergefreiter.

But the fresh-faced young leutnant was efficient where the hapless obergefreiter was slapdash. He read the daily communiqués. He knew about the enemy agent suspected to have been landed in the vicinity of Caillons.

The young leutnant was also ambitious. He had heard about the new man Graf who was shaking things up in Caillons and whose name was on the communiqué about the enemy agent. Taking an agent would be a great achievement for the leutnant in its own right. But even if he failed in that, perhaps it would be no bad thing to let this man Graf know that here in Houlgate was a leutnant who was vigilant and fervent in his wish to serve the Reich.

The leutnant told his driver to stop the truck a good two hundred metres away from the cottages. Lights out, engine off. He led eight of his men quietly along the lane and dispersed four of them around the priest's cottage. He stationed a pair on each side of the doorway. Then, as any civilised visitor would at this hour, he knocked gently and apologetically on the door.

No answer. He knocked again, a fraction louder. This time he was rewarded by the sound of a sleepy voice within, then a clunk and a groan as something was stumbled into, then the voice again, still sleepy but moving closer. Light showed beneath the door.

As soon as the door began to open, the four troopers pushed in. Two threw the night-shirted priest to the floor and kept him there at gunpoint while the others searched the place – which was rapidly done because there were only two rooms, one downstairs and one upstairs, and precious little in the way of furniture and hiding places. They returned empty handed but the leutnant knew that was not the end of it; everything would be cleared into the truck and searched thoroughly. He flicked the light off and on to signal the truck to approach. Time to rouse and search the other cottages. Short of raiding every home in the area, that was as much as could be done tonight.

An hour later all the white cottages had been searched and Père Mathieu, his books, papers, clothing and other belongings were on their way to Houlgate.

'It's the crows,' said Graf a couple of hours later.

'Crows?' queried the fresh-faced young leutnant.

'The black crows. The priests.'

Houlgate's Kommandantur, the Villa Onexis on boulevard Saint-Philbert, was peaceful now. In the basement a couple of the leutnant's men were tidying things up, hosing down the walls and rolling Père Mathieu's corpse into a blanket, the easier to lug it upstairs and out to the truck. Graf neither knew nor cared how or where they

271

would dispose of it; Houlgate was the young leutnant's headache, not his.

The two men stood side by side on the open first-floor balcony, taking their ease in the cool night air after their labours with the priest: fruitless labours, for neither Père Mathieu nor his few modest possessions had told them anything. Despite that disappointment, the young leutnant was enjoying this comradely interlude, Graf and he, just the two of them, man to man, for Graf had made it clear that the leutnant had done exactly the right thing in arresting the priest and sending for him. The fact that the oberleutnant had been silent for the last few minutes, deep in thought, did not matter; in fact, it was even better this way, a sort of privileged access, a form of trust.

Now Graf nipped his cigarette end between finger and thumb and flicked it into the darkness. The glowing stub, trailing sparks like a tiny comet, sailed in a pleasing parabola over the narrow strip of lawn to land in another little explosion of sparks on the street below, where the black Citroën was parked. The young leutnant contemplated how agreeable it would be to cruise about in a sophisticated machine like that, dashing wherever he was needed, in the way that Jürgen Graf had sped into Houlgate tonight.

On the other side of the boulevard, beyond where the cigarette had landed, stood a church, l'Église Saint-Aubin de Houlgate. Unlike Mathieu's little white-painted place of worship, it was large and imposing with many elegant Gothic windows and doorways and its fair share of spires, and built of good brick and stone. Graf nodded in its direction.

'You see those holy bastards over there?' he said. 'Look at the place. They're as rich as Jews, the priests. You think there might be a network. Well, I agree. That's the network.

272

It's them – the priests, the crows.'

'France is full of priests,' said the leutnant, gratified that his idea was being well received. 'Normandy is full of priests.'

'It's *alive* with them, like a rat is alive with fleas. There's one particular holy bastard in Caillons.'

'You plan to arrest him?' The leutnant felt a twinge of anxiety. Action in Caillons would cut him out.

'One day. But not tonight.'

The leutnant was relieved.

'That might be where the trail begins,' continued Graf. 'But it's not where it's going.'

'No, it's not.' Agreement felt safe.

'And that's what matters. Caillons to Houlgate. Work it out.'

The leutnant tried. But fortunately Graf was speaking for his own benefit. It was he who had worked it out.

'The Atlantic Wall, that's where it goes. Look at the facts. The agent is dropped in Caillons – one of the few places in Normandy where we haven't yet started building the defences. That's why they land him there – doesn't make his purpose too obvious if he's caught, but close enough for him to get to the Wall here in Houlgate – which is exactly where he came. Not right into Houlgate – again, too dangerous – but safely outside. And where does he go with the priest? Directly to the coastal defences. That's who the other priest was – the agent.'

'Yes, that's it.'

'So now the question isn't why Caillons. It's why Normandy.'

Graf wrested his thoughts away from that question and focused on the leutnant. He knew the young man had no clue, but he could still serve a useful purpose.

'I have to get back to Caillons,' Graf told him. 'But

there's a job for you to do here. Vital to the security of the Reich. I can tell you with certainty that the trail will go from here to Cabourg, then continue along the coast. I guarantee it. This man is masquerading as a priest and those black crows are his network. We have to stop him.'

'I can't arrest all the priests from Cabourg onwards, Herr Oberleutnant. Even if that was possible, I don't have authority beyond Houlgate. My major –'

'You don't have to arrest every priest. That's the worst thing you could do. The agent would hear about it and go to ground. The priests you should look for aren't in big fancy palaces like that eyesore.' Meaning l'Église Saint-Aubin. 'You're after the ones who are tucked away, like our friend tonight.' Down on the boulevard two troopers were loading a rolled blanket into the back of the truck. 'Not all crows are big and noisy. Look in the countryside, off the beaten track. Talk to them but be discreet. Have a pretext. Don't alarm them. Sniff around where they live. See if anything feels off, suspicious. If it does, bring them in and send for me. No wholesale arrests, no sweeps. Precision work. Got it?'

The leutnant nodded. Precision work. He liked the sound of that. He felt purposeful, chosen.

'You may have done even better tonight than I thought, Leutnant. Any questions?'

'Thank you, Herr Oberleutnant. Yes, I have one question.'

'Ask.'

'The priest tonight, he kept mumbling about somewhere called Oissel. There seemed to be a woman involved, a widow I think. None of it made sense.'

'It's their tactic to foil interrogation – concentrate on something and keep thinking about it and nothing else. This Père Mathieu, he may have seemed unskilled but that was part of his skill. He was in fact highly trained, that's why we couldn't break him.'

'Experienced too, perhaps.'

'Highly experienced.'

The leutnant nodded. This Oberleutnant Graf was so wise.

Père Gilbert Trèves greeted Benedict like an old friend on his return to Varaville. But the rheumy eyes behind the heavy spectacles were anxious.

'I feared I wouldn't see you again, Nicolas. Thanks be to God for your safety but I believe you're in grave danger.'

'Dangerous times for all of us.'

'Things have been happening. Better to speak inside.' As before, he led Benedict into the back room, his stiff limbs seeming to creak as he hurried along. 'I've made a list. It may not be complete –'

'A list of what?'

'Priests across this part of Normandy who've suddenly been arrested for no obvious reason. I don't know which of my brothers in Christ have been helping you, but it may mean the Boche are onto you.'

'Show me the list.'

It took only a moment for Benedict to scan it. A melancholy moment. He recognised four of the names and locations: Mathieu in Houlgate, Vincent in Douvres-la-Délivrande, Hugues in Arromanches, Philippe in Vierville. But there were other names he did not know, suggesting that the trawl was based on hunch and luck rather than solid information.

'They're following my route but I don't think they have hard intelligence,' he said. 'You're the one who may be in danger, Gilbert. You could be next.'

The old man shrugged. 'Priests are difficult torture subjects. We look to the next world rather than seeking to

275

alleviate our pain in this one. What can the Boche threaten me with?'

'I have one more thing to ask of you, Gilbert.'

'I know.' The priest cast a glance at the black telephone in the corner. 'The instruction was to wait, to see if you made it back this far. And you have, by the grace of God.'

'You remember what to say?'

'All I need is for you to tell me how many.'

'One pair. Only one.'

'I'll make the call at the appointed time. Don't worry – God will see to it that the Boche don't get to me first.'

'Nothing lackadaisical, then.'

In Caillons it was that moment, precious and fleeting, when afternoon finally slipped into dusk. As Jeanne watched, the fields and the headland turned from green to burnished gold; soon the empty lantern panes of the lighthouse would seem to be on fire.

She made her way down towards the port, watching the boats as they returned to the bay. The gulls' hopeful cries as they pursued the nets mingled with the chimes of the mairie clock reminding her that curfew was only half an hour away. But that was fine; she had time enough.

Gérard Leroux's boat was already moored. He was walking along the breakwater when he saw her. He crossed to the road where she could reach him, then turned and stood looking out to sea while he rolled a cigarette. No one was within earshot. She walked past behind him, a couple of metres away, slowing her pace only marginally.

'Our losses have been heavy, Gérard. Our ranks are depleted.'

'I know two men who are willing. Reliable men who know guns.'

'Speak to them and decide. I trust your judgement. I have

276

a request – will you be my second-in-command?'

He bent his head to light the cigarette. 'I'd be honoured.'

'Good. France has work for us.'

She would wait until midnight. Then she would recover the MP40 from the cleft in the beech tree where she had hidden it. For eternity, she had thought. But eternity would have to wait.

She continued walking, her thoughts running as clear as the ocean.

'Yes?'

'Is this Élysées three-five-nine, two-two-eight-three?'

'It is.'

'So this is the workshop of Monsieur Cazarin?'

'It is, but we're closed now.'

'Can you take my order? It's for a pair of candlesticks. I know which design. I only want one pair. Only one.'

'One pair is no problem, but you'll have to call back tomorrow.'

'I see. I apologise for disturbing your evening. Goodnight.'

Gilbert heard the footsteps approach outside. He replaced the telephone handset as gently as possible, breaking the connection without making the bell resound, and moved away to distance himself from the apparatus. If his voice had been heard he could claim to have been praying – a lie but in a good cause.

The knock on the door that came a moment later was restrained and polite. Gilbert sighed and opened the door. The fresh-faced young leutnant who was waiting outside removed his battledress cap and smiled apologetically.

'Père Gilbert Trèves?'

'Yes.'

The young leutnant's smile grew broader. 'If ever a

277

church and its priest could be said to be tucked away, off the beaten track, that's certainly you, Monsieur.'

He stood aside and the four armed troopers accompanying him marched into Gilbert's little house.

16

The morning sun was sending broad shafts of light across Klaus Ebermann's office. Leutnant Ernst Neiss stood rigidly at attention as the major, now returned from Germany, arranged on his desk the reports that the leutnant had worked so diligently to compile in his absence. They could not have made happy reading; they were not what a man wanted when he was burying and mourning his wife and children.

Neiss sighed quietly. Truth, the poet had written, was a torch; but he had also warned that it could burn.

The major set the last report in place.

'Let me summarise,' he said. 'Correct me where necessary.'

'Yes, Herr Major.'

Ebermann positioned a forefinger on the first report. 'Graf has not apprehended the enemy agent – if the agent exists. Alternatively, if the purpose of the enemy aircraft was to deliver arms or other matériel, he has not uncovered any such items. Indeed, on the night in question his troops failed to impede or damage or deflect the aircraft in any way, allowing it to inflict massive casualties. All this in addition to the explosions on the railway line at La Vierge and the access lane to the barracks, which the oberleutnant failed to prevent and in connection with which he has made no arrests. The nearest he came was the STO evader Charles Meslin, whose death seems to be the result of Graf's ineptitude while attempting to capture him.'

'Yes, Herr Major.'

The finger moved to the next report.

'The oberleutnant arrested the man Colinet on strong evidence of his involvement in the earlier assault on Wehrmacht personnel but failed to prevent the prisoner's suicide. Thus a captive was lost to us who could have provided valuable intelligence on Resistance activities and participants, and who may also have had information on the enemy aircraft and whether an agent really has been landed and what his mission was or may still be.'

'Yes, Herr Major.'

Ebermann sighed; the finger moved on.

'The oberleutnant was responsible for the destruction of a memorial to the Weltkreig dead of Caillons, a wanton and vindictive act likely to achieve nothing other than bringing the Reich into disrepute among the occupied population. The French war dead of that earlier generation may have been our forefathers' enemies but we're not animals, Neiss. We honour the fallen, of whatever era, and whether friend or foe.'

'Yes, Herr Major.'

'Then there was the death of the man Clavier, another STO evader and who might have been a source of intelligence on others of his kind. The deaths also of the Voinets, father and son, both ordinary tradesmen with no charges against either of them. And most disturbing of all, there was the killing of an innocent child, Olivier Sulot, seven years old. Have I overlooked anything so far?'

'No, Herr Major.'

Ebermann shook his head and repositioned the forefinger.

'Next we have the shooting of the elderly Adalard Fougeret, admittedly a man who was armed and had clear intent to kill. You acknowledge that there is disagreement between you and Graf as to whether the target was Graf himself or a French female civilian who was in close proximity to him at the time. Depending on one's view on that, there is the possibility that Graf did not follow proper procedure, thereby bringing the Reich into disrepute. I note that your account and your opinion that Graf was not the primary target are supported by the Wehrmacht messenger.'

'That is correct, Herr Major.'

'I have to admit that as regards that particular incident I would be prepared to excuse Graf's action to a degree, given the emergency in which he found himself and irrespective of the gunman's target – for example, if the oberleutnant had only wounded the man in order to disarm him. Had he fired only once and even if that shot had been lethal, perhaps I might still excuse him since he had to act in the heat of the moment. But he fired several times – and then he shot the man in the head. This after examining the body, which would have given him ample opportunity to see that the man was already dead or at least incapacitated. This sequence of events suggests an act of calculated malice, for which there can be no excuse.'

'No, Herr Major.'

'All this on top of the summary execution of ten civilians on the night of the screening of the Ministry for Public Enlightenment and Propaganda's information films.'

'With respect, Herr Major, you provided signed approval for that. I have it on file.'

'I regret it now. I allowed the oberleutnant to convince me it was a necessary measure. In fact, he requested permission to execute twenty or even thirty men. Instead of merely refusing that request, I should have seen it for what it was – a warning sign of his instability. Now we have bodies beginning to come to shore, most of them not even in my own zone of control, causing confusion to other jurisdictions.'

Ebermann drew his hand down his cheek. He looked very tired. He set the report down and went to the window. The square below was almost deserted in the early morning.

'And now we have the girl, Hélène Dupré,' he said softly.

'Yes, Herr Major.'

Unseen by Ebermann, Neiss quickly mopped his brow, for they were now entering dangerous territory. Hélène Dupré, daughter of the major's former lover. Or possibly to-be-renewed lover, depending on which way the wind might be blowing.

And the major had just buried a daughter of his own.

By any measure, then, dangerous territory.

'The accusation you've made against Graf is very grave.'

'Yes, Herr Major.'

'She's a child.'

'Two years older than the age required by French law, Herr Major, but illegal under our law.'

'A child, Neiss. Physically impaired. He has abused his authority as a representative of the occupying power. Unsoldierly. Inhuman.'

'Yes, Herr Major.'

'How strong is the evidence?'

'Irrefutable, I'm afraid, Herr Major. There's an old cottage –'

'There are witnesses, you say.'

'Yes, Herr Major. Patrols saw them entering and leaving. On multiple occasions. Further, an obergefreiter has reported seeing items belonging to the oberleutnant in Hélène Dupré's home when it was searched.'

'And it turns out that the Dupré girl is the female civilian who was in proximity to the oberleutnant when the gunman Fougeret attacked.'

'Yes, Herr Major.'

'Possibly lending weight to your view that it was she who

was his primary target – as a collaborator, for example.'

'That's possible, Herr Major.'

Ebermann returned to his desk. 'Tell me something, Leutnant Neiss.'

'Yes, Herr Major.' Neiss would have liked to use the handkerchief again. This talk of collaborators was very unsettling. There were those in Caillons who saw Jeanne Dupré in that light; surely the major knew that.

'How could our situation in Caillons be worse? What could reduce further the low regard in which the population of Caillons holds its German occupier? Or the low regard in which Graf's troops must now hold him? Tell me, Leutnant Neiss. I'd be most interested to know.'

Neiss had no answer.

Next door, in the Villa Normandie, Jeanne heard the outer door open and close as Madame Guinard arrived. She called a greeting and heard the old woman's reply. She broke off from her polishing of the great table in the dining hall – a table at which still sat the ghosts of her mother and father and where she still saw a young Jeanne and Pierre Rochard and, later, her own Hélène and Isabelle and Michel – and went out to the entrance hall, cloth and tin of polish in hand.

'So the major's back from Germany,' said Madame Guinard.

'Late last night.'

'I'll get breakfast under way.'

'No need. He's gone already. He's at work in the mairie.'

'No stopping him. Lunch, then.'

Jeanne made to return to the dining hall, then turned back to Madame Guinard as though an idea had that moment occurred to her.

'Perhaps something special for his dinner tonight.'

'Why? To welcome him back? He's Boche.'

'He's a bereaved husband and father.'

Madame Guinard fixed a hard gaze on Jeanne and said nothing.

'That dessert he likes,' Jeanne persisted. 'The one with almonds. Gebrannte Mandeln.'

'Hmph,' grumped the old woman, and continued on to the kitchen.

An hour later, as the rich odours of vanilla and cinnamon and almonds and caramelised sugar drifted through the halls and corridors of the Villa Normandie, Jeanne finished her cleaning duties and unlocked the door to the sous-sol. Ten minutes after that she left the Villa Normandie and returned to La Croisette. Her cleaning basket was hooked as usual over her arm. It was the heaviest the basket had ever been.

On a shelf well out of sight in the sous-sol of the Villa Normandie sat her tins of polish and her neatly folded cleaning cloths.

In London's Baker Street there was a hum of activity that the colonel sensed as soon as he entered the vestibule. The place was always busy but this morning things were buzzing at a distinctively elevated level. Clerks and planners rushed up and down the staircase, some of them so preoccupied that they even failed to notice him. Far from taking umbrage, for a few moments he indulged himself: the years were shed and he was part of a team again, no more and no less important than any other member, rather than the grand old man who ruled all of them with Olympian detachment and was expected to know all the answers.

Then someone bade him good morning and he was the grand old man again. He climbed in his ponderous way to the first floor, keeping a firm hold on the banister with his good hand and staying well out of the way of the young tornadoes as they flew past.

'We're bringing Avignon out,' explained the thin man, who clearly had not slept or shaved. 'Our man in Paris received the phone call last night. He passed the word to us and we alerted Danton by radio. Our message was acknowledged and the correct code words were used at Danton's end to confirm no enemy intervention. So everything's in order, everything will be ready. It's game on.'

'When do we fetch him?'

'Tonight.'

The colonel raised an eyebrow. Short notice indeed; that explained the extra buzz about the place.

'Time for me to tell you about Danton, though,' added the thin man.

'Problem?'

'Not with Danton. Possibly with Paris, according to Danton. Our communist pals, to be precise. Danton's had suspicions for some time. He's been running a check on them. The snare tightens today.'

The colonel eased himself behind the desk and dug out his pipe and tobacco. All these long years at this game and he still felt his pulse quickening as things came to a head.

'So tell me,' he said as he began to pack the pipe.

Bertrand Mercier's sawmill lay deep in the heart of the bois de Caillons. This morning, as on so many of these long, empty days without work – even the felling and preparation of Graf's three execution stakes had been denied the sawmill – the place was deserted, its machinery shut down and weeds creeping through the carpet of wood shavings and sawdust.

Jeanne had stepped into the clearing at the same moment as Gérard and Paul Leroux, all three of them having made their way up from the village and the port separately, to avoid drawing attention. She joined the brothers in the long shed that housed the great conveyor and the circular saw, its blade rusting and dull. Insects buzzed around them and birds swooped beneath the shingled eaves. Coarse grasses pushed through splits in the belt of the conveyor. Jeanne tore off a handful of seed heads and let the seeds fall through her fingers. Even in this dead place, life could not be quashed.

'The Germans executed Bertrand Mercier's brother and two cousins in Évreux last year,' said Gérard. He spoke very quietly, not much more than a whisper. 'They were résistants. Bertrand has been begging for months to be allowed to join us. I've always told him I was no résistant and had no idea what he was talking about. He's a hunter, so he's knowledgeable about firearms. And he has three or four good rifles hidden away.'

'Useful. And Auguste Sulac?'

'Also a hunter. He and Bertrand hunt and trap together. He's a thatcher by trade and also works for Bertrand – or he used to, when the work was there. They're good friends, they know each other's ways, they'll operate well together. Auguste had Jewish family connections in Germany. Now the Jewish relatives are all gone – the death camps. You may remember his wife, Valérie?'

'Died a few months ago. Tuberculosis.'

'Like Bertrand, Auguste has also wanted to join us for a long time but in his case Valérie was the problem – she was too frightened to allow it.'

'So now he's a free man.'

'As free as any of us can be.'

Paul, who had stationed himself where he could watch the

woods, raised a hand.

'They're here,' said Gérard.

A few moments later Mercier and Sulac appeared at the end of the shed. Jeanne had not heard their approach. It was a good start; they knew their hunters' craft.

'Don't waste your time,' Mercier told Paul, who was still watching the woods. 'There's not a German in France who could follow us.'

Brisk handshakes followed. There was preliminary talk, brief and in low voices, of what weapons and ammunition the new arrivals could provide and of what was expected of them as cell members.

'Gérard is my second-in-command,' Jeanne concluded. 'He'll tell you more when you need to know more.'

'You mean if you decide we can be trusted,' said Mercier.

'Yes, since you ask. That's also why we're meeting here instead of the cell's usual place. Gérard has vouched for you but we take one step at a time.'

'I don't have a problem with that,' said Sulac. 'Neither does Bertrand. Did you bring us here merely to meet us?'

'No time for that,' said Jeanne. 'We have an immediate task. It needs both of you.'

Gérard was frowning. 'Immediate? Tonight?'

'No, today. Daylight hours. Night is when this cell has always mounted its operations. So it's time for a different strategy.'

'Has this been authorised by Danton? You said these things have to be.'

This time the question was from Paul Leroux. Mercier and Sulac turned to him, puzzled by a name they did not recognise; but they said nothing, sensing his tension.

'I said that Danton's authorisation is needed for actions of an exceptional nature, such as something that might cut across cell territories.'

'I'd call an operation in broad daylight exceptional. And it'll be risky moving around with weapons in daylight and setting up.'

'We'll have explosive as well,' Jeanne told him. 'Detonators, magneto.'

Paul looked even more unhappy but said no more.

She looked around them, much as she had looked around on that night when she had taken on the cell's leadership. She waited for further questions. Or challenges.

It was Bertrand Mercier who spoke.

'Night's fine for trapping but daytime's best for hunting. We're here to hunt, aren't we? So let's hunt.'

Gaspard forced down a cup of Sulot's coffee – the fake stuff, to his chagrin, not Graf's reserve – by way of breakfast while he listened to the talk in Café du Marché. There was no real news, nothing but the usual moaning and groaning, plenty of it about Jeanne Dupré, plus a new theme for the assembly to get its teeth into: Jeanne's Nazi-loving daughter, whom many had seen cosying up to Graf in place de l'Église when old Adalard almost did for them both. There were even those who were adamant that Graf had put himself deliberately between Adalard's gun barrel and her, the little vixen. Young love, they cackled humourlessly. Blood will out, was the consensus.

Sulot himself was still teary over the death of little Olivier, as were the two or three sisters who lumbered into and out from the kitchen, so no fresh gossip was forthcoming from any of them. Gaspard collected some debts and agreed a couple of small loans, recording everything in his notebook, then lit a Gitane to get rid of the taste of the coffee, settled the oilcloth cap in place and cycled for home.

The little professor sprang from the bushes as he arrived

at the cottage – the same bushes that had given cover to the Jewish woman and her charges. Gaspard swung the pushbike sharply to one side and skidded to a stop.

'You'll be the death of me, Professor.'

Behind the tortoiseshell spectacles the stray eye sought the far distance while the good one focused on Gaspard.

'My apologies. But if you knew the journey I've had.'

'No vélo today?'

The professor pushed some of the shrubbery aside with his foot. Gaspard saw part of a grimy black frame and wheel.

'Had to hide it – you weren't here,' the professor said accusingly as he followed Gaspard indoors. 'My God, what a journey. Mail train from Paris, middle of the night, I wasn't even awake. My Ausweiss is of alarmingly poor quality as forgeries go – even I can see that. But I was on the train before I knew this. My people in Paris are in so much panic I think they simply accepted whatever they could get. But it's my neck. The guard on the train, he looked and looked at the Ausweiss. You know how they do. Put a man of a certain type into a uniform and he thinks he's God. Awful night, awful journey. My God.'

'Cheer up, Professor. Think of the heroic tales you can tell about yourself when this is all over. Think of the memoirs you'll write.'

'My God, if I survive.'

'God this and God that. You're in a profane mood this morning. But you're a communist, you don't believe in God, so you have no right to take his name in vain.'

The professor looked hurt. The large eyes swivelled. 'An innocent turn of phrase.'

'With no potency for an atheist. Pick someone meaningful. You should be swearing by Nietzsche or Kant.'

'A German or a Prussian?'

Gaspard scratched his chin. 'Fair enough. Then you do need God after all – and not only for swearing by.'

'Do I?'

'Certainly, because you need what our German friends call angst – in your case existential angst. You think you're stricken by it but in fact you need it. Can't get by without it. But if God exists, you can't have it. A logical impossibility. So you can't allow God. You'd have no purpose. There'd be no point to you, Professor.'

'Oh dear. No point – but isn't that my point? In the meantime, do you have anything for breakfast? That would be a purposeful way to take the discussion forward.'

His host was already fetching platters and tins from the larder. 'You're in luck, I need a decent coffee, you can join me for that. Bread too. And butter, though it's German style this time. Are you too much of a patriot for German butter, too proud to stoop to that?'

'Never too proud when it comes to butter. Real coffee, bread and butter. Any sugar for the coffee?'

Gaspard nodded.

'An entire book of coupons,' said the professor. 'I hope you're in no hurry to get yourself a radio man.'

'Don't get me wrong, Professor – I enjoy your visits and I appreciate the comrades in Paris helping me out, sending you here with my messages. But I need my own radio operator, here on the spot.'

'What happened to your previous one? I've often wondered.'

Gaspard cocked his thumb and mimicked a gunshot. 'They never last long, radio operators. The Boche are getting good at triangulating the signals. So you enjoy your jaunts down here, do you?'

'They're dangerous but they have their compensations. I trust they're worth your while too. This one should be no exception. I have more news for you, my friend.'

'I figured as much.'

The good eye winked conspiratorially. 'Two nights, they said to tell you. That's what.'

Gaspard set plates on the table. 'Two. You're sure? Not one, not three?'

'Two nights.'

'Counting from when?'

'Last night.'

'So – tomorrow night.'

'How's breakfast coming along? Someone I know said always to eat first when there's news.'

'At least some of your intellectual influences are sound.'

With so many Germans in Deauville and Trouville, there was plenty of work in the two towns. And plenty of work meant plenty of people crossing pont de l'Union in both directions each morning. All Benedict had to do was slip in among them, one more nondescript figure in the crowd. No detour this time, no little boat in the moonlight, no drunken boatman.

As he crossed into Trouville a Wehrmacht truck came rattling and bumping past him. Up in the cab beside the driver sat a fresh-faced young leutnant with a fervent glint in his eye, the glint of a young man with his sights set high. Too high, as it happened, to notice the priest pedalling along in the stream of people on the road below.

As for Benedict, he was not minded to gaze up at every Wehrmacht truck that passed. He kept his head down and pushed doggedly on.

'Important work – and soon,' Gaspard had said.

The coffee jar was on the windowsill of La Croisette, exactly where Père Lachanau said he had found the first one. Jeanne picked it up and examined it: same squat glass jar, same English text, same illustration of an elegantly robed Arab. And inside, a small folded square of paper. All exactly as before.

She slipped the paper into her pocket, took the jar into the cottage and hid it safely away. Then she set off for the icehouse and the one-time pads.

'You have to call off today's operation,' was Gérard Leroux's verdict an hour later. 'This takes priority.'

'No. We go ahead as planned. But we do it without you.'

'What?'

'You stay behind. If today goes against us and I don't get back, you take over.' She held up the transcription. 'Which means you deal with this.'

'What if none of you gets back?'

'Then you do this alone. I'll tell you everything you need to know.' She put a match to the transcription. 'Luc Clavier showed you how to handle the explosive, how to set it up. Yes?'

'Yes.'

'Then I need you to show Paul how to do it.'

Route du Littoral began at the crossroads of La Vierge, followed a long curve on its approach to Caillons with a few sharp turns along the way, and finally merged with rue du Phare on the outskirts of the village. About a kilometre before that merging of roads, there was a place where the land on one side rose high enough and was wooded enough to afford a person a perfect location from which to set an ambush on the road below, should they be that way inclined.

Jeanne was that way inclined.

There was a drain that carried a stream beneath the road. But the stream was only a stream when enough rain had

292

fallen to feed it. The rest of the time, as now, it was merely a dusty hollow. In that circumstance the clay drainpipe provided a ready-made receptacle for a large quantity of Nobel 808 explosive, should a person be inclined to pack it full.

She was that way inclined too.

The explosive had been laid and the cell was now installed in position on the wooded slope. She had arranged the team in two ranks: the new members in front, five metres apart; herself and Paul Leroux above and behind them. She had her left hand on the magneto plunger but her right on the MP40. She released the safety.

'If you make a wrong move,' she told Mercier and Sulac, 'if we think you're infiltrators, we shoot you.'

'In the back?' said Mercier.

'In the back of the head. You won't even know.'

So the afternoon sun beat down and they waited.

A familiar chug-chug announced the approach of an armoured patrol car. It rounded the bend in the road and came towards them. Two troopers sat up front, two stood in the rear, one of them manning a heavy machine gun. Jeanne had come deliberately without field glasses, the danger of a telltale reflection in daylight being too great, so she strained to make out the men's features as the vehicle ambled closer.

Still holding the MP40, she flexed her grip on the plunger and sensed the surge in tension in the others. She focused on the patrol, scanning the faces.

The vehicle rolled past, continuing towards Caillons. The chug-chug faded.

'Jeanne?'

It was Paul Leroux. She ignored him.

'Something wrong, Jeanne? Jeanne?'

'There were only four of them. We can do better.'

They waited again.

This time it was a truck. She let it too pass.

'It must have had a dozen men aboard,' hissed Leroux. 'What do you want, Jeanne – the whole garrison?'

She was aware that Mercier and Sulac had turned to stare at her, quickly turning away when she looked at them. Their thoughts were plain enough: perhaps Jeanne Dupré had lost her nerve, perhaps they were putting their lives on the line for nothing.

The next vehicle was a half-track. She wiped sweat from her eyes. But there was no need to strain this time. The figure of Jürgen Graf in battledress and helmet was unmistakable. He was standing in the hatch, smoking. She had what she had waited for.

But Graf suddenly barked an order and the half-track came to a stop three metres short of the drain, its engine still running. Graf hoisted himself over the side of the hatch and vaulted down to the road.

'What's he up to?' whispered Leroux.

Mercier raised his hunting rifle and settled into position.

'I can take him,' he said.

'But not all of them,' said Jeanne. 'So hold your fire.'

Graf was the only one she wanted but she had no proof of Mercier's accuracy. He could miss. It was a chance she dared not take. Nobel 808, by contrast, made no mistakes.

Graf strode to the rear of the vehicle. They heard two loud clangs as he kicked the rear hatch.

'Loose door. They'll be on the move now.'

Graf returned to the side of the vehicle. He had one boot on the side plate and was about to climb up when a German voice called out.

'Halt!'

The trooper who had shouted was staring back along the road. He had raised his submachine gun. Two others did the same. Jeanne followed their gaze and their aim. A cyclist, a black-suited figure, had rounded the bend to come into plain view of the troopers. He had stopped as commanded.

Her heart lurched. It was Avignon.

'Herr Oberleutnant,' said the trooper. 'It's a priest.'

Graf looked slowly around, indifferent. A priest? In a land where, as he had lately pointed out, they swarmed like fleas. It was probably that old black crow Lachanau, the last person he wanted to be bothered by today.

But it was not Lachanau. It was a man he had never seen before.

Hardly daring to believe that at last his luck might be on the turn, he ordered the three troopers to hold their positions, detailed two others to accompany him, unholstered his pistol and strolled slowly towards the stranger.

Benedict was furious with himself. How many blind bends in roads and lanes had he approached with proper caution, always stopping to check what was waiting unseen around the corner? Such measures were a nuisance, they slowed him down, but they had kept him alive and his mission safe. And now today, the final day, in his hurry to get back to Caillons, he had behaved like an amateur.

He watched the oberleutnant who was priming his Luger as he approached, as casually as if he were promenading on a Sunday afternoon.

'Who are you?'

'Père Nicolas Marot.'

'Your business here?'

'Passing through on my way to Quinéville.'

'Passing through. So you're not from here?'

'No.'

'I see.' He looked Benedict up and down, then started to

walk slowly behind him. 'Quinéville's a long way.'

'A couple of days' cycling.'

'It's also in the other direction.'

'What?' Benedict swivelled around to look at him. 'Are you sure, Oberleutnant?'

'Quite sure.'

Benedict turned to look back the way he had come, then at the surrounding countryside. He shook his head, mystified.

'I must have taken a wrong turning.'

'Perhaps someone changed the signposts. They do that.'

'It's a disgrace.'

'But in any case, Quinéville is a closed zone – as is this area. You shouldn't be in either one if you're not a resident.'

'I have travel permits and I'll be resident in Quinéville.'

'I see. So where have you come from?'

'Rouen. By train as far as permitted and then by vélo. I brought my vélo on the train.'

'You have your ticket, of course.'

'It was one way, so I didn't keep it.'

The German pursed his lips. 'Unwise. Why are you going to Quinéville?'

'To take up duties in my new parish. That's why I don't have a return ticket.'

The German had prowled back to stand in front of Benedict again. He was standing too close, deliberately. Part of the intimidation treatment. A cloying odour of some kind of perfume or cologne poured from him. He extended a gloved hand.

'So – your papers and those permits, please.'

Benedict slipped a hand inside his jacket. His fingers brushed the Browning. One semi-automatic against five submachine guns plus others in the half-track. Not good odds. His hand moved on and withdrew his identity papers, his travel Ausweiss and the two letters, one from the archbishop and the other from the Militärbefehlshaber authority.

'What's all this?' said the German, examining the envelopes.

'Letters, my permits. They confirm my permission to travel through coastal areas like this to reach my parish. It's the shortest route.'

'But still a couple of days' travel, as you said. So where will you stay at night?'

'With friends.'

'Priests?'

'Of course.'

A broad smile spread over the German's face. He slipped the identity papers and letters into a chest pocket of his battledress and closed the flap with an air of finality.

'But, Oberleutnant –' protested Benedict.

The German motioned to one of the troopers, who came forward and took the pushbike from Benedict.

'Search his bedroll. As for you, Priester – hands behind your head and turn around.'

Benedict turned around. He felt the weight of the Browning.

'Avignon,' said Paul Leroux. 'Wasn't that what he called himself?'

'Yes.'

'If they arrest him they'll take him with them and they'll get moving again. We can still go ahead once they reach the drain. Do it then, Jeanne. Too bad for Avignon. He's not our problem. Fortunes of war.'

'He *is* our problem. He's under our protection.'

Mercier and Sulac were watching her again. They

exchanged a glance.

'Are we doing this or are we just here for fun?' hissed Mercier.

'If anyone opens fire he gets a bullet in the head. From me. That's your last warning. That includes you, Paul.'

She watched as Graf and the troopers approached the Englishman. Neither she nor the others could hear any of the exchange that followed, but it was easy enough to guess its overall direction. They saw Graf prowl around Avignon, they saw papers being handed over and not returned, they saw the trooper unfurling the bedroll and Avignon turning away from Graf and beginning to raise his hands.

Then they saw the Englishman spin full circle, his right arm lowered again and a pistol in his hand. A single pistol against an entire patrol unit. Madness.

She drove the plunger home.

The blast blew Benedict off his feet and flat on his back. The half-track bucked a full metre clear of the road, one tracked side returning to earth half a second before the other, so that the men inside were flung from side to side, crashing against the armoured superstructure. Heads split open, bones splintered, a spine snapped. One of the caterpillar tracks burst apart and flicked out like a whip, crushing one of the troopers who had accompanied Graf along the road. Chunks of asphalt and clay pipe rained down, inflicting more injuries and adding to the troopers' confusion.

Graf was blown forward, colliding with the pushbike. The Luger flew from his fist and landed somewhere in the grass by the roadside. He found himself staring at the head of one of the troopers, complete with helmet and chinstrap but minus body. The eyes were still open. Then the headless body crumpled to the ground beside him.

The shooting began, a barrage of single rounds and submachine-gun bursts. The bodies of still-dazed troopers jerked and fell to the ground or collapsed back into the half-track as the volleys found their marks.

Benedict scrambled to his feet. Instinctively he looked towards the place that was most likely to be the origin of the gunfire, the lightly wooded slope up ahead. As he did so, a figure rose from the undergrowth, a slight figure in an oversized leather blouson and armed with a submachine gun. He leapt to the side of the road, well clear of the gunfire that continued to pin the Germans, and sprinted towards her.

Graf stayed concealed behind the headless body. He had no choice, it was his only cover. He had no weapon and to his frustration the body had been parted from the trooper's submachine gun. The weapon lay only a few metres away – but a deadly few metres, too perilous to cross. Nor could he shift the trooper's body to get at the pistol beneath it. He was helpless.

A movement to one side and behind him signalled that the priest had survived. Not only that, but he was running from the road. More fortunate than Graf had been, he still had that pistol in his hand and was firing at any trooper who still showed signs of life.

But where was he running to?

Graf risked a cautious glance around the body, showing himself as little as possible. What he saw made a cold fury boil up within him. All his suspicions were proven. He pulled back quickly out of sight, cursing more than ever his lack of a firearm.

There she was, submachine gun spitting death at him and his men while the priest – beyond any doubt the elusive enemy agent, and now most assuredly no figment of Graf's imagination – ran towards her, protected by her covering fire. There she was, the filthy little murderess.

Jeanne Dupré.

17

They raced from the scene, weapons in hand or slung over shoulders. Lisieux led the way into a wide tract of woodland.

'You're early,' she accused Benedict as they zig-zagged between the trees. 'The message we received said it would be evening.'

'I made better time.'

'So we have to hide you for longer. And you got in the way of today's operation. Wrecked it and endangered us.'

They ran on for several minutes with no more said. Eventually she slowed to a stop and steadied herself against a tree trunk while she caught her breath. She clutched her side.

'Was Graf dead?' she demanded of Benedict. 'The oberleutnant, the one who challenged you. He didn't return fire. None of them did. Did we kill him? Did you see?'

The others had stopped as well, all of them out of breath and sweating. One of them overheard her questions. He was the only one Benedict recognised from the night of his arrival. He was carrying a magneto box, coils of cable and a short spade.

'Of course Graf's dead,' he said before Benedict could reply. 'They're all dead. If the explosion didn't get them our bullets did. No one came out alive. We got all of them.'

She looked unconvinced. She turned back to Benedict. 'Well?'

He shook his head. Why was one particular German so

important to her?

'He went down, that's all I can tell you. Could be alive, could be dead.'

It was not the answer she wanted. She questioned the other two but neither could claim a direct hit, neither could say they had seen the oberleutnant take a bullet or shrapnel from the blast.

She let the subject drop. They heard a distant whine of vehicle engines, the first sign that the search for them was getting under way. Time to press on.

They left the woods and crossed more fields, always keeping to hedges and walls, sometimes jogging, sometimes slackening their pace to a walk; then came more woodland and patches of thick ferny undergrowth. As they drew closer to Caillons, the other three peeled off in different directions. A touch on Lisieux's shoulder, a hand raised in farewell, then each man was gone.

'My understanding is that you depart tonight,' she said to Benedict. 'I hope that at least is still correct.'

'Yes.'

'Good. The arrangements have been made.'

They were following a wide arc that he reckoned would bring them to the headland and the icehouse. She slowed down to pick her way over logs that had been laid across a small stream.

'I need to talk to you,' he said when they were both across. 'When this is over, you and I –'

It was as far as he got, as if she knew she had to stop him. She rounded on him, her gaze fierce. 'When what is over? This war? You're still thinking like that? There is no you and I, Avignon. You know nothing about me, not even my name. All you know is someone called Lisieux – and who is she? No, tonight you go back to England and I stay here, waiting for the communists to take over if you're to be

302

believed. You and I? A different time, a different place –
who knows? But not this time or this place.'

'People have to keep living,' he reminded her. 'Your
words.'

'Yes, and you should do that. Go back to England and do
exactly that. Now stop wasting time.'

She turned away and resumed running.

After the stream came marshland as damp as any claggy
Lewis peat bog despite the heat. Each step was a struggle
but she pushed ahead with more urgency than ever.

'I'll take you to the icehouse, then I have to get home. If
Graf survived and saw me he'll arrest my daughters. I have
to reach them before he does.'

'Then what?'

She shrugged, shook her head. It was the first time he had
seen uncertainty in her. 'That's not your concern.'

'You saved my life today.'

'I never wanted you here, Avignon, you know that. But
you were entrusted to my protection. Trust has to be
honoured.'

They reached the headland and the cliff. The sound of
Wehrmacht engines was stronger and more insistent. More
vehicles had joined the pursuit. She led him down the
treacherous path in silence. As he was about to pass through
the curtain of undergrowth she slung the MP40 from her
shoulder and handed it to him along with a fresh magazine.

'Your handgun isn't enough. Take this. Let's hope you
won't need it. Return it before you depart tonight. Leave it
on the ground, someone will collect it.'

'Will you be there?'

'If I'm there I'll be out of sight, you won't see me. In any
case it depends on what I find when I get home.' He
thought her expression softened. 'We won't meet again,
Avignon. Go back to England. Find another time, another

place.'

To his surprise she extended her hand to him. They shook hands. Then she looked up and smiled at him. It was uncertain, the smile, marred by the anxiety he knew she was fighting to control; but it was still a smile, the only one he had ever had from her.

Graf was very much alive. Bloodied, bruised and battered, but alive. Livid with anger. And more determined than he had ever been in his life.

Everywhere throughout Caillons, both village and port, his troopers tramped the pavements, clearing people off the streets and ordering them to stay in their homes. It was a daylight curfew, unprecedented in the place's troubled history.

On his orders the shops in rue du Centre were forced to close. Sulot was told at gunpoint to empty Café du Marché immediately and lock up until further notice, leaving coffees and platters of dubious saucisson abandoned, tables unwiped, fat congealing on stacks of unwashed dishes to feed the fat flies. The pétanque players were sent scurrying from allée d'Acadie. Fishing boats returning to port were made to moor up and were forbidden to set out again. Boats scheduled to depart had their passes cancelled. Troopers whose normal job was to make sure that fishing catches went straight to the barracks and in theory were not plundered by local people commandeered a boat and made its crew take them out to the mussel bouchots, where they ordered those inspecting the crop back to port.

Père François Lachanau stared open-mouthed as armed troopers advanced up the aisle of l'Église de Notre Dame de la Mer, chasing away the handful of faithful who were waiting for afternoon confession. When he protested, he was pushed aside by an insolent uniformed youth whose downy cheeks looked as if they had never yet known a razor.

The school was emptied, the terrified children sent fleeing to their homes in tears. Little Hervé Meslin ran the fastest. This time there was no nonsense from Maître Péringuey or Maîtresse Lavisse, though Péringuey's heart was in his mouth until a certain little black-eyed girl was safely out of sight, a Cuisson twin gripping each of her hands as if the child's life depended on their solicitude; which in fact it did.

With the entire garrison engaged in the task, Caillons became a ghost town within the half hour. It was accomplished in almost complete silence: no shouting by the troopers, no screeching trucks, and the population too cowed to argue or raise a whimper of complaint.

Graf positioned his men to encircle La Croisette, directing them over the fields on the windowless sides of the cottage and moving them into locations where they would remain invisible until their time came. No smoking, no talking, and with orders to open fire only on direct command from him and him alone.

Then it was time for him to pay a social call.

Hélène and Isabelle were at home. It was Isabelle who opened the door to him. He knew he presented a shocking sight, his face caked in dirt and blood, a long graze down one side of his jaw, a purple bruise beneath one eye, his battledress torn by the blast and streaked with the blood of his decapitated trooper. But she did not bat an eyelid.

No surprise there, was his thought; as icy as the north wind, this one. He would enjoy his time with her. Younger than Agathe Lanery and Estelle Rousselot, she would provide many hours' satisfying exercise.

'Go away,' she snapped. She tried to close the door but

305

his stout Wehrmacht boot had been placed to block it. He shoved the door open, swatted her aside and entered.

Hélène rose from the table, fear already etched in her face. Ah, this one he would enjoy most of all. More, even, than the mother.

The dark eyes that had once lanced his soul grew wider as she took in the state of him.

'Jürgen, you're safe. I was worried sick. But look at you – let me see. What happened? You're injured.'

'As if you care. No more lies. Sit down – stay where you are.' He turned to Isabelle. 'You too – sit.'

He unholstered the Luger, none the worse for its temporary loss. Hélène stared at it. Her hand went to her throat and closed on something there. It was the fine gold chain he had given her. He reached down and tore it from her neck. She cried out in alarm and pain. A thin streak of blood appeared where the chain had cut into her flesh. He flung the chain down on the table, scattering its broken links to the floor.

'Jürgen, what have I done?'

'Done? Absolutely nothing. That's the problem. Told me nothing, gave me nothing.'

'I gave you everything.'

'You made me think so. I fell for it. What a family, this family you couldn't bear to leave. For once you'll do some real talking.'

'Talk about what?'

'About him.'

The sisters looked at one another.

'Who?' they said in chorus.

'You stay here, both of you, at this table. You don't move from here and you don't say a word – you'll talk later but for now you shut up.'

He removed his helmet and marched about, looking the

place over. Not much to see, only this one room and what looked like an attic or loft above. Worse than he would give a dog.

He clattered up the open stairs to where he could wait unseen.

Deep beneath the Villa Normandie, in the sous-sol that ran the width and length of the great house, Major Klaus Ebermann had heard nothing of the explosion and gunfire far distant at La Vierge. His mind was on other matters, matters that for him were just as devastating.

Nothing could bring him peace. He mourned his family, he loathed the despicable Graf for the damage he had done to the name of Germany, he loathed the German leadership, which had wreaked enough damage even without the oberleutnant's efforts.

But most of all he loathed himself. He had betrayed everyone and everything he held dear: his family, his country, the honour of his uniform. Even Jeanne Dupré. He had used her for the comfort she gave him. He had made her no better than a whore; he had brought that calumny upon her. He should have known that would be the outcome of his use of her. There was not an occupier in history who had not inflicted that status on the occupied. He was as bad as Jürgen Graf. To abuse the daughter or abuse the mother: where was the difference? Which also made him a hypocrite.

Père Lachanau would not absolve him. He had thought to find a priest in Germany who would come to his aid but Catholic priests were becoming few and far between these days and his time there had been short and all spoken for: the funerals, the legal processes. The old priest's warning haunted him, would not dislodge from his mind: 'Your Führer will take you to hell with him.' What if it was true?

What if the sins of the leadership were visited upon all who served it, whether or not they were the ones who pulled the trigger, who turned on the gas, who pumped out the air, who injected the acids, who removed the living organs? What if indeed he could not be absolved without renouncing the entire Reich and all its acts and servants, as the old curé insisted?

Today he had roamed the Villa Normandie from top to bottom, wandering restlessly through room after room. Jeanne Dupré was everywhere in the house wherever he turned. He saw her bent to her cleaning or followed her padding barefoot through the corridors, like the ghost of her own past. He saw her in his bed, once her own marital bed. He saw her when the Villa Normandie had been her childhood home. The old photographs from that lost era before a foreign occupier came to trample her life were still in the house somewhere, probably down here in the sous-sol. Rochard, he thought her family was called. He had no excuse for not being certain; Lachanau had spoken of them often enough.

Thus began his search. In the corridor that led to the kitchens the air was ripe with the scents of vanilla and cinnamon and almonds. Madame Guinard had been busy with that dish of hers that she erroneously thought he enjoyed so much; he had never had the heart to disabuse her. He passed along the corridor, opened the door to the sous-sol, found the light switch and descended the steep stairs to the shadowy spaces below.

He had been down here only once before, the day he arrived to take command of Caillons and the Villa Normandie. All around him were racks of wine, shelves of brandies and cognacs, rows of game birds hanging to age, wheels of cheese, blocks of butter, jars of flour, preserves, sugar, spices and all the raw materials of Madame

Guinard's art, if it could be called that. No shortages here, no call for coupons, no queues. Was that part of his guilt too?

He continued to the furthest area where old furniture and household items were stored, far beyond Madame Guinard's realm. Here the smells were of dust, ancient wood and mouldering books. This was where the photographs would be; he remembered seeing great leather-bound albums as well as boxes with framed scenes of hunting parties, family gatherings, stern patriarchs and sober wives, children dressed like perfect little mannequins.

He frowned, his thoughts interrupted by some vague unease, a sense of something out of place. He stopped walking and looked back where he had come from, the photograph albums forgotten. What was it that troubled him, that had intruded? He closed his eyes and waited.

Then the answer came. He opened his eyes and looked around again. The sous-sol was vast; the foodstuffs area was at least twenty metres behind him. The stairs back up to the house ascended five, six metres. Why then could he still smell Madame Guinard's gebrannte Mandeln all the way down here, in this most distant corner? Why could he still smell almonds over these fusty odours of old rugs and mould?

The reason, when he found it, shook him to the core.

There were two beds, separated by a curtain. Judging from the clothing hanging from nails, this side of the curtain was occupied by the daughters. Graf glanced down to check that nothing was going on with them. Nothing was. Hélène was weeping quietly, the younger one was watching her, looking as surly as ever. He went to the other side of the curtain, the mother's side. An old trunk, books, photographs, more clothing, wooden sabots and one pair of leather shoes. Nothing under the bed. He flung the sheet back. Nothing in the bed or the thin bolster. He swept everything from the top of the trunk, the resulting racket provoking startled gasps from downstairs, and tossed the contents over the floor, including the blue cape that Jeanne Dupré had worn in the square that morning.

There was nothing of any interest or consequence. He returned to the girls' side of the curtain and repeated the exercise, with the same result. All he found were his gifts to Hélène: the small phial of perfume, some of the chocolate, the silk underwear.

Then he saw the book. It was almost hidden by the bolster. It was his copy of Jung's *Wirklichkeit der Seele*. Reality of the soul? She had no soul. That was her reality. As he picked the book up it fell open and he saw the notes, faint pencilled lines in the margin of the dense black German text. He took the volume towards the stairs, where the light was better. The sisters looked up. He scowled and they quickly turned away.

The notes were in French. He scanned a few, then turned the pages rapidly until he had seen all of them. His heart seemed to fill his whole chest, squeezing the air from his lungs. He recognised these passages. He had translated them aloud for her. Sleepy approximations, his mind more on her soft body than on the text, as they lay together in the cottage out by chemin des Mesliers. But somehow she had committed his drowsy words to memory long enough to be able to write them into the book afterwards, every word carried with her as carefully as a child would bring a bright insect in her cupped hands to wonder at and treasure.

He retreated from the stairs and sat down heavily on the bed. When had she done this? Where? In this hovel? Had she found solitude and quiet, secret minutes snatched alone in this cramped shack, to do this?

310

In that moment the dreams came flooding back. Their dreams. Their life together in a glorious Reich. With her devotion at his command, what could he not have achieved?

But everything was ashes now. She had told him nothing but she must have known everything her mother was doing. Had they laughed together over it? Laughed about his humiliation. Nothing could undo that, no number of books could change the fact. She could transcribe every word he had ever uttered to her but it would count for nothing. Everything she had said and done was a lie. Leaving him with nothing.

He sat there, staring at a future that would never be.

At last Jeanne was within sight of La Croisette. Here where the long grass hid her she could watch the cottage, the yard and outbuildings. She forced herself to wait, however agonising her need to see Hélène and Isabelle. She removed the Luger from her waistband. The pistol was her only weapon now that Avignon had the MP40.

The place was quiet and peaceful, as if sleeping in the sun. She could hear the chickens but not a sound from the house, no splash of water from the sink, no clang of cooking pots, no voices. No movement at the window, none outside. A thread of smoke drifted from the chimney. None of these things meant her daughters were there, just as none of them meant the opposite. If the girls were absent – either of them or both – it could easily be because her fears had been realised and Graf had survived the attack and already had them under arrest. Not just Isabelle, for he would turn on Hélène like a wolf, whatever delusions she had about his so-called love for her.

Time seemed to thicken as she lay there, each second crawling past. The sound of Wehrmacht engines had ceased, suggesting that the pursuit might have moved away from the countryside. In which case house-to-house searches would be the most likely next step. Perhaps they were under way even now.

When she could stand the waiting no longer she broke cover, dashed along the march of pines on the margin of the third field and flung herself into the yard of the cottage. No bullets felled her. No German voices shattered the silent afternoon.

She crept to the window and peered in. She could have wept in joy and relief. There at the table sat Hélène and Isabelle.

A final quick glance to check that no German uniform was in sight at the end of her path or in ruelle de la Baie, and she was at the door, lifting the latch, hearing its familiar rusty scrape as if to reassure her that all was well. She hurried inside and made straight for her daughters.

But Hélène and Isabelle did not rise from the table to greet her or press themselves into her open arms. They stared up at her in wordless dismay, their eyes red and puffy, their cheeks grubby with tears.

She froze, her heart suddenly a dead weight in her chest.

'Willkommen, Madame,' said a guttural voice overhead, followed by the hoarse ratchet of a Luger semi-automatic being primed. 'Please put your weapon aside. Stolen Reich property, I see.'

Two fields behind her, Benedict witnessed her dash to the cottage. He watched her enter. He saw the Wehrmacht troopers who, as soon as she was inside, emerged from the hedgerows she had passed and from the hawthorn bushes at the foot of the path, their rifles and submachine guns pointed not at the cottage but at all directions from which a rescue or an attack might be attempted. Which meant that someone was already in the cottage, waiting for her. Whether or not that was the oberleutnant called Graf, a trap had been set and she had walked right into it.

She would not be killed; not immediately. She would be interrogated first. And unlike the priests in whom creaky old Père Gilbert Trèves of Varaville had such confidence, she would break, however courageous she might be. Not to save her life, which she would know was impossible now, but simply to end it, since that was the only way to end the pain.

She would tell her interrogators everything: about local Resistance personnel and activities, certainly, but also about the agent she knew as Avignon, including where he was to be found. Whether she could hold out until he was safely beyond reach was anybody's guess; but it was not a guess on which the colonel and the thin man in Baker Street would wish Benedict to risk his mission: and he knew they would be right.

He felt cold sweat prickle his chest and forearms. There was one option. Only one.

The cardboard cartons were concealed behind an upended mattress and an ancient armoire adorned with ornate carvings. Ebermann had to push both the armoire and the mattress aside in order to assess the extent of what there was, but someone who wanted only to remove a single carton or part of its contents could simply worm their way behind the obstacles. Especially if that someone was slight in frame. Someone like Jeanne Dupré, whose tins of wax polish and carefully folded dusters had been left here, he now discovered, all the way behind the mattress and armoire.

The cartons were blank and anonymous. Had they been in the foodstuffs area, they could have passed for innocent goods. Except for that smell of almonds at close quarters. There were perhaps thirty of them. Each carton held twenty small packets. Each packet was about the thickness of a good solid Bratwurst, but shorter, with flat ends, as if it had been neatly chopped. The packets were wrapped in shiny waxed paper. On the paper were printed the identity and provenance of the contents: Nobel's Explosive No. 808. British made and supplied by the SOE to Resistance groups here in France. And where better to hide it than here? Madame Guinard's cooking had taken care of any odour that arose when quantities were withdrawn.

With every box he opened the truth edged a little further into the light. Shame came creeping after it. His shame. The old woman might have stirred the pot, but the menu was Jeanne Dupré's. And he had swallowed every lie she served him.

He bowed his head. He had used her? Was that what he condemned himself for? That he had made a whore of her? Yes, he had used her. But no more than she had used him. Which had come first – his oafish fumblings or her calculating machinations? He would never know, and it hardly mattered now. They were both whores. His betrayal was worse, far worse, than he had thought, his dishonour was many magnitudes greater. There were sins here that lay far beyond Père Lachanau's remit.

There was one carton that was smaller, flatter than the others. He opened it. The interior was divided into five sections, each protecting a slim metal tube. He withdrew one carefully. Half its length was brass, the other half copper. A thin coloured band ran around the top. This one was red, but the others were black, green, yellow, blue. He slid the tube back into the carton. They were timing fuses. The coloured bands indicated the degree of delay, from ten minutes to twenty-four hours.

He closed the box and returned it to the shelf. But he left the mattress and the armoire pushed aside.

Graf searched Jeanne. She knew it for what it was: not only a precaution but also a deliberate act of humiliation, the more so since it was done in full view of her daughters.

He began with the leather blouson, making her remove it so that he could check the pockets and lining. Then he turned her to face the wall, her legs spread, her arms outstretched to the wall, and ran his hand over every part of her body. He took his time. The only mercy was that she was wearing Michel's old trousers. He moved in close behind her as he explored her breasts and she felt him against her buttocks. She drew away, bending her body closer to the wall, but he pressed against her again.

'You see what kind of beast he is, Hélène?' she said.

His hand squeezed her breast so hard that she cried out.

'Your daughter had no complaints,' he said. 'Always begging for more. She was a furnace.'

He swung Jeanne around to face him. 'Today's attack – who was with you?'

'I acted alone.'

'I saw their gunfire – at least three other shooters.'

'You imagined it. Just as you imagined Hélène ever cared for you.'

'And the priest – where is he?'

'Probably in the church.'

His head tilted back in surprise.

'Père Lachanau is usually in his church,' she added.

'Very funny. The priest you rescued today.'

'There was no other priest. Something else you imagined.'

'I know he's the agent.'

'What agent?'

Eventually he ordered Hélène and Isabelle to their feet and prodded mother and daughters over to the door. He swung it open and Jeanne saw the troopers at the foot of the path. She stepped outside and looked to left and right: in her fields stood more troopers. He had left nothing to chance. Meticulous as ever.

'Walk,' he ordered. On his signal the nearest troopers closed in, their weapons now turned on the captives.

Jeanne took her daughters' hands. 'Heads high,' she whispered.

'Silence,' barked Graf.

'Proud daughters of France. Remember.'

So they walked, their heads high, down the path and past the little kitchen garden. Behind them they heard the scrape of the rusty latch as the door of La Croisette swung shut.

Gaspard reached out and tapped the watch on the gefreiter's wrist. A nice piece, Swiss, leather strap, gold-plated casing, jewelled movement. It was he who had sold it to the young German a few months ago.

'How is it?' he asked.

The gefreiter grinned. 'Good. Very good.'

'Keeps good time?'

'Ja.'

'Good German time?'

They laughed. Behind the gefreiter the other troopers looked on, some amused, some po-faced behind their chinstraps.

He had come upon the patrol, six youngsters smoking and slouching against their armoured vehicle, where the road he was following crossed the heath outside Caillons. They stepped forward and blocked his path but more from boredom than any motive more threatening.

'So what's going on?' he asked the gefreiter, dropping his

voice to a confidential level.

'Go into Caillons if you like but you might have to stay the night.'

'Sealing it off? I heard an explosion and shooting. Anything to do with that?'

'Haven't been told. But I hear they've made some arrests.'

'Good. You can't come down hard enough on these people.'

'The roads might be open again before curfew. Won't know until we get further orders. So you can pass now but it's a gamble whether you can leave again. You have somewhere to stay if necessary?'

Gaspard winked. 'She's very accommodating.'

More laughter.

'If it's true they've caught someone, I might open a little book. Interested?'

A grin. 'Ja.'

Gaspard clapped him on the arm and cycled onwards. He winked confidently at the other troopers as he passed but his stomach was in knots.

It was Benedict's first sight of Lisieux's daughters, one of whom he saw had a limp. A clumsy brace encircled her calf.

The little procession turned the corner into ruelle de la Baie, where it was lost from his view. He bided his time as the remaining troopers crossed the fields and filed past the cottage. If Lisieux and her daughters were on their way to the barracks at Le Manoir he was powerless. His only hope was that they would be taken first to the Kommandantur in the Villa Normandie or to the mairie, where their arrests would be registered and all three of them charged.

He pictured the geography. The Villa Normandie and the

mairie were close by each other in place de l'Église. From the right vantage point he could cover both.

He ventured over the fields, crouching along ditches and walls. He turned away from Lisieux's cottage and down towards the port, still holding to the margin of the field until he reached the row of cottages near the top of rue du Port. Here he turned again, staying close to the back walls of the cottage yards, and headed uphill towards the square.

The final cottage had once had a low woodshed or coal store built against the wall of its yard. Most of the structure had collapsed, leaving only a stub of wall protruding at right angles. It was a metre or so high and about the same in width. He crouched behind it. The bricks were irregular, a jumble of discards and broken halves thrown together with skimped mortar. It took him only a few minutes to scrape away enough mortar with his dagger to allow him to ease out one of the bricks.

He peered through the gap. On the left of place de l'Église stood the Villa Normandie, its doorway guarded by two armed troopers, and to its right and directly opposite him, the mairie, draped in huge Nazi banners. Next to the mairie was the church itself. While the Villa Normandie was guarded by two armed troopers, the mairie had not only its two armed guards but a further ten or twelve troopers hanging around outside, smoking and looking restless. It was, perhaps, confirmation that the prisoners were indeed still here in Caillons, in the mairie, rather than at Le Manoir. The troopers were their escort.

Something else caught his eye. In the gravelled courtyard of the mairie stood three tall wooden stakes. They looked recently cut and stripped, but their pale surface bore dark stains. It took little thought to fathom their purpose or to guess at what had caused the stains.

He became aware of an unnatural hush over the village.

318

To the right of his field of view, rue du Centre ran off from the square. On the corner stood a charcuterie bearing the name Voinet. It was boarded up, Nazi posters plastered across its windows and door. He knew there were other shops and a café in the street; yet he could hear no buzz of activity, no conversation, no scrape of chairs: only the low voices of the troopers outside the mairie and the ring of their steel-shod boots on the pavement.

On the other side of the cottages were rue du Verger and rue du Port, both as empty as rue du Centre. No civilian entered or left place de l'Église; yet at the very least the mairie should have had a steady stream of civilians coming and going at this hour. He thought back to what he had seen below him as he left the icehouse: the lack of activity in the harbour, the only signs of life being Wehrmacht troops and vehicles.

There was only one explanation: the place was under curfew.

He checked the MP40, slipped the barrel into the gap and ensured that there was enough space for him to sight along it. It was an imperfect situation for an imperfect weapon but it was the best he would achieve. He had to hope it would be good enough.

'I want to see my confessor,' said Jeanne.

She and Hélène and Isabelle stood in what had once been a waiting room of the mairie. Now it was stripped of furniture except for two chairs and a trestle table. The armed troopers who had escorted them from La Croisette stood guard on either side. Graf prowled back and forth, the Luger still in his hand, while Leutnant Ernst Neiss sat at the table before a block of blank forms and a typewriter. Graf's helmet was also on the table, clearly in the leutnant's way; every now and then Neiss nudged it another centimetre or two to the side.

Jeanne knew how things would go. Once the processing was over and the leutnant's forms were all filled in and signed and countersigned, she and her daughters would be moved to the cells deep beneath Le Manoir. It was what had happened with Pierre and the others. Then, unless a miracle intervened, they would return to the mairie. For one last time.

There would be no miracle.

'My confessor,' she said again.

Again Graf ignored her. But his thoughts seemed to be following a similar path to her own.

'My three stakes will be used again, Neiss, exactly as I promised you.'

'There'll have to be a trial first, Herr Oberleutnant. For Madame Dupré, that is.'

'There'll be a trial for all of them – a good military trial – and there'll be a verdict. The same good verdict, three times.'

'Two of the accused are children. Under Reich law they can't be tried in military court.'

'They look like adults to me.'

Neiss removed his spectacles and rubbed his eyes. 'I understand that Père François Lachanau has birth records for all members of his congregation. If we ask him to attend Madame Dupré as she has requested, he can bring her daughters' records with him.'

Graf looked at him for a time, saying nothing. Then he crossed the room and spoke briefly in a low voice to an obergefreiter, who nodded and went outside.

Graf returned to Neiss.

'You were saying?'

'I'm suggesting that Père Lachanau may be able to help.'

'And you think I'd believe any records in this place?

Especially that old crow's. Are you sure he can write?'

Jeanne snorted. 'You're an idiot, Graf.'

The back of his gloved fist whipped across her face, though mercifully only the fist, not the Luger. Hélène and Isabelle screamed. Jeanne felt consciousness slipping from her. She fought not to succumb. She felt her daughters' arms around her, supporting her, until the troopers separated the three of them and pushed them back to their places. Her mouth filled with a metallic tang. She spat out blood.

The door opened as the obergefreiter returned. Graf went to him and took the man's Luger from its holster.

'Let's simplify the matter,' he said. 'On your feet, Neiss.'

'Herr Oberleutnant?'

'On your feet – stand up.'

He caught Neiss by the shoulder and steered him to the middle of the room, then pushed Isabelle into place beside Hélène. The obergefreiter stepped behind Jeanne, seized her arms and pulled her aside.

Graf cocked the borrowed Luger and thrust it into Neiss's hand.

'Shoot one of the daughters,' he said.

'Herr Oberleutnant –'

'It's a simple instruction, Neiss. I don't care which one you shoot. You can choose. We'll get all the intelligence we need from the mother in exchange for letting the other one live.'

The room was deathly quiet. Hélène and Isabelle could have been carved from marble, they were so still. Jeanne made no sound, terrified of tipping either Neiss or Graf over the edge. The obergefreiter tightened his grip on her.

Neiss stared at the weapon in his hand as if he had never seen such a thing before. His body began to shake.

'No,' he said at last. The single word seemed to cost him

great effort.

'What's this? You'd disobey a direct order?'

Sweat rolled down Neiss's face. 'You have no authority to issue such an order. Nor to try children in a military court. I'll inform Major Ebermann. He'll add these matters to the others.'

'Others? What others? Oh, you mean the little tales you've been telling him? Well, let's see if you live to tell any more.'

The gun that Neiss had been forced to hold was pointing at the floor. Graf raised the leutnant's arm with the barrel of his own gun so that Neiss was aiming in the general direction of Hélène and Isabelle. Then he stepped back, cocked his weapon and took aim at the leutnant's head.

'It's one of them or you, Neiss. Your choice. You have until the count of three.'

The leutnant's arm was shaking so hard that it seemed to be completely out of his control. The muzzle of the Luger jerked from side to side. There was every chance the weapon might discharge accidentally.

'One,' counted Graf.

Neiss brought his left hand up and wrapped it around his right to steady it.

'Two.'

'No!' screamed Jeanne, a long, endless plea that she could no longer restrain. She flung herself forward with all her strength to block the bullet. But the obergefreiter's grip was like steel. She stayed exactly where she was. She continued screaming.

An instant before Graf's final count, Neiss swung around, arms still outstretched, and discharged the Luger directly into the oberleutnant's face.

There was a dry click.

He fired twice more, to the same effect.

Graf burst out laughing and lowered his own weapon. 'You're an old woman, Neiss, not a soldier. You couldn't even tell that the magazine was empty. Did you really think I'd trust you with a loaded weapon?'

Neiss continued firing. Click after useless click. Graf wrested the Luger from his trembling hands.

'Arrest this man,' he ordered. 'Attempted assassination of a Wehrmacht officer.'

Two troopers stepped forward, their rifles pointing at Neiss. Graf pushed him back down on the chair. The leutnant's glasses fell to the floor. He retrieved them and shoved them back in place.

'Do the paperwork, Neiss. It's all you're good for. You heard the charge.'

Jeanne felt the obergefreiter's grip loosen. Another trooper took over.

'My confessor,' she demanded again. Her jaw had become stiff; her words were slurred.

Graf returned the Luger to the obergefreiter.

'Send the men door to door. Lift the curfew. The harbour's still off limits – no fishing, no boats – but the village is open. I want people in the streets. I want them out there, in the square, in time for when we move these three out. Get them here for that. I want them to see everything. I want them to see these three pretty little murderers – tell them there won't be many more chances. I want them to see the good work we've done for the Reich today.'

He planted himself before Jeanne and wrenched her head up to make her look at him. A blast of pain shot through her.

'And fetch the priest for this one,' he added. 'But no birth records.'

He snatched up his helmet from the table, sending the stack of forms flying to the floor.

* * *

Gaspard hurried past François Lachanau as soon as the priest opened the door.

'Is it Jeanne?' he asked. 'Has she been arrested?'

Lachanau nodded. 'And the girls. Graf has them all.'

'Merde.'

'Succinctly put.'

'What happened?'

'I'm still trying to find out. You heard the explosion?'

'Who didn't? The shooting too. Jeanne's doing?'

'It looks that way.'

'Has Avignon reached Caillons yet?'

'No idea.'

'It's bad timing, François. The worst. What was Jeanne thinking?'

The priest looked mournfully at him. 'Graf, I suspect. That's what. Graf and Hélène. I saw him as he brought them to the mairie. Covered in blood. Not his, regrettably, he looked unscathed other than a few scratches. But I'd guess he was Jeanne's target.'

Graf and Hélène. Gaspard sighed. He looked at the priest.

'Again I have no one but myself to blame, François. I knew about the oberleutnant and Hélène. I should have seen this coming. Especially with Jeanne making one attempt already. Old Adalard got there first, otherwise it would have been Jeanne who was dead in the gutter.'

'Well, if it's confession time, then mine is that I knew when it started between Graf and Hélène. It was rape. I never imagined it would develop as it did. That was my first mistake. My second was allowing Jeanne to silence me and prevent me from doing anything about that monster. We're a pair of old fools, Gaspard.'

They were interrupted by a loud knock on the door. Gaspard withdrew to the kitchen corner. A German voice addressed the priest.

'Oberleutnant Graf orders you to come to the mairie. A prisoner wants to see you.'

There were scuffling sounds as Lachanau snatched up his black briefcase, then the door was slammed shut.

An hour passed before the priest returned. His hands were trembling as he put the briefcase back in its corner, drew out a chair and joined Gaspard at the table. He took a Gitane from the packet by his friend's elbow and lit it. Gaspard could not remember the last time he had seen him smoke. The priest took several drags in silence. Gaspard waited.

'I've been with Jeanne,' Lachanau said finally. 'Avignon has arrived safely – and is still safe, as far as Jeanne knows.' He smoked some more. His gaze had never strayed from the briefcase. 'She made her confession to me. She took communion.'

Gaspard waited again. Lachanau stubbed out the cigarette.

'And now there's something you have to do, Gaspard. Something Jeanne requires of you. She has sent very specific instructions. She won't be dissuaded – God knows, I've tried. It's something you haven't done for a while.'

Ebermann stood on the galleried balcony, watching the empty square but seeing nothing, only Jeanne Dupré and her daughters being marched into the mairie by Graf, a scene that played over and over before him.

There came a time when a man could fight no more. Like the bull falling to its knees for the death thrust, a man surrendered to the inevitable. Tired, finished, ready to leave the field. Even a man whose business was to fight. Perhaps above all such a man, for there could be honour in surrender, whether or not he was really made for war in the first place. Surely that was God's code too, not just the battlefield's.

He returned to the sous-sol and made his preparations.

Gaspard cycled as if the devil himself was on his tail. He stayed well clear of the roads and the heath, using only his own hidden routes through the woods; this was not a journey with leisure for encounters with Wehrmacht patrols, however friendly.

This time, thankfully, no professor or any other uninvited visitor waylaid him at his door. One minute inside to fetch what he had come for, and he was on his way back to Caillons, the devil still there right behind him.

Benedict had seen the villagers gather in the square as the curfew was lifted. He had seen the tall, white-haired priest hurry into the mairie. The villagers waited patiently. They looked enquiringly at one another and shrugged. After a time the priest emerged. Some of them tried to speak to him, but he shook his head and hurried away.

Benedict sat back on his haunches. Whatever was going on, one thing was plain: with the square now packed with people, his imperfect situation had become worse.

Gaspard hurtled up the spiral staircase of the lighthouse two and three steps at a time. When he reached the enclosed gallery at the top his head was spinning, so that he had to take a minute to steady himself. He set down the waxed canvas sleeve and unbuckled its straps. The sleeve was similar to the kind used by fishermen for their rods, but shorter and wider; its contents were a good deal heavier than fishing gear.

A good sniper never gave up his weapon. A wise commander knew that and turned a blind eye to the

326

hardware that was not returned at the end of hostilities – particularly a captured piece that had no place in his arsenal and regarding which no record existed and no questions would therefore be asked.

Gaspard slid the Mauser from the sleeve and balanced its familiar weight in his hands. Today's Wehrmacht had more advanced versions – better actions, more powerful telescopic sights – but this original was still an inspiring weapon. Throughout the years of that wretched earlier war it had been a part of himself: by his side when he slept, within reach when he ate, slung over his shoulder when he marched, oiled and always clean and ready for use at a moment's notice; as it still was today. Every death it delivered back then had been a small shard of hope for France.

Thirty years on and France was struggling for that same hope all over again. Today it fell to him to deliver another death in its service.

'Herr Oberleutnant, secure transport is on the way.'

Graf flicked his cigarette butt into a corner. He rose from his chair and faced Jeanne.

'Outside,' he ordered. 'Cabaret time.'

'Jürgen –' began Hélène.

'Shut your mouth.'

'He's right,' said Isabelle. 'Don't waste your breath on him.'

For a moment the evening sun blinded Jeanne as she stepped outside. She squinted through the haze as she descended the steps to the courtyard, followed by Hélène and Isabelle. The waiting troopers closed in. Her vision cleared and she saw that the square, deserted earlier, had now filled with people. A tremor passed through them when they recognised her. A low murmur arose. She scanned the faces. All of them were known to her. Some were dark with sorrow, some wore expressions of grim satisfaction. Among the sorrowful ones she saw Bertrand Mercier, Auguste Sulac and the two Leroux brothers.

She searched for Gaspard Baignères. He was not there.

Strong hands grasped her arms from behind and pulled her back against one of the three stakes, the middle one where Pierre had been tethered, and held her there. Hélène was on her right, Isabelle on her left, both of them pinned the same way.

Graf appeared at the top of the steps. It was the villagers' first sight of him since the attack at La Vierge. Jeanne saw surprise in the faces and realised how carefully he was arranging things. There had been ample opportunity for him to wash and change out of his bloodied clothing but he had not done so. That was no accident. It was all part of the performance. Meticulous again.

He came down the steps to the courtyard. Behind him followed Ernst Neiss, an armed trooper guarding him on either side.

Graf turned his attention to the crowd. He raised his arm to encompass Jeanne and her daughters.

'People of Caillons, these criminals murdered many loyal German soldiers. They brought reprisals on you and your families. Like all who defy Reich law, they face German justice. Here before you is where they'll pay for their crimes. Today is a preview. The next time they stand here will be when the sentence of the court is carried out.'

A booming voice interrupted him. François Lachanau had arrived.

'Justice? You call this justice, Graf? What kind of justice declares verdict and sentence in advance? You're a fraud, Graf. Your justice is a fraud, as perverted as yourself.'

Jeanne closed her eyes. The voices faded. Now all she

heard was the wood pigeons calling their creamy notes and the gulls crying as they wheeled over the bay. All about her she heard the buzz and whir of life that never ceased or rested from the struggle for survival. Over the sound of the surf breaking beneath the headland she heard her daughters' laughter as they fell into their father's arms, she heard her own laughter and Michel's as they followed the secret tracks down from the headland to the shore. Her nostrils were filled with the sharp note of juniper, with bright sage and soft myrtle. She saw joy and tears in her mother's eyes as she watched little Hélène, her first grandchild, dance like Chauviré, her legs perfect then, her swan wings folding and yielding to inevitable death.

Jeanne opened her eyes again. Gaspard Baignères was not there.

She was ready. The empty lantern panes of the lighthouse blazed with fire. She closed her eyes.

Graf's speech had given Benedict time to settle the barrel of the MP40 in the gap in the brickwork. Not too far forward, lest it be visible, but far enough for stability and balance. In the distance he heard a truck approaching. It would be transport to take Lisieux and her daughters to Le Manoir.

We won't meet again, Avignon.

He closed his finger gently on the trigger – an untested trigger whose pulling weight was unknown to him; gently was the only way.

A shot rang out. But not his shot.

18

The telescopic sight gave Gaspard three times magnification. When the troopers moved apart, she was there in the cross hairs. The evening sun was behind him and full on her. There was a moment when she seemed to be looking directly at him.

'This time death has a purpose,' was the message she had sent via François Lachanau.

One chance, one kill. It had to be her rather than Graf. Her orders. Other Grafs would simply be sent to fill the space he left. And Gaspard's chance would be lost. She had seen all of this.

Her daughters she left in François Lachanau's hands. A fair apportioning, it seemed to Gaspard: give each old fool his opportunity to make amends.

Her body did not fall back with the first bullet. It arched towards Gaspard, embracing death. He fired again. The bloom of red on her chest was joined by a second. Then a third. With that she caved away from him. Released by the trooper who had been restraining her and was now diving for cover, her body slid to the gravel.

It was a kill that would never be entered in Gaspard's notebook. Maître Aristide Péringuey had a point after all: some things were best not remembered.

There was chaos in place de l'Église. More than he could take in through the confines of the telescopic sight. Was there time to deal with Graf after all? It was tempting. He panned from side to side, looking for the oberleutnant among the mêlée of panic-stricken villagers and the battledress uniforms that were still visible, stretched across the pavement or on the gravel of the mairie courtyard.

Suddenly he understood why the uniforms remained visible, why their wearers were still in the open and not taking cover. The wearers were dead. Only with this realisation did he consciously hear the submachine-gun fire. It had been there since immediately after his first shot, he was convinced of that now, but in his concentration he had been deaf to it. There was another shooter somewhere. But who? Paul and Gérard Leroux were down there in the square; he had seen them. Also Mercier and Sulac. There was no way any of them could have concealed such a weapon. So who?

He glimpsed movement on the corner of rue du Centre. Troopers were regrouping there, possibly with a view to heading his way. A good sniper knew when to stop. The sun behind him had concealed his muzzle flashes but enough was enough.

Another burst of automatic fire sounded, clouds of debris kicked up from the corner of rue du Centre, two of the troopers sheltering there fell to the ground. His fellow shooter was giving him cover.

He gathered up the three empty bullet casings and flew down the spiral staircase, packing the Mauser away as he went. Within seconds he was cycling for home, the Mauser across his back and his oilcloth cap pressed tightly in place. Behind him the firing continued, then ceased. Either his unknown comrade-in-arms was dead or, like him, had decided to make himself scarce.

Gaspard cycled onwards, that old devil at his back again.

'Maman!'

The scream was Isabelle's as the first bullet hit and she

saw her mother's body arch, a stream of blood spurting from her chest. She found herself suddenly released by the trooper who had been holding her and flung herself towards Jeanne, oblivious to the two shots that followed, oblivious to any possible danger to herself, oblivious to everything but her mother.

Graf was not oblivious. He saw so much in that instant, the space of one heartbeat, which was all it took for the three bullets to find Jeanne Dupré. He saw his loss of her, just as he had lost Meslin and Colinet and Clavier. Yet again he saw everything he had tried to achieve turn to ashes.

From the corner of his eye he saw someone lunge forward, towards him it seemed. His reaction was instinctive, a reflex, the same reflex that had responded to Adalard Fougeret. Wehrmacht training ran deep. He spun on his heel and shot. Isabelle Dupré fell without a sound, without so much as a moan, and now he saw even more, but again too late: that he himself had destroyed yet another chance. For once there would be no coup de grâce.

Only Hélène Dupré was left. Only she could tell what she knew. Resistance identities, locations of arms and munitions caches, plans: she would know everything. The whereabouts of the agent and why he was here: she was sure to know these things too.

But when he turned to seize her she was nowhere to be seen.

François Lachanau saw Jeanne Dupré die. That was planned, God forgive them all, him and Gaspard and Jeanne herself. He also saw Isabelle die. That death was not planned. He was not sure he could find it in himself to ask his saviour's forgiveness for the perpetrator of that death.

The villagers had scattered or thrown themselves to the

ground. The place was a bedlam of screaming civilians and shouting troopers who were trying at one and the same time to seek cover, organise themselves for response and find the sources of the gunfire. It was clear by then that there were two shooters, and for that Lachanau had no more explanation than did Gaspard Baignères. But, like the matter of forgiveness for Graf, it was a dilemma for another day.

The timing of Gaspard's shots was something over which he, François Lachanau, had no control. They had both known that would be the case. Thus, when Gaspard seized his moment, Lachanau was further from the mairie than he would have wished – too far to reach Hélène and Isabelle, which had been his hope, and too far to stop that shot of Graf's. But as Isabelle fell, the oberleutnant's gaze lingered on her for a few precious seconds. Graf could not help himself – a killer had to follow his prey to the ground.

Ernst Neiss also saw that moment. His armed escort had lost interest in him as soon as the shooting began. Now he leapt forward, ignoring the hail of gunfire, clenched his arms about Hélène, who had also been released by the trooper holding her, and locked his hands together – he was no strongman, she was as tall and perhaps the same weight as himself and he knew there would be no second chance – and half carried her back towards the mairie. He pushed her to the ground in the lee of the steps, safe from the gunfire; and safely beyond Graf's view.

From a few metres away François Lachanau watched it all.

The air was alive with bullets. Even Graf could not stand there forever, looking for Hélène. Finally his nerve broke; he flung himself towards rue du Centre and cover.

Neiss met Lachanau's gaze. He nodded almost imperceptibly at the priest. The compact was sealed.

Benedict had done as much as he could. As much as he dared.

His last volleys were the ones that pinned Graf and two or three troopers in rue du Centre. They and their comrades who had survived were returning fire now, though it was as yet fairly random – a carpet of rounds that fanned across the general area rather than pinpointing his wall. But that would change. It was too dangerous for him to respond now; they would be watching for exactly that.

The arrival of the truck gave him both his opportunity and the final incentive he needed. It roared into the square from rue du Centre and skidded to a halt, narrowly missing some prone villagers. Troopers leapt from the back; Graf immediately started bawling orders at them, pointing in Benedict's general direction. Evidently the marksman's location was still unknown. His weapon had fallen silent, so it was likely that he had made good his escape. Which made it Benedict's turn.

He gripped the MP40 beneath his arm and ran.

Shielded by the truck and unseen by Graf, who now had other things to attend to, Lachanau made a dash for the mairie steps. Neiss blinked up at him. One of the lenses of his spectacles was cracked.

'I don't know how to thank you,' said Lachanau.

'The deed is everything, Monsieur le Curé, the glory nothing.'

'Goethe?'

Neiss nodded. 'The gate between the rear courtyard of the mairie and your churchyard is unlocked, Monsieur. There's no one in the mairie. You won't be seen.'

'That gate's always locked, on the major's orders. For security.'

'I unlocked it this morning.'

'Why?'

'I don't know. I myself find it strange.'

The priest looked steadily at him. 'God moves in mysterious ways, Leutnant.'

Lachanau raised Hélène to her feet, then lifted her up bodily in his arms. She made not a sound, her gaze was vacant, her body slack so that he had to cradle her head against his shoulder. She did not reply when he spoke to her. Only the fact that her eyes were open indicated that she was even conscious. But being conscious and being in possession of her senses were not the same thing.

He hurried into the safety of the rear courtyard.

'Graf!'

The voice rang out across the square.

Graf looked up to see Ebermann standing on his galleried balcony.

Surely not. He wiped dust from his eyes and looked again. But it was no illusion, the major was there. Graf shook his head; here he was, in the middle of a gun battle, his men dead or dying on all sides, and Ebermann was standing there as unruffled as if he was a general inspecting his troops.

'Come here, Graf!'

The man was mad. Graf glanced up again and jabbed a hand towards where he thought the shooter was, the one with the submachine gun. Surely it was obvious even to Ebermann what their priority was.

A shot cracked through the air. Another chunk of debris flew from the brickwork immediately in front of Graf.

'Herr Oberleutnant –' stuttered an anxious trooper.

'I know,' snapped Graf. 'Our own major's shooting at us.'

'Now, Graf!' bellowed Ebermann. 'Right now!'

Graf hunkered down on the running board of the truck, on the far side from the shooter, and ordered the driver to take the vehicle across the square. They got there safely.

'This better be good,' he muttered as he thumped upstairs.

It was not good.

'Herr Major, this is not an ideal time.'

'It's the right time.'

Ebermann was standing in front of the gallery window. On a small table beside him was a white folder, fat with papers of some kind.

'Herr Major, with respect –'

'You no longer have permission to speak. You will remain silent and listen. I will be brief.'

Graf stared at him. Intolerable. That Ebermann should dare –

But the major's next words cut the thought short.

'Your career is at an end, Graf. Your command has been withdrawn. You no longer have authority over any serving Wehrmacht soldier. At the end of this interview you will be placed under arrest and held under guard until the time of your court martial. The charges against you are detailed here.' Ebermann tapped the white folder but left it closed. 'I will summarise them.'

It took fifteen minutes. Graf recognised the reports filed by Neiss. He recognised the names and the incidents: the enemy aircraft, the elusive agent, Meslin, Colinet, Clavier, the Voinets, the seven-year-old boy, the old man. There were other things too, things that stung in their different ways. The first were the demolition of the war memorial and the summary execution of the ten Caillonais.

'As regards the executions,' said Ebermann, 'you persuaded me with false evidence.'

Such a lie.

Ebermann drew a deep breath. 'And then we come to Hélène Dupré.'

The name fell on Graf like a curse. The words that followed were poison: seduction of a minor, taking advantage of a crippled civilian, neglect of duties, bringing the Reich into disrepute, a relationship that jeopardised security.

It was too much.

'You had her mother, Ebermann. You're preaching to me about security?'

'You do not have permission to speak. But since you mention Jeanne Dupré, that brings me to your latest failure. You knew her value, yet you failed to safeguard her. Everything she could have told us is lost. You gave the attackers all the time and opportunity they needed to neutralise her while you stood there showing off.'

Ebermann turned around to look through the gallery window at the scene below, where Graf's troops were cautiously moving forward. The shooting seemed to have ceased. The major began to describe the procedure that would follow Graf's arrest.

But Graf was no longer listening. His gaze went from the white folder to Ebermann's back. This thing he had in mind, this idea that had formed while Ebermann was spewing his accusations, it could be done. He had witnesses to the shot that the major had fired. It was the act of a deranged man. Deranged by grief at the loss of his family, deranged by guilt because of his relationship with the résistante Jeanne Dupré. Probably he was still besotted with her; and he had seen her die today, that too had made his mental state worse. A textbook case.

This thing could be done. Indeed, it seemed to Jürgen Graf, he had no alternative. He would find Hélène Dupré and eliminate the awkwardness that she constituted. He would destroy that white folder, of course. Then eliminate Neiss, who was due a coward's death sentence anyway, and destroy his records too, those reports.

It could all be done. All he needed was for Ebermann to turn around, to face him. And that could be arranged. Very easily.

He drew the Luger and loaded a round into the chamber. Sure enough, Ebermann turned at the sound, though he seemed neither alarmed nor in any great hurry.

Graf fired. The major fell to his knees, staring at Graf. He made no attempt to draw his own weapon. A weakling to the end.

Graf fired again. Ebermann folded backwards. Graf went to him and delivered the coup de grâce. There was no ricochet. He wrapped the dead hand around the major's Luger, made the hand draw the gun from its holster and placed Ebermann's finger around the trigger. With his hand over the major's, he fired a round from Ebermann's own gun into the wall behind where he had been standing.

The pauses between the four shots would fit well enough – Ebermann shot first but missed, the next two shots were Graf's in self-defence; the coup de grâce was a matter of respect for an officer whose life should be properly terminated after his crime.

On a day of such confusion, all this could be claimed and believed. It could be done.

Graf went to the table, picked up the plump white folder and opened it. Exactly as Ebermann had said, it was filled with charge sheets. But the one on top was blank. He tossed it aside. The next one was blank too. And the next. All the sheets were blank.

Scheisse. What the fuck was going on?

Down in the sous-sol the cupric chloride solution released

from the ampoule crushed by Klaus Ebermann half an hour ago ate through the last microns of wire restraining the striker of the detonator in the timing fuse. The striker struck home.

'Reporting for duty, mon colonel.'

Gaspard returned the salute. 'At ease, soldier.'

The coin was already waiting on the table, a one-franc piece that had originated from no official mint: on one side Marianne with her wheatsheaf within the legend 'République Française', on the other 'Liberté, Égalité, Fraternité' and the impossible year 1943.

'Deliver it immediately, soldier.'

'Yes, mon colonel.'

Suddenly the deep thunder of an explosion shook and filled the cottage, louder than anything Gaspard had heard or felt since Verdun. Mirabaud did not flinch but the walls trembled, the animal snares and traps bounced on their hooks, pine cones clattered on the roof, rattling like gunfire.

Gaspard frowned. What was this? It sounded and felt like every stick of explosive in Normandy had just gone up. The very ground beneath his feet reverberated.

'Hostilities may be recommencing, soldier,' he told Mirabaud. 'Proceed with all possible speed and vigilance.'

'At once, Colonel Mauser.'

Gaspard winced; no longer so pleasing, that nickname. But Mirabaud pocketed the coin, snapped to attention for a parting salute and marched fearlessly from the cottage.

Caillons shook to its foundations.

The Villa Normandie seemed to hoist itself entire and intact from the ground, the outer walls tearing free from their foundations. They fell back as the inner structure disintegrated and collapsed into itself. The delicately pointed turrets and chequerwork chimney stacks folded like paper, allowing the outer walls, untethered from these anchorages, to crumple. Great sheets of ochre brick and cream stucco fell inwards, followed by the huge timbers that had criss-crossed the upper floors and formed the open gallery from which Ebermann had once surveyed his Reich-given demesne.

As the walls fell, so did the thousands of dark red tiles of the roof, tumbling like rubies into the dust. Gargoyles and shepherd boys and minstrels crashed to earth and shattered into fragments. Spiralled gutters stood unattached, then wilted and collapsed. Flames began to lick at the timbers and wainscoting.

L'Église de Notre Dame de la Mer quivered. Mortar showered from the walls of the mairie and long splits zigzagged down the courses of brick. The giant Nazi banners billowed out with such force from the front of the mairie that they snapped the ropes that held them. They fluttered slowly to the courtyard, turning it scarlet as if filled with blood.

Crockery and goods came crashing down in homes and shops, window frames twisted apart and cracked their panes, shutters fell from their hinges. Bottles smashed to the floor in Café du Marché.

Dogs cowered and whimpered, cats crouched in fear, wanting to flee but not knowing where, uninterested in the rats and mice that emerged from every crevice and now scurried in mindless circles. The cobblestones of place de l'Église were shaken loose, sending dust rising like smoke from the ground as if hell was opening.

The ripples of the quake spread outwards. Wooden shingles shook free from the roof of La Croisette, leaving scars of tarred paper behind them and crashing into the henhouse and Jeanne's vegetables. The row of cottages at the top of rue du Port trembled, the stub of wall that had shielded Benedict finally falling along with several of the yard walls. Windows shattered in the little schoolhouse in rue des Châtaigniers. One of the chestnut trees that had shaded Jeanne wrenched its roots from the earth and lurched across the lane.

The villagers who lay trapped in the square were deafened by the roar of the blast and could not hear their own screams. Among them was little Hervé Meslin, who had already seen much in his short life that no child should ever see. He struggled to grasp what was happening as this latest terror struck. The roar of the explosion seemed to be not around him or outside him, but was passing right through his body so that he was a living part of it. He felt it in his chest, in his wildly shaking limbs; it resonated in his head. At any moment his body might fly into pieces, like the fragments of bricks and roof tiles that were now raining down.

As the debris fell, deadly chunks that had escaped the vortex of the explosion, the paralysis immobilising the villagers was broken. People scrambled to their feet, helping each other as much as they could, and ran for the cover of any open doorway. Those troopers who had not been detailed to pursue the sniper or the other shooter joined them. There they huddled, French and German alike, occupier and occupied, peering fearfully out at the destruction.

Benedict was halfway down the path to the icehouse when he heard the blast. A second later he felt the ground tremble beneath his feet. He halted his descent in case the cliff face should shear. The bushes and undergrowth around him were shivering, as if a breeze riffled their blossoms and leaves. Then all became still again. He stood for a moment, listening for clues, but all he heard in the distance was the

341

familiar whine of Wehrmacht engines starting up. He hurried on. Whatever had happened, it might give his pursuers something other than him to think about.

Père François Lachanau gasped as his house shook around him and the noise of the explosion filled his head. Books fell from their shelves, the oak dresser trembled and rattled, its contents crashing down. A splintering sound followed by the tinkle of falling glass told him that the window of his downstairs room had fallen in. Hélène remained silent and limp, either hearing and sensing nothing or still indifferent to everything beyond her own horrors. He guided her into a chair.

Behind him the door flew open. Madame Guinard half fell into the room. She was white with fear.

'Merciful God, what was that?' she panted. 'Are we being bombed?'

'I don't know, but I need to find out. I must go. Madame, would you –'

'Go, mon père. I'll look after the girl. It's why I followed you, to see to her.'

Lachanau raced back to place de l'Église. His brain could barely process the sight he found there. Along the side of the square where only minutes previously the Villa Normandie had stood, there was now only a huge mound of rubble, of burning timbers and crushed brick. Through the clouds of dust and smoke he made out bits of furniture and interior fittings, treads of a staircase that no longer led anywhere. A few shocked Wehrmacht troopers stood about, looking helpless and confused. More were drifting back, their search for the gunmen abandoned. Like Lachanau, they stared in disbelief. The villagers stared too. Lachanau tasted dust in his mouth. When he spat, the spit was orange with brick dust.

He came upon Ernst Neiss.

'Shots were fired,' the leutnant said. 'Four shots.'

'Where? In the Villa Normandie?'

Neiss nodded. 'I heard them, so did others. Immediately before the explosion. All the gunfire had stopped by then.'

'And Major Ebermann?'

Neiss shook his head hopelessly as he looked at the rubble. 'In there somewhere. We'll dig, of course. We don't have suitable equipment but we'll organise and dig by hand. We won't give up hope.'

'Very laudable. Who'll do the organising?'

Neiss peered up at him. The spectacles were now caked in dust. 'I will, Monsieur. In the absence of more senior officers I'm in command.'

'Congratulations.'

'It's only temporary.'

'As is everything in this world, Leutnant.'

Lachanau walked on towards the remains of the Villa Normandie. No one could still be alive beneath that mound of destruction. The little leutnant would be wasting his time.

The priest sighed. There was one thing he himself could do. Only one, but it mattered. He raised his right hand and made the sign of the cross over the rubble.

'Ego te absolvo,' he whispered.

Neiss had followed him. He had seen and heard.

'Oberleutnant Graf's in there too,' he pointed out.

'How unfortunate. An exemplary Wehrmacht officer and leader.'

'He was going to court-martial me.'

'I can't imagine what your misdemeanour could have been. Were there other witnesses?'

'All dead. Paperwork's all gone too. Up in smoke.'

'It's an ill wind, Leutnant.'

'I was wondering, Monsieur – do you include the

oberleutnant in your absolution? Not that I believe in these things. Just wondering.'

Lachanau pondered. Then he shrugged. 'Fortunately that's not up to me. My saviour accepts all sorts – I'll leave it to him to decide.'

The two men stood together, listening to the crackle of the flames. Then they heard the metallic clunk of the mairie's Henry-Lepaute, elegant and unscathed, as the minute hand nudged forward.

19

An old moon, so weary that its final waning glimmer was no more than the faintest chalk line among the stars, crept along the black sky. Gérard and Paul Leroux paced Jacques Colinet's salt meadow, setting out the hurricane lamps at the intervals that Jeanne had instructed Gérard. Half a dozen pairs of eyes followed their progress – the sheep from one corner of the field, Bertrand Mercier and Auguste Sulac from another.

The lamps had been hard to come by, to replace the ones lost previously. Some were Gérard's own, from his boat; the others he had begged from fellow fishermen.

'Do we even know if the plane will come?' said Paul as they finished.

'Why wouldn't it?'

'And the agent, this Avignon fellow – what if he doesn't show up?'

'Why wouldn't he?'

'After what happened today.'

'Nothing that happened changes anything. You said he got away with all of you after the attack at La Vierge, and he wasn't arrested with Jeanne.'

'Are you sure you know what you're doing, Gérard? Last time the plane came, we set up decoy explosions.'

'And maybe we'd do the same tonight if we had any explosive left. Or maybe we wouldn't bother. But strangely enough, we don't have any, not until we receive further supplies. So that makes for an easy decision. Now stop arguing, Paul.'

Even in the darkness, Gérard could sense his brother stiffen.

'Don't talk to me like that, Gérard. You're not my cell leader.'

'You think not?' said Gérard soberly. 'Something was waiting for me on my boat tonight. I can't say I'm thrilled. Bring your cigarette over here.'

The coin was barely visible in the dull red glow but both men knew what it said.

Matters settled, they slithered into the ditch alongside Mercier and Sulac.

Benedict straightened up as he emerged from the curtain of undergrowth and assessed the night sky. As dark as pitch. Tillman would not be happy. Or whoever it might be this time.

He slung the MP40 over his shoulder and set out along the path.

The touch of steel on the back of his neck and the voice came at the same time.

'Avignon.'

He calculated. The Browning was in his waistband; it would be better at close quarters than the awkward submachine gun. Or he could try to unbalance the man and send him to the foot of the cliff.

Then the voice spoke again.

'I'm a friend, Avignon. My gun is a precaution only – in case you're jumpy. Relax.'

The cold pressure went away. Benedict heard the sound of the pistol being uncocked. He turned to see a man with thick grey moustaches watching him. An old oilskin cap was pressed tightly on his head.

'Who are you?'

346

'Like I said, a friend. There's nothing for you to worry about. Your transport is on its way and everything at this end is in hand – I had a look before coming here. You can find your way to the landing area?'

'I can.'

'This time things should be calmer than your arrival. Our German friends are preoccupied tonight. There'll be no problems.'

'You ambushed me to tell me that?'

'I came to ask a favour. I want you to take another passenger.'

'Impossible. No spare seat, no parachute.'

'Yes, there are. I know SOE's aircraft. So do you.'

'Who is this passenger?'

'A girl. Her name is Hélène Dupré. You saw her today, I think.'

'How would I have done that?'

'Because that was you in the square. With that submachine gun you're carrying. One of ours, I believe. Be sure not to take it with you.'

'Is this the girl with the caliper?'

'She's not safe here. If the Germans don't get her, the locals will.'

'For collaborating?'

'Of which she's completely innocent. Most people today were too confused to know what was happening. Some of them think she's dead. It won't be hard to convince the rest. We took the bodies of her mother and sister away. Simple enough to say hers was there too. I'll make sure mouths stay shut. So you'll take her with you?'

Benedict nodded.

The man thought for a moment, stroking his moustaches. 'Be kind to her, Avignon. It's not only her leg that's damaged. You understand?'

347

'I understand.'

'One more favour. Don't worry, it's not another passenger.'

'What then?'

'This.'

He pressed something into Benedict's hand. The night was too dark to see what it was, but Benedict knew the feel of a one-franc piece. He suspected he also knew what was engraved on it.

'When you get to London, to that club, contact Pascal. You know the procedure. Give him this message. Tell him the problem is Paris.'

'A cuckoo?'

'See – you know Pascal. Yes, a cuckoo. Cost us the lives of three good men. But tell him it's not the professor. Our little professor isn't clever enough. He thinks he is but he's out of his depth. He'll tell plenty of tall tales when this is all over but he's harmless. Someone else in Paris is the problem. I can't give Pascal any more than that. I don't have a name. Pascal will have to do the rest. At least I've narrowed the odds for him.'

'I'll let him know. Where's the girl?'

The man nodded towards the top of the cliff. 'When you get up there, someone will be watching for you, he'll bring her to you. His name's Mirabaud. He's slightly damaged too. Perhaps we all are, nowadays. Go safely, Avignon.'

Benedict had turned the corner in the path when he heard the man's voice again, a hoarse whisper from the darkness.

'Avignon?'

'Yes?'

'Would you have shot her?'

'What are you talking about?'

'In the square today, that's why you were there. You took a big risk. Would you have shot her?'

'Who?'

'Jeanne. Well, would you?'

'Did you?' said Benedict as he turned away.

He had her name now. Jeanne Dupré. He resumed climbing. Even an Englishman knew which way was up.

L'Église de Notre Dame de la Mer was filled with dust. Even now, long after the explosion, a visible haze still floated in the air, flaring into tiny sparks when the flames of votive candles caught the motes, so that it seemed as if the place was inhabited by fireflies.

Père François Lachanau stood motionless and silent before the altar and its crucifix. He was not praying; he was not communing with his saviour who gazed down on him with infinite compassion. He was listening. When he was sure that the square outside was as quiet and empty as when he had passed along it just now, when he was satisfied that he could hear no German boots or whining engines approaching, he drew the large ring of keys from beneath his soutane, chose one and slipped it into the lock of the door that led to the church spire.

François Lachanau knew about wireless valves. They were delicate and temperamental. Look at them wrong and they expired. Tap them with a fingernail at the wrong moment as they cooled or warmed and they exploded. Heaven alone knew what damage might have been caused today.

But SOE's engineers had not let him down: this equipment was built to survive parachute drops; what did the occasional explosion matter? There was a thick layer of dust on the suitcase and debris all around it, but it bore no marks or dents. He raised the lid. The anode and crystal tuning dials were intact, as was the crystal holder. When he removed the internal cover, the transmitting and receiving valves looked undamaged. The aerial wire that ran up to the outside of the spire was unbroken. The earth wire had detached from the spire's copper earth but it took only a moment to reconnect it.

Everything glowed reassuringly as the set warmed up. An acrid aroma stung his nostrils. He tapped his wreck of a nose and smiled. Nothing to worry about. Quite the contrary. Just hot wireless valves. Just hot dust.

The night was black. The Lysander was black. The little aircraft was there in the meadow almost before Benedict could bring it into focus. He set the MP40 on the ground as instructed by Lisieux. He corrected himself: as instructed by Jeanne Dupré. As he laid it in the grass, it felt as if he was laying the woman herself to rest. Then he lifted her daughter into his arms and ran towards the aircraft.

'Welcome, stranger,' called Tillman. 'Room for two more at the back.'

Benedict helped the girl up the ladder and into the rear cockpit. It took a moment or two to arrange her in the narrow space, her clumsy caliper banging against the steel struts and brackets that were the Lysander's skeleton. But eventually he installed himself on the bench seat and slammed the canopy shut. He clapped gunner Smith on the shoulder and felt the craft surge forward.

As they left the ground he looked back in time to see the lamps go out one by one. Somewhere down there a priest and a man with fierce moustaches were listening and watching, straining to see the aircraft and relieved if they could not make it out. Perhaps the Germans would be watching and listening too, however preoccupied they might be.

'If I'm there I'll be out of sight, you won't see me,' Jeanne had promised. And perhaps she was there. Perhaps she too was watching.

The barracks at Le Manoir would be passing beneath him now, invisible in the darkness this time, and to starboard there was the tall shadow of the old lighthouse. An instant and it vanished. France slipped away; now there was only the sea beneath him.

He felt the girl rest her head on his shoulder. Such a simple act of trust. And trust had to be honoured.

He lifted his gaze to the sky. Above him the moon was fading to nothing.

The night belonged to the stars.

Hervé

So, my friend, the tale was told.

It was the Englishman's last day in Caillons. We decided to stretch our legs so that he could have a final look around. We walked out as far as the schoolhouse on rue du Père François Lachanau and returned to stroll beneath the pines in parc des Trois Martyrs. The sweet scent of the pines was heavy in the air. The only sounds were the clack of boules from the pétanque pitches and the calls of children playing. In the distance beneath us the waters of the bay sparkled as if someone had gathered together all the sequins in the world and scattered them there. A flat-bottomed chaland moved unhurriedly between the mussel bouchots. Caillons was at peace.

After a while we turned out of the little park. We stopped for a minute before the war memorial in allée Jacques Colinet. I like how it incorporates broken pieces of its ruined predecessor – at Père Lachanau's insistence, I remember you saying. I think of it as embedding the past within the present. As we always should. Now it has two wars to commemorate. And beside it stands the obelisk dedicated to our résistants. A whole long list of names, including my father's.

'How did your father die?' the Englishman asked me.

'We never found out. The last members of Jeanne's original cell who were there that night, Gérard and Paul Leroux –' I indicated their names on the obelisk. '– were killed in a later action.'

'I'm sure he died bravely.'

'He wasn't always buried in the churchyard, where you found his grave. There was a place where all the résistants' bodies had been dumped. Nothing more than a pit. After the war Père Lachanau arranged for it to be opened and for the bodies to be reburied properly. It turned out that someone had attached nameplates to them, so identification wasn't a problem.'

We made our way back to place Dupré and Claude's café. There was time for a last coffee together.

'The notes are my grandmother's,' he said. 'Written by her over many years.'

Ah, those notes of his, that mysterious folder. At last.

'They tell her story – and my grandfather's.'

'Daniel Benedict was your grandfather.'

He nodded. 'The intelligence he brought back from his mission in Normandy was crucial to the D-Day landings and the Allies' victory in Europe. But I knew nothing of his story until I read what my grandmother had written. It was only after her death last year that her notes came to light. She and I were very close but she never spoke about her wartime past or my grandfather's. That's simply how that generation was. It was she who taught me French. It was the only language we ever used with each other, from as far back as I can remember. She was French, you see.'

'And her name,' I ventured, 'I think perhaps it was Hélène?'

He smiled. 'In her new life in England it was Helen. Daniel and she married, a child was born – a boy, my father, their only child. Helen went to university, a rare achievement then for a woman. She qualified as a psychologist, in those days still a relatively new field. She specialised in child psychology. Her gift was helping children who were psychologically or emotionally damaged in some way: by violence, by extreme neglect, or most of all by sexual abuse, the prevalence of which was little recognised then – she was a pioneer. Later she returned to the academic world, researching and teaching, extending her understanding and passing on her skills. I was never lucky enough to be one of her students, though my father was, but like him I too followed in her footsteps – he was a child psychologist and so am I.'

'Family business.'

'In more ways than one, you see.'

We had reached the square. He paused before the Villa Normandie. We studied its fine timbered façade together.

'You didn't seem surprised to learn of its destruction,' I said.

'I already knew. Daniel's mission couldn't have succeeded without the help of many brave people – not only Jeanne Dupré and her cell, including your father, but also the ordinary Catholic priests who had risked their lives for him. He knew that some had been arrested and killed, but the picture was incomplete. So he returned to Normandy with another mission – to find out what had happened to his contacts and where possible gather evidence that could be used later in the trials of those who had tortured and executed them. Naturally Daniel started his search here in Caillons. That was when he discovered what had happened to the Villa Normandie. His account is in my grandmother's notes. He never returned to Caillons after that. Helen never returned at all.'

'Sad but understandable.'

We took our usual table beneath the café awning. He leafed through the folder as he had done on our first morning together. Then, as so often before, his gaze returned to the Villa Normandie.

'You were going to tell me how it came to be rebuilt,' he

reminded me.

'Ah yes.' I finished my coffee and lit a cigarette. 'After the war, it transpired that Gaspard Baignères was the owner of certain portions of land – all the land surrounding Le Manoir, in fact, including the roads leading to it. The owners of Le Manoir had died in exile, without heirs or surviving relatives, so the state got its hands on the château and its farmland. Our politicians wanted to develop Le Manoir into a shopping area but Gaspard held them to ransom.'

'That sounds in character.'

'A deal was struck and he ended up part-owning the development. One thing led to another, as it usually did with Gaspard, and in time he owned it outright. He called his company Groupe Loisirs Danton. The old fishing cottages in rue du Port, including the one you've been staying in, he bought them too and developed them into holiday accommodation. Also La Croisette and the places around it, suitably modernised, of course. If God had been selling the air we breathe, I think Gaspard would have snapped that up too.'

'But the Villa Normandie – that he did snap up.'

'For a song, what was left of it, which wasn't much. It too had fallen into state hands. Gaspard rebuilt it as it had been. Almost. The original plans were found in La Croisette, so he replicated the outside appearance of the building – every brick and tile, every statue. Plenty of work for local stonemasons and carpenters. The interior had to be different, of course, given its intended new use. But there's a dark side to the story.'

'Which is?'

'As they cleared the site, they found what was left of Graf and Ebermann – not much, only bones, shreds of uniform, boots, pistols. Ebermann had taken three bullets – one in the head, Graf's trademark – but there were no bullets in Graf's body. The fourth bullet – four shots had been heard that day – that fourth bullet was never found. Obviously three had been fired by Graf's weapon, one by Ebermann's. The major's bullet was the one that was missing. Lost in the rubble, I suppose. Exactly what went on between the two men remains a mystery, along with what caused the explosion. So the Villa Normandie still keeps some of its secrets. Perhaps the ghosts of Ebermann and Graf are still duelling there.'

'Ghosts or not, the new Villa Normandie is obviously doing well.'

'Groupe Loisirs Danton is one of Normandy's most successful companies and a major employer.'

'And the little German leutnant – what became of him?'

'Ernst Neiss? He was captured by the Allies as they advanced and held as a prisoner of war. François Lachanau vouched for him to make sure that none of Graf's war crimes could be laid at his door – to some of the Caillonais, after what they'd suffered one German was much like another and equally deserving of the noose. But Père Lachanau saw to it that no such mistake was made and Ernst Neiss was safely repatriated to Germany at the end of the war. They kept in touch and the following summer Ernst returned to Caillons. He came to visit but he never left. Some people never accepted him as a member of our community but what better protectors could a man have than Père François Lachanau and Gaspard Baignères? Ernst and my mother became firm friends. My mother told me that Père Lachanau tried his matchmaking skills on them, but I suppose they preferred things as they were. Ernst was like a father to me and my new little brother; and as I grew up he remained a dear friend.' I stopped and thought about what I had just said. 'And he still is,' I added.

356

'He's still alive?'

I shook my head sadly. 'He died a few years ago. But, as he was fond of saying, what we have in our hearts is not lost in death. His grave is the only one you missed in the churchyard – he wasn't a Catholic, not even a believer, but I persuaded our curé to stretch a point for him. I think Père Lachanau would have approved. So that's Ernst's story.' I paused and looked at him. 'And now I have a question for you.'

'Go ahead.'

'The Villa Normandie, La Croisette and the Dupré land – arguably you have a legal claim of ownership.'

He was smiling, those blue eyes full of amusement. 'And I'd spend the rest of my life tangled in French law trying to prove it.' He shook his head. 'No, Hervé, I'm content as things are. My grandmother would be, too. So I think my business in Caillons is concluded.'

As we walked to his car, he paused by the plaque at the corner of the square, the one he had asked me about on that day we first met.

Place Dupré
Hélène, Isabelle et leur mere, Jeanne,
massacrées par les nazis

'"Slaughtered by the Nazis",' he said. 'So tell me now, Hervé – what do you think? Is that the truth?'

We contemplated the question in silence.

'Close enough,' I concluded. 'Practically the bare wood.'

We shook hands for the last time. He glanced at the mairie clock.

'A Henry-Lepaute,' he said, though to himself as much as to me. 'Keeps perfect time. I wonder if the mechanism is original.'

Then he climbed into his big four-wheel drive and was gone.

So here we are, my dear old friend, just you and I again.

What a wonderful thing you did when you wrapped your arms about Hélène Dupré that terrible day and swept her out of Graf's sight. What a gift you gave the world: not only Hélène but two generations thereafter. God blesses the healers, but he also blesses those who make their healing possible. And I think he does that whether you believe in him or not, so don't waste my time arguing about it.

I've brought you some flowers. Violets today.

Rest in peace, my friend. As does Caillons now.

Also by KEVIN DOHERTY

PATRIOTS

Russia. The 1980s. The Cold War is still raging.

Mikhail Gorbachev's strict vision for Russia is driving out the economic corruption that riddled the old Soviet regime.

Nikolai Serov watches as traitors in positions of the highest authority are forced into revealing their hands, knowing that he does not want to fall victim to the same fate of arrest and execution.

As head of the KGB's First Chief Directorate and one of Moscow's leading black marketeers and drug kings, Serov recognises that he has only one chance to construct a sophisticated plot that will ensure his own freedom.

Serov's intricate plan unfolds in a calculated web of murder and betrayal as he activates a Russian mole who has lain dormant for the past twenty years and now is at the top rung of Britain's MI5.

His vision for the future stretches far and wide as his secret master plan succeeds in influencing East and West policy and dictates the fates of governments on both sides.

Patriots takes the reader right to the heart of Russia. Meticulously researched, complexly plotted, explosively violent and ruthlessly authentic, it is the first novel to deal with the darker side of Gorbachev's programmes of perestroika and glasnost.

'A brilliant tale of treachery and power politics' – Tom Kasey, best-selling author of *Trade Off*.

9/22 NEW
10/22
12/22
2/23
3/23
4/23
5/23

Printed in Great Britain
by Amazon

77049698R00210